CHRISTABELLE

Titles available in this series

Yannis
Anna
Giovanni
Joseph
Christabelle

CHRISTABELLE

Beryl Darby

JACH

ISBN 978-0-9554278-4-8

Printed in Great Britain by the
MPG Books Group, Bodmin and King's Lynn

First published in the UK in 2009 by

JACH Publishing
92 Upper North Street, Brighton, East Sussex, England BN1 3FJ

website: www.beryldarbybooks.com

For Lilian,
who has been such a good and
supportive friend over many years.

Reviews for *Yannis* – the first title in the series

The Daily Mail (National Newspaper)

Yannis makes for a most interesting and enjoyable read.

Evening Argus (Local Newspaper)

Brighton based Beryl Darby is a compulsive writer and *Yannis* is the first of six novels she has written about the same Cretan family. Her saga is built around actual events in the island's history, although the characters are fictitious.

Essentially Worthing (Local Magazine)

A gripping read. You'll get hooked into the atmosphere of this exciting and sometimes harrowing tale, based on actual happenings at the leper colony of Spinalonga near Crete.

C.M.P.C.A (Local Area Magazine)

This is a chilling story, and even more disturbing because it all actually happened. But while everything certainly doesn't end happily ever after, you are not left sad. In fact, after living through the many triumphs and tragedies of these people for 700 odd pages, you are sorry to bid them farewell. Beryl has a comfortable style, an acute ear for dialogue, and total mastery of her subject. *Yannis* works on many levels: it tells a story too long untold, depicts a Greece few of us know at all – with human emotions at their most intense. I promise, once you've been drawn into this close Cretan community you'll be hooked.

Written by D. Shorley FCLIP Sussex University

Uckfield Lending Library (Michael Hollands)

I asked the library to buy *Yannis* and finished it at Easter. I thought it was absolutely wonderful how you got into the minds and situations of the characters and brought it all so vividly to life. There were moments that were really moving.

Ian Rees – Elektros Bookshop, Elounda

A remarkable read, I was unable to put the book down.

Readers' Reviews for Yannis

I started to read *Yannis* at 9.00 p.m. and when I lifted my eyes from it the time was 3.00 a.m.!!

* * *

Thank you so much for such a lovely story. I don't have a lot of time to read, but I couldn't put *Yannis* down.

* * *

Have only this morning closed *Yannis* with regret. There are moments in life when words seem so inadequate to the occasion – and this is another. A massive story – full of the keenest observation of the human condition and the compassion that strings us all together.

* * *

I just had to write to tell you how much I loved your book. It was compulsive reading and beautifully written – I read every single word! I found that whilst I was reading I was also seeing all the characters, places and situations in my mind and I think that is the sign of a great author. You are up there with the best of them and I can't wait to read *Anna* when it is published.

* * *

I just wanted to say how much I enjoyed the novel – if enjoy is the right word to use for such a tragic subject. I didn't realise leprosy was still a problem in this century, particularly the way the lepers were treated so thank you for opening my eyes to this subject. I kept imagining it as a film. It's got all the ingredients. Such a mixture of emotions and human conditions.

* * *

I have just finished reading *Yannis* and really enjoyed it.

* * *

I have read *Yannis* during my holiday and thoroughly enjoyed it. Wonderful! It made me cry.

Readers' Reviews for Anna

I couldn't put *ANNA* down and was trying to finish it with misty eyes when it all comes together at the end – that wonderful mixture of happiness, sadness and completion.
M. Hollands (Uckfield Library)

* * *

I have just finished reading *ANNA* wonderful. The end had me in tears.
S. Beard

* * *

I just had to tell you how much I enjoyed *ANNA*. I just could not put it down.
P. Jones

* * *

The characters are so real that I feel I know them.
D. Mason

* * *

I fell in love with Anna's nephew.
Y. Owens

* * *

I loved *YANNIS*. I thought *ANNA* was even better and I cannot wait to get my hands on *GIOVANNI*.
G. Newman

* * *

I become so involved in the plot of each book that I await the outcome as anxiously as if the fictitious characters were my own family.
G. King

* * *

Each time I finish a book by Beryl Darby I am eagerly anticipating the next. Please write many more about this family.
J. Wilson

Readers' Reviews for Giovanni

The plot widens out even more internationally and into the realms of crime. I think it is incredible the way you construct and move the plot forward, handle the dialogue and relationships, the scope and complexities of the places and situations. I put you up there with Maeve Binchy, Jeffrey Archer, and Colleen McCullough.
M. Hollands (Uckfield Library)

* * *

Thank you for giving me so much pleasure with your writing.
R.. Shepherd

* * *

This series of books is the best I have read in thirty years.
C. Taylor

* * *

I absolutely love your books and cannot wait for *JOSEPH*.
S. Wood

* * *

These characters have become a part of our family. We talk about them as if they were real.
G.. Hiscox

Readers' Reviews for Joseph

I could not put *JOSEPH* down.
C. Grant

* * *

I cannot tell you how much I enjoyed *JOSEPH*. The characters have become so real to me.
J. Evans

Family Tree

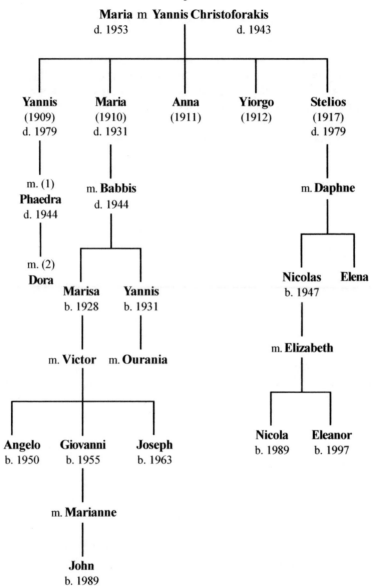

Family Tree

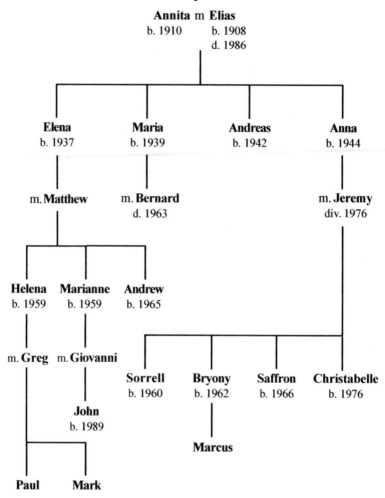

Author's Note

1994 – 1996

Christabelle studied herself critically in the full length mirror. As long as she could remember she had heard people compliment her mother on having such a beautiful daughter. She was just eighteen, well proportioned and with long shapely legs. She held her hair up on her head. That certainly gave her a sophisticated appearance. She spent some minutes fixing it in place before looking again at the magazine that lay open on her bed. She copied the pose of the model, shoulders back, hips thrust forward and her head tilted to the right, her left arm extended above her head and slightly to the side as if she were leaning against a column.

She turned the pages until she came to the next advertisement, sat down at her dressing table, rested her chin on her hand, and stared intently into the mirror. For the next hour she amused herself by experimenting with her hair in different styles. It was a shame that so many of the models were blonde or were wearing their hair straight. It made it difficult for her to compare her own looks with theirs. Finally bored she flipped through the magazine to see if there were any articles that would interest her, anything to delay starting her homework that she needed to hand in the following day.

Unable to put off her school work any longer she pulled the books towards her. Provided she handed in something she really did not care what kind of a grade she received. Her only interests were travel and fashion. She looked at the questions that were meaningless to her. She would telephone Dolores. If she couched her questions and remarks carefully she could usually rely on her friend giving her the answers that she needed.

Picking up her papers she went down to the lounge, grimacing as she saw her mother leaning back on the sofa, Henry stroking her leg whilst he alternately whispered in her ear and kissed her neck.

'I need to use the phone.'

Anna frowned in annoyance at her daughter's intrusion and pushed Henry away from her. She had just been about to suggest that they retired to her room where they would be more comfortable and Henry could carry out his whispered suggestions.

Christabelle turned her back on them and dialled Dolores number. 'Hi, Dol, how you doing? Isn't that homework the pits! What did you make of it?'

For half an hour Christabelle monopolised the telephone, making notes as Dolores unwittingly gave her the information she had been seeking, finally replacing the receiver with a pleased smile on her face. She collected her papers together and without a word to her mother left the room, closing the door firmly behind her. She was thankful there was the bathroom between her room and her mother's bedroom so she would not have to hear them when they would undoubtedly mount the stairs to complete the activities they had started on the sofa.

Christabelle sipped her orange juice thoughtfully. She would have to have a portfolio of photographs taken and she was not at all sure how much that would cost her. If she did not have sufficient in her savings account it would be no good asking her mother for a loan or some extra money. Anna always pleaded poverty.

She debated whether to take Dolores into her confidence. It was possible that she would lend her some money. She would promise to repay it by giving her the money she earned at the supermarket stocking shelves at the weekend.

'I do wish you would knock before you come bursting into the lounge,' Anna complained as she saw her daughter sitting at the kitchen bar.

Christabelle ignored her.

'It's bad manners, you know. Henry was most embarrassed.'

Christabelle slipped off the stool at the eating bar. 'I think I should be the one to be embarrassed. You and Henry were behaving disgustingly as usual.'

'We were not. We were just having a little cuddle.'

'With his hand up your skirt! Dirty little man.'

'He's not. He's a very nice man. He's taking me out for dinner tonight.' Anna smiled contentedly. 'I'm going to wear that new dress he bought me last week.'

'Really. Well, I hope you enjoy yourselves and behave better in a restaurant than you do when you're at home.'

'We may come back afterwards, so please knock if you want to come into the lounge and use the phone.'

'I'll do no such thing. I live here. I should be able to walk freely into the lounge whenever I wish. Tell Henry to keep his hands to himself then he'll have no need to be embarrassed.' Christabelle picked up her jacket and her bag of books and slammed the kitchen door behind her.

Christabelle opened the folder of photographs and studied them critically. Brajowski had done a good job. Each one did justice to her undeniable beauty and perfect figure. She shuddered involuntarily as she pored over those of her naked and in risqué poses. How she had hated the way he had touched her as he had altered her position, his hands had lingered unnecessarily on her breasts and legs and it had taken all her will power not to scream and run from the studio.

For a while she sat lost in thought, then a secretive smile crept over her face. She would get her revenge for the indignities she had suffered. First she would decide on the number of copies she wanted. A second visit to the studio would give her the opportunity to check on her idea and when she collected the extra prints she would be prepared to carry her plan through. What a shock he would get! She giggled to herself at the unintentional pun as she sorted the photographs, selecting only those where she was fully clothed to show her mother.

Anna looked at them cursorily. 'You certainly photograph well. I'll look at them properly later. I'm meeting Kurt for dinner and I really should get showered and changed or I shall be late.'

'Kurt?' she asked.

Anna smiled happily. 'He's so good looking. I'm sure you're going to like him.'

Christabelle raised her eyebrows. 'Really? What's happened to Henry?'

'Oh, I got tired of Henry. Kurt is so delightful. His family came over here from Germany after the war. His father was in the army, of course, but he's really a carpenter. He has his own business. Kurt had the opportunity to go into it with him, but he says he's no good with his hands.' Anna gave a little giggle. 'His family live in San Francisco and he's promised to take me there.'

Christabelle bit at her lips in frustration and annoyance. Why did her mother never have time for her? 'I really wanted to talk to you about them.'

'Surely we can talk later, dear? What's so urgent about a few photographs?'

Christabelle took a deep breath. 'I plan to send them off to modelling agencies.'

Anna raised her eyebrows. 'What makes you think you're attractive enough to be a model?'

'You've just said I photograph well. I know I look as good as any of the models in the magazines. It's just a question of showing them to the right people.'

'And how are you going to meet the right people? What on earth do you want to be a model for anyway?'

'I want to travel. I want to see America and go over to Europe.'

'You could be an air hostess and do that.'

'I'd never see anywhere. No sooner have you arrived than you have to get the plane ready for a return journey. I want to be free to travel around wherever I fancy.'

'You'll probably change your mind over the next couple of years.' Anna rose and handed the photographs back to her daughter.

'I'm not waiting a couple of years. I want to start now.'

Anna frowned. 'You haven't finished high school yet. You can't possibly think about a modelling career until you've completed your education.'

Christabelle drew herself up to her full height. 'I intend to start as soon as possible. If I wait until I've finished college I shall be too old. You need to start young if you are to get to the top and I'm already eighteen.'

Anna smiled deprecatingly. 'You think you will become a top model?'

'I intend to be the most famous model in the world, not just America,' stated Christabelle, a determined set to her mouth.

'Very ambitious of you. I'll talk to Kurt about your idea and see what he thinks.'

'This has nothing to do with Kurt.'

'Oh, it could do. He is such a delightful character. I think I may have met the one man who would make an ideal daddy for you.'

Christabelle's lips curled in disgust. 'How many times have you said that to me about your different boyfriends? I've had more prospective 'daddies' than I can count.'

'Kurt is different. Now, I really must go and have my shower or I shall be very late.'

Christabelle looked mutinously at her mother as she left the room. There was no way she was going to stop her from achieving her ambition. She collected up the photographs and returned to her bedroom. She needed the reprints and a contract; then would be the time to deal with her mother and Kurt also if the need arose.

First she would get her own back on Dolores. She had only asked for a loan of two hundred dollars to buy the smart suit she had seen which would be suitable for her to wear when she visited modelling agencies. Dolores had refused immediately, despite having a considerable sum in her bank account ready for University. It was so unjust. Now she would have to use the remainder of her own dwindling savings.

The following day dawned hot and sultry. Christabelle picked up the telephone. 'Hi, Dol, what you up to today?'

'I haven't really decided. It's so humid.'

'Do you fancy going out to the lake? We could take some lunch with us and have a swim. How about if I call in at the supermarket and come on to your place?'

Dolores hesitated. It was tempting, although Christabelle did not usually suggest going to the lake however hot it might be as she was unable to swim. She would paddle or sit on the edge of the bank whilst Dolores enjoyed the cool water.

'Make it in about an hour. I've a couple of jobs I want to get done first.'

'Sure. See you.' Christabelle replaced the receiver with a feeling of elation tinged with apprehension. The idea had come to her suddenly. It would be interesting to see if she could accomplish it.

The girls walked slowly to the lake and Christabelle scanned the area. She did not want to be too close to any other visitors.

'Let's go under that tree,' she suggested. 'We're close to the water and it will give a bit of shade.'

'I'm going straight in to cool down,' announced Dolores. 'Are you coming?'

'I'll stay on the edge.'

'I'll teach you to swim if you like.' Dolores made the offer regularly.

Christabelle shook her head. 'I'd like to learn to swim, but not in here. You never know what might come out of the reeds or river bank.'

Dolores shrugged. 'Provided it isn't an alligator I'm not too worried.' She stripped off her blouse and shorts and ran down to the edge, letting the cool water run over her feet, before running further in and plunging under, swimming strongly out from the shore.

Christabelle followed slowly. She had spoken truly when she said she was frightened that something unpleasant would come out from the reeds. She was not at all sure if water snakes lived amongst them. She stood on the edge and watched as Dolores began to swim slowly back towards her.

Screwing up her courage Christabelle began to wade out into the water and towards a reed clump. She pretended to examine it, then beckoned to Dolores. 'Come and see this.'

Dolores swam over, wading the last few feet. 'What have you found?'

'I'm not sure. Look, down there.'

'Where? I can't see anything.'

'Bend down.'

Dolores bent and as she did so Christabelle grabbed her shoulders and pushed her head beneath the water. Struggling and gasping Dolores tried to claw her way back up to the surface, but she was no match for the strength Christabelle had in her arms. She thrashed wildly in the water and to Christabelle's consternation she heard someone calling.

'What's going on? Are you in trouble?'

Christabelle maintained her grip on Dolores, but turned her head. The man was already wading into the water towards them.

'Please help. My friend seems to be tangled in the reeds. I can't pull her out.'

As he reached them, Christabelle cupped her hand beneath Dolores chin and held her head above the water. Strong arms lifted Dolores and he pulled her easily free from the weeds, almost toppling backwards as he had expected more resistance. He carried the unconscious girl to the river bank and laid her down on her side.

'Call the emergency services.' From the pocket of his discarded shirt he pulled a mobile 'phone and passed it to Christabelle. Her hands trembling, Christabelle dialled the number and spoke in a low, hesitant voice, giving only vague directions to their location. It seemed only a few moments before the sound of a siren reached her ears.

The man turned Dolores onto her stomach and began to pummel her back until a stream of water gushed from her mouth and she coughed and moaned. Almost immediately paramedics arrived and took over from him.

'Can you tell us what happened, miss?'

Christabelle gave a shudder and collapsed dramatically onto the grass. 'It was so awful. I thought she was going to drown. I had been trying to hold her up for ages before this man arrived.'

'Can she swim?'

'Oh, yes. She's a good swimmer. I think she'd got tangled up in the weeds. I kept pulling at her, but I couldn't move her. It was so frightening.'

Dolores coughed again and expelled more water from her lungs.

'We'll take her back to the hospital and get her checked over. If you'd like to collect up your belongings and come with us, miss. It would be helpful to have you there to give us her details and let us know where we can contact her parents.'

'She's not going to die, is she?'

'No. She's had a very nasty experience, but thanks to this gentleman she should make a full recovery. I don't think either of you will fancy swimming again for a while.'

'I can't swim,' replied Christabelle firmly. 'It took all my courage to go into the water. I hate the thought of something swimming against my legs.' She shuddered dramatically again.

'Then it was extremely brave of you to go in to help your friend. She's very lucky to have a friend like you around.'

Dolores's rescuer frowned as he picked up his shirt. Everything had happened so quickly. He must be mistaken about the depth of the water, yet he was sure the girl holding her friend had been on her knees when he arrived and when she straightened up the water had been no more than waist deep. Even if the girl had become tangled in the reeds there should have been no reason why she could not keep her head above water.

Marianne and Giovanni wandered through the medieval town on Rhodes hand in hand. Marianne consulted her map. 'I think I really have seen everything in the Old Town now. If we do the wall walk this afternoon we could go to Lindos tomorrow and visit the Acropolis.'

Giovanni took the map from Marianne and finally decided where they were standing. 'That should lead us to another gate; the Athanasiou.' He pointed to a route that was devoid of any attractions.

Leisurely they strolled down the cobbled streets, finally entering a small, neglected square. Giovanni pulled the map from his pocket and looked at it again. Marianne peered at it with him and traced a road with her finger.

'If we go through that side turning we should be by the walls. If we follow them we're bound to end up at a gate.'

Giovanni held Marianne's hand a little tighter. 'I don't think this is a very good area to be walking in.'

Marianne looked at the dirty walls that hemmed them in. 'I don't think I've ever been in a red light area before.' She insisted on dawdling along the narrow road, reading the names of the girls that were scrawled above the entrances.

'I wonder what they're like?' mused Marianne.

'There's one in her doorway,' whispered Giovanni. 'You can see for yourself.'

Marianne slowed even more and looked curiously at the girl who was lounging against the stone wall of her doorway. As they drew level with the doorway they could read the name *'Suzi'* painted above and a man could be seen sitting in the courtyard in a wheelchair. He looked out at them. Giovanni stiffened perceptibly whilst Marianne drew in her breath sharply.

'Still the golden boy? Still Uncle Yannis's favourite nephew?' the mocking voice floated out from the man in the wheelchair.

'Giovanni…'

'Walk on,' he ordered his wife.

As they passed, the woman glared at Marianne with hatred in her eyes. She should have accepted Giovanni when she had the opportunity. She spat after their retreating backs.

By the time they turned the corner Marianne was shaking and Giovanni put his arms around her.

'It was them, wasn't it?' she asked. 'They looked so awful!'

Giovanni nodded. 'Something must certainly have happened to Joseph to put him in a wheelchair. Maybe he had a car accident. I have to go back.'

Marianne looked at her husband in horror. 'Why? It could be dangerous. You know what Joseph is like.'

'We may be able to help him.'

Marianne looked at Giovanni in disbelief. 'Help him? After what he did to you? He tried to kill you!'

'I owe it to my parents to find out what has happened. I'm going back now.'

'I'm coming with you.' Marianne held up her hand as Giovanni was about to protest. 'If Joseph turns nasty I can threaten to telephone the police. There may be nothing wrong with him and he's just sitting in that chair.'

Giovanni tucked her hand into his arm. 'I want you to wait by the gate. If there's any sign of trouble you leave immediately. I can look after myself.'

Silently they retraced their steps into the old town and after taking only two wrong turnings they ended up outside the wooden door that led into the small courtyard. Joseph was still sitting in the wheelchair and Giovanni stood in the doorway.

'May I come in?'

Joseph scowled. 'What do you want?'

Giovanni stepped into the courtyard and Marianne followed him. Sorrell looked at her cousin, spat again in her direction and walked back into the house.

'What's happened to you, Joseph?'

'Why should it concern you? I had an accident. Damaged my spine; that should satisfy you, shouldn't it?'

'It doesn't satisfy me at all. I don't like to think of you being confined to a chair for the rest of your life.'

'Why should you care?'

'I'm your brother.'

'You should have remembered that years ago when you threw me out of your night club.'

'If you had behaved decently I would have been only too willing to employ you. If you had proved yourself to me I'm sure Uncle Yannis would have employed you eventually.'

'I don't believe you and it's too late now.'

'Is there anything we can do for you?'

Joseph looked at his brother cunningly. 'You could give me some cash. You don't get much for a disability.' He jerked his thumb towards the house. 'She doesn't bring in as much as she used to.'

Giovanni pulled out his wallet. He removed all the notes that were in there and thrust them into Joseph's hand. Without counting the money Joseph pushed it into his pocket. He reached for his crutch and swung it into the air. Marianne took a step forward; sure he was going to attack Giovanni.

'Now get out. Your curiosity should be satisfied. Get out of my house and don't come back.'

Giovanni looked at his brother in disbelief and felt Marianne pluck at his arm.

'Let's go, please, Giovanni.'

Giovanni gave Joseph a withering glance. 'You haven't changed, have you? I came here willing to help you in any way I could, but you're as evil as ever. What a fool I was!'

Joseph swung his crutch closer to Giovanni, who turned on his heel, pushed Marianne through the doorway and strode off up the road. He was shaking with anger.

Marianne sat beneath the trees with her husband, the tears running down her cheeks. Giovanni squeezed her to him. 'There's no reason for you to be so upset.'

'Will you tell your parents we've seen Joseph?'

'What for? It would distress them to know that he's crippled. My mother would want to take him back to Italy and look after him. My father would never let her. They would fight and argue; eventually they would hate each other. I cannot do that to them.' Giovanni shook his head sadly.

'What about Bryony and Grandma?'

'Would either of them want to know that Sorrell was working as a prostitute? No, Marianne, put them right out of your mind. Had we not walked that way we would never have known they lived on Rhodes. As far as I am concerned we have never seen them.'

'They've really managed to spoil this holiday for me.'

Giovanni tilted her chin up and wiped her tears gently with his finger. 'Don't let them do that. We were having such a good time.'

'I don't want to go back into the Old Town.'

'You don't have to. We can walk back to the hotel by the top road. Let's go back now and we can have a swim before lunch.'

'Suppose we meet them?'

'Why should we? They don't know where we're staying and why should they want to meet us anyway?'

Marianne shrugged. 'I just feel so unsettled. After what Joseph did to you before, I'm frightened,' she admitted.

'There's no need to be frightened. I'll tell you what; we'll hire a car for our last three days and drive all around the island. We don't have to go back into the Old Town. There'll be plenty to see elsewhere.'

'I do wish we hadn't seen them,' Marianne said miserably.

Christabelle returned to the photographic studio with the excuse that she wanted some reprints of her photographs. Mr Brajowski was working when she arrived without making a prior appointment and frowned.

'I cannot see you now.'

Christabelle smiled sweetly at him. 'I don't mind waiting until you've finished. May I make myself a cup of coffee?'

'Of course.' He turned back to the mother with the fractious little boy. 'If you could persuade him to kneel on the floor beside the toy train, and we will try again.' He sighed. How he hated these sessions with small children.

Christabelle entered the small kitchen and studied the kettle and plug intently as she made her coffee. She was sure she could carry out her intention on her next visit. It seemed an eternity before she heard the photographer bid farewell to his client and she emerged clutching her portfolio.

'I would like three reprints of each one, please.'

Mr Brajowski smiled. 'You could have left your instructions on the answer phone. There was no need for you to wait.'

'I thought you might want the originals.'

'I have the negatives. You want thirty in all. They will be ready for you,' he looked in his diary, 'the day after tomorrow.' He eyed her up and down appraisingly, making her flesh crawl.

'That's fine. What time shall I call?'

Again Mr Brajowski consulted his diary. 'I am busy until eleven; then I have nothing more until twelve fifteen. Between eleven and twelve if that suits you.'

Christabelle nodded. 'I'll be here, and Mr Brajowski, I would like the negatives of all my photos, please.'

Mr Brajowski raised his eyebrows, but made no comment. He could easily duplicate them. You never knew when a negative would be useful in the future.

Christabelle deliberately waited until twelve thirty before arriving at the studio. 'I'm so sorry,' she apologised. 'I was held up. I don't mind waiting. I'll help myself to a cup of coffee, if that's all right.'

Mr Brajowski frowned in annoyance. He was more interested in the voluptuous blonde who had not hesitated to remove her clothes at his suggestion and giggled each time he touched her to improve the suggestiveness of her pose. She gave the impression that she was not averse to his overtures. He sighed. He could always offer to take a few more photos and he would make sure he locked the door after Christabelle left.

Christabelle made a cup of coffee, then removed a small screwdriver from her purse. It took no more than a few minutes for her to make the adjustments and she was innocently sipping her coffee when Mr Brajowski called to say he could spare her a few moments whilst his subject changed her clothes. Christabelle placed the half empty cup on the side and entered the studio.

Apologising yet again for her late arrival, Christabelle accepted the envelope and paid, pushing the receipt into her purse. 'I really am grateful to you, Mr Brajowski. I shall obviously use you again should the need arise, and, of course, I will recommend you.'

'It was a pleasure, my dear. If you come again maybe we could discuss a little discount.'

'How kind,' murmured Christabelle, shuddering inwardly. She had an idea she knew what he would suggest to earn a discount.

'Good luck with your career. I feel sure you will be successful. I look forward to seeing photographs of you in the future. I will be proud to know that I took the first ones that gave you fame and fortune.' He said the same thing to each girl who came to him requesting a model portfolio.

'Thank you, Mr Brajowski.' Christabelle made her escape, as the blonde emerged from the changing room wearing tight trousers and a low necked top ready for her next series of photographs.

Christabelle returned to the small house she shared with her mother and immediately replaced the screwdriver in the box of tools that was kept beside the washing machine for simple running repairs.

She felt feverishly excited. She had done it. She must now put her actions out of her mind and concentrate on approaching modelling agencies in the hope of securing a contract.

It was four days before police officers called and Anna agreed they could wait until Christabelle arrived home. She tried to draw the reason for their visit from them, but was told they were making routine enquiries and she had no need to worry.

The sound of the front door opening signalled the return of her daughter and Anna called out to her. 'Christabelle, can you come here right away.'

Christabelle poked her head around the door to the lounge and saw the two policemen. An icy hand seemed to clutch at her heart. 'Give me a moment. I need to go to the bathroom.'

Before anyone could answer her she had run upstairs to the toilet and locked the door behind her. She stood taking deep breaths and looked at herself in the mirror. With her dark colouring they would not know if she had gone pale. She stretched out her hands; there was not a tremor. She flushed the unused toilet and returned to the lounge completely composed.

The policemen stood and invited her to sit before resuming their seats. The older one cleared his throat. 'I am Detective

Hidalgo and this is my assistant, Detective Greenburg. You are Miss Christabelle Bartlett?'

Christabelle nodded.

'We have a few questions we would like to ask you, just routine, nothing to worry about. I understand you knew Mr Brajowski, the photographer?'

'Yes.'

'When did you last visit his studio?'

'On Friday; I was collecting some reprints.'

Detective Hidalgo nodded. 'What time were you there?'

Christabelle appeared to think. 'I was a little late. I arrived about twelve thirty. He was busy and I had to wait awhile.'

'What did you do whilst you waited?'

'Nothing. I made myself a cup of coffee.'

'Did you notice anything about the kettle when you used it to boil the water?'

Christabelle looked puzzled. 'Notice anything?'

'Yes. Did you have any problem getting it to work?'

Christabelle thought swiftly. 'I had to give the plug a little wriggle. I hadn't pushed it in quite far enough.'

'Which plug was that? The one into the kettle or the socket in the wall?'

'The kettle,' answered Christabelle quickly.

Detective Hidalgo nodded. 'What did you do after that?'

Christabelle could feel her heart pounding. 'Do?'

Detective Hidalgo gave a little shrug. 'Did you investigate the plug on the kettle to see if there was a fault?'

'No. I didn't give it another thought.'

'So how long did you spend in the kitchen?'

'Not very long. I hadn't finished drinking my coffee when Mr Brajowski called and said he could see me. Why?'

'Unfortunately Mr Brajowski met with an accident later in the day. As a matter of routine we are interviewing anyone who had an appointment with him last Friday.'

'I didn't have an appointment.'

'We know you were not in his diary, but the young lady who was with him between twelve fifteen and one fifteen said someone had called and waited. She gave a description that fits yourself and there is also a copy in Mr Brajowski's receipt book of a payment you made to him.'

Christabelle nodded. 'That's quite right. I have the receipt if you wish to see it.'

'That won't be necessary at the moment. Having collected your photographs how much longer did you stay at the studio?'

'I left immediately. I had no reason to stay, and Mr Brajowski wanted to continue with his work.'

'Did you return later by any chance?'

'No. Why are you asking me these questions?'

'It appears there was a fault on his kettle; the one you had used earlier in the day. Mr Brajowski suffered an electric shock. I would say you are a very lucky young lady.'

Christabelle's hand flew to her mouth. 'How awful! Is he all right?'

Detective Hidalgo shook his head. 'The pathologist thinks he died instantly.'

Christabelle's eyes widened. 'Dead!' She began to tremble. 'It could have been me! If there was a fault on that kettle – and I used it.' Christabelle passed a shaky hand across her eyes. 'It's terrible. I feel quite sick at the thought.'

Detective Hidalgo leaned forward. 'I'm sorry to have to ask you, miss, but did you in any way tamper with the kettle? Try to repair the plug in any way?'

Christabelle shook her head. 'No. As I said, I gave the plug a little wriggle. I thought I hadn't pushed it in quite far enough. The kettle boiled and I made my coffee. If I had thought it was broken I would have told Mr Brajowski. I would not have known how to repair it.'

The detective nodded. 'I'm sorry we had to trouble you.'

Christabelle shrugged. 'It was no trouble. I'm just rather shocked,' she murmured as she rose to show the two detectives out.

'Naturally. Thank you for your help.' Detective Hidalgo shook her hand, surprised at the strength of the grip she returned.

Detective Greenburg grinned at his companion. 'Some looker!'

Detective Hidalgo nodded. 'A very attractive young lady. What did you think?'

'I think she was genuinely shocked and surprised. She was quite open about being in the kitchen and making coffee. Volunteered the information about the plug. I can only think she was very fortunate not to be the one who was electrocuted.'

'Very fortunate indeed.'

'So? Case closed? Accidental death?'

Detective Hidalgo pursed his lips. 'People really should be more careful about their electrical appliances. When we make a press release maybe we could ask them to highlight that to their readers. I guess Brajowski had tried to repair the fault himself. It would have been more sensible to take it to an electrician or buy a new kettle.'

Detective Greenburg started the engine and drew away carefully into the traffic. 'I would have hated to see that beautiful young girl laying there. She really is something else.'

Fernando Hidalgo laughed. 'She's also far too young for you! Your daughter must be nearly her age.'

David Greenburg grinned sheepishly. 'There's no harm in admiring from a distance. If I was twenty years younger it might be a different matter.'

She returned to the lounge where her mother had switched on the television and was choosing a channel.

'That was rather a nasty experience.'

'Mmm.' Anna was already distracted by the chat programme. 'Oh, I haven't seen this one before.'

Christabelle looked in disgust at her mother. Any normal mother would have wanted to talk to her daughter and try to minimise the effect of the sudden death of an acquaintance and a visit from the police department. Without another word she left the lounge and retired to her bedroom, where she lay on her bed with her hands behind her head, a pleased smile on her face. He might have been a fantastic photographer, but he was a dirty, lecherous old man and had received his just desserts in her eyes. She had only intended the photographer to receive an electric shock. The fact that it had killed him showed just how clever she had been. She knew the detectives had no reason to suspect that she had manufactured the fault. Her acting had been superb.

Mike Able spread the photographs across his desk. He could tell at a glance that Brajowski had taken them all. The poses the man used never varied, but this girl could have potential. Her features were classical, with high cheekbones and almond shaped eyes. It was difficult to judge her height, but her figure was good and her legs long and shapely. He wondered about her ethnic origins. She was not dark enough for a black American, but neither did she look Spanish or Puerto Rican, maybe she originated from Mexico. He shuffled the collection together and walked over to his colleague, fanning the photographs out in front of him.

Peter Martinez selected one and gazed at it critically. 'Who is she?'

'Christabelle Bartlett. I've never heard of her but these came in the post this morning. There's a covering letter saying she's available for work and hopes to hear from us.'

'Let me see the others.' Mike placed them on Peter's desk and waited for a reaction. 'She looks good here. Ask her in. We'll see what she really looks like. You can interview her and if you think it's worthwhile we could do a few shots ourselves. Take it from there.'

Christabelle walked into the building that housed the fashion magazine and took the elevator to the fifth floor. She had dressed with deliberate care, knowing a white blouse under a powder blue suit with white accessories would compliment her colouring. Her hair was piled up on her head and she wore the minimum of make up, just her eyes and lips accentuated. She had seen the admiring looks from both men and women as she had slid from the taxi, ignoring the driver's offer to take her to Bermuda for the weekend. She took a deep breath and knocked at the door marked Martinez and Able.

'Come in.'

Christabelle entered and approached the receptionist. 'I have an appointment at ten thirty with Mr Able.'

The receptionist gave her a quick glance and ran her finger down the list of appointments. 'You must be Miss Bartlett. Please take a seat until you are called.'

Christabelle sat demurely on the straight back chair and resisted the urge to cross her legs. She picked up a magazine from the table and began to idly flick the pages. Beautiful young women and handsome men were featured on each page, often with exotic backgrounds that she guessed were no more than blown up photographs used as a back-drop. The door to the inner office opened and she studiously ignored it, allowing the man who stood there to examine her for a few moments.

'Miss Bartlett?' Christabelle smiled and replaced the magazine on the table. 'Please come in.' He opened the door wide and watched as she walked across the room. She moved well, not the false, high-stepping walk of the catwalk model, but a natural, easy gait.

'I'm Mike Able. I'm pleased to meet you, Miss Bartlett. Please have a seat.'

Christabelle knew her every movement was under scrutiny. She must not appear too languid, nor must she appear hurried and over anxious.

'Good morning, Mr Able. Thank you for agreeing to see me.'

Mike Able cleared his throat. This girl could be dynamite. She was totally breathtaking. His brain was reeling. He glanced down at the photographs of her that lay on his desk. Brajowski had done a good job, but his photographs did not do her justice.

'It's my pleasure, Miss Bartlett,' he managed to say and was relieved that his voice did not squeak with excitement. 'We are always looking for new talent. You won't mind if I ask you a few questions? Some of them may be a bit personal, but I assure you they are essential.'

Christabelle raised her well-shaped eyebrows. 'If I find them too personal I shall decline to answer them.'

Mike Able was totally taken aback. He was not used to such self-assurance, almost arrogance, from an applicant.

'Quite,' he managed to utter, drawing a pad and pencil towards him and trying hard to collect his thoughts. 'First I have to ask your full name.'

'Christabelle Bartlett, but I want to work under the name of Christabelle. No surname.'

'Why is that?'

'I like my name. I don't want it to be shortened to Chris or Christa and that would probably happen if I used my surname.'

'And what kind of work do you have in mind?'

'Fashion photography for your magazine to start with.'

'Have you any previous experience?'

Christabelle looked at him scathingly. 'If I had experience it is very doubtful that I would be applying for an interview. It would be more likely that you would be contacting me offering work.'

Mike Able gave a choke, which he turned into a cough. 'What made you apply to our company?'

'Your magazine has the widest circulation and the best reputation. I believe in starting at the top.'

'How old are you Miss Christabelle?'

'I was eighteen last month.'

'Do your parents know you wish to have a career in modelling? Are they agreeable?'

'I have spoken to my mother.'

'Your father? What does he have to say?'

'I have no father.'

'I'm sorry.'

Christabelle shrugged. 'There's no need to be sorry. I never knew him, so I don't miss him.'

Mike leaned forward, his elbows on the desk. 'May I ask your ethnic origins, Miss Christabelle? I have tried to guess from the photographs and I came up with Mexican. Now I see you I know I'm wrong.'

'My mother is Greek.'

'And your father?'

Christabelle turned a limpid gaze on Mike Able. 'I have just said I never knew him.'

'Quite. I wasn't thinking. Now, I have to ask about your health. Do you consider that you are fit and well?'

'I certainly do.'

'Do you have any allergies – feathers, perfumes, materials of any sort?'

Christabelle shook her head.

'Any birthmarks or scars that would be difficult to cover with make-up?'

'No, nothing.'

'No trouble with your feet or back?'

'No.' Christabelle looked surprised at the question.

'You often have to spend long hours standing around. Backache and sore feet show in the face. Do you suffer with colds?'

'Not often.'

'Any asthma?'

Christabelle smiled. 'Maybe it would be easier if I told you I have had measles, rubella and chickenpox as a child. I do not take drugs, smoke or drink. I have no skin complaints, allergies, corns, bunions or in-growing toenails, and nor do I have any monthly problems.'

Mike Able looked embarrassed. 'I have to ask, you understand. Now, you say you wish to do fashion photography. What exactly did you have in mind?'

'I would be happy to do evening or cocktail wear, smart and casual fashion, lingerie, beach wear; advertisements for beauty products. I am prepared to be flexible, but I don't want to appear with animals or children.'

'Why is that?'

'I have no experience of either. I wouldn't know how to interact with them.'

Mike Able nodded. 'Some of your photographs are quite provocative. Were you also thinking of breaking into the male magazine market?'

'No,' answered Christabelle quickly. 'I am certainly not prepared to do nude or even topless. Mr Brajowski told me they were a necessary part of a portfolio.'

Mike Able smiled to himself. He had always thought Brajowski to be a lecher. 'Maybe it is for some companies, but not ours. Now, if we decide that we could use you, what do you expect in the way of remuneration?'

'That would depend upon the terms of my contract.'

'What do you mean?' Mike Able frowned. This interview was not running along the usual lines where the applicant was only too eager to work for next to nothing to try to make a name for herself.

'If I am contracted to you for six months I expect to be paid a monthly retainer and commission on each photo shoot. If you are only prepared to pay me each time you use me I shall consider myself freelance and appear in other magazines or advertising as requested of me.'

'Do you have a contract with another magazine?'

Christabelle smiled complacently. 'I have an interview with 'Select' tomorrow, one of your rivals, I believe. Who knows what they might offer me?'

'Exactly.' Mike Able tapped his pencil on the desk. 'Will you excuse me for a few moments? I need to have a word with my colleague, Mr Martinez; then maybe we could arrange to take a few shots of you.'

'If you wish.' Christabelle settled herself more comfortably in the chair.

Mike opened the door that connected his office with Peter Martinez. 'All right to come in and have a word, Pete?'

Without waiting for an answer he closed the door behind himself and sat on the edge of Peter's desk. 'I need your help. I've got that Christabelle girl next door. Wait until you see her! Trouble is; she's trying to drive a hard bargain. Wants a six month contract and commission on all photo shoots, otherwise she says she'll consider herself freelance. She also says she has an interview with *'Select'* tomorrow, and I can assure you we wouldn't want them to get hold of her.'

Peter raised his eyebrows. 'What does she specialise in?'

'Says she's flexible, but no animals or children. She's not interested in nude. That was Brajowski's idea.'

'I bet it was,' grinned Peter. 'He always had good ideas! I'll come and see her. You phone through to William and tell him to be ready in ten minutes.'

Peter Martinez walked through to the office Mike Able used and regarded the composed young woman. She rose and shook his hand.

'Mr Martinez?'

Peter nodded. 'And you are Miss Christabelle.' He was surprised at the firmness of her handshake. 'I believe Mike has gone through all the preliminaries with you and we are arranging to take a few photos of you. Do you have any other clothes with you?'

Christabelle looked faintly amused and indicated the small case beside her. 'Of course.'

'Fine.' He was used to girls dragging in large cases and producing numerous different unsuitable outfits. 'Mike is arranging for William to take some shots of you and I'll ask make-up to get you ready, if that's all right. Now, as regards this contract that you have asked for, we need to discuss a few details, always assuming that we think you are suitable once we have seen our photographs.'

'Naturally.'

'You have asked for a six month contract. That is somewhat unusual. We normally contact an agency and ask them to send someone.'

Christabelle looked at him steadily. 'Are you always happy with the model they send? You probably have to pay them extortionate amounts for the service. If I were contracted to work for you it would need only a telephone call and you would know I was the right girl for the job. Also there would be no chance of seeing me in a rival magazine advertising a similar product.' Christabelle held up her hand, as Peter was about to interrupt. 'Please allow me to finish, Mr Martinez. I cannot agree to work exclusively for you without the guarantee of a regular income. You might only use me once in a month and I would hardly be able to live on that kind of money. If you are dissatisfied with me at the end of six months we can conclude the contract and no doubt I can move on.'

Peter Martinez shook his head. 'We have never given a model a contract.'

Christabelle smiled sweetly at him. 'Now would be the chance to experiment and see if it is profitable to you. I would suggest that I have a retainer of a thousand dollars per month and a further five hundred each time you use me. We're probably talking ten thousand maximum.'

'I'll need to talk to the accounts department. We have to stick to a budget.'

'I'm not prepared to work exclusively for you for less. If I were freelance I would probably make more, even going through an agency.' Christabelle relaxed back into the chair. 'Maybe you could discuss it with accounts whilst I'm having my test photographs. Obviously if you are not satisfied with them you would not be interested in me. All I would ask then is that I am given the negatives and my expenses for travelling here today.'

Peter Martinez found himself nodding agreement to her. He felt totally out of his depth. Never before had he met such a young girl who seemed so much in command of the situation and prepared to drive such a hard financial bargain. He forced a smile onto his face.

'I'll consult with accounts and also my partner. The final decision is not mine alone, you understand.'

'Quite. Would you like to direct me to make-up and we can take it from there.'

Peter Martinez sat across from Mike Able and laid Christabelle's proposal before him. Mike frowned. 'What's she up to? We usually offer the conditions they work under and they are only too grateful.'

'She's done her research. What she says is true. She probably would earn more as a freelance, she could work every day, and even deducting their commission she'd be earning more than she's asked us for.'

'So what's the advantage to her?' asked Mike.

'We're not going to call her every day, leaves her plenty of time to herself. It also means she doesn't have to worry for the next few months. If she's planning to go to *'Select'* tomorrow and tells them we turned her down they'll probably snap her up and offer her more. We could do a feature on her *'Amazing New Model'* a couple of photos and a page about her background, could be a selling point.'

'No doubt she'd want extra for anything we wrote about her.'

'Probably, but I think it could be worth our while in the long run. We could run that in the next issue, and then tell readers there will be an exclusive photo shoot of her in the next. Wet their appetites. In four months we'll be advertising for the summer season and we could use her for our beachwear collection.' Peter leant back in his chair and smiled. 'She could appear in the '*après sun*'. What to wear after a day on the beach or by the pool; casual for barbecues, semi-evening for dinner with friends. By that time we'll know whether the public like her and either extend her contract or cancel. We could then expose more of her in swim wear.'

'You've certainly been charmed by her! Let's go down and see how she works. We don't want any prima donnas putting William into a state. You know how he gets with a new face.'

'Tippy-toes, darling. Head back and arms stretched. The man of your dreams has just entered the room, remember. No, don't look at me. I want your profile. Lovely. One more. Relax. Now, hold up the skirt of your dress, both sides, like wings. Pretend you're an angel. Head to the right. Same pose. Facing me. Fine. Sitting at the table, chin on hand, gazing into his eyes, let the love pour out. Bend forwards a little more. I want a hint of cleavage. That will do nicely. We'll call it a day there. Get yourself changed whilst I get these processed.'

Christabelle nodded demurely and walked back into the changing room. She had noticed that Mike Able and Peter Martinez had entered the studio and ignored them. She knew they would talk to William and longed to know the form their conversation was taking.

'How was she?' asked Mike.

William made a circle with his thumb and forefinger. 'A dream. Knew what I wanted and gave her all. No problems. I'll get these processed and send them up.'

Peter looked at Mike. 'I'll take her for coffee when she's dressed. Sound her out about a feature. If it's just an informal chat I might pick up something that she wouldn't let drop during an interview.'

Mike nodded thoughtfully. 'Provided those photos turn out well we could be on to a winner.'

Christabelle returned home feeling thoroughly pleased with herself. She had assured the men that it was no problem to wait for her contract to be typed up and she had signed it happily. Now with a copy in her purse she felt secure. There was no way they could go back on their agreement unless they were prepared to pay her a very expensive settlement. She would certainly stay for the six months, but it could be worth her while to put out a few feelers towards the end of that time to see if a rival magazine was prepared to offer more. It would be something to hold over her current employers and maybe they would be willing to increase her retainer. At this rate she could soon be a very wealthy woman. She lay on her bed, her eyes half closed, as she envisaged herself wearing exclusive gowns and visiting exotic places around the world.

Anna was incensed when Christabelle told of her success that evening. 'I totally forbid it. You have to finish your education first. And as for giving an interview, that's out of the question.'

'Why? It's a reputable magazine. I'm not doing 'girlie' shots. It's fashion. There's nothing wrong in me giving an interview and them printing up my background. I've nothing to hide.'

'I won't have it. You're only eighteen. You don't know what you're getting into. An interviewer will twist what you say to make you sound more interesting and goodness knows where that could lead.'

'If they don't print the truth I will sue them,' Christabelle remarked coldly. 'I've signed a contract with them and there is no way I'm breaking it.'

'You have to. I'll speak to them. I'll tell them you're too young and did it without my knowledge or approval.'

'You will not. In fact you cannot. I've had my eighteenth birthday so I am considered of an age to make my own decisions. You can't do a thing, mother, so forget it.'

'But your education!' Anna could see her monthly income from Christabelle's father stopping immediately he heard she was working. Having all the household expenses paid by her mother the additional amount he contributed meant she lived very comfortably.

'As far as I'm concerned I've finished my education. I am now embarking on my career.'

'And what will you have to fall back on in a few years time when your looks and figure have gone? Nothing. You'd do far better to wait a while and get into the film industry. I know people who could help you.'

'You, know people who would help me? There would be only one thing they would want from me and I'm not prepared to start my career laying on my back for any one. I'm not like you, mother.'

Anna's face flamed. 'What do you mean?'

'You know what you are, mother. A slut. I've realised over the years that all these 'boyfriends' you have are just meal tickets to you. You don't care about any of them. I'm not prepared to live my life like that. I'll make my way on merit, not sex.'

Anna jumped to her feet and hit Christabelle a stinging blow across her cheek. 'How dare you! How dare you speak to me like that? You've no idea what I've given up for you. If you don't listen to me and do as I say you'll regret it.'

'Is that a threat?' sneered Christabelle.

'It's a warning. When you find yourself on the scrap heap I won't be able to afford to keep you. Where will you get a job? You'll end up in a supermarket stocking shelves if you're lucky.'

'By the time my looks and figure have gone I shall have saved enough money to live very comfortably without needing to work. I should have at least ten years ahead of me, probably twenty if I look after myself.'

'Anything could happen to you that could ruin all your grandiose plans. You're just a silly child.'

Christabelle's eyes flashed. 'I am not silly and I am not a child. You'll find that out very soon.'

Fury at her mother's reaction and the slap she had received was rising in her and she retired to her bedroom. Her mother would have to be dealt with, but she would have to be very careful how she proceeded.

Kurt arrived in response to Anna's frantic phone call. 'I don't see what I can do,' he remonstrated. 'She's headstrong, I admit, but she's also correct in saying that now she's eighteen you can't stop her.'

'You talk to her, Kurt. She might listen to you.'

'You know she won't. She doesn't even like me. My advice is to let her get on with it. If it works out well then be thankful, if it doesn't she'll still have time to return to her education, and might also have learnt a valuable lesson.'

Anna wrung her hands. 'You just don't understand!'

Kurt shrugged. Maybe it was time his relationship with Anna came to an end. It had been enjoyable at first, but now she had become somewhat of a nuisance, continually demanding more of his time and money. He would let her ride out this storm with her daughter and when he felt the time was right he would put her out of his life.

Christabelle sat in the kitchen, her hands hanging limply between her legs and her head bowed. She shuddered intermittently.

'She's in shock.'

'Naturally, but I still have to ask her a few preliminary questions.' The policeman placed his hand on Christabelle's shoulder. 'I'm sorry to have to trouble you at a time like this, but it is necessary. Could you answer a few questions for me?'

'I'll try.' Christabelle's voice was a whisper.

'Just tell me what happened this afternoon, from, say lunch time onwards.'

'I went shopping.'

'What time did you get home?'

'I don't remember, around three probably.'

'And what did you do when you arrived home? Did you go straight into the lounge?'

'No, I went up to my room.'

'How long did you spend up there?'

Christabelle shrugged. 'Maybe five minutes. However long it takes to hang up a jacket and wash my hands.'

'And then you came down to the lounge?'

'No. I came to the kitchen. I was going to make some coffee.'

'Just for yourself?'

'I called out to,' Christabelle's voice broke, 'my mother to ask if she wanted a cup.'

'Take your time. What did you do then?'

'She didn't answer, so I thought she hadn't heard me.'

'Why wouldn't she hear you?'

'The television was on. I switched it off - later.'

'So you thought she hadn't heard you,' prompted Detective Mullen.

'I opened the door to the lounge and that's when I found her. I thought she'd fainted and I went over to her.'

'Having thought your mother was in a faint what did you do then?'

'I knelt down beside her and tried to lift her up.' Christabelle looked at the blood on the sleeve of her blouse. 'It was then that I realised she was hurt.' Christabelle was struck with paroxysms of shuddering.

The doctor stepped forward and took her pulse. 'I really would like to sedate her as soon as possible. She has had a terrible shock.'

'Of course. Do you have anyone we could contact, miss? A friend or relative who would come and stay with you.'

Christabelle shook her head. 'There's no one.'

'What about a neighbour?'

'Oh no, they'll only be nosey and want me to talk about – about – my mother,' she finished lamely.

'I think it would be better if Patty stayed here with you tonight. I don't like to think of you being in the house alone. She'll let the doctor know how you are in the morning.'

Patty put her arm round Christabelle's shoulders, feeling the girl's body stiffen under her touch. 'Come upstairs and get into bed. The doctor will give you a shot and when you wake up you'll feel better.'

'I'll be all right,' Christabelle protested.

'You'll be surprised how difficult you'll find it to get to sleep without a bit of help. Do as the doctor says and it will help you in the long run.'

Without further protest Christabelle allowed Patty to take her up to her room. It was obviously to her advantage to comply with their requests. So far her acting had been perfect.

Detective Mullen finished typing up his report and placed it in the folder. All he needed now was the autopsy report and that would be the end of the case he had been called out to in the late afternoon. Another hour and he would be off duty. With luck he would not receive another call out now and could leave at a reasonable time and get a full night's sleep.

He felt so sorry for the young girl. How terrible to return home and find her mother had suffered a fatal fall. He wondered idly if the woman drank or was on any form of medication that might cause her to lose consciousness. The girl had been negative about both questions, but maybe her mother kept a few secrets to herself. No doubt the autopsy report would bring anything untoward to light.

The Detective entered the precinct office ten minutes early for his duties. He turned on his computer and filled a polystyrene cup with coffee from the vending machine. E-mails first, then he could get on with the routine work. The result of the autopsy on the Bartlett woman should be through by mid-day; then he would have to visit the house again and talk to the daughter about funeral arrangements. He would phone Patty at about ten to see how the girl was coping. If necessary he would ask the police doctor to call in.

Patty reported that Christabelle had slept until early that morning. She had complained of a headache and seemed very quiet and lethargic, probably still suffering to some degree from shock.

Detective Mullen nodded to himself. It was only to be expected. At least she had not become hysterical. Once he had told her that the funeral arrangements could be made and she had something to occupy her she would feel better. He'd give the doctor in the mortuary a call and see when he thought the results would be through.

'Ah, Dennis. I was just about to call you. I'm a bit busy today. Could you come down? There's something I'd like to discuss with you about this woman you sent in yesterday.'

'Can't you tell me over the phone? I'm also busy.'

'If I tell you, you'll still have to come down. See you in, say, half an hour.'

The line went dead and Dennis Mullen looked at the receiver. There was only one reason why Doctor Hendrix would want him to go to the forensic laboratory. He was obviously not happy about the Bartlett woman fainting and hitting her head. There had to be more to it than that. With a sigh the Detective replaced the papers he had been working on into a folder and retrieved the one marked Bartlett. He would take it with him, and also a junior detective.

'Oliver, are you working a case today?'

'Nothing particularly, just routine.'

'Come with me, then. It's a mortuary job first, then on to the family.'

Oliver raised his eyebrows, but asked no questions. He knew Dennis would give him the details as they drove to the other side of the town.

Dennis disliked the mortuary. The smell of formaldehyde seemed to permeate everything and made him feel sick. He was grateful that Doctor Hendrix was waiting in his office and he did not have to talk to him whilst he was carrying out an autopsy.

'I received your report on the Bartlett woman's accident and expected it to be straightforward. There are a few things that need to be explained.'

Dennis sat forward on his chair and instructed Oliver to make notes.

'There is a fresh bruise on the left side of the jaw that is not consistent with her fainting and falling backwards and hitting her head. There is also bruising around her throat and on her shoulders. The damage to her skull could have been done with a sledgehammer. It's splintered.' Dr Hendrix regarded the detective calmly, waiting for his comments.

Detective Mullen frowned. 'Do I understand this right? You're saying someone hit her, tried to strangle her and then smashed her head in?'

Dr Hendrix nodded. 'That's about it as far as I can see at the moment. She may have had a heart attack or some sort of seizure, but that doesn't explain away the bruising or the damage to her skull. A person who faints is usually relaxed when they fall.'

'And with a heart attack?'

'Same sort of thing. Bruising at the point of impact, but nothing more. Depends to a certain extent what they hit their head on, of course.'

'It appears that she landed on the stone fireplace surround.'

'With considerable force, I would say.'

'You haven't examined her heart yet?'

Doctor Hendrix shook his head. 'I thought you ought to see what I've found so far. I've taken photos, of course, but I'd like you to have a look before I go any further.'

The two detectives followed the doctor down to the autopsy room where the body of Anna Bartlett was laid on a slab and covered with a plastic sheet. Doctor Hendrix drew the sheet back to reveal her head and shoulders.

'Look, there,' he pointed to the mark below her chin on the left side. 'It's fresh. You can tell by the colour. It couldn't possibly have happened the day before. Same with these.' On each side of the woman's throat was a dark mark, with lesser bruising showing on each shoulder. 'Hold on, I'll turn her over.'

With practised ease Dr Hendrix turned Anna's body over. On both shoulders there were four dark marks, evenly spaced, and the base of her skull was a mess of congealed blood and bone splinters. 'Seen enough?'

Detective Mullen nodded. He had seen more than enough. He was just thankful that the doctor had not yet opened up the body for further exploration. That really did turn his stomach.

Dennis sat in the car with Oliver. 'Well, what's your opinion?' he asked the young man.

'I'd say that someone did that to her deliberately.'

'I would too. The question is who? Her daughter found her when she came in from shopping.' Dennis sighed. 'We'd better get over there and break the news to her. I warn you, the girl is something to look at. Don't get ideas.'

Oliver grinned cheerfully. 'I'm not likely to. I'm not into girls.'

'Oh!' Dennis was taken aback and gave the young man a surreptitious look.

Detective Mullen had a quick word with Patty before asking to see Christabelle. 'We'll go into the kitchen again. I'd just as soon the lounge stayed untouched at the moment.'

Christabelle entered the kitchen dressed in black trousers and sweatshirt, her hair pulled back from a face devoid of makeup.

'Please sit down, miss.' Dennis indicated the stool at the eating bar.

'We could go into the lounge. I don't mind. I've got to go back in there sooner or later.'

Dennis shook his head. 'Here will do fine. Patty could put the kettle on whilst we talk. I could do with a coffee, if you don't mind.'

Christabelle shrugged. He could have as much coffee as he wanted.

'I'm sorry to have to trouble you again, but I'd like to go over yesterday's events again with you. You said you went out shopping. What time did you leave the house?'

'After lunch, about one thirty, I think, maybe a little later.'

'And where did you go for this shopping?'

'The local shops. I wanted some toiletries from the drug store.'

'What time did you return?'

'I think it was about three.'

Detective Mullen raised his eyebrows. 'It can't take more than ten minutes to walk from here to the shops. Why did it take you so long to buy a few toiletries?'

Christabelle gave a ghost of a smile. 'I was looking at the magazines. I'm going to be a model. I like looking through them to see the latest fashions. I tend to lose track of time.'

'Now, would anyone else have been at the house whilst you were out? A repairman? An acquaintance? Anyone at all?'

'Only Kurt.'

Detective Mullen stiffened. 'Who is Kurt?'

'A friend of my mother. He was just leaving as I came in.'

Detective Mullen made eye contact with Oliver who was standing behind Christabelle and taking notes.

'Can you give me his full name and his address? Maybe he saw someone.'

'His name's Kurt Schwaber. I don't know his address. He works at '*Blue Boys*' in the evenings.'

'How long did you say your mother had known him?'

'I'm not sure. Probably a few months.'

'And you have known him for the same amount of time?'

'More or less. He was just here one day when I came home from High School.'

'And after that he was a frequent visitor?'

'Fairly. He seemed to be here two or three times a week.'

'Did you like Mr Schwaber?'

'What difference does it make whether I liked him or not?' asked Christabelle. 'He was my mother's boyfriend.'

'When you say he was her boyfriend, do you know the extent of their relationship? This is a little delicate, particularly under the circumstances, but were they intimate friends?'

Christabelle shrugged. 'I expect so. My mother never told me and I didn't ask.'

'But you never saw anything that would make you suspect that they were more than friends?'

'Detective Mullen, this may sound rather callous under the circumstances, but my mother had a succession of boyfriends. They usually lasted between six and eighteen months. She told me only last week that she was going to tell Kurt that she was not going to see him again. She had met someone else.'

'Who was this person she had met? Did she tell you his name?'

'No.'

'Was she specific about when she planned to tell Mr Schwaber that she no longer wanted to see him?'

'No.'

'She could have done so yesterday?'

'I suppose so.'

'Now, Miss Bartlett, I want you to think very carefully. You had been shopping and were coming across the road when you saw Mr Schwaber leaving the house. Did he say anything to you?'

'He waved his hand and hurried away.'

'Was that usual if you met outside?'

Christabelle frowned. 'No, he usually stopped and asked how I was, had I enjoyed my day. The usual kind of pleasantries.'

'But he didn't do so on this occasion.'

Christabelle shook her head.

'Why do you think that was?'

'I assumed he was in a hurry.'

Detective Mullen placed his fingertips together. 'You told me last night that you came in and went up to your room. Tell me again exactly what you did up there.'

'I put away the toiletries I had bought. Hung up my jacket and washed my hands.'

'So what were you wearing when you went out?'

'A denim skirt, white blouse and denim jacket.'

'Where are these items now?'

'The shirt is in the laundry box, it has some blood on it, and the skirt and jacket in my wardrobe.'

'You won't mind if we take these clothes away with us? We will need to do some tests on them.'

Christabelle looked at him in surprise. 'Tests? Why?'

'I'll explain to you in a moment. Now, Miss Bartlett, I know this is going to be difficult. Take your time. When you came back downstairs you went to the kitchen and called out to your mother. You received no reply. Please tell me exactly what you did after that. Every little detail.'

Christabelle took a deep breath. She must make sure she kept her story plausible. 'She didn't answer me and I had heard the television on as I passed the lounge.'

Detective Mullen stopped her. 'Was the lounge door open or closed?'

'Open, well, not shut, just kind of half closed.'

'Maybe you could show me later. Please carry on.'

'I pushed the door wide open and walked inside. That was when I saw her. I thought she must have fainted. I went over to her and knelt down. I spoke to her, you know, "Mom, Mom, what's the matter?" and she didn't move. I took her hand and it was limp. I put my hand under her shoulders to lift her up and that must have been when the blood got onto my blouse. As I began to lift her I saw the blood where she must have hit her head on the fire surround.' Tears entered Christabelle's eyes and she brushed them away with her hand. 'I laid her back down and immediately phoned for the paramedics. You know what happened after that.'

'Now, whilst you were upstairs did you hear a noise at all that could have been your mother falling?'

Christabelle shook her head. 'I can't recall hearing anything.'

'Miss Bartlett, I have to ask you not to enter your lounge until I give permission. I received the autopsy report on your mother this morning. It appears that this was more than an unfortunate accident. According to the doctor there are marks on your mother's body that are very recent bruises and the damage to her skull that killed her is too extensive to have been caused by a normal fall, whatever she hit her head on.'

Christabelle buried her head in her hands. 'That's awful; just so awful. Are you sure?'

'We can't be sure of anything at this stage. We will need to get a specialist team up here to examine your lounge and probably the hall. You never know what they might find. There may well have been an intruder. You won't object to us taking your fingerprints, will you? They are bound to be everywhere and we can then eliminate them from any others that we find.'

Christabelle shook her head. 'Whatever you need to do, but why do you need my clothes?'

'It is quite possible that you may have some blood on them that does not belong to your mother. It is very likely that she tried to defend herself and may well have scratched her assailant. If she drew blood it could be on her clothing and also transferred to yours. It would obviously help with the identification of a suspect.'

'Shall I get my clothes for you?'

'Just show Patty which ones you were wearing. She'll bag and label them. Now, are you sure you have no one we could contact to be with you? No relatives at all, even friends from your school, a neighbour?'

'No, and I really would rather no one knew what had happened.'

'I appreciate that, my dear, but if, as it appears, your mother was the recipient of foul play the news media will start to hound you.'

Christabelle looked at him in horror. 'You don't mean it! That kind of publicity could be so … so hurtful to me.' She had been going to say harmful and changed the word just in time.

'If they do try to contact you just say 'no comment', or put the phone down. Don't answer the door to them. I'll leave Patty here with you for a bit longer. If they do start to pester you she can deal with them.'

'I can look after myself,' protested Christabelle weakly.

'I'm sure you can, but you had a terrible shock yesterday and I've had to give you another today. It all adds up. If you want to talk Patty is here.'

'She didn't make your coffee,' observed Christabelle.

'I expect she forgot. I can manage without it. Just remember what I said. Please don't use the lounge until I say you may and be very careful if anyone comes to the front door. There could be some maniac at large. You can't be too careful at the moment.' Detective Mullen stood up. 'We'll be off. I'll arrange for the finger-print crew and I'll probably be back to see you again tomorrow. If you would just show Patty the clothes you were wearing.'

Christabelle nodded. She must be patient just a little longer.

Dennis and Oliver sat in their unmarked patrol car. Oliver was about to start the engine when Dennis shook his head. 'Patty should be out in a minute. I want to hear what she has to say.'

As if on cue, Patty waved to them and walked down to the sidewalk. 'You forgot this, Dennis.' She lowered her voice as she handed him a small notebook. 'I checked the clothes as I bagged them. Nothing visible, except on the blouse.'

'Has she talked to you at all?'

'She's hardly spoken. Spends most of the time sitting and staring into space; seems to be in a world of her own.'

Detective Mullen nodded. 'That will be the shock, no doubt. I'll probably be able to relieve you tomorrow. Right, Oliver, let's go.'

'How did you know she would come out?' asked Oliver as he put the car into gear.

'Deliberately placed this on the table as I left. She knew I'd want a word alone with her.'

Oliver sniffed. 'Why didn't you just ask to speak to her privately?'

'I don't want the girl to think she's being watched and reported on.'

'You don't think she did it?' Oliver shot his chief an incredulous glance.

'No, but she may know who did. Now I think we'll proceed to '*Blue Boys*' and see if they can give us the address of Mr Kurt Schwaber.' Dennis relaxed back in the seat. He could get used to being chauffeured.

Kurt looked at Detective Mullen in disbelief. 'She was absolutely fine when I left her. She had just turned the television on to watch a show.'

'Did you see her daughter as you left, sir?'

'Yes. She was just coming across the road and I waved to her and called out.'

'What did you call out?'

'I don't really remember. Something like 'Hi, how are you' or 'how you doing?''

'And what did she reply?'

'I caught the word 'good', she may have said 'pretty good', 'feeling good'; something like that.'

'And what exactly was your relationship with Mrs Bartlett?'

'We were friends. Had ….'

'Intimate friends?' interrupted Detective Mullen.

Kurt nodded. 'We have been for about six months. I took her out to dinner occasionally, visited her at the house once or twice a week. If she needed something fixed I'd do it for her. She appreciated having someone to discuss her problems with.'

'Problems?' Detective Mullen raised his eyebrows. 'What problems?'

Kurt shrugged. 'Her daughter has just signed a modelling contract and Anna, that's Mrs Bartlett, wanted her to finish her education first. Apparently they had quite a row over it. Mrs Bartlett wanted me to talk to Christabelle, that's her daughter, and get her to change her mind.'

'And did you talk to her?'

'No. I said let her go ahead. If it didn't work out she could always go back to her education and would have learnt a lesson into the bargain.'

'How did Mrs Bartlett accept this piece of advice from you?'

'I think she felt I should have agreed with her, but I'm not the girl's father. I have no influence over her and it really isn't anything to do with me.'

'Quite. Thank you for your time, Mr Schwaber. I may have to call on you again at a later date.'

Detective Mullen left Kurt with a bemused look on his face. Who would have thought that Anna Bartlett would have been found murdered in her own home!

'Well, Frank, have you anything more for me?'

Dr Hendrix shook his head. 'Apart from the bruising and the crushed skull there was nothing physically wrong with the woman. No trace of drugs or excess alcohol in her system.'

'Any theories about who could have inflicted the injuries – man or woman?'

'Considerable strength had been used to force her head back. That indicates a man, rather than a woman.'

'What about the size of the bruises? Do they give any indication?'

'Not really.'

'Anything under the finger nails?'

'No, scrupulously clean.'

'And the punch to the jaw?'

'Again, I can't commit. All I can do is repeat that in my opinion the injuries were inflicted by someone using considerable force.'

'Thanks for your help. If anything else should occur to you give me a call.'

Kurt was surprised to see the detectives at his apartment for a second time that day. He was dressed in a pair of shorts and his body glistened with sweat from his exertions. 'What do you want now? I thought I'd answered all your questions this morning.'

'I'm afraid we have one or two more questions for you. You don't mind if we come in?' Dennis Mullen pushed the door open as he spoke.

'Can I have a shower and get dressed? I've been working out and I don't want a chill.'

Dennis nodded. 'We can give you ten minutes. Have you got your own gym?'

'No, just a couple of bits of equipment.'

'May I see?'

'Go on through,' called back Kurt as he headed into the shower.

Dennis and Oliver walked into the bedroom. A rowing machine and a punch bag were on view, obviously having been used recently. Dennis ignored them and opened drawers and cupboards swiftly, giving the contents a cursory glance.

'Thought I might as well take advantage,' he grinned at Oliver as they walked back into the lounge. 'Do a quick check and make sure he is in the shower.'

Oliver returned and nodded. 'Turned the water off just after I poked my head round the door and I saw him step out. He's pretty muscular.'

Dennis made no comment and the two detectives sat in silence waiting for Kurt to finish dressing and return to the lounge.

'Can I get you anything, gentlemen? Coffee, soft drink or something stronger?'

Detective Mullen shook his head. 'We're fine, thanks. I'd just like to go over your movements for yesterday again. You have the right to have the services of an attorney before you say anything more to us if you wish.'

Kurt shook his head. 'I don't need an attorney. I've nothing to hide.'

'Good. Now, what time did you say you arrived at Mrs Bartlett's house?'

'I can't say for certain, sometime between quarter to two and the hour.'

'Did you always visit at that time?'

'No. It varied. Depending upon my schedule.'

'So Mrs Bartlett would not have been expecting you?'

'She was expecting me, but I hadn't given her a firm time. Just said after lunch.'

'Did you plan to spend the whole afternoon with her?'

'Not on this occasion. My brother was in town and I'd arranged to meet him for a drink before he caught his flight home.'

'Where did you meet him?'

'At the airport. More convenient for him than coming into town to me.'

'Quite. What does your brother do for a living?'

'He's into computers. Trouble shooting. Gets called all over the States.'

'And where exactly had he been called to on this occasion?'

Kurt frowned. 'Carmans, Sharmans, Shermans – some name like that. I didn't take a lot of notice.'

'How long had he been in the area?'

'I'm not sure. He called me from his hotel to say he would be here for a few days and could we meet up for a drink before he left.'

'Do you see your brother frequently?'

'No. Only if he comes down this way. The last time was over a year ago.'

'Do you have a good relationship with him?'

'Yes, we're friends as well as brothers.'

'So why didn't you arrange to meet at a time when you would be able to spend longer together?'

'He had arrived in the early hours and booked straight into a hotel. He spent the next days with the firm sorting out their problems. I work in the evenings. Meeting up at the airport was the most sensible solution. We've done that before.'

Detective Mullen nodded. 'You'll be able to give me his address and a contact number I presume?'

'Of course, but why is it necessary?'

'We may need to corroborate your statement.' Dennis Mullen consulted his notebook. 'So you arrived at Mrs Bartlett's at approximately two and you left at what time?'

'I told you, about three. I'd arranged to meet Wilhelm at five and I wanted time to allow for the traffic. As it happened I got there a bit early and had to wait half an hour for him.'

'What were you wearing when you left yesterday afternoon?'

Kurt looked at the detective in surprise. 'Shirt and jeans.'

'Where are those clothes now?'

'The shirt is at the laundry. The jeans are in the wardrobe.'

Dennis raised his eyebrows. 'Was it necessary to send the shirt to the laundry?'

'Today is laundry day. I send everything. Sheets, towels, clothes. I have no facilities here.'

'Could you give us the name and address, please?'

Kurt frowned. 'Yes, of course, but I don't see why you should need it.'

Detective Mullen closed his notebook. 'I would like you to come down to the station with us to make a formal statement. You'll come willingly, I hope, sir. If you refuse I can get a warrant for your arrest.'

'My arrest? Whatever for? I've done nothing.'

'Then you'll have nothing to worry about, will you, sir? You can telephone a lawyer from the station if you wish and in the meantime I suggest you say nothing further to us. If you'd just like to get your jacket and keys.'

Having deposited a thoroughly bemused and slightly frightened man at the precinct station, Dennis turned to Oliver. 'What do you think of him?'

'He seems genuinely puzzled by your request that he makes a formal statement at the station. Do you want me to track down this brother of his?'

'Not at this stage. I think we'll pay another visit to Miss Bartlett. Ask her for a little bit more information about her mother's boyfriend.'

Patty informed them that Christabelle was lying down when they arrived and they sat in the kitchen to await her. Movement could be heard in the lounge where every inch was being examined minutely for any information.

'I'm sorry we had to disturb you, miss. I hope you weren't asleep?'

Christabelle shook her head. 'No, just resting. Trying to come to terms with events. What can I do for you?'

'I just wanted to tell you that we have taken Mr Kurt Schwaber to the station to make a statement. He's not been charged with anything at this stage, but we want to check up on one or two things and ask him a few more questions. We'll keep him in custody until we are satisfied with his answers.'

'Oh, that's a relief. I feel much safer now.'

'Safer?'

Christabelle bit at her lip. She must be really careful. She smiled at the detectives. 'I wasn't strictly honest with you yesterday, about the time I was out.'

Dennis regarded her sternly. 'In what way?'

'I did go out about one thirty to the drug store and spent some time looking at the magazines, but I was home about two thirty. I didn't know Kurt was here until I had entered the house. I heard him shouting at my mother and thought they were having a row. I didn't want to get involved so I slipped back out and waited across the road until I saw him leave. Everything else I told you is true.' She turned an innocent gaze on the two men.

'When you say shouting; could you hear what he was saying?'

Christabelle shook her head. 'No, when I say shouting, it was more that his voice was raised and he sounded angry.'

'Did you hear your mother?'

'I left as quickly as I could.' She shivered. 'I didn't want Kurt to think I had been eavesdropping.'

'So you have no idea what could have made Mr Schwaber angry?'

'I told you my mother was planning not to continue the relationship. She may have told him and that could have caused his anger.'

'Did Mr Schwaber have a quick temper?'

'I don't really know, Detective. I avoided him if I could.'

'Why was that, miss?'

'I didn't like the way he looked at me.'

'Can you describe the way he looked? Was it menacing or threatening?'

Christabelle appeared to consider. 'Not exactly, it was more speculative. As if he was thinking what he could do to me.'

'Mr Schwaber told us that you and your mother had a disagreement about you starting a modelling career. She had asked him to speak to you, try to dissuade you.'

Christabelle gave a small smile. 'We did have an argument when I first told her. We then both calmed down and discussed it sensibly. I have signed a six-month contract. I assured her that I would go back to my education if I wasn't successful at the end of that time.'

'Why didn't you tell us yesterday that you had seen Mr Schwaber in the house?'

'I was frightened,' she said simply. 'When I found my mother I thought it was an accident. I was so shocked. It was so unexpected. I could hardly think straight. When you told me she had been,' Christabelle moistened her lips, 'murdered, I knew it had to be Kurt. If he knew I had told you about their argument he might have returned and done something to me.'

'Well I don't think you need to worry about that now. I'd like you to accompany us down to the station and make a full statement.'

She looked at the detective in alarm. 'Are you arresting me?'

Dennis smiled reassuringly at her. 'Certainly not. It's just a formality. Your statement will be used to help us put pressure on Mr Schwaber and hopefully he will make a full confession. If he continues to protest his innocence it will take that much longer to get a conviction, but we should be able to keep him in custody. You'll have nothing to fear.'

Christabelle relaxed visibly. 'You've been very kind to me.'

Christabelle returned from the precinct station feeling elated. All she had to do now was rid herself of the continual presence of Patty and she could get her life in order. She needed to decide on the image she planned to present to the world. It could be to her advantage to continue to act as a charming, innocent young girl, coming to terms with a tragedy.

'Patty, can you give me some advice?'

'If I can.'

Christabelle frowned. 'I presume I shall have to arrange a funeral for my mother. How do I go about that?'

'First of all you have to wait for notification that her body has been released. That should be any time now. You have to register her death and then take the certificate to a mortician at a funeral parlour. They'll be able to advise you on procedure after that.

Did your mother leave a will? She may have left instructions regarding her wishes.'

'A will? I've not thought about that. I suppose I'll have to look through her papers.'

'Did she never mention it to you?'

Christabelle shook her head. 'She obviously didn't expect to die yet.'

'Do you know the name of her lawyer?'

'Would she have one?'

Patty smiled. 'How would I know? Most people do. There should be papers around regarding the deeds of this house. If they're not here the chances are they're lodged at a lawyer's office.'

Christabelle sighed. 'I'm not looking forward to the next few weeks.' She frowned. 'I ought to telephone Mike Able. I don't feel I can give an interview at present.'

Patty looked at Christabelle curiously. 'Interview?'

'I start work in a couple of weeks. My modelling job. They wanted to do an interview with me about my life as part of an advertising feature. I don't think I can cope with that at present.'

'It wouldn't be advisable. You might say something that could have a bearing on the outcome of the trial of Mr Schwaber.'

Christabelle pulled a face. 'They'd relish in the details. No, I'll phone Mr Able and ask for an appointment to explain the position to him. I'm sure he'll understand. I am able to go out and about as I wish, aren't I?'

'Of course. You can do as you please. The sooner you get back into a normal routine the quicker you will recover from the trauma. You do seem to be coping quite well.'

'I'm trying.' Christabelle gave a tremulous smile. 'It still doesn't seem real. How much longer are you staying, Patty?'

'Detective Mullen told me I could leave when I felt you were able to be left alone. I wish you did have someone who could come and stay with you, for a few days at least.'

Christabelle shook her head. 'Now Mr Schwaber's in custody I feel considerably happier. It will take time, of course, to get over what happened to my mother. Once I start working it will be easier. Take my mind off it. Tell Detective Mullen that you can leave whenever it suits you. I'm very grateful to have had you here, but there really is no need for you to stay any longer.'

'Are you quite sure?' Patty sounded doubtful.

'Yes,' replied Christabelle firmly. 'I'm going to be busy going through my mother's papers, then making funeral arrangements. I'd like to have everything sorted before I start work. I don't want to have to ask for time off if I can help it.'

'I'll leave you my phone number. You can call me any time if you suddenly get a bit low and want some company.'

'I'll really appreciate that. Now, I must make an appointment with Mr Able. That will be the first job out of the way.'

Mike Able looked at the young girl as she sat in front of him. Black did nothing for her and the quicker she came out of mourning the better. He was shocked; such a tragedy for her.

'Of course I understand, my dear. Naturally it would be impossible for you to give an interview under the circumstances. Do you feel up to commencing work in a week or so? We could delay for a short while if it would help.'

Christabelle shook her head. 'I want to start as soon as possible. It was just the interview that was worrying me. I'd find it very difficult to talk about my life with my mother at the moment.'

'Don't hesitate to contact me if there is any way we can help you. Are you,' he hesitated, this was a little delicate, 'sound financially? There can be a lot of expenses at a time like this.'

'I don't know. I still have to go through my mother's papers. Find her will. Once I've done that I should be able to have access to her bank account.'

Mike Able took a chequebook from the drawer. 'Maybe a little on account would help.'

Christabelle's eyes filled with tears. 'Everyone has been so kind to me. I'll not use it unless it becomes necessary. I will repay it from my salary. Thank you, Mr Able. I really did not expect that,' she said honestly.

'You take care of yourself. Call me if any problems arise, otherwise we'll see you in two week's time.' Mike shook Christabelle's hand and ushered her from his office, immediately entering Peter Martinez's room to apprise him of the situation.

Wilhelm Schwaber was surprised when the police drew up outside his house. He answered the door swiftly, convinced they were bringing him bad news about one or both of his elderly parents. The policeman shook his head at his anxious enquiry.

'To the best of my knowledge both your parents are fit and well. May I come in Mr Schwaber? We have a couple of questions we would like to ask you about your visit to your brother. Nothing to be alarmed about.'

'Has he met with an accident?'

'No, but he is in somewhat of a difficult situation. Were you aware that he was friendly with a lady by the name of Anna Bartlett?'

'I knew there was a woman in his life by the name of Anna. I don't think he ever mentioned her surname to me.'

'Have you any idea how long they had been acquainted?'

Wilhelm shook his head. 'Not really, some months. What is this about?'

'Unfortunately Mrs Bartlett was found dead shortly after he had left her house. On the day in question he says he was meeting you at the airport. We would just like to confirm a few facts with you regarding that meeting. What were you doing in New Orleans?'

'I work as a trouble shooter for a large computer firm. If they have a serious fault that cannot be put right over the telephone I am asked to visit the company and sort things out for them.'

The policeman nodded. 'And this was the purpose of your visit on that occasion?'

'Yes. I had flown in earlier in the week. I telephoned Kurt and we arranged to meet at the airport before I flew back to Washington. We hadn't seen each other for well over a year so it was a good chance to catch up.'

'If you could just give me the name of the firm you were called to, the hotel where you stayed and your flight details I'd be grateful'

Wilhelm frowned. 'What do you need those for?'

'Just routine. Instructions from the New Orleans police.'

'I work for *International Trouble Solutions*. They had a call from Carmans. My secretary booked my flights and a hotel close to their offices. She can confirm that for you. I have to hand over all my receipts.'

'Would you have a bill from the airport bar?'

Wilhelm shook his head. 'No. Kurt bought the drinks. If I had done so I would probably have thrown the bill away. Entertaining my brother would not have been acceptable on my expense sheet.'

'Was your brother on time to meet you?'

'He was early, he was waiting for me.'

'And how did he appear to you?'

'What do you mean? He was no different from the last time I saw him.'

'He didn't seem anxious, stressed in any way, nervous?'

Wilhelm shook his head bewildered. 'He was just the same as always. What's this all about?'

'Mrs Bartlett appears to have been murdered and your brother, Kurt Schwaber, was at her house only a short while earlier. He was seen to leave no more than ten minutes before her body was discovered.'

Wilhelm's face turned ashen. 'My brother had nothing to do with that.'

'How can you be so sure, sir?'

'He's not a violent man. He never has been.'

'Mr Schwaber claims he is innocent, but the police have to make enquiries, you understand. If you could tell me of anything that appeared out of character to you about his demeanour or behaviour I'd be grateful.'

Wilhelm shook his head. 'I've told you, there was nothing. He was waiting for me, we had a beer together, well, I had a beer; he had a soft drink as he was driving.'

'What did you talk about whilst you were together?'

Wilhelm shrugged. 'Nothing of any great importance. We talked about our parents. I told him Michelle and I are planning to go to Vegas for our wedding anniversary.' He frowned. 'I really cannot think of anything out of the ordinary.'

The policeman shut his notebook. 'Thank you, Mr Schwaber. That will be all.'

'Can I contact my brother?'

'You would have to contact the police department in New Orleans. I have no jurisdiction there. I was simply asked to make some enquiries of you and report back to them.'

Christabelle went to the bureau. Now she had the house to herself she could go through her mother's papers at leisure, hopefully she would find a Will and also a bank statement which would give her an idea how much she had to live on in the immediate future.

Two hours later Christabelle slammed the last drawer shut in frustration. There was nothing. No Will, no bank statements, no deeds to the house, no letter from a lawyer. They had to be somewhere. She sat back on her heels and thought carefully.

There was nothing locked in the kitchen or bathroom so they would hardly be stored in there. They could only be in her mother's bedroom. Sighing deeply she stood up and stretched her cramped limbs. She might as well start the search now.

The drawers and wardrobe revealed nothing other than the items they were designed to contain. Christabelle looked around the room. There was the bedside chest of drawers and a blanket box beneath the window. She pulled out the two spare pillows that lay on the top, followed by a spare duvet and there beneath it was a small metal cash box. She lifted the box out, surprised at how light it was, and placed it on the bed. Clicking her tongue with annoyance as she found it locked, she began her search for the key, finally discovering it inside a small vase that stood on the windowsill.

She turned the key in the lock and looked in at the meagre contents. There was a savings book, some bank statements, an address book and a sealed envelope. Christabelle flipped open the savings book and smiled as she saw a balance of over seventy thousand dollars. Eight hundred dollars had been deposited regularly each month over the years and at times further sums had been added. Each month a withdrawal had been made, but always less than the amount deposited. The bank statements covered only the last three months and showed very little monetary movement and a final balance of five hundred dollars.

Curiously she opened the address book, finding the contents sparse in the extreme. There were no addresses and everyone was listed under their first name. Bryony, Elena and Matthew, and Matthew had been crossed through, Helena and Gregory, all with local telephone numbers.

In the section for 'K' there was just a telephone number, no name. Presumably they were acquaintances of her mother and she could contact them later.

The telephone ringing startled her and she reached out a tentative hand for the extension by her mother's bed. 'Hello?' She was surprised how nervous she sounded.

'Detective Mullen here. I just wanted to let you know that you can start to make funeral arrangements. The police surgeon has issued the death certificate so all you have to do is register it and contact funeral parlour.'

'Thank you. Patty told me the procedure.'

'Are you all right there alone? I could ask Patty to come round.'

Christabelle gave a shaky laugh. 'I'm coping well. The telephone surprised me. I thought it might be the press.'

'I've managed to stall them temporarily. Sent them off to another part of the town where there was an incident. We'll have to give a press release when the case eventually comes to trial, but that won't be for a long time.'

'I do appreciate your help, Detective.' Christabelle spoke sincerely.

'All part of the service. I'll leave you in peace now.'

'Thank you. Goodbye.' Christabelle replaced the receiver and turned her attention to the envelope. She assumed it contained her mother's Will and she opened it carefully. Inside were four sheets of paper.

The first one she looked at appeared to be a financial agreement. It declared that Rudi Ersoy would deposit eight hundred dollars a month into the account held in the name of Anna Bartlett until such time as their daughter Christabelle finished her education. It was signed by Rudi Ersoy, followed by an address, and also by someone called Elias Kzantarou.

Christabelle sat down heavily on the bed.

The second and third sheets of paper were folded together and she opened them curiously. It was her birth certificate and Rudi Ersoy was named as her father. Rudi Ersoy was her father! It couldn't be *the* Rudi Ersoy. He was famous. Surely her mother would have told her if her father was a well-known film star? The other sheet of paper declared that her name had been changed back to Bartlett and consequently the original birth certificate was no longer valid.

The final sheet of paper had a heading giving the name and address of a firm of lawyers and was an agreement regarding the house where she had lived all her life. Christabelle read it through a second time, trying to understand the full implication of its contents.

'Provided Anna Bartlett keeps the conditions imposed upon her by her parents the house is for the sole use of Anna Bartlett and her daughter Christabelle. All utility bills and maintenance expenses, up to a maximum of five hundred dollars a month, will be paid by Elias Kzantarou or Annita Kzantari directly into the account of Anna Bartlett.

In the event that Anna Bartlett remarries or co-habits the expenses will no longer be paid by them.

Upon the demise of both Elias and Anna Kzantarou the house will be bequeathed to Anna Bartlett and she may remain living there or sell as she thinks fit.

In the unlikely event that Anna Bartlett dies before her parents the house in its entirety will return to them as part of their estate.'

There were three signatures at the foot of the declaration and Christabelle read it through again in disbelief. She was, in effect, homeless, unless, of course, these Kzantarou people were already dead. This was something she had not foreseen. She had always assumed the house belonged to her mother and she would inherit it upon her death. Christabelle rubbed her hand across her head. This upset her plans to sell the house and rent an apartment closer to the town. Should she contact the firm of lawyers and see if the document was legal, and if so, how long she had before she would be required to vacate the property?

She gave a little smile. Obviously she was not thinking clearly. If she had never found the agreement she would not know about the conditions. She would just stay in the house and plead ignorance if confronted at a later date. She would leave the paper locked in the box and hidden beneath the duvet and pillows, no one could prove that she had found it unless they knew the other papers were with it, and that was highly unlikely.

Carefully she refolded the paper and replaced it inside a new envelope that she fetched from the bureau in the lounge. Taking a pillowcase from her mother's bed, she wiped both the inside and outside of the cash box before placing it carefully into the blanket box and covering it with the duvet and pillows. With the same pillowcase she wiped the outside of the blanket box, then proceeded to strip the rest of the bedding and take it down to the washing machine where she bundled it inside.

Returning to her mother's room, she collected the remaining papers and the address book. They could sit innocently in the bureau until such time as she had a use for them. Sitting in the twilight in the lounge, Christabelle began to make plans for the following day.

First she must collect the death certificate; then visit a funeral parlour. She would use a call phone to telephone a solicitor, give a fictitious name and just check that everything legally belonged to her if her mother had not left a will. After that a visit to the bank was a necessity to transfer the money from her mother's account into her own. She also had to deposit the advance she had on her salary.

Feeling satisfied with the way events were progressing she prepared a salad, added some cheese and two slices of rye bread. She turned on the television to watch the news, hoping there would be a film afterwards to interest her, whilst she ate a leisurely meal. Later she would spend an hour exercising before having a shower and retiring to her bed, safe in the knowledge that she would fall asleep as soon as her head touched the pillow.

Christabelle, Detective Mullen and Patty were the only people who attended Anna Bartlett's funeral. Christabelle kept her head bowed during the service, thanked the police officers briefly and prepared to hurry away.

Detective Mullen took her elbow. 'I'll be happy to take you home, Miss Bartlett. Patty and I will be going your way. We can have a little chat on the way.'

Christabelle felt her heart lurch. She forced herself to smile. 'Thank you. It hasn't been the best of days.'

Dennis opened the car door for her and Patty slid inside at the back.

'What did you want to talk to me about?' asked Christabelle.

'Just wanted to ask how you were feeling?'

Christabelle sought her words carefully. 'A little disorientated. I keep expecting to go home and see my mother there.'

'Have you had a chance to look for any legal papers?'

'I've been through the bureau and found her bank statements.'

'Was there no copy of a Will?'

Christabelle shook her head. 'Nothing like that at all. I haven't found any deeds to the house or the name of a lawyer. I'll ask at the bank when I go down to sort out the finance. They will probably be able to help me.'

'Quite likely. You could even find they hold a copy of her Will.' Dennis moved into the main stream of traffic. 'Could you just tell me again exactly what happened the afternoon that you found your mother?'

'I've told you and I've also made a statement,' Christabelle protested.

'I know, but Mr Schwaber insists that he had no disagreement with your mother and that he called out to you when he saw you outside.'

Christabelle raised her eyebrows. 'It certainly sounded as if they were having an argument. Had they been talking normally I would not have gone back out.'

'Maybe it was the television you could hear?'

Christabelle shook her head. 'It was definitely Kurt's voice.' She wrinkled her brow. 'I didn't hear any other voices. I don't think the television could have been on.'

'But it was on when you returned home the second time?'

'I told you that was why I thought my mother hadn't heard me call out to her. I remember switching it off. I did that before I called the paramedics. I wanted to make quite sure I heard what they said to me.'

Dennis nodded. 'You're quite certain?'

'Absolutely.'

'Mr Schwaber says he called out to you and you replied, he wasn't quite sure what you said, but is adamant that you did so.'

She shook her head. 'He just waved his hand and hurried off.'

'Did you know Mr Schwaber was interested in body building?'

'No, but as he works as a security man at a night club I'm not surprised. He would need to be fit.'

'Do you go to a gym at all, Miss Bartlett?'

Christabelle looked at him in surprise. 'Goodness, no. I'm not interested in physical activities at all.'

Dennis smiled as he drew the car to a halt in front of her house. 'We'll keep in touch, Miss Bartlett. Let you know how things are progressing.' He watched her enter the front door. 'Poor kid,' he observed to Patty, who had joined him in the front of the car. 'She obviously has no one in the world to turn to.'

'She's a strange one. Shows very little emotion. She didn't shed a tear today.'

'I think she's still in shock. Keep in touch with her, Patty. She might need a good deal of help in a few weeks.'

Christabelle stretched herself lazily on her bed and thought about Rudi Ersoy. Tomorrow she would try to find his telephone number and set up a meeting with him. She wondered idly what kind of a reception she would get, but certain that she would come off better in any encounter.

It took Christabelle over a week before she was finally able to make an appointment to meet Rudi Ersoy. She had searched the telephone directory, not expecting to find a number, tried the film casting agencies to no avail and finally film studios who were able to give her the telephone number of his secretary. She had tried to sound very professional whilst she spoke to the cool young woman who tried to deter her. Christabelle insisted that she was carrying out an investigation on behalf of the bank and she had confidential business with Mr Ersoy, the detailed nature of which she was not able to disclose. All she could say was that the bank needed their representative to meet with him to verify a signature. Her persistence finally paid off and the secretary confirmed his address and made her an appointment at ten thirty the following day.

Dressed in her powder blue suit, Christabelle took a taxi to the address and walked confidently up to the door. To her surprise Rudi opened the door himself and she took stock of the figure she had only ever seen before on a cinema screen.

'Good morning,' his white teeth gleamed as he smiled at her. 'I presume you are the young lady from the bank who needs to verify my signature?'

'That is correct. May I come in?'

Rudi opened the door wider and Christabelle stood in a large octagonal hall. 'My study would probably be the most suitable room, I think.' Rudi pushed a door on his left and ushered her inside.

'You have a very fine house, Mr Ersoy.'

'Thank you. Do have a seat, Miss …? I regret I don't know your name.'

'I didn't give my name to your secretary. Had it become necessary I would have given her a false one.'

Rudi frowned. 'Why on earth would you do that?'

'Because had I given her my real name I am sure you would not have agreed to see me.'

'This isn't an interview for some tabloid is it?' he asked suspiciously.

'Certainly not,' replied Christabelle firmly. 'But I would like to ask you some questions.'

Rudi stood up. 'I think not. You have obviously tricked your way into my house and I have absolutely nothing to say to you. Please leave now.'

Christabelle settled herself back into the chair. 'You may have been able to get rid of me that easily once, but not this time.'

'What do you mean? I've never seen you in my life before. You've come to the wrong person. I don't wish to be rude, but I am asking you for the last time to leave or I shall telephone the police.'

'That would be very foolish of you, Mr Ersoy. I suggest you listen to my proposition before you call anyone.'

'I've told you, no interviews.' Rudi towered above Christabelle who did not move.

'The interview will not be about you, but about me.'

Rudi sat back down in the chair. 'I really do not understand what you're talking about.'

Christabelle straightened her back. 'Then I will spell it out very simply for you. I would like confirmation from you that some eighteen years ago you had an affair with a woman named Anna Bartlett.'

'I don't see that my private life has anything to do with you.'

'It has a great deal to do with me, Mr Ersoy. I am Anna Bartlett's daughter – your daughter.'

Rudi shrugged. 'I don't believe you. You have no proof that I ever knew your mother.'

Christabelle raised her eyebrows. 'On the contrary, I have a birth certificate and it names you as my father.'

Rudi shrugged. 'That proves nothing. You can put down whatever name you want on a birth certificate. She'd probably seen me in a film and become a fan.'

'I agree, she could have been, but it is somewhat of a coincidence that you then agreed to pay Mrs Bartlett eight hundred dollars a month for the keep and education of this daughter you know nothing about.'

Rudi's jaw sagged. 'What rubbish has your mother been telling you? This is a pack of lies. If you don't leave immediately I shall throw you out.' He rose again, bunching his fists menacingly.

Christabelle smiled at him. 'Do sit down. I haven't stated the purpose of my visit yet.'

'Your visit is over.'

'I think not. You see, I have been asked to give an in depth interview for a magazine. I think the story of how I discovered my father would make quite interesting reading, don't you?'

'Mrs Bartlett was quite well known for the favours she bestowed. I doubt if she would know who fathered any of her children.'

Christabelle felt the heat rushing to her face. 'Mr Ersoy, both you and I know that you are my father. We can keep that knowledge just between us or I can tell most of the population of America. The choice is yours.'

Rudi slumped into the chair. 'Are you trying to blackmail me?'

Christabelle shook her head. 'I just want to come to an arrangement with you. Sadly my mother died a short while ago and when I was going through her papers I found the agreement that you signed agreeing to pay for my education. I am still only eighteen, so would probably be continuing my education for at least another three years. That would be a minimum of twenty four thousand dollars that you would be paying. Who knows, I might decide to end up a professor, how many years does that take?' Christabelle smiled at him.

'How did your mother die? Was it illness or an accident?'

'Unfortunately she was murdered.' Christabelle spoke calmly.

'Murdered! How? By whom?' Rudi was obviously startled.

'The police have arrested a man who was a friend of hers. I can't say any more than that obviously.'

'Did he do it?'

Christabelle shrugged. 'The evidence certainly points to him.'

'That's terrible.' He passed a hand over his forehead. 'So what is it you want? If you are asking me to recognise you as my daughter I'm not prepared to do that.'

'I have no wish to be anyone other than Christabelle Bartlett. I have managed for eighteen years without a father so I really don't think I need one now; but as you are my father I consider that you have a responsibility to me. I am not planning to continue with my education, but I think a lump sum payment to help me to get started in my career would be in order.'

'And when you've spent that you'll come back again for more.'

Christabelle shook her head. 'I, too, am willing to sign an agreement with you. You give me a cheque for twenty four thousand dollars, and provided the bank honours it, I'll leave you in peace. You can continue with your life and I can start mine.'

'And if I refuse?'

'Rudi, may I call you Rudi? It would be very foolish of you to refuse me. I have signed a contract to begin a modelling career in five days time. Originally they wanted me to do an interview about my life as advertising propaganda. Obviously after the death of my mother I said it was out of the question at the moment. I may feel able to give such an interview in a few months time. It could be quite a story. Losing my mother in such tragic circumstances, but finding my long lost father.'

Rudi gave her a look of pure hatred. 'You are blackmailing me.'

'Not at all. As I pointed out, if I had decided to continue with my education you could be paying out a lot more than twenty four thousand. My mother left me very little and I have to live until I am well known and sought after. I shall invest most of the money. I don't plan to end up destitute at some time in the future.'

'What makes you think I have that kind of money?'

Christabelle curled her lip scornfully. 'Please, don't try to plead poverty. You are known to be one of the wealthiest and most successful film stars. You certainly live in an extremely opulent house.'

'It costs money to live like this.'

'I'm sure it does. I would love to have the opportunity. The house where I lived with my mother is a shack compared to yours, but it is home. Now, your chequebook, Rudi; then I'll not bother you again.'

'What about the agreement you mentioned?'

'I have it ready. Once you have given me the cheque I will give you the agreement.'

'I'd like to read it first.'

'Very well.' Christabelle took a sheet of paper from her purse. To her surprise he perched a pair of glasses on his nose and read it slowly.

I, Christabelle Bartlett, daughter of Rudi Ersoy and Anna Bartlett, have accepted a gift of twenty four thousand dollars to help me start my career as a model. This exempts Mr Ersoy from his regular payments of eight hundred dollars per month and absolves him of any future responsibility for me financially.

'You haven't signed it.'

'You haven't given me the cheque,' she retorted quickly.

Reluctantly Rudi took his chequebook from a drawer in the desk. 'I should never have got mixed up with your mother,' he growled.

'Oh, I'm pleased you did. I wouldn't be here otherwise, would I?' Christabelle watched as he signed the cheque with a flourish.

'The agreement,' he reminded her, still holding the cheque.

'Of course.' She placed her signature on the piece of paper.

'I don't trust you. Suppose you come back again in a few months and ask for more?'

Christabelle raised her eyebrows. 'That's not a very nice thing for a father to say to his daughter. Provided the cheque is honoured

I doubt if I shall have any reason to contact you again. I won't mention to anyone, particularly your wife, that you are my father.' Christabelle took the cheque from between Rudi's fingers and placed it safely in her purse. 'There's just one other thing; I would like to be introduced to my half brothers at some time.'

'Never. They are much younger than you, just children.'

'I would still like to meet them.'

'It's out of the question. Now get out.'

Christabelle gave him a dazzling smile. 'You've been so good to me. I do appreciate it.'

Rudi showed her out of the front door and returned to his study. He beat his fist on the arm of the chair. The little gold-digger; she took after her mother there. Grudgingly he had to admire her. She had obviously planned carefully before confronting him. He just hoped she would keep to the agreement that she had signed and not keep coming back for more. His money would not last for ever and then he would have no way to keep her quiet. He doubted that his two boys would have as much nerve and audacity in similar circumstances.

'Mr Schwaber, let us go over the events again. Maybe you will remember something.'

'I've told you. I didn't hurt her. I kissed her goodbye, she switched on the television and probably went over to her chair to sit and watch whatever was on.' Kurt was exhausted with the continual questioning from his attorney.

'You didn't actually see her sit in her chair?'

Kurt shook his head. 'I was out of the room by the time I heard the television.'

Arthur Delaney pursed his lips. 'Are you quite sure you didn't return. Maybe you had forgotten something?'

'I went straight to the front door and out.'

'Mr Schwaber, I want to believe you, but I'm finding it very difficult. You must tell me the truth.'

'I am. I swear I am. I didn't lay a finger on her.'

'Have you ever suffered from amnesia?'

'No.' Kurt looked surprised.

'Had you been drinking?'

'No, I was driving.'

'Do you take drugs in any form, either medicinal or recreational?'

'I had antibiotics last winter for a chest infection, but I don't take anything regularly except multi-vitamins.'

'Were there any cross words between you – an argument?'

'No, nothing.' Kurt shook his head in despair.

Mr Delaney looked at the miserable man in front of him and tapped his pen on the table. 'According to the statement given by her daughter she heard you raise your voice, she said you sounded angry. Were you angry about anything?'

'No. I had no reason to be.'

'Had Mrs Bartlett, perhaps, told you that she no longer wished to see you?'

'No.'

'Would that have made you angry had she done so?'

'Not angry. Upset, hurt, maybe, but not angry.'

'You work as a security man at *'Blue Boys'* I understand?'

'Yes.'

'How long have you worked there?'

'About five years.'

'Your job means you have to stay physically fit, I presume. I hear you have a small gymnasium in your apartment.'

'I like to work out, keep in trim.'

'Do you consider yourself physically strong?'

'Reasonably.'

'So a woman of Mrs Bartlett's physique would not have been a challenge to you?'

Kurt frowned. 'I don't understand what you're getting at.'

'Considerable force had been used on the lady. If, and I repeat if, you had molested her it is quite possible you used more force than you realised which resulted in her injuries.'

'I didn't touch her.'

'Have you ever injured anyone whilst performing that duty?'

'Nothing worse than a few bruises that I know of.'

'Mr Schwaber, are you quite certain that when you kissed Mrs Bartlett goodbye you did not hold her rather too hard, maybe pushing her head back, enough to leave bruising?'

'I bent down to kiss her. I had my hands in the small of her back. Her hands were at the back of my neck.'

'You did not, I suppose, whilst you were talking, accidentally bump her on the chin? These things can happen.'

'I did not,' replied Kurt firmly.

Mr Delaney closed his brief case. 'Well, I'll think over all that you've told me and be back tomorrow.'

'I've told you the truth. I swear it.'

'So you keep saying, Mr Schwaber.'

Christabelle looked through the address book that had belonged to her mother. She didn't want any of these people turning up unexpectedly on her doorstep. She would telephone the first number this evening and see what kind of a reception she received. A man answered the telephone at the third ring.

'Could I speak to Bryony, please?'

'I'm sorry, she's not here at present. Can I take a message or ask her to call you back?'

'I'd rather speak to her in person. When would a good time be to call again?'

'She should be in tomorrow evening after seven. Are you sure I can't give her a message? Tell her who called?'

Christabelle ignored his offer. 'I'll try again tomorrow.' She replaced the receiver quickly and turned to the next listing. It rang persistently six times; then an answering machine cut in. Christabelle slammed the receiver down. She would try the last number and if they were not available she would not bother to call them again. Once more she was unsuccessful; a recorded message cutting in to say the number was no longer in service. She shrugged her shoulders. She would try this Bryony person tomorrow and forget the others.

'Mr Schwaber, if you continue to claim your innocence you realise you will be tried for homicide.'

'But I am innocent.'

'So you keep saying! If you put in a plea of manslaughter – she provoked you – you hit her – you tried to catch her, but she fell and hit her head.'

Kurt shook his head. 'I didn't touch her.'

'Look,' Mr Delaney sat forward. 'I'm going to lay it on the line. You are going to be tried for homicide. If you don't come up with any defence you're going to get a death sentence.'

'What do I have to say to convince you?' Kurt had a note of desperation in his voice. 'You're supposed to be my attorney, supposed to do your best to ensure I receive justice. All you seem to want to do is convict me.'

'Mr Schwaber, I will do my best to secure your freedom, but you have to tell me the truth. You can plead mitigating circumstances or diminished responsibility, but just to keep repeating that you're innocent means I have no defence to put up on your behalf.'

Kurt looked at the attorney before him. 'There is nothing else I can say. I am innocent. If you can't take my word for it and believe me then I'd better appoint another attorney.'

Mr Delaney sighed deeply. 'Maybe you should, Mr Schwaber. I really do feel that I cannot help you.'

'Hello, is that Bryony?'

'Yes.' The voice was wary.

'I'm sorry to telephone you like this, but I believe you knew Anna Bartlett?'

'Yes,' again the voice sounded suspicious of the caller.

'I'm afraid I have some sad news for you. Mrs Bartlett died some weeks ago.'

'Oh! I don't believe it! How? Was she ill?'

'Unfortunately she was murdered.'

'Murdered! How? By whom?'

'I really don't feel I can go into details over the telephone. The police have a man in custody.'

'Are you calling from the police department?'

'No. I'm her daughter.'

'Her daughter!'

'Yes.'

'Then you're my sister.'

'I think you must be mistaken there. I have no brothers or sisters.'

'No, wait, listen. Where are you?'

'At home.'

'In Hollywood?'

'Hollywood – goodness no. I'm in Gulfport, Louisiana.'

'How long have you been there?'

Christabelle gave a small laugh. 'All my life.'

'I don't understand. Hold on a moment, please.'

Christabelle could hear a conversation in the background and finally a man came back on the line.

'I'm Bryony's husband. You've obviously given her a bit of a shock and everything seems very confused. We live in Gulfport also. Could we come over and meet you? Maybe we could get a few things straightened out.'

Christabelle hesitated. Did she really want to get involved with these people? 'I guess so,' she agreed.

'Give me your address and we'll be over. We have a car so it will be no problem.'

Christabelle dutifully relayed the address of the house and deliberately vague directions to where she lived.

'Right. Give us about half an hour and we'll be with you.'

Before Christabelle could reply the line went dead and she frowned at it in annoyance. She had not expected them to want to visit her and certainly not at such short notice. Now she only had a short time to ensure the house was reasonably tidy and decide whether to change her clothes or greet them in a tee shirt and jeans.

It was nearer an hour and a half before a car drew up outside and Christabelle peered curiously through the curtains. A tall, thin man opened the passenger door for a small, plump woman. She looked totally bewildered and he gave her shoulders a squeeze as they walked up to the door.

Christabelle took her time in answering their knock and ushering them into the lounge. 'Please sit down. I can only offer you coffee or a cold drink, I'm afraid. I don't have any liquor.'

'That's quite all right. We're teetotal. I'm Marcus and this is my wife, Bryony.'

Christabelle shook their hands. 'I'm Christabelle.' She was pleased she had bothered to change into a pair of black tailored trousers and a white blouse, dressed her hair and made up her face. She felt vastly superior to both of them, neither of whom was smartly dressed and Bryony's face was devoid of make up.

'How did you know where to find me?' asked Bryony as soon as she was seated.

'I found an address book when I was turning out my mother's belongings. It had the name 'Bryony' and a telephone number. I thought the least I could do was telephone her friends and let them know of her death.'

Marcus sat forward. 'Are you able to tell us what happened? It won't distress you too much?'

Christabelle shook her head. 'I'm over the shock and I've dealt with all the horrible formalities. I've told the police department so many times that telling it again won't hurt me.' She explained to them how she had returned from her shopping trip, heard Kurt's raised voice and waited until she saw him leave the house; then a few minutes later discovered her mother's body.

'That must have been very traumatic for you,' Marcus sympathised. 'I presume this man Kurt is the one the police have in custody?'

Christabelle nodded. 'I was certain he had killed her and I felt much safer when they arrested him. I thought he might come back and do the same to me as I had seen him leaving the house.'

'Very understandable. Have you been able to hold a funeral yet?'

'A couple of weeks ago. I had to wait for the autopsy to be completed before I could make any arrangements.'

'She was my mother, too. I hadn't seen her for years, but I would like to have attended her funeral.' Bryony's lip trembled.

'I'm sorry. I didn't find the address book until afterwards. I didn't feel I could go through her personal possessions at first. It didn't seem right.' Christabelle turned large, sad eyes on them. 'Mom had always been there and suddenly I was alone.'

'You're not alone any longer. You have family now. I don't know whose idea it was that we shouldn't know you, but it was very wrong of them. We could have helped you and stood by you. You certainly shouldn't have had to face this on your own.' Marcus reached across and patted Christabelle's hand.

'Grandma said mother was living in Hollywood, but you say you've lived here all your life?'

Christabelle nodded. 'Mom never said she had any relatives. When I asked her she said it was just the two of us.'

Bryony shook her head in disbelief. 'You mean, she never told you that you have three sisters, cousins, grandparents?'

'Three sisters?'

'Yes, well, strictly speaking you have. We have no idea where either Sorrell or Saffron is living now. You see, Jeremy, he was Saffron's father, and my mother had an almighty row and he walked out taking Saffron with him. Grandma said mother had gone to Hollywood with a film star. Sorrell and I went back to boarding school and spent the holidays with Grandma and Grandpa. Sorrell left to go travelling as soon as she was old enough. I haven't seen her since before I was married and I don't know where she is now.'

Christabelle's head was reeling. She wished she had never tried to telephone any of the numbers in her mother's address book. 'Did your mother – our mother – never visit you?'

Bryony shook her head sadly. 'Grandma always said that the time wasn't right and she wasn't able to get away from her work in Hollywood. I suggested I visited her, but she said that it wasn't convenient and mother moved around a good deal so she didn't always have her current address. After I tried two or three times I got the message that she didn't want to know me, so I didn't bother any more.'

'Why should they say she was in Hollywood when in fact she was living here in Gulfport?'

'I can only think that her relationship with this so called film star had failed and she didn't want to lose face by admitting to them that she was living close by.'

Christabelle shrugged. 'All her relationships seemed to fail. They usually lasted from six months to a year; then someone new would appear on the scene.'

'I'm afraid Mom had a problem. If it's any consolation to you I have no idea who my father is and nor has Sorrell.' Bryony turned towards her husband. 'You wouldn't mind if Christabelle came and stayed with us until she gets back on her feet, would you?'

'Not a bit. We haven't very much room, but we can fit you in. You'll be welcome.'

Christabelle shook her head. 'It's very kind of you, but there really is no need. I have a home here and I'm starting work in a couple of days. You're under no obligation to look after me.'

Inwardly Bryony breathed a sigh of relief. She had felt obliged to make the offer. 'If you're sure - if there's anything you need you will tell us, won't you?'

'I'm sure I'll be fine. I was given an advance on my salary to help me with current expenses and once I actually start work I should be able to save a considerable amount. I'm a photographic model and the magazine seems to think I have quite a future before me.'

Bryony nodded. She felt dowdy and unkempt beside the young girl who exuded glamour. 'We'll leave you our address. It would take too long now to tell you about all your other relatives and the family history. Maybe we could meet up properly one weekend, make a day of it and get to know each other properly?'

'I would really appreciate that. I feel a bit overwhelmed at the moment. I don't think I could take in any more information this evening.'

'I think Bryony is feeling much the same. It has obviously been a shock for both of you.' Marcus squeezed his wife's hand. 'Let's set a date for a proper get together before we leave.'

'I don't know what my commitments are to the magazine. You set a date and I'll contact you if I can't make it for any reason.' Christabelle had no intention of attending a family reunion.

Marcus and Bryony consulted his diary and finally settled on a date three weeks in advance. Christabelle dutifully wrote down their address and the date, promising that she would telephone and confirm nearer the time, assuring them that she was certain she would be free over a weekend.

'I'm so pleased we have found each other.' Bryony's eyes were moist with unshed tears as she hugged her half sister. 'I just wish mother was still here.'

Christabelle did not return the hug, but Bryony did not seem to notice. 'So do I. I'm sure she would have been delighted. I do appreciate that you bothered to come round to meet me. I'm very fortunate to have found such lovely relatives.'

Marcus looked at his wife quizzically as he drove away from Christabelle's house. 'Well?'

'What do you mean – well?'

'What did you think of her?'

'She seemed nice enough. It's hard to form an opinion under the circumstances. I'd like to get to know her better. After all, she is my sister.'

'Half sister,' Marcus corrected her.

'I wonder what Grandma will say when we tell her?'

Marcus frowned. 'Do you think it's a good idea to tell her?'

'Why ever not? She has to know that my mother is dead.'

'Does she? It would distress her terribly. It took me almost an hour to calm you down. Why not leave things as they are?'

Bryony looked at him doubtfully. 'Would that be right? What about Aunt Elena and Uncle Andreas? Should we tell them?'

'Why don't we wait until we've met her again? See how she feels about suddenly having a crowd of curious relatives. It's a lot for her to have to deal with on top of everything else.'

Bryony sighed. 'I suppose you're right. It's been eighteen years since anyone heard from my mother so I guess another month or so won't make any difference.'

Christabelle enjoyed her time in front of the cameras and rushed to buy a magazine the first time she was featured advertising perfume. She was disappointed that it only showed her head and shoulders and did not give her name, but it was a start. She was surprised when she visited her local drug store to see the same picture staring back at her from the perfume counter. She would wait until she received her first cheque and see whether she was paid any extra for the advertising.

The week before her intended meeting with Bryony and Marcus she telephoned them. 'I'm so very sorry. I've been asked to go out of town for a week to do some location work. I'm not going to be able to make our date.'

Bryony sounded genuinely disappointed and suggested two other weekends, but Christabelle refused to commit herself. 'I'll pencil them in, but I will obviously have to cancel if I'm sent out of town. You do understand, don't you?'

'Of course. Your career seems to be taking off. I'm so pleased for you. It will be lovely to have someone else famous in the family.'

'Someone else? Who else is famous?'

'Uncle Andreas. He writes plays and has had one turned into a film. His name features regularly in television credits.'

'What is it? I'll look out for him.'

'Andreas Kzantarou. I forget you don't know about the rest of the family. I tell you what I'll do, I'll draw you a family tree and write a little bit about everyone. Then when we meet up you'll know who I'm talking about.'

'Would you really? That would be a tremendous help. I feel terribly ignorant and I don't want to offend anyone.'

'I'm sure you wouldn't. Actually, Marcus and I agreed that before you were introduced to the rest of the family you should really just come and meet us properly. We can talk and get to know each other. It would be rather inconsiderate of us to expect you to cope with meeting everyone at once.'

Christabelle breathed a sigh of relief. 'That's very thoughtful of you. It would be a bit of an ordeal. I'll look forward to receiving the family history and do my best to make our next meeting.' She replaced the receiver thankfully. If she were only to meet Bryony and her husband again it would not be so difficult.

A thick envelope arrived for Christabelle and she looked at the contents with interest. The family tree that Bryony had promised showed her grandparents had four children; one of her aunts had twin girls and a boy and her mother having four girls. Both of the twins were married and had children of their own.

Christabelle settled herself on the sofa and began to read the closely typed pages. Her grandparents, Annita and Elias Kzantarou had come to America when her grandfather was given a research grant and had stayed in the country. Her grandfather had died eight years ago, both their older daughters had been widowed and her uncle had never married. Bryony was scant of details about her aunt Maria, who was now in Brazil, but wrote considerably more about her aunt Elena and her twin daughters, one of whom had married a relative and lived in Crete. Their brother, Andrew, was working at the New York Stock Exchange and she was unsure whether he was married or single. Of her uncle Andreas she gave details about his writing career, but no mention of his private life.

Christabelle looked at the family tree again. So this Elias Kzantarou had been her grandfather. It was his signature on the agreement with Rudi and also on the tenancy conditions of the house. Maybe she would keep her next weekend appointment with Bryony and see what further information she could gather that could be of use to her in the future.

Christabelle examined the statement that had arrived with her cheque carefully. The advance on her salary had been taken off, but she had been paid commission for the three photo shoots she had completed. There was no mention of extra commission for advertising. She lifted the telephone and requested an appointment to meet with Mike Able and was gratified to be told he could accommodate her the next morning.

She donned her new cream suit with a toning lemon blouse and surveyed herself in her mirror. It had been worth the investment. One new item of clothing per month she was prepared to allow herself, but she was determined to always put at least five hundred dollars into the savings account, knowing the day would come when her looks were no longer in demand.

Mike looked at her appraisingly as she entered. It was good to see a model make an effort and not turn up in jeans looking like any other girl in the town.

'It's good to see you, Christabelle, and may I say how that colour suits you. What can I do for you?'

From her purse Christabelle withdrew her statement. 'I would be grateful if you would clarify something for me. The perfume advert I did for you, should I be receiving commission for the local advertising?'

Mike smiled. When he had prepared the account he thought she might query it and he had his answer ready. 'Of course. Unfortunately the contract came in too late for this month. You'll receive it next time.'

'How much?'

'An extra one percent.'

Christabelle shook her head. 'Not enough. Three percent.'

'Out of the question. We only make four percent ourselves,' he lied glibly.

'I expect two.' Christabelle rose. 'Two, or I withdraw my permission for any photograph of me to be used outside of your magazine. There was no mention of outside advertising in my contract; therefore you are in breach of our agreement.'

Mike Able waved her back into the chair. 'Hold on, now. It was the decision of the drug stores. Originally we had another girl lined up for the job. They pointed out that it would look rather contradictory to have two different people advertising the same product and we were forced to agree with them. We withdrew Mandy Jo and used you. This happens, you understand.'

'I do understand, but I feel I should have been advised.'

'I apologise. I didn't think. My fault entirely.' Mike smiled at her. 'We're very pleased with you, Christabelle. I think you'll find you're working your tail off very soon.'

'Good. I'd like to show a little bit more of me than just my face. People will think I haven't got a body to back up my looks.'

'All part of our exposure of you. Your next assignment will be for jewellery and we'll go down to your waist. Following that I have plans for eveningwear. Keep the public guessing and wanting to see more of you. When we start advertising the summer beachwear range they'll get their wish and see your legs.'

'That sounds a little more exciting than lipstick, perfume and shampoo. And the advertising percentage?'

'Two,' he stated firmly. 'I'll add it into your contract.'

She gave him a dazzling smile. 'I knew I could rely on you, Mike.'

'If you had an agent they would be responsible for the negotiation of deals,' he reminded her.

'If I had an agent I would be working freelance and you would not have an exclusive on me. Whilst I'm here I'd like to ask if there's a chance of any location work. I've never been outside New Orleans and I'd appreciate the experience of visiting new places.'

'At our expense, I bet you would,' Mike thought. He smiled at her. 'It's early days. Location work can be pretty demanding.'

'I'm not afraid of hard work. Eventually I want to be on the cat walk for the most exclusive designers. I'm determined to get to the top and be the most sought after model in the world. Success doesn't come from sitting at home dreaming about it.'

'Stick with us and you could find you achieve that ambition. Let me organise your exposure and you won't regret it.' Mike looked pointedly at his watch. 'I've got to rush. I've an appointment down town. Can I give you a lift?'

Christabelle shook her head. 'I have a few errands to run whilst I'm in this area. Thanks for the offer and your help. I can pick up my amended contract when I come up to work next.' She extended her hand. 'I hope you don't think me too pushy, but I have to look after my interests.'

After Christabelle left, Mike entered Peter's office. 'That girl will go far,' he observed. 'Did you listen in?'

Peter nodded. 'I thought you handled her very well. I wonder where she has in mind for location work - the Bahamas?'

'I wouldn't put it past her! See you in a couple of hours. I'm off to the jewellers to select the items we need for next week.'

'Mr Schwaber, a provisional trial date has been set for January of next year. Is there anything you can tell me that would help your cause?' Eric Delaney looked at the forlorn figure before him.

Kurt shook his head. 'Nothing. I've told you the truth. I can't do more than that.'

Mr Delaney sighed heavily. He knew the man before him could expect a life sentence for homicide, possibly the death sentence. 'Very well. I'll be in touch. Let you know how things are progressing. We're proceeding with character references at present. Show the court that you have a blameless past. You'll need to have medical tests nearer the time, to show you are of sound mind and physically fit, but I'll let you know the dates set for those in good time.'

Kurt nodded. He really did not care.

'It's wonderful to see you, Helena, and you Greg. The boys have grown so much. John's looking forward to having them to play with for a couple of weeks.' Marianne loaded their luggage into the car. 'We have about an hour's drive ahead of us. Tell the boys to give me a shout if they need to stop.'

Marianne looked at her sister, taking in the immaculate make up and perfectly styled hair. She was comfortable in her shorts, tee shirt and flat shoes, but doubted that her sister felt the same in the high heeled sandals she was wearing. They were going to be totally impractical and Marianne hoped she would have more suitable footwear with her.

Helena looked at the straggling, unkempt buildings on the outskirts of the town. This was not how she had imagined Crete.

'I've given you a bungalow close to the taverna. I don't know what you plan, but it's the closest to the beach. When I come up in the morning I can leave you the car if you want to go for a drive,' Marianne offered.

Greg looked at the scooters wheeling in and out of the traffic. Everyone seemed to be taking their life in their hands. 'Is it as busy as this everywhere?'

'It is during the season. It quietens down in the winter.' Marianne braked sharply to avoid a taxi that pulled out in front of her without a signal. She shouted rudely at the driver who shrugged and continued on his way.

'You won't have to worry about cooking. If you get yourselves some breakfast we can make arrangements for lunch and then I expect you to join us for the evening meal. Everyone is looking forward to meeting you so much. You'll have to bear with Aunt Anna and Uncle Yiorgo. I've told them you're coming and who you are, but they neither of them remember from one day to the next.'

'Mum said that where you live is beautiful.' Helena sounded doubtful.

'It is,' Marianne assured her. 'Take no notice of this suburban sprawl. We live right by the sea and have a wonderful view of Spinalonga. You'll have to go over and see where old Uncle Yannis lived. They take boat loads of tourists over every day, but I thought we could go early one morning before they start arriving.'

'Have you got a boat?' asked Paul. Maybe this holiday was not going to be as boring as he had imagined.

'Just a little one with an outboard motor. Do you like boats, Paul?'

'I think so. Dad has taken us out on the lake.'

'You'll find the sea is a bit different and there are strict rules. You have to wear a life jacket.'

'I won't need that. I can swim.'

'I'm pleased to hear it, but you'll still wear a jacket when you're in the boat. If you fell over the side it would keep you afloat until we hauled you out. Now, we're just driving through Malia. This used to be a tiny village, just the main street. There's an archaeological site here that you might like to visit.'

Helena looked at the shops they were passing. Covering almost every square inch of space were brightly coloured dresses, embroidery and beach goods of every description. Tourists were milling around on the narrow pavement and Marianne was forced to drive at a crawl.

'Once we get passed here we can travel a bit faster again. They have talked about building a new road to bypass the town. The traffic is frustrating for everyone.'

'I'm surprised those things they have hanging up stay clean,' remarked Helena.

'They don't. They use the same ones for display all summer. Never buy anything from outside, always show them what you want and they'll get it for you from their new stock.'

'I want one of those,' announced Mark, pointing to a large inflatable dolphin.

'You can't,' Helena informed him. 'They're dangerous. The wind can blow you out to sea.'

'You can play with John's,' Marianne promised and saw the annoyed look on her sister's face. 'He's allowed to have his provided it is tied to a rock.'

'You don't let him on the beach alone, do you?' asked Greg.

'Of course not. He can just about swim now, but he's not allowed down there without an adult yet.' Marianne increased the speed of the car. 'You'll start to catch glimpses of the sea now. We'll take the cut over the hills so we can go to your bungalow first to drop off the luggage. Giovanni is up at *'ANNA'S'* and John is with him. I'll wait whilst you get changed into something comfortable, then I'll take you down to the house.'

'Does John speak English?' asked Helena.

'Of course he does. He also speaks Greek and is picking up a bit of Italian from Giovanni.'

Helena sighed in relief. 'My Greek is pretty rusty. I never use it now.'

'Not even when you visit grandma?'

Helena shook her head. 'I don't manage to get out to her very often. I'm so busy with the boys and everything.'

'I'm sure it will come back to you. We always speak Greek at home as the family don't speak anything else. Mum coped all right when she came. What about the boys? '

'I've never bothered to teach them. It didn't seem worth it as we're American now.'

Marianne slowed to a halt. 'Have a look at the view from here. There's Spinalonga.'

Helena and Greg looked across the sparkling blue water where the small island could be seen shimmering in the distance.

'Can we go in the sea when we get there?' asked Paul.

'Not today. By the time we've unpacked it will be too late.'

Marianne raised her eyebrows. 'The boys can come back with me whilst you do that. I'll take them down for a swim with John. If you don't mind, of course.' She spoke in Greek, knowing the boys would not understand.

Helena frowned. 'Maybe. I don't want them getting chilled.'

Marianne laughed. 'They won't get cold in August.' She started the car again and they began to cruise down the hill.

Marianne drew up outside the taverna and sounded her horn. John came bounding out followed more slowly by his father. He looked at the two boys and was not impressed. Their shorts and open neck shirts were clean and pressed, and they were both wearing socks with their sandals.

'Hello, scruff,' said Marianne, taking in his grubby shorts and dirty tee shirt. 'What have you been up to?'

'Mending my bike. The chain came off.'

'Come and meet Mark and Paul, and say hello to Aunt Helena and Uncle Greg.' Marianne was quite used to seeing John in dirty clothes. He started off immaculate each morning, but had an inability to stay clean for more than about half an hour. She was amused by the obvious disapproval on her sister's face.

Giovanni helped Greg to take their cases from the boot of the car, placed them on a hand trolley and began to wheel them towards a bungalow.

'It won't be noisy here at night, will it?' asked Helena anxiously. 'The boys won't be able to sleep if it is.'

Marianne looked at her in surprise. 'It won't be noisy,' she assured her. 'The boys will probably be so tired by the end of the day that they would sleep through an earthquake if we had one.'

Helena was horrified. 'Earthquakes! I hadn't thought about that. Is it safe here?'

Marianne shrugged. 'As safe as anywhere else. Now, do you want the boys to get changed into swimming trunks and come back with me?'

Greg nodded to his wife. 'Might as well. They'll only be a nuisance nagging us to get to the beach.'

Helena hesitated. 'Are you sure they'll be safe?'

'I promise I'll stay with them the whole time. You get sorted out up here and let Giovanni know when you're ready to come down to the house. He'll be at the taverna or round and about. It's not usually busy at this time of day; most people are out enjoying themselves. I'll let him know the arrangements and grab John.'

Marianne walked back to the taverna and spoke to her husband. 'I'm going to take the boys down for a swim. Helena thought it would be too late by the time they had unpacked for them to go.'

'How long will unpacking take them? It's only three now.'

Marianne shrugged. 'I'm not sure this will be an easy fortnight.'

By the time Giovanni arrived at the house with Helena and Greg it was nearly six.

'Where are the boys?' asked Helena as soon as she stepped out of the car.

'Playing with John in his room.'

'I'd better go and see them. They didn't get sun burned, did they?'

'I put cream on them, but they're both dark enough not to burn easily,' Marianne assured her.

'You can't be too careful. Where's John's room?'

'I'll show you.' Marianne led her sister into the house. By the noise emanating from one room it was obviously where the boys were playing. Marianne opened the door and there was an immediate hush. 'What are you doing?' she asked sternly, looking at the rearranged furniture and the bedding spread all over the floor.

'We're camping and we've just been attacked by wild animals,' explained John.

'Wow! Pretty scary! Anyone hurt?' asked Marianne, pretending to be serious.

John shook his head. 'We fought them off.'

Helena was horrified. 'Just look at this room! Boys, I'm disgusted with you. What a way to behave.'

'Leave them, Helena. They're only having fun. It can all be cleared up later. How long are you camping for? Have you got enough supplies with you?'

'Just 'til supper.' John waved an empty crisp packet at his mother. 'We had a packet each.'

'They boys won't eat their supper,' announced Helena.

'I'm sure they will. They were probably hungry after the beach. Come and meet Aunt Anna and Uncle Yiorgo, then we can sit out on the patio and have a drink.'

Marianne drove her sister and her family to the airport with a feeling of both sadness and relief. As she had predicted, the fortnight had not been easy. Helena had worried the whole time that the boys would fall if they climbed on the rocks, would be burnt by the sun, drown in the sea or die from food poisoning. When they had visited Knossos she insisted their boys accompanied them and then complained that they had both been a nuisance all day, continually nagging at their parents to return to Elounda and go on the beach. Their trip to Spinalonga had been hardly any more successful as she insisted they held her hand or

Greg's and did not go anywhere near the ruined buildings as they might fall and injure themselves.

By the end of the first week John was walking around with a permanent scowl on his face as after their first riotous evening in his room Mark and Paul had been forbidden to play the same game again and they had spent the time pushing model cars around or playing board games, with Helena checking on them every half an hour or so to ensure they were behaving.

'They're babies,' he complained to his father. 'If Mark doesn't win he cries and Aunt Helena thinks I've hurt him, and Paul cheats. I'll be glad when they go home.'

Giovanni felt much the same way. How could twin sisters be so different? Helena asked for the car windows to be closed so that her hair would not get blown about, she was continually applying sun tan cream to herself and the boys and saying the sun was too hot, or screaming at them to be careful. She had insisted on visiting a hair dresser in Aghios Nikolaos and then complained that they had no idea how to style her hair, despite it looking no different from the way it had when she first arrived. By the time she had showered, applied her make up and repainted her finger nails it was mid morning and Greg would have kept the two boys amused until she was ready to accompany them. Giovanni was thankful that he was married to Marianne.

Helena relaxed back into her seat. 'Thank goodness we are on the way home. I don't think I could have lasted there very much longer. How does Marianne put up with that kind of life?'

'It didn't seem too bad to me,' commented Greg.

'Not too bad! She spends all her time rushing around from one place to another. Even when she's at home – and it isn't their home – she has to look after that old aunt and uncle.'

'She seems happy.' Greg tried to placate his wife, not wishing to hear all her complaints about the holiday he had enjoyed.

'How can she be! What has she got to look forward to?

Throughout the summer she admits she works her fingers to the bone. She hasn't got a home of her own; it belongs to Giovanni's uncle, and what happens when they get old? She'll be expected to look after them as she does the other relatives. What a waste of her education, after all the money Pappa spent on her. Going to University in England and training to become an international lawyer; a lot of good that did her.'

'Your Pappa would have done the same for you. You decided you wanted to get married. Do you regret that now?'

Helena looked at her husband sharply. 'Of course not. Do you?'

'Not a bit,' he replied cheerfully. 'You're just different. Marianne seems quite content with her life the way it is.'

'How can she be?' asked Helena scornfully. 'She never goes to the hairdresser or beauty parlour. She doesn't even seem to have any friends to go out with occasionally. Not that there is anywhere to go except a taverna. Her son is so badly behaved; probably because he has to spend so much time amusing himself.'

'I thought they spent a good deal of time with him.'

'That was probably because we were there. I expect they're usually too busy working to take any notice of him.'

'I didn't get that impression.'

Helena glanced at her husband in annoyance. He was supposed to agree with her.

'We're taking off,' announced Mark, his face glued to the aeroplane window.

Paul gave a deep sigh. 'I wish we were just arriving.'

Greg smiled at him. 'You enjoyed yourself?'

Paul nodded. 'I wish I lived there like John does. He's so lucky. Fancy having your own beach! Can we come back again next year?'

'We won't be able to afford it,' Helena answered quickly. 'It costs a lot of money to go to Greece from America.'

Paul's face crumpled and his lip trembled.

'Don't start howling. You're too big to behave like a baby.'

'Maybe they could come and visit us?' he suggested, blinking rapidly to try to disguise the tears in his eyes.

'They haven't any money to go travelling like we have,' announced Helena smugly.

Greg looked at her in surprise. He had never heard her speak so spitefully about her sister before. 'You really didn't enjoy yourself?'

Helena shook her head. 'If we had stayed in a hotel it might have been better. At least we could have had a separate room for the boys and some privacy and we could have eaten the kind of food we're used to instead of the things Marianne dished up with all that salad.'

'I quite enjoyed trying some of their local dishes. I thought that grilled octopus was great.'

Helena gave him a scathing look. 'I'm surprised we didn't all have food poisoning or bad stomachs at the very least. Those sausages! Did you see that old aunt with the bowl between her legs stuffing the skins. So unhygienic!'

Greg took her hand. 'Well, we didn't. I'm sorry you didn't enjoy visiting your sister. Maybe if we went on our own when the boys are older it would be better. You two would be able to go off on shopping sprees and I could just lounge around on the beach.'

'You just don't understand, do you, Greg? Marianne and I might be twins but we are as different as chalk and cheese. She would probably be as miserable going shopping, if they have any decent shops, of course, as I was laying on the beach. I'm not surprised Grandma took the opportunity to leave and come to America. I have no desire to visit Greece again. I find it difficult to understand why Mamma goes out each year. She surely can't enjoy herself.'

'I'm sure she likes to see Marianne and John. If we moved away I'm sure she'd want to come to visit us.'

'That's different.' Helena picked up the in-flight magazine signalling an end to the conversation. 'I thought I might buy some of that perfume they were advertising on the way out. It's only forty dollars a bottle. I could buy two and give one to Mamma.'

Christabelle looked at her bank account. It was growing steadily. She had resisted buying any of the ornate and expensive jewellery she had modelled, despite the offer of a discount, but had succumbed to a small gold Rolex wrist watch. When she had first seen it on her wrist she had fallen in love with the elegant timepiece and spent the whole of that month's salary to purchase it. She had spent frugally since then, only one new pair of shoes and a blouse.

Detective Mullen had sent her a brief unofficial communication that the trial of Kurt Schwaber for the murder of her mother would probably be held in January and she would be called upon to give evidence. She shrugged the information off. She felt quite capable of dealing with that event when it happened. She knew now where she had inherited her talent for acting.

Her day spent with Bryony and Marcus had been interesting, but she had avoided making a further date to meet with them and requested that the rest of the family were not yet told of her mother's death.

'Kurt is coming up for trial in January, but apparently the dates often change due to delays. It will probably be in the newspapers, so my relatives will have to know before then. I'm thinking particularly of my grandmother. Why distress her before it's necessary?'

Bryony bit at her lip in indecision. 'What do you think, Marcus? Should we tell them now or wait until nearer the trial?'

'I think we should wait,' replied Marcus firmly. 'We don't know how they will react to the news. As Christabelle says, why distress any of them until we have to?'

Christabelle smiled with relief. All the time her grandmother thought her daughter was alive and well she had the house to live in and no expenses. She certainly did not want to have to think about renting an apartment; it would interfere with her savings plan.

'Elizabeth! Do you mean it? Are you really coming over? I can't wait to see you. You'll never believe the way Plaka looks now. Don't be silly, you'll stay with us, not in a bungalow. You're our guests, you're family. Would you charge me to come and stay with you? Of course not, so we don't charge you. Give me your flight details. I'll be there to meet you. Of course it's no trouble. Monday week. Wonderful.'

Marianne replaced the receiver. 'Giovanni! Giovanni! That was Elizabeth. They're coming over in two weeks. Isn't it wonderful?'

Giovanni smiled at her excitement. 'Great news. Where are we going to put them? We're fully booked.'

Marianne frowned. 'They'll stay here with us. I don't want to move Aunt Anna or Uncle Yiorgo. It would upset them too much. We could move into Uncle Yannis and Aunt Ourania's spare room – I'm sure they wouldn't mind. Elizabeth and Nicolas can have our room with a bed for Nicola.'

Giovanni nodded. 'I'll leave it up to you to organise. I must go and tackle that drain again.'

'Who's Elizabeth?' asked John, looking up from the model ship he was constructing.

'She's my best friend. We went to Athens together and she met Nicolas. He's one of Dad's relatives. I came over to see her, we visited Crete and I met your father.'

'Do you think that piece goes there?' John was more interested in his model.

'No, try it further over. They're bringing their daughter Nicola with them. She's near enough your age.'

'Yuk!'

'What do you mean – yuk? You'll like her.' His mother's tone of voice forbade him to disagree.

'I've got glue on my fingers.' John made the excuse and grinned. 'She'll no doubt have to spend all her time with her parents – as she's a girl,' he added.

'I'm sure you'll like her.' Marianne crossed her fingers behind her back as she saw the sceptical look on her son's face.

Marianne drove Elizabeth, Nicolas and Nicola up to Plaka where Giovanni was working. Nicola had hardly opened her mouth since she had arrived and Marianne was worried. She wanted to spend time with Elizabeth and Nicolas and that could be difficult if they had to think about entertaining a child continually. She had been so confident that John and Nicola would immediately become friends, but now she was seriously concerned. The girl was so quiet and withdrawn.

Giovanni emerged from the taverna, a bottle and glasses in his hand. He set them on a table and embraced his visitors affectionately. Nicola hung back and he approached her carefully.

'Hello, you must be Nicola. I remember you as a tiny baby and I'm sure you don't remember me at all.' He held out his hand and Nicola took it shyly.

Marianne could see John up at the crazy golf pitch where he appeared to be practising his golf swing.

'Come on,' she said to Elizabeth. 'We'll leave the men here to talk for a while and go up and surprise him. He's looking forward to meeting you.'

To Marianne's embarrassment when they were only a few yards from the golf course John was heard to swear loudly in Greek. Immediately Marianne chastised him and he looked suitably abashed.

'I didn't know you were there,' he mumbled.

'That's no excuse for using language like that. Don't you ever let me hear you say such a thing again. Now come and meet Nicola. Maybe you could show her how to play crazy golf whilst I show her parents all the work we've done up here.'

Meekly John walked forward. 'Hello.'

'You swore,' said Nicola, smugly.

'You wouldn't know. I said it in Greek.'

'I speak Greek.'

'Bet you don't.'

'I sure do.'

'Say something then.'

Nicola shrugged. 'What shall I say?'

'You could tell me my golf is very good.'

'I could play better than that,' she said in Greek.

'You could not,' John answered, his face darkening.

'I'll show you.' She opened the gate and walked inside the fenced area, picking up a discarded golf club.

Marianne looked at Elizabeth and laughed. 'I suggest we leave them to argue it out and go back down. John, look after Nicola and be down at the taverna in an hour to come home with your father.'

John raised his hand in acknowledgement, not taking his eyes off Nicola as she prepared to hit the golf ball.

Both Elizabeth and Nicolas were full of admiration for the changes that had been wrought at Plaka. 'If Spinalonga was not sitting out there in the bay I would never believe this was the same place that I visited nearly ten years ago. I felt sorry for anyone who had to live here then, but now I feel envious.'

'There's a tremendous amount more that we want to do, but it all takes time. Have you seen enough? I ought to go back to the house and prepare a meal for Aunt Anna and Uncle Yiorgo. Are you hungry, Elizabeth? We don't usually eat until Uncle Yannis and Aunt Ourania return from Aghios Nikolaos, but you could have something earlier if you wanted.'

'I'm fine. Just leave a bowl of olives near me.'

'It's a good job we had a large crop this year! We had always used them ourselves, but it was Aunt Ourania's idea to have them packaged with our own label and sell them in the shop. The tourists love it. They feel they are really buying something authentic to take home with them.'

Upon their return Marianne retired to the kitchen and the savoury smell that wafted out to them made Elizabeth regret her decision to wait until later to eat. She was gone for a considerable amount of time and finally returned shaking her head.

'Sorry about that. Uncle Yiorgo decided he had to go up to the fields and bring the sheep down. It took a while to persuade him that Uncle Yannis was up there doing the job.'

Nicolas looked at her in surprise. 'What sheep? I didn't know you still had any.'

'We haven't, but Uncle Yiorgo forgets and the only way to put his mind at rest is to tell him that Uncle Yannis is herding them in. Now, what do you two plan to do with yourselves whilst you're here? Sight seeing or swim and sun bathe?'

'A bit of both. Neither Nicolas or I saw enough of Crete on our earlier visits, but I don't think Nicola will be very enthusiastic. She was fed up with being dragged off by her grandmother to be shown off to various neighbours. The week we spent in Athens was more than enough for her. We managed to take her off to the beach each day, but she even found that boring. There was no one for her to play with. I just hope she and John will get on together.'

'We'll soon know. I can hear Giovanni arriving. If John is smiling all is well. If he's looking sulky you'll know there's a problem with them.'

John rushed out onto the patio. 'Mum, can Nick and I go swimming before supper?'

'Give me half an hour and I'll come with you.'

'Can't Nick and I go down now? We won't go in the water.'

'Promise you'll stick to the rules?'

'I promise, Mum.'

'All right. You and Nicola can go down, but no rock climbing or swimming until I get there.'

John sighed heavily. It would be no fun sitting on the decking waiting for his mother who would probably not arrive for at least an hour. He wanted to show Nicola how proficient he was at swimming and diving. 'We'll get changed,' he said glumly.

Nicola whispered something to him as they made their way into the house. John's face lit up and he nodded. Marianne gave a sigh of relief. It was obvious that John and Nicola were becoming friends.

Elizabeth shook her head in disbelief. 'Nick!' she said. 'She's never allowed anyone to shorten her name before.'

John and Nicola emerged from the house wearing their bathing costumes below their shorts. John had his hand deep in his pocket and Nicola carried a beach bag.

'What have you got in there?' asked Elizabeth.

'Just my towel and some bits and pieces.' Nicola blushed.

Elizabeth raised her eyebrows, but said no more as Giovanni joined them, bringing another bottle of wine with him. 'Not for me,' said Elizabeth. 'I'm limiting myself to one a day now.'

'But you haven't had any yet.'

'I know; I'm planning to have a glass with our meal.'

John and Nicola hurried out of their view and down the steps to the small private cove.

'This is fab!' exclaimed Nicola. 'I wish I lived somewhere like this. We have the lake in the park, but this is a proper beach.'

'When Mum comes we can explore properly. There are rock pools just over there and all sorts of things get stranded in them. I'm not allowed to go scrambling when I'm alone down here. Mum's frightened I'll fall and hit my head.'

'Would the sea come in and drown you?' asked Nicola, wide-eyed.

'No, we hardly have a tide. It's just that she doesn't like to think of me laying there hurt until someone comes looking for me. That's the problem when you're an only child. Everyone is so concerned about you. Don't you find that?'

Nicola nodded. 'Shall I tell you a secret? You're to swear on your life that you'll not tell anyone at all.'

'I swear,' promised John solemnly.

'My Mum's going to have a baby. I'm not going to be an only child any longer. She doesn't know that I know, but I heard her and Dad talking. Dad was worried that flying might be harmful and she was assuring him that it would be no problem.'

'She doesn't look as though she's having a baby,' frowned John.

'It's early days yet.' Nicola spoke knowledgably as she opened her bag and removed two plastic cups, a carton of fruit juice and a packet of biscuits. 'Did you bring a pack of cards?'

John pulled them from the pocket of his shorts. 'I'll get some pebbles. Whoever wins can have the last biscuit. There always seems to be one extra in the pack when you try to share them. The loser has to buy an ice cream tomorrow.'

'I'll sneak down in a few minutes and see what they're doing,' said Marianne. 'I know they were up to something. John always has such an air of innocence about him when he's planning to do something we might disapprove of.'

'He's a boy,' smiled Nicolas. 'He should be getting up to all sorts of diabolical things. I did, didn't you, Giovanni?'

'Why don't we all join them for a swim?' suggested Giovanni.

Elizabeth finished her fruit juice. 'I hope my costume fits. I seem to be expanding rather fast this time.'

'Does Nicola know you're pregnant?'

Elizabeth shook her head. 'I thought I'd wait a while before I said anything. I just hope she'll be happy to have a brother.'

'How do you know it will be a boy?'

'I'm sure it is. I am so different this time. I haven't had any sickness and I can't bear sweet things. We've even decided on a name – Stephen Michael, after the grandparents.'

Marianne smiled in amusement. 'Well, if you're wrong she can always be Stephanie Michelle, I suppose. Come on, let's get changed or I won't have time for a decent swim before I need to help Aunt Anna and Uncle Yiorgo into bed.'

Marianne placed a finger on her lips. 'We'll go down quietly and surprise them. See what they're up to.'

She led them down the steps in single file, suppressing a giggle and moving to one side to let Elizabeth see. Giovanni and Nicolas peered over their shoulders.

'Can anyone join the party or is this an exclusive gambling club?' called out Giovanni and both children started guiltily.

John shrugged his shoulders. 'We had to do something whilst we were waiting for you. We thought you'd be hours.'

'Can we go in the sea now?' begged Nicola. 'I'm really hot.'

Giovanni nodded. 'Be sensible, both of you. No further out than the rock.'

'Which one?' asked Nicola, looking at the low cliffs that rose up from the tiny beach.

'That one.' John pointed to the dark patch on the water that indicated a submerged rock a short distance from the shore. 'I'll race you there and back.'

'I don't want to go back to Athens. I want to stay here. I like it here. It's better than at home. Why can't we live somewhere like this instead of in a city?' Nicola turned over in her bed feeling close to tears.

'You want to go back and see grandma again, don't you? She's looking forward to seeing you and hearing all about your holiday over here.'

Elizabeth tried hard to be patient with her rebellious daughter, although she had no wish to return to Athens for the last week of their holiday.

'If we lived here we could go and see her in the winter. I hate Athens when it's hot. I want to stay here and go swimming with John.'

'Once the holidays are over John has to go back to school like everyone else. The weather turns cooler and no one goes swimming then.'

'At least he can climb on the rocks and look for things. All I have at home is silly dancing classes and silly walks in the park.'

'I thought you enjoyed your dancing classes.'

'I used to enjoy them. I want to go swimming now, not silly dancing.'

'You could have some swimming lessons instead of dancing.'

Nicola's mouth set in a stubborn line. 'I want to go swimming in the sea, not some silly pool.'

Elizabeth sighed. 'Well, if it's a silly day there's nothing more to be said. We have to go home. Everyone has to go home at the end of their holiday however much they have enjoyed it. Now, if you do want a last swim you'd better get yourself up. If you stay in bed sulking you'll not have time to do anything and I shall be taking you to the airport in your pyjamas. That really will look silly.'

1997 – 1999

'I'm sorry, Mr Schwaber, the date for your trial has had to be cancelled.'

Kurt looked at the prison warder bleakly. 'I doubt if it will make any difference.'

'The reason,' the warder persisted doggedly, 'is that Mr Delaney has suffered a slight heart attack. The doctors have ordered him to rest for at least six months.'

Kurt shrugged. 'What's another six months to me? I've already been here nearly two years.'

'That's not my fault. I've just been asked to deliver the message and offer you the opportunity of appointing another attorney.'

'I might as well. Mr Delaney didn't believe I was innocent so I doubt if he will mind one way or the other.'

'Very well. Do you know of anyone to take his place?'

'I'll think about it. Ask my brother the next time he visits. He said he would come again in a couple of months.'

The warder left the small cell. The man was an enigma. He seemed totally resigned to his fate, despite protesting his innocence. His only request was for a continual supply of books relating to Yoga and he would be seen standing for hours in one position or sitting meditating. He was the least troublesome prisoner in the whole block.

Christabelle received the news of the trial delay with a frown. This had upset her plans. She had decided that once the trial was over she had the perfect excuse to go to New York to enable her to avoid any adverse publicity. Now she would have to renew her contact with Mike Able and Peter Rodriguez again; but she would definitely be asking for a higher rate of commission for each photo shoot. She was steadily working towards her goal of being a multi millionaire.

If the trial of Kurt Schwaber had not taken place by the next time her contract was up for renewal she would ask Detective Mullen if she was able to leave Louisiana and go to work in New York. It was time she moved on. She had made her long term plans; first a move to New York, then eventually over to London, Paris and Milan and she was anxious to make a start. When she had become a household name in Europe she would take a trip to Australia, visiting Greece, Turkey and Egypt on the way.

Confident that her career would move forward as she had planned she curled up comfortably on the sofa with a pile of magazines where she had been featured. She never tired of looking at and admiring herself on the glossy pages. She spent hours in front of her mirror, trying different hairstyles, new ways to accentuate her eyes and mouth or posing to see the effect.

She was no longer just a face or body on a page. Captions everywhere read *"as Christabelle wears"* or *"uses"*. It was so gratifying when she walked into the town and she saw heads turn and heard people saying *"that's Christabelle, the model."*

She had cultivated an image for herself. She walked languidly, never leaving the house without being dressed immaculately and wearing makeup; when she paused to look into a shop window she checked her pose in the reflection. Shop keepers were delighted when she patronized them. Customers would come in just to see her and usually made a purchase before leaving.

Once in the privacy of her home she removed her make up and the smart, expensive clothes. She did press-ups, sit ups and squats in the kitchen each day to keep her muscles in trim; after the exercises she would run on the spot for an hour before taking a shower. Whilst reading a magazine or watching the television she would use a power ball to strengthen her fingers. No one was going to see her in a gymnasium getting sweaty, nor were they going to find any keep fit equipment in her home. Her natural firm handshake had been replaced with a limp touch. She did not want the world to know that she had enough strength in her hands to open the lids on jars that would defy most women or that she could easily out sprint a pursuer. The image she projected was one of languid fragility combined with charm, instilling a desire in people to protect and care for her.

'Marianne, Elizabeth had the baby yesterday.'

'Stephen Michael?'

'No, a little girl, Eleanor.'

'Eleanor?' Marianne was surprised.

'We decided we would call her after my sister.'

'How is Elizabeth?'

'She's a little tired. Nicola is disappointed – she wanted a brother like John.'

Marianne laughed. 'John has thrown out a few hints about having a sister. You'll have to come back and visit us again as soon as you can.'

'We will, that's a promise. Elizabeth should be home in a couple of days and she said she would telephone you to have a long talk. I was just to tell you the good news and say that all is well.'

'I'm so pleased for you both, Nicolas. Thank you for calling and love to all of you.' Marianne replaced the receiver. She was genuinely happy for her friend, but she had no wish to add to her own family. At least it would be something to tell her mother when she made her weekly telephone call.

Bryony drew up outside her grandmother's house and sounded

her horn twice before she disabled the steering wheel. There was probably no need to do so, she always locked the car, and there was not a great deal of crime in this area.

She walked up to the front door and gave her customary two rings on the bell, waiting to hear her grandmother calling 'I'm coming, I'm coming, don't be impatient.'

There was silence from inside the house. Bryony rang the bell again; maybe Annita was upstairs or in the bathroom. Everything seemed very quiet and still.

Bryony bent down and called through the letterbox. 'Grandma, it's Bryony. Are you there?'

No answering voice came to her. Bryony had a sick feeling in the pit of her stomach. She moved to the window and peered through as best she could, seeing very little. She tried the gate that led to the back of the house. If she could get round there the kitchen door might be unlocked or maybe a window.

The gate did not yield and Bryony bit her lip. Should she telephone the emergency services? She would call at the neighbour's house, ask them if they had any information about her grandmother, and if necessary use their phone. She walked back towards the front door and it was then that it dawned on her that her grandmother's car was not in the usual place. Her grandmother was out!

A feeling of annoyance overcame her. She always called on a Wednesday evening after she had finished work. The drive took almost an hour each way, and she always spent at least two hours at the house, often longer, meaning that she rarely arrived home before ten. She climbed back into her car and slammed the door. She would wait for fifteen minutes, then leave.

The time dragged and Bryony was just about to start her engine when she saw her grandmother draw up. Annita got out and hurried towards her.

'I'm so sorry. I was held up. I didn't realise the people would talk for so long. Have you been waiting ages for me?'

Bryony forced herself to smile. 'Not long. I was a bit worried at first when I didn't get an answer, then I realised you were out.'

Annita opened the front door. 'I thought I would be back much earlier. I haven't even got a meal prepared. We'll have to send out. What would you like – pizza or Chinese?'

'I really don't mind. Whichever you prefer.'

'Chinese, then. I've such a lot to talk to you about – and I want your opinion.'

Bryony followed her grandmother into the kitchen where she was handed a take-away menu. 'Choose what you want. I'll make some coffee; then I'll tell you where I've been.'

Bryony raised her eyebrows. 'I'll have a chicken in lemon sauce and egg fried rice, please. Do you want me to phone?'

Annita nodded. 'I'll have the same. A portion of prawn sesame toast would be good, and some seaweed. Do you want some spring rolls?'

'I'll never eat that much!'

'I can always freeze anything that's left. I'll take the coffee through. Come and join me when you've ordered.'

Bryony telephoned the order through and set plates ready on the worktop before joining her grandmother in the lounge.

'Now what is it that you think you've decided?'

Annita smiled. 'It's good to see you. I need someone to talk to about my idea. This house is getting far too big for me now.'

Bryony waited. Was she going to ask her and Marcus to live there with her? She loved her grandmother dearly, but did not want to live with her. As her grandmother became older and infirm she would be honour bound to give up work and care for her. She had never wanted to be a nurse and the thought of having to wash and care for someone, even someone she cared about, revolted her.

'It was lovely when it was a family house, but now half the rooms are closed up and I never go into them. If Elias were here it might be different.' Annita looked at his photograph and shrugged. 'I sat here thinking about it the other evening, wondering what I should do when I really cannot cope with the stairs, shopping and cooking. Then I remembered the Berkendorfs. Do you remember them? They lived down the road a way, but we were always on friendly terms.'

Bryony nodded. She remembered how the old man had always scowled at her whenever he saw her and his wife had never given her more than a thin smile.

'Well, they decided that their house was no longer manageable and they went into a retirement home about six months ago.' Annita smiled conspiratorially. 'I decided they had had time to settle in and it would be neighbourly of me to call and see how they were getting on. It also gave me a chance to have a look around and see what a retirement home is really like these days. They seem to be happy enough there and I must say it appeared very nice. It was very clean and furnished attractively, nothing garish or looking threadbare. Mrs Berkendorf asked if I would like to have tea and she rang a bell and asked for it to be brought to their sitting room as she had a visitor.

'We sat there making small talk for a while and then I asked them if I could see the rest of their suite. I say "suite" but it's really only a lounge, bedroom and bathroom. I admired everything, of course, and then I asked them how much they were paying. They stopped being so hospitable then. They said the fees differed depending upon your accommodation and the amount of care you needed and it would be better if I spoke to the manager.' Annita dropped her voice. 'I think the social are contributing.'

Bryony shook her head. 'Grandmother! You are awful. Fancy asking them for a start what they were paying. They probably told you the truth when they said the fees differed. Why should you think they're on social?'

'They only rented the house they lived in. He was a taxi driver and she was a teacher until she had her daughter. Never went back to it afterwards, so what kind of savings would they have?'

Bryony giggled at her grandmother's reasoning. 'They could have inherited money or won it gambling. You can't possibly know whether they are receiving financial help.'

Annita waved her hand airily. 'I was just speculating. It's beside the point anyway. I couldn't possibly live there. It's called *'Copse House'* and the locals call it *'Corpse House'!* Well, having seen their accommodation I thought it would be a good idea to find out a little more about retirement homes, so I made some appointments round and about and I've been visiting them. That's where I was today. I thought I would be back long before you arrived, but the time just flew by. The people there were so nice. They took me all over the building and I met some of the residents. The only problem is they all seemed so old.'

Annita sighed. 'They knew everyone who lived there and all their little idiosyncrasies. There's one lady who believes all the library books belong to her, so she never returns them. When the shelves begin to look empty they have to ask if they can 'borrow' them, so they can replace them. Anyway, by the time I left *'Green Vistas'* I had made up my mind – I think. I shall put my name down on their waiting list ready for when I have to leave here.' Annita sat back and looked at her grand daughter anxiously. 'Do you think that's sensible of me?'

'Very sensible,' Bryony agreed swiftly, relieved that her grandmother had not expected her to care for her. 'You may never need a place, but it's as well to know where you want to go should the need arise. Aunt Elena could choose one for you and you might not be happy there. If you think this one is right for you, put your name down by all means.'

'Elena would put me into the first one in the telephone directory. I'm not saying it wouldn't be a good home, but I want to choose where I go, not be shuffled off anywhere just to suit her. What I would like, Bryony, is for you to come with me for a visit. I'd like your opinion. I'm sure you'll think of things to ask them that had never occurred to me.'

'Of course I will, grandma. I can ask for an afternoon off when you've made an appointment.'

'I made one whilst I was there. I thought a Wednesday would be most convenient for you as that's the day you visit me. Two weeks today at three in the afternoon.'

Bryony shook her head in amusement. 'Suppose I had said no?'

'I could have cancelled, or just gone back alone for another look.' Annita held her head on one side. 'That sounds like our meal arriving. Can you go and let them in and bring me the bill? You're not to pay; it's my treat.'

A date had still not been set for Kurt Schwaber's trial and Christabelle decided the time was right to approach Mike Able.

'I don't quite know how to say this, Mike, but I hope you'll understand.'

'Another increase in your salary?' he smiled.

Christabelle shook her head. 'My contract is up for renewal at the end of the month. I'm not going to sign it.'

'What?' Mike looked at her in amazement. 'Why ever not?'

'I'm going to New York.' Christabelle held up her hand as he was about to interrupt her.

'I've been told that the trial has been delayed for at least another six months. I'd planned to go to New York after that, but for all I know there could be one delay after another and it could be another year or more before I have the opportunity to go away. I've spoken with Detective Mullen and he says there is no reason why I shouldn't go anywhere I please. I just have to leave an address where I can be contacted and be prepared to return when a trial date has finally been set.'

'How long do you plan to stay there? We could post-date your contract or give you a month or two off.'

'I hope to be away considerably longer than a month. I'm planning to look for work in New York. Once I'm known there and this trial is over I plan to go to London. I want to try to work freelance for a while, just to cover my expenses and get my face known in Europe. London and then over to Paris, maybe Milan. I can't be tied to a contract if I don't know when I'll be back.'

'You're quite certain you want to take a chance on being successful elsewhere?'

'Of course I shall be successful.' Christabelle looked surprised at the idea of failure.

'I'll take my collection of advertising photographs with me and I won't have any trouble getting work.'

Mike frowned. 'You can't take any of the photographs that we've used of you.'

'I don't intend to. I simply cut the adverts from the magazines. Anyone can buy a magazine and see me.'

'And when you return? What do you plan to do then? Come back to us?'

Christabelle smiled at him. 'Maybe. I will keep in touch. You were good enough to give me my first opportunities to break into the business. I believe in loyalty, but I may have other ambitions by then and modelling may not be one of them. I don't believe in making a promise that I can't keep.'

'There's nothing I could say or do to make you change your mind and stay here?'

'Nothing.' Christabelle spoke firmly. 'I've always wanted to see what the world is like outside of New Orleans.'

Mike smiled, defeated. 'I knew you were a very ambitious young lady when you first approached us. I think you'll do well in New York. I do have a contact there. Would you like me to speak to him? Give you a foot in the door, so to speak?'

'Would you? I'm sure that would be a great help to me.' Christabelle smiled gratefully.

'I'll do it today. He can probably recommend a decent hotel where you can stay without paying the earth. If you do need anything you will contact us, won't you? We're going to miss you.'

'You'll only miss the money I bring in to your magazine,' thought Christabelle.

She rose and extended her hand. 'Thank you, Mike. I really appreciate all you've done to help me.'

'Bryony, come and sit down. We need to discuss something.' Marcus waited until his wife was seated beside him. 'I talked to Mr Montgomery today when I collected his insurance money. I always thought him such a nuisance, refusing to pay direct through a bank so I had to drive out to him once a month. I'm sure the firm only allowed it because he was such a long standing customer. He said he didn't trust a bank to look after his money after the Wall Street crash.'

'How on earth does he manage?'

Marcus shook his head. 'I don't know, but it isn't my problem. He's finally admitted he can't live alone any longer and is going off to live with his daughter in Biloxi. He said she planned to sell his house for whatever she can get for it. She's not interested in doing repairs. I asked what figure she had in mind and he didn't know, but he has given me her phone number. What do you think? Should I phone her and see how much she's going to ask?'

'Do you think we should?'

'There's no harm in asking her. We can find out the price for property in the area that is in good condition and see if she's being reasonable. It will need a fair bit spent on it. I don't think he's ever touched it since he moved in.'

Bryony hesitated. 'I'd like to have a look at it before I decide. I don't want to find I'm in the depths of nowhere.'

'I wouldn't do that to you. If you don't think you'll be happy there we don't have to move. We can always stay here. It's not very big, but there's a fantastic view of the ocean and a small garden. There's only one down side. If we did go ahead we'd have to put off our visit to your cousin in Crete. We would have to take out a mortgage, of course, but the rest of our savings would probably go on repairs. I have a few ideas that could make it really outstanding.'

Bryony felt unreasonably disappointed. She had been looking forward to the projected visit for some months. Over the years that she had corresponded with her cousin she had longed to visit and see for herself all that Marianne described to her. Marcus had finally decided they could afford such an expensive trip as his bonus dividend had been extremely good for the last two years.

Bryony swallowed and tried to smile. 'We could always go another year.' She felt annoyed with herself for feeling so disappointed. You could not compare a holiday with owning a house, rather than an apartment; and Marcus was obviously full of enthusiasm for the move.

'Marianne? I have some bad news, I'm afraid.'

'Grandma?' It was most unusual for her mother to telephone.

'No, it's Helena. She's had a miscarriage.'

'Oh, Mum, what a shame. She told me she was pregnant the last time I spoke to her. How far was she?'

'About four months she thought.'

'How is she?'

'Not very well and she's feeling very depressed, of course. I obviously can't leave her at the moment. I'm staying at their house and looking after the boys and everything. I don't know how long it will take her to get back on her feet again. It means I can't make any plans to visit at the moment.'

'Of course not. I understand.' Marianne felt a degree of guilt at the relief she felt over her mother's cancelled visit. 'When she's well enough to leave maybe you could bring the boys over here with you. We'd love to see them again.'

'Maybe.' Elena sounded doubtful about the idea.

'Do give Helena my love. When would be a good time to call and talk to her? I don't want to disturb her if she's resting.'

'You can talk to her now if you want.'

'Fine. Put her on the line, and, Mum, if there is anything I can do from a distance do let me know.'

'I will. Here she is.'

Marianne replaced the receiver and grimaced. Half an hour she had spent listening to Helena describing in detail all her symptoms and the final outcome, finally she had cut her sister short and ended the call by insisting she had to collect John from school. Bryony had e-mailed her the previous week to say she and Marcus were unable to come as planned and now her mother had cancelled. She shrugged. There was nothing she could do about it. No doubt Giovanni's parents would make their annual visit and she always enjoyed their company.

Christabelle took a taxi and drew up outside Rudi Ersoy's house. She had not telephoned to make an appointment as she was sure he had left instructions that if ever she telephoned she was to be told he was not in residence. If he was truly not at home then all she had wasted was her taxi fare.

She rang the bell and waited until the door was opened by a small attractive woman. Christabelle wondered if she was his wife or whether he kept a maid.

'Good afternoon,' she smiled sweetly. 'I've come to see Mr Ersoy. He is expecting me.'

The woman frowned. 'He didn't mention having an appointment this afternoon.'

'It must have slipped his mind. He told me I could call at any time.'

'What name shall I tell him?'

'There's no need to give him a name. He'll remember me as soon as he sees me.'

Giving Christabelle a doubtful look, the woman tapped on the door Rudi called his study. 'Rudi, there's a young woman here to see you. She says you're expecting her.'

'I'm not expecting anyone. Get rid of her.'

Christabelle pushed past the woman and opened the door wider. She walked in, her head held high and her hand outstretched. 'Hello, Rudi. It's good to see you again. I hope this isn't an inconvenient moment to call.'

Rudi's jaw dropped. Quickly he recovered his composure. 'It's all right, Lynda. I had forgotten I'd arranged this meeting.'

Lynda eyed Christabelle up and down. 'Shall I make some coffee?'

'Not on my behalf, please. I can only stay a very short while. This is more of a courtesy call than a social visit.' Christabelle smiled and sat down on the easy chair.

'This will only take five minutes.' Rudi assured his wife. 'If you would put some coffee on I'd like a cup.'

Lynda gave Christabelle a suspicious glance and left the room.

'How dare you come here! You said you would never trouble me again. I didn't believe you at the time. You're not getting another dollar out of me.'

Christabelle looked at him sadly. 'What a nasty suspicious mind you have. I hadn't even thought about money. I came to say thank you for the help you gave me in the past and to tell you that I'm off to New York. You've no doubt seen the advertisements I've done for various products. Now I'm off to become a household name elsewhere. Of course, if you were to offer me a little something towards my travelling expenses I would not refuse.'

Rudi pulled a ten dollar bill from his pocket and placed it on the desk. 'Take that and leave.'

Christabelle picked up the note and held in between her fingers. 'Poor Rudi. You must really be poor, Rudi, if that is all you can afford to give your daughter as a farewell gift. Well, I suppose it's the thought that counts. Is that lady your wife? I would like to be properly introduced. I'm sure we'd have a lot to talk about.'

'That's none of your business. Here. Now get out.' Rudi placed another two hundred dollars on the table and Christabelle seized it quickly.

'Thank you, Rudi. That's *very* generous of you. I do appreciate it. I imagine you put more than that in the charity box when they come around collecting. I must say Lynda is very attractive. Was my mother attractive, or would you have called her beautiful?'

Glowering at her, Rudi produced a further five hundred dollar notes from the drawer of his desk. 'I haven't any more money in the house. It's no good you trying to get anything more out of me.'

Christabelle folded the notes and placed them in her purse. She gave Rudi an amused smile. 'I'll call again when I return from New York, whenever that may be.' She rose gracefully from the chair. 'Do say goodbye to Lynda for me. It was a pleasure to meet her, albeit briefly. I can see myself out.'

Christabelle walked down the road towards the waiting taxis, a pleased smile on her face. She really had been rather clever. She had taken a chance and it had paid off literally. She would make a point of visiting him again at some time in the future when he was least expecting her.

Bryony was excited when Christabelle telephoned to tell her she was leaving for New York the following week. 'I'm so envious. How I would love to go to New York. You'll have to tell us all about it when you return.'

'That probably won't be for a while. Once I'm well known in New York I plan to go to London, then Paris, Milan, maybe Athens. I could be gone for a few years. I'm beginning to feel quite excited at the prospect. I've always wanted to travel and I should have plenty of free time to visit places of interest.'

'Oh, Christabelle. How I would love to go to Europe, Greece particularly, to look up our relatives there. You will keep in touch and tell us about England and France. Do you really think you'll go to Italy and Greece as well?'

'I'll have to see how much in demand I am. I don't want to have to touch my capital if I can help it. I'm saving for my old age. It's just such a nuisance that the trial has been delayed. I shall have to return for that and it's bound to be at a most inconvenient time.'

'I'm so pleased we still haven't said anything to Grandma.'

'So am I,' thought Christabelle.

'As I said, no point in distressing any of the family until it's necessary.'

'I tell you what,' Bryony had an idea. 'If you do go to Greece would you visit our cousin, Marianne? I'm sure she'd love to meet you. I'll send you her address.'

Christabelle frowned. A visit to relatives had certainly not been on her agenda. 'Don't send it yet. I would probably lose it within a few months. I'll let you know if my plans extend to travelling to Greece.'

'Of course. I understand. It's just in case you go over to Crete. It could be useful for you to have an address. Can we meet up before you leave? Come over for supper and tell us your itinerary. Marcus is going to be so interested. He keeps promising me a trip to Crete to see Marianne. I'll probably have to wait until he retires. Only another twenty five years!'

Reluctantly Christabelle agreed. She wished she had never telephoned Bryony in the first place. Her half sister wanted to become a close friend, in constant touch with her, and Christabelle had no time for such intimacy, skilfully managing to avoid many of the meetings that Bryony had suggested.

Yiorgo coughed harshly. His chest hurt. Breathing shallowly he walked slowly to the window and peered out. It was raining again. He ought to go and bring the sheep down and make sure the donkey was under cover. Muttering to himself about the inclement weather he struggled into his jacket and opened the patio door.

Leaning heavily on his stick he walked the length of the patio and turned onto the driveway that led up to the road.

'Uncle Yiorgo, it's time for your supper.' Marianne tapped on the door and opened it at the same time, never sure whether Yiorgo would hear her from outside.

'Uncle Yiorgo.' Marianne raised her voice. 'Are you in the bathroom?'

There was still no answer and Marianne opened the bathroom door. Yiorgo was not in there, nor his bedroom or the small sitting room. She was sure he was not in either the kitchen or the family lounge. Maybe he had gone to his sister's room.

Marianne knocked on Anna's door.

'Is it lunch time?' asked Anna.

'No, I came to tell you that your supper was ready. Is Uncle Yiorgo with you?'

'He's not back from the fields yet. You should have called me earlier and I would have cooked a cheese and spinach pie for you.' Anna made the same offer almost every day.

Marianne smiled. 'That would have been nice. No one makes a pie as good as yours. Have you seen Uncle Yiorgo?'

'I told you, he's not back from the fields. Can you keep his hot for him?'

'Of course. You come along now and have yours.'

Marianne settled Anna at the table and served her meal. 'I'll be back in just a moment,' she assured her and hurried back to Yiorgo's room. The patio door was ajar and she looked outside. There was no sign of the man. Hurriedly she went from room to room; finally satisfied that Yiorgo was not in the house. She picked up the telephone and called the taverna where her husband was painting the walls.

'Giovanni, Uncle Yiorgo's not in the house. His patio door is open. Aunt Anna said he was out in the fields, but you know how unreliable she is. I'll have a quick look around outside and call you back. If he has really gone out I hope he thought to put a coat on.'

'Give me ten minutes and I'll be there. I only need to put my brush in soak and lock up.'

Marianne checked that Anna was eating steadily, put on her jacket and tied a scarf over her head. It was becoming dark early that afternoon and it was miserably damp and depressing outside. She hurried up the driveway to the main road, hoping she would be able to see Yiorgo, but there was no sign of him. He could easily have turned the wrong way and be walking into Elounda rather than towards Plaka. She wished she knew how long he had been gone, but knew it would be useless to ask Anna. Hoping she had guessed correctly she began to jog towards Plaka.

Giovanni replaced the lid to the paint, wiped his brush and placed it into a jar of water. He would have preferred to wash it out so it would be ready for the next day, but at least it would not harden over night. He wiped his hands on an old tea towel and picked up his jacket. He doubted that Anna was correct in her surmise that Yiorgo was in the fields. It was most unlikely that he would be able to walk the distance from their house to Plaka and Giovanni hoped he would see him resting on a wall as he drove down the road.

Marianne had only jogged a short distance along the road when she saw the crumpled form lying on the ground and rushed towards him. 'Uncle Yiorgo!'

To her relief he turned his head at the sound of her voice. She placed her arm beneath his shoulders and helped him to sit up. 'Giovanni will be here very soon with the car to take you home. I was so worried when I couldn't find you.'

'The sheep.'

'Yannis is seeing to the sheep. There was no need for you to come out,' she soothed him. Whenever Yiorgo began to fret about the sheep being out on the hill he was assured that Yannis would get them as he had when he was a boy.

Yiorgo shivered. 'Cold,' he muttered.

'Of course you're cold. Your clothes are wet. How long have you been laying here? We'll soon get you home and Giovanni will help you to have a hot bath. When you've got some dry clothes on you'll feel better.'

Yiorgo coughed, deep and rasping, pressing his hands to his chest. The doctor had prescribed a cough mixture and advised him to give up smoking. The mixture had helped a little, but had no intention in giving up smoking at his age. His cigarettes and a nightly glass of brandy were the only pleasure left to him in life now.

Marianne was relieved when she saw Giovanni driving slowly down the road and waved to him. He accelerated and drew up a short distance from them.

'Have you found him?'

Marianne nodded and moved closer to her husband. 'I don't know how long he's been out here. He's soaking wet and says he's cold. I've promised him a hot bath when we get home and I think we ought to call the doctor out.'

Between them they raised Yiorgo to his feet and he stumbled the few feet to the car, sinking into the seat gratefully.

The doctor examined the elderly man and shook his head sadly. 'He has pleurisy. He's probably had it for a few days. Has he complained about chest or back pain?'

Giovanni shook his head. 'He refused to give up smoking. He probably thought if he told us he was in pain we would take his cigarettes away from him. What can you do for him?'

'Not a lot, I'm afraid. I'll give you a prescription for an anti-biotic. Apart from that he needs to be in an even temperature and resting. See if you can take those cigarettes away.'

Anna took the news of Yiorgo's death calmly and asked to be taken up to the taverna. She sat and looked across at the hills, lost in her memories. Yiorgo had loved the farm, unlike Yannis and Stelios, who had no inclination to be out in all weathers toiling manually. The war years had been the hardest. Trying to keep the farm going, caring for her invalid mother and looking after Marisa and Yannis with Italian soldiers billeted on them had been difficult. No doubt it had strengthened her, both mentally and physically, but who would have thought she would have outlived her siblings? Poor Maria; who had died so young in childbirth; then Yannis and Stelios dying in the same year. She sighed heavily. Had Yiorgo enjoyed his life? He had changed after the war. Before he had always been quiet and seemed content with his own company, but he had become bitter and withdrawn. The only time he had spoken about his war time experiences was when Michael had visited. Michael! Despite the intervening years the pain she had experienced when his daughter had told her about his death was still as sharp. A tear rolled down her cheek and she brushed it away impatiently. She should be mourning her brother, not the man she had loved. She gave herself a mental shake. She would call Marianne and ask her to take her back to the house. She always became maudlin when she sat and looked at the hills.

Yannis sat with Giovanni. 'What's wrong with your father?'

Giovanni turned anguished eyes on his uncle. 'I don't know. He says he's having some tests. It could be an ulcer.'

'Do you believe that?'

'I'd like to.'

'It makes for a problem with Uncle Yiorgo's funeral. There's no way we can carry the coffin from here to the church. Victor doesn't look as if he has the strength to walk and I'm pretty unsafe without my stick. John's not tall enough, so that would only leave you. I've decided we'll ask the undertakers to provide pall bearers and we'll walk beside it. We'll also walk from the taverna.'

Giovanni raised his eyebrows in surprise. 'But we always go from the house.'

'We go from the deceased's house. The taverna was Uncle Yiorgo's home. We're all getting on in years. We're not fit enough for such a long walk. Up the hill from the taverna to the church will be enough for all of us.'

For the first time Giovanni took stock of his uncle. He tended to forget that he and Ourania were already in their seventies. Yannis looked weary and he hoped that he was not going to develop an illness as his father appeared to have done.

Giovanni smiled. 'Whatever you think is best, Uncle Yannis.'

Yannis nodded. 'That's settled then. I'll speak to the undertakers.'

'Can't you stay for another week?' asked Giovanni.

Victor shook his head. 'I have to go back. You know what your mother is like. She's nagged me for years to lose weight and now when I'm finally losing a few kilos she's worried about me. I insisted that I postponed my hospital appointment so that I could come for Uncle Yiorgo's funeral, but I ought to keep the next one.'

'What do they think is wrong?' Giovanni was concerned. He had never heard his mother nag her husband about being overweight; nor could he ever remember his father having more than a heavy cold.

Victor shrugged. 'It's probably just old age creeping up on me. I'm nearly seventy seven. Look at your Uncle Yannis. He's not as old as me and he's succumbed to a stick.'

'You'll telephone me with the results?'

'Of course, but I doubt if they'll find anything to be worried about.' Victor smiled confidently. He knew the pain he had deep inside had nothing to do with his age and he doubted that any medication the doctors were able to give him would cure it.

Christabelle looked out of the window as the aeroplane circled in to land at La Guardia airport. So this was New York. Her heart gave a little jump of excitement. She planned to make good use of her time whilst she was here. Once she had secured some work she would visit the most famous areas as she had dreamt of doing as a child. She would also make sure that she attended events where she would be seen and noticed by people who could help her career to move forward.

'I have over two years experience in fashion modelling in New Orleans. You can see I have been successful.' Christabelle fanned out the handful of photographs of herself. 'I am happy to continue to work in the business, but I would also like to try for television commercials.'

'That has different requirements. You need to be able to act a bit and move well.' Reuben Neumayer looked at her speculatively above his half spectacles. Mike Able had talked to him at length about the girl who sat before him and he was sure she had the potential to go far, but he was not prepared to make it easy for her. He opened a large desk diary and began to turn the pages. 'There are a couple of companies that are asking for girls to screen test for the adverts they are making in the next few weeks. You'll be up against the pros who've been working in that media for some years. I can add your name to the list if you want the experience. It's pretty doubtful that you'll be offered anything so be prepared for disappointment.'

Christabelle swallowed her annoyance. She knew how accomplished she was at acting. 'If they turn me down I hope they will give me the reason. I shall then know what is expected of me the next time. Is there anything else available before these tests? I don't want to sit around and do nothing.'

'If you want me to act as your agent, my commission is thirty five percent.' He glanced at her keenly. 'Is that acceptable?'

'How much do I earn for each shoot?'

'That depends upon the company and the advert. My terms are the same for all contracts.' Reuben pulled a second desk diary towards him and ran his finger down the page. 'I could send you out tomorrow. It's a tooth whitening advert for a magazine.'

Christabelle shuddered inwardly. 'I don't really feel that promotes my image. If people think I need to whiten my teeth what else will they think is not natural about me?'

'Hair spray? I presume you use it. They want someone on Thursday.'

Christabelle nodded. 'I'm happy to do that. What else do you have?'

'How much work do you want?'

Christabelle shrugged. 'Two or three days a week suits me, but if I was needed for a longer stretch I'm amenable. I plan to give myself plenty of time to go sight seeing whilst I'm here.'

Reuben nodded. 'I'll book you in definitely for Thursday for the hair.' He pressed the bell on his desk and his secretary entered. 'Dearly, call Eisenhowers and let them know that Miss Christabelle will be with them on Thursday at ten. Give her the address. Make her a list of other suitable assignments over the next month and she can have a look at them. Come back to me tomorrow and tell me which ones you're prepared to take. You can sign your contract at the same time. Dearly will have it typed up by then.'

'Yes, Mr Neumayer. If you'd like to come through to my office, Miss Christabelle.'

Christabelle followed the woman back into the cubby hole she called an office and sat and waited whilst Dearly compiled a list of possible modelling contracts.

'Is Dearly your real name?'

Dearly flashed a smile at Christabelle. 'Everyone always asks me that question. It certainly is. Dearly Beloved to be exact. My parents left it a bit late to tie the knot. They were at the church and the vicar had just said *'Dearly beloved we are gathered together'* when my mother went into labour. She managed to get through the service and I was born in the vestry. There's the address of Eisenhowers.' She handed a business card over and

Christabelle tucked it safely into her purse. 'Now if you can just give me the usual details for me to fill in on your contract for Mr Neumayer, then we're done.'

Christabelle enjoyed the experience of making a commercial. It had certainly not been demanding of her. She had obeyed the director's instructions to the letter and walked carefully to avoid the cables that were stretched across the floor from one set to another as the wind machine blew her hair around her. She had stopped in surprise when he called "Cut". She had not been aware of an error on her part.

A diminutive girl hurried forward, brush, comb and hair spray in her hand. Whilst Christabelle sat she styled her hair back the way it had looked before the wind machine had done its work. Her face was re-powdered and she took up a new pose on the steps before a backdrop of the ornate facade of a building. She waited whilst two other girls had their hair blown by the wind machine before joining her. She looked immaculately groomed whilst they looked windswept.

'Cut. You're supposed to be pleased to see your friends, Christabelle. Smile, you know you look ten times better than they do. You're wearing the new hair spray, remember.'

Christabelle nodded and the scene was replayed six more times before the director considered it was ready to film. When he finally declared it was satisfactory she was surprised to find that the two minute advertisement had taken well over four hours to complete and she felt exhausted.

'Not bad,' he said grudgingly to her as she bade him farewell. 'You can tell you're a novice, but you might shape up in time.' He had no intention of telling Reuben Neumayer that the session had gone smoothly and he was delighted with Christabelle. She had done whatever he had asked of her without either complaint or argument, unlike so many of the other girls he had to try to work with.

Christabelle made two more advertisements for the same company, one for a washing machine and the other for lip gloss. She had steeled herself to kiss the cheek of the young man who co-starred with her, to prove that the lipstick did not come off, but the ordeal had not been as bad as she had feared.

'Try not to step on my foot in the next take,' he commented. 'It's hard to keep a smile on my face when my foot hurts.'

'I am so sorry,' Christabelle apologised insincerely and went to her chair for her make up to be touched up. Inwardly she was seething. She had not stepped on his foot, merely touched the edge of his shoe.

Controlling her emotions Christabelle completed the shoot to the director's satisfaction. Told to 'cut' she trod back very deliberately and was rewarded by a howl of pain as she ground her stiletto heel down hard onto Enrico's foot.

'Oh, dear, I've done it again. You really must learn to keep your big feet out of the way.' She tossed her head and walked away from him, a smile of satisfaction on her face.

Within six months Christabelle was gratified to see that her photograph was looking back at her from advertising hoardings and magazines. People recognised her as she walked along the street and entered shops where the assistants hurried to serve her. She had decided to stay in a small hotel, rather than rent an apartment. The novelty of keeping a small house clean and tidy, having to shop and be responsible for her food had palled; besides, she had an image to keep up. No one would expect a famous model to scrub her own kitchen floor or clean the oven.

'So when do you go into hospital, grandma?' asked Bryony. 'Give me the date and I can have some time off to go in with you.'

'There's no need for that! I appreciate the offer, but I am quite capable of taking myself to the hospital.'

'I know you are, but who is going to drive your car back? You can't leave it parked there for a fortnight.'

'I hadn't thought of that,' admitted Annita. 'I suppose if you left your car at my house you could drive mine back and pick yours up.'

'Are you sure you should be driving?'

'Of course. I'm only having a hip replacement. I won't be able to drive for a few weeks afterwards; then I shall be back to normal.'

'Who's going to look after you?'

'The hospital, of course.'

'No, I mean when you come home.'

'No one. I won't need looking after. They've assured me I shall be free of this awful pain and able to live a normal active life. I'm quite looking forward to walking round the shops again.'

'So what date are you being admitted?'

'Ten days time. They want me in the day before they operate. Such a waste of time, but the rules are the rules.'

Bryony consulted her diary and bit her lip in annoyance. 'Right. I've got that date marked down and I'll get the day off. I'll drive out to you in the morning and check you have everything you need with you, then after lunch we can go to the hospital. I can stay with you whilst you get settled in, then I can drive your car home. Have you told Aunt Elena?'

'Not yet. She'd only fuss. I'll tell her a couple of days beforehand. She's sure to have an unbreakable appointment for something booked by then and I can tell her that you're coming with me. That will be a relief to her!'

'Grandma, you really are a wicked old lady.'

Annita sighed. 'I'm not wicked. I know my family.'

Bryony waited anxiously for the return of her husband. Her grandmother's operation could not have come at a worse time for her. After weeks of negotiation with Mr Montgomery's daughter they had finally completed the purchase of the near derelict house. It had taken months to have the property repaired and redecorated; stretching their finances to the limit, and now it was finally ready for them to move in. She had already booked a week's leave to enable her to finish the packing at the apartment and unpacking at the house. The very day they were to move was the day her grandmother was to be admitted to hospital and she had now committed herself to being with her.

Marcus was understanding. 'Of course you must go with your grandmother. She relies on you. I can finish up here on my own and go over to the house in time to see the furniture in. Just remember to come home to the correct address.'

'I'm just disappointed. I was so much looking forward to being there from the very beginning so we could decide together where we wanted the furniture. I wanted to cook our first meal in my new kitchen.'

'If you don't like where I've had the furniture placed we can always move it again until we decide where it looks right. I can have a meal ready for you when you return or we can order in and you can cook the next night.' Marcus was as disappointed as his wife.

'I won't tell grandma we're moving that day or she'll insist that she goes in alone. I can't let her do that. Suppose something happened whilst she was under the anaesthetic? I'd never forgive myself.' A tear crept from the corner of Bryony's eye.

'Don't be dramatic, Bryony. If the hospital thought there was any problem they would not have agreed to operate. You know how careful they are. One hint of malpractice and they get sued, besides, I have a sneaky feeling that your grandmother will outlast us all.'

Bryony gave a shaky smile. 'She's eighty nine, Marcus!'

'Let me see you walk, grandma.' Bryony watched as her grandmother rose confidently from the chair and walked across the room with the aid of two sticks.

'Once I'm home I shall be able to throw these away,' she announced. 'They're supposed to give me confidence at the moment and it keeps the nurses happy to see me using them. I don't really need them.'

Bryony frowned. 'I think you should use them for a day or two when you get home. You don't want to have a fall and end up in here for another three weeks. Is anyone coming to check up on you for the first few days?'

'I've got that all sorted. Sharon Mulready said she'd call in on her way to work, pick up a shopping list if I have one and then drop by on her way home. Until I can drive again I shall have to rely on her for my perishables, but I've got plenty of meals in the freezer. I certainly won't starve.'

'You know you can always call me if you need anything, grandma. I'll telephone you each day before I leave work and if there's anything at all that you need I expect you to tell me. I can easily drop it by for you.'

'You're a good hearted girl, Bryony. When am I going to see this new house of yours? It was very naughty of you not to tell me you were moving on the day I came in. I could easily have made some other arrangements. Marcus must have been so cross with me.'

'Of course he wasn't. He understood that I had to be with you. It was just lucky we had both booked time off so he was able to deal with everything. I think you'll like it. It's probably no bigger over all than the apartment, except for the kitchen. That's big enough for us to have a table out there so when we are on our own that's where we eat. When we've saved up a bit we plan to have an extension built on the back and make that into a dining room. The best thing of all is having a garden. It's not very big, but the old man who owned the house was a keen gardener and he designed it beautifully. Even better is that it's low maintenance as neither Marcus or I know anything about gardening. From the front there is a lovely view of the ocean. We want to put larger windows into that room so that we can look at the view whilst we're sitting there. I'll come up and collect you when you feel ready and you can come down for the day, provided you don't think an hour each way in the car will make you too stiff and uncomfortable.'

Annita smiled contentedly. 'I'm sure it won't. Now where is that doctor? I would like to be home by lunch time. If I have to eat here they'll insist that I have an hour's rest afterwards. It's really just to give the staff a break. We don't need to rest just because we've had something to eat.'

2000 – 2002

'So what do you think, grandma? Did we do the right thing in buying this?'

'I think so. It's a delightful little house and you have a wonderful view over the sea.' Annita followed Bryony from room to room, leaning heavily on her stick. Her hip replacement had rid her of the pain, but not made walking any easier for her. She had an idea that the other hip needed the same treatment and she would have to prepare herself for another spell in hospital. 'When do you plan to start building the extension?'

'We can't afford to do that for another six months at least. You sit down and I'll show you the plans. We're going to knock out the whole of the back wall and extend the side walls by five feet. It will give us a lovely big room and an even better view of the garden. I can't wait to get rid of that little window so we can see out properly. Marcus has other plans as well. He thought we should make use of the flat roof. He's suggested that we have the window in the upstairs room replaced with a door so we can walk out onto the roof and use it as a patio.'

'Why do you need a patio up there when you have the garden?'

'We don't need it. Marcus just thought it would look more attractive if the roof had railings around it with a few pot plants and garden furniture. From up there you'll be able to see for miles.'

Bryony settled herself comfortably beside her grandmother

and unrolled a sheaf of plans. 'These are the ones that have been drawn up by the architect for the extension.'

Annita cast her eyes over them, they meant very little to her.

Bryony unrolled two more large sheets of paper. 'Marcus has drawn this,' she announced with pride. 'This is how we want the inside to look after the work has been completed.'

Annita looked at the drawing for the interior of the room. The kitchen had been designed with an island to separate it from the living area and Bryony pointed out that it would be large enough for them to sit at to eat and would have a shutter that could be pulled down to close off the entire area.

'I thought that could be a good idea. If we have friends over for a meal they won't want to sit and look at dirty dishes, so when I've cleared the table I just close the shutter.'

Annita nodded. 'Very practical; and what kind of furniture do you plan to have?'

'Something light; cane or bamboo. We want it to feel as if this room is an extension to the garden. We'll still keep our other furniture in the living room. This is Marcus's idea for the roof.'

'Suppose you need the room for a different purpose in a couple of years?' Annita wished her granddaughter would start a family.

Bryony shrugged. 'I doubt if we will.'

Annita raised her eyebrows, but said no more. It really was none of her business.

Christabelle opened the recorded letter with trepidation. It was as she feared. A date had finally been set for Rudy Schwaber to stand trial for the murder of her mother and she was officially called to attend and give her evidence.

She had enjoyed the time she had spent in New York, rarely working more than three days in any one week, leaving her ample time to visit the places of interest.

She travelled to the top of the Empire State Building, pretending to feel quite faint from the height, which gained her the attention of the other visitors.

Whenever she visited Carnegie Hall she made sure she arrived at the very last moment and all eyes would be turned on her as she took her seat and gave a little wave to the crowd as if she were royalty.

She knew that most of the audience would recognise her from the commercials that were broadcast regularly on the television network, but she was tired of seeing her smile advertising toothpaste, her hair running through her fingers to promote a shampoo, close ups of her glossy lips assuring people that the lipstick she wore would not smudge or leave a mark on a glass. She was worth more than this. The fact that she had to give Reuben Neumayer thirty five percent of all her earnings, including the small percentage she earned each time a commercial was shown, annoyed her. She did the work. All he did was ask his secretary to pick up the telephone.

Having to return to New Orleans could be beneficial. It was time for her to move on and London seemed like the next logical location. She would renew her acquaintance with Mike Able and ask him if he had any contacts in Europe that might be able to help her.

For three days Christabelle sat and listened as the council for Kurt Schwaber's defence described his blameless character, that he had no reason to be violent towards Anna Bartlett and their relationship was not about to end. His attorney pointed out that no blood at all was found on any of the clothing owned by Mr Schwaber. A worker at the laundry gave evidence that she had certainly not seen any suspicious stains on his shirts.

The prosecution suggested that the shirt in question had been disposed of, but could offer no proof. Mr Delaney rose to object to the insinuation and as he did so he clutched at his chest. His breath was being squeezed from his body and the pain was excruciating. He toppled forward and various people rushed to his aid as the judge called for a recess and the court to be cleared.

Detective Mullen telephoned Christabelle the next morning at the hotel where she was staying. 'I'm very sorry, Miss Bartlett. The trial has had to be adjourned. Mr Delaney suffered a fatal heart attack yesterday. Unfortunately the defence don't feel they can continue at this stage without him.'

'So what happens now?' Christabelle was thoroughly annoyed. She would need to change her plans.

'Another member of the firm will be appointed to take over the case. It will cause a considerable delay. They will need to review the evidence against Mr Schwaber and decide how they will present his defence. When they feel ready to proceed they will have to apply for a new date in court. We could be looking at anything from six months to a year, maybe longer.'

'What am I supposed to do in that time? It is most inconvenient. I terminated my contract in New York to return specifically for the trial. I had planned to go to Europe once it was over.'

Detective Mullen considered. 'It would obviously be better if you could stay locally for a while. The new defence lawyers will certainly want to speak to you. They could also be difficult and decide to apply for a subpoena to prevent you travelling out of the State.'

'What!'

'I'm only looking at the worst case scenario. Once they've sorted through Mr Delaney's papers they will probably ask for an interview with you fairly quickly. They will be as anxious as you to get the trial moving again.'

'I see.' Christabelle bit at her lip and thought rapidly. If she was expected to stay in New Orleans for an unspecified amount of time it would be practical to open up the house and live there rather than stay in the hotel where she had spent the last week. She would also approach Mike Able and see if he could provide her with some work. She tried to sound unconcerned. 'Oh, well, there's obviously nothing I can do. I'll just have to make the best of it.'

Christabelle entered the house that had been closed up for over a year. It smelt musty and slightly damp and was certainly in need of cleaning. She went from room to room opening up the windows; then checked that the electricity and water supplies were in order. She would contact a cleaning firm and stay in the hotel for a further week until they had made the house habitable again. She ought to contact Bryony, surely her aged grandmother was no longer alive and that would mean she could sell it.

Mike Able and Peter Rodriguez were delighted when she approached them and assured her they would be able to provide her with plenty of work.

'I cannot sign a contract, you understand. I will obviously need to have time off when this new trial takes place and as soon as it is over I want to go to London.'

Mike Able frowned. 'That means you could work freelance.'

Christabelle shook her head. 'I'm happy to sign an agreement to say I work exclusively for you, but I cannot be tied down to specific dates. I realise that means I would not have a monthly salary to rely on, but I'm sure the commission for my work could be increased so that I am not out of pocket overall.'

Peter Martinez was busy making calculations on the side of his notebook. He looked up at Mike and smiled. 'I think we could give you a five per cent increase on what you were earning before.'

'That's not enough. Twenty per cent would be more appropriate. Prices have risen and salaries with them. I might only have one or two commissions from you and then I would be badly out of pocket. Remember I can always go freelance. You also have to bear in mind that I have far more experience now having worked in New York.'

Peter frowned. He knew her request was reasonable, he also knew that she would find no shortage of work as a freelance model. The moment the other magazines found out she was available for work they would be falling over themselves to employ her.

'Ten per cent,' he offered.

'Fifteen,' Christabelle spoke firmly. 'I'll not accept less if I'm to work exclusively for you.'

Mike raised his eyebrows and gave an imperceptible nod to his partner. They could not afford to refuse her.

'Mr Schwaber, I do believe you when you say you did not harm Mrs Bartlett.' Kurt's new attorney sat forward in his chair across the table from the accused man. 'The problem is, as I see it; that only leaves one other person. Mrs Bartlett's daughter.'

Kurt looked at Rory in disbelief. 'She couldn't have done that to her mother.'

Rory shrugged. 'I'm afraid I am going to have to go through all your statements to Mr Delaney again, which will be pretty tedious for you, but I want to see for myself if there's anything he didn't pick up on.'

'I kept telling him I was innocent.'

'I know, but on the face of it, circumstantial evidence is against you. I want to put a few ideas to you and see how you feel about them. All the requisite tests regarding your physical and mental health have been completed, so there will be no need to go through that again. Was Mrs Bartlett expecting you?'

'I telephoned her during the morning.'

Rory McMahon nodded. 'Now, can you remember the exact time you arrived at Mrs Bartlett's house?'

Kurt shook his head. 'Not to the minute.'

'Did you see anyone when you entered?'

'No.'

'Would anyone have seen you? A neighbour; a passer by? Anyone?'

'I didn't notice anyone, but someone could have seen me.'

Rory made a note to make enquiries in the area. He knew it was unlikely that anyone would remember seeing Kurt Schwaber due to the time that had elapsed.

'What about when you left?'

'I saw her daughter, Christabelle.'

Rory nodded. 'I understand from her statement that she had entered the house earlier and heard you having an angry discussion with Mrs Bartlett.'

Kurt shook his head. 'That isn't true. We spent a pleasant hour chatting. I was telling her about my brother and his family. I promised to take her out for dinner later in the week. There was no argument over that.'

'Did you say anything with a raised voice? Anything at all that could be misconstrued by someone who overheard you?'

'Nothing.'

'When you left the house you saw Miss Bartlett approaching. What did you do?'

'I called out hello to her. I can't remember exactly what I said; it was probably *"hi, Christabelle, how you doing?"* or something similar.'

'What was her reply to that?'

'I couldn't hear. She waved her hand, smiled and said something, probably *"fine"* or *"feeling good"*. The usual sort of thing.'

'Miss Bartlett claims that you only raised your hand to her and hurried away.'

'I was in a hurry, but I definitely called out to her and she replied.'

'Did you hear Miss Bartlett come into the house earlier, as she claims?'

'No.'

'Would you have heard her?'

Kurt shrugged. 'Not necessarily. She's not a noisy person. Shuts doors quietly, walks quietly.'

'Did you like Miss Bartlett?'

'I didn't dislike her. She seemed very reserved. If she was in when I called she greeted me politely enough, then usually made some excuse to leave the room.'

'Could this have been tact on her part? Leaving you and Mrs Bartlett alone together.'

'Possibly. I never really thought about it like that. I just assumed she disliked me.'

Rory tapped his pen against his teeth. 'Now, you say you did not hear Miss Bartlett enter the house. Suppose someone else had entered the house? Would you have heard them?'

'Someone else?'

'An intruder. Someone who had no business to be there.'

'If they had broken in I would have heard the noise, no doubt.'

'I'm thinking more of someone who was in the house before you arrived. Someone who had gained access and was hiding, upstairs maybe, or in another room.'

Kurt frowned. 'I certainly didn't hear anyone else in the house.'

'Did you have occasion to go upstairs?'

'I only went into the lounge.'

'How did you get into the house, Mr Schwaber? Did you ring the bell or did you have a key to let yourself in?'

'I always rang the bell.'

Rory closed his notebook. 'We'll leave it there for today. If you think of anything you feel could be useful, you know where to contact me. I'll go over what you've told me today and check it out with your previous statement. If I come across any discrepancies or need clarification I'll be in touch.'

Christabelle stood demurely in the witness box. Under questioning by the prosecution she described how she had returned to the house and departed swiftly upon hearing angry voices. She saw Kurt Schwaber leaving the house, appearing to be in a hurry and that was when she had re-entered. Having deposited her purchases in her bedroom and used the bathroom she had returned to the kitchen with the intention of making coffee. She had called out to her mother to ask if she would like a cup. When she did not receive a reply she had entered the lounge and found her mother on the floor. Thinking she had fainted she had tried to lift her, subsequently getting blood on the sleeve of her blouse. When she realised she was badly injured she had called the emergency services and later given a statement to Detective Mullen. Encouraged by the prosecution she confirmed she had told the detective that her mother had planned to finish the relationship. Tears came to her eyes at appropriate moments and she could see she had the sympathy of the jury.

Rory McMahon had been unable to produce any new evidence and Kurt Schwaber continued to protest his innocence. At the end of the week the jury were asked to retire to consider their verdict. Christabelle sat in an agony of apprehension. What would happen if Kurt Schwaber were set free? Would the police reopen the investigation?

To the surprise of Christabelle, but no one else in the court house, the jury returned within two hours with a unanimous verdict. Kurt Schwaber was guilty of murder in the first degree as charged and they were recommending the death penalty.

Christabelle looked down at her clenched hands. She did not want anyone to see the triumphant gleam in her eyes.

Kurt Schwaber stood motionless. 'I'm innocent,' he protested. 'I swear I'm innocent.'

Rory McMahon rose to his feet. 'My client will lodge an appeal, your Lordship.'

The judge looked at the defence counsel sadly. 'That is Mr Schwaber's right provided you can produce some new evidence that could overturn the verdict of this court. In the meantime the verdict stands.'

Christabelle telephoned Bryony. 'I thought you would want to know the outcome of the trial.'

'I read about it in the newspapers.'

'That's the kind of publicity I can do without. Thank goodness that serial killer has just been arrested and he's been making the headlines. I'm very grateful to him.'

'Christabelle!'

'You know what I mean. So you know Kurt Schwaber was given the death sentence?'

'That's so awful.'

'He deserved it. Anyway, how's Grandma? Did you have to tell her?'

'She doesn't have a newspaper. She says they're always full of bad news, besides, she's in hospital.'

'Is she ill?' Christabelle crossed her fingers.

'Not a bit,' replied Bryony cheerfully. 'She's having a second hip replacement. She should be able to come home any day now. Are we able to meet up? Do you have some free time?''

Christabelle shook her head vehemently. 'I thought I ought to let you know that I'm off to England. I'd planned to go earlier; then I had to hang around.'

'Send me a postcard of Buckingham Palace and give me your mobile number.'

'Whatever for?'

'Just in case anything happens to Grandma. You'd want to know, wouldn't you? I wouldn't expect you to come back or anything.'

'Yes, of yes, of course. You don't think anything is going to happen to her, do you?' Christabelle's hopes soared.

'No, of course not. I've got a pen and paper. Tell me your number.'

Kurt Schwaber awaited the visit from Rory McMahon with trepidation. It was all very well saying that he would be appealing against his death sentence, but if no new evidence could be produced he would not be granted permission to proceed.

Rory looked sympathetically at the dejected man sitting before him. 'I have to admit that I was not surprised by the verdict. The girl had the jury eating out of her hand.'

'What can I do? I know I'm innocent. Even if an appeal is successful and the death sentence is commuted they'll give me life.'

'We have to start back at the beginning. I have to find some evidence to prove that the verdict should be overturned. I talked to your brother after the trial. He believes in you and is willing to try anything to prove your innocence. With your permission I'd like to get a friend of mine involved. I'll ask him to make some enquiries with the neighbours, just in case they saw anyone in the area. I'll be back in touch as soon as possible. In the meantime I'd like you to think about that afternoon again. Try to remember every little detail. There could be something you think to be insignificant that turns out to be vital.'

Christabelle breezed into Mike Able's office with a complacent smile on her face. She sank down in a chair. 'Thank goodness that ordeal is over. I really felt quite faint when the jury returned with their verdict. I was so relieved.'

Mike raised a quizzical eyebrow. 'He was found guilty?'

Christabelle nodded. 'The judge has given him the death penalty.'

'I reckon he deserved it. From what I've heard it was pretty cold blooded.'

Christabelle decided it was time to change the subject. 'What I've really come in for is to talk about my future.'

'You're leaving us?'

'You know I always planned to go to Europe once all this,' she shuddered dramatically, 'horrible business was over. I'll obviously finish my outstanding assignments with you.'

'We will miss you, Christabelle.'

'I don't plan to stay away for ever. I thought I would work for some months in London, then Paris, followed by Milan, maybe Athens. I'll probably be away about a couple of years.'

'I can only wish you well. I'm sure you'll be successful.'

'I hope you'll be willing to give me work when I return.'

'You don't plan to go back to New York?'

Christabelle shook her head. 'I enjoyed the experience, but I wouldn't want to live there indefinitely. I shall return to New Orleans when I've seen all I want of Europe.'

Mike wrote swiftly on the back of a calling card. 'There's the name and phone number of a colleague in London. I'll have a word with him and you call him when you arrive. I know he'll help you all he can.'

Christabelle arrived at Heathrow airport in pouring rain. For the first time she wondered if her idea of visiting London during the winter months was such a good idea. It seemed even colder here than it had been in New York. The countryside that she saw from the windows of the coach looked bleak and drab beneath the grey skies and she shivered. Thank goodness she had ignored the prejudice against animal fur and brought her coat with her. She was going to need the warmth it offered.

From Victoria Station, where the coach deposited her, she took a taxi to the hotel Mike's contact had recommended and booked herself in for a week. At the end of that time she should know whether she was going to be able to find work easily or if she needed to go elsewhere. Having had a shower and a short sleep she telephoned down to the reception desk and asked them how she could make a local call.

'Just press nine on your telephone dial and follow it with the number, including the area code. The cost of the call will be added to your bill.'

The anonymous voice replaced the receiver and Christabelle pulled a face. To have addressed her as madam would have been courteous.

Hesitantly Christabelle dialled the number Mike Able had given her and was reassured by hearing the telephone ringing at the other end. She was about to replace the receiver when it was lifted.

'Hello?'

'Good evening, may I speak to Mr Donaldson, please.'

'Speaking.'

'I'm sorry to interrupt your evening, but Mike Able told me to call you when I arrived in London. I'm Christabelle.'

There was a momentary silence. 'Oh, yes, I didn't know exactly when you were arriving. Can I call you back in about ten minutes? I was in the shower when you rang.'

'Certainly. I'm at the hotel you recommended and my room number is two zero three.'

'Fine. Speak to you again soon.'

It was less than ten minutes before Benjamin Donaldson telephoned Christabelle. 'Have you eaten yet?' he asked immediately.

Christabelle looked at her watch. 'What time is it?'

'Seven thirty in the evening, although I doubt if your body knows that. I'd like to take you out to dinner, we could get to know each other and I can tell you what Mike has asked me to do for you.'

Christabelle frowned. She did not want her life organised for her. 'I guess so,' she answered grudgingly.

'Right. I should be with you in about an hour.' The phone went dead and Christabelle looked at it surprised. Were all English people as abrupt over the telephone?

She looked out of the window. It was still raining. No doubt it was cold out and she had no idea what would be suitable to wear. Wearily she opened her case and began to remove her clothes and hang them in the wardrobe. Having done so she looked at them speculatively and finally decided on a white cashmere trouser suit. Beneath the jacket she could wear a silk camisole top which would give her additional warmth, her long white kid boots she returned reluctantly to the wardrobe, not wanting to get them marked with rain, and decided instead on her black ankle boots.

Having piled her hair up on top of her head, accentuated her eyes and lips and applied an expensive perfume, she surveyed the finished effect in the full-length mirror. She looked what she was – a top model. She turned on the television to a news channel and watched the English news without interest until the telephone rang and Benjamin Donaldson announced that he was waiting for her in the reception area.

As she exited the lift a tall, blonde man stepped forward and extended his hand. 'You must be Christabelle.'

Christabelle nodded. 'I assume you are Mr Donaldson?'

'Ben, please call me Ben.' He surveyed the girl before him with a practised eye. She certainly lived up to Mike's description of her. 'As it's such a horrible evening I thought you might prefer to eat at the hotel. We can see what they have to offer and if there's nothing you fancy we can always take a taxi to somewhere else.'

Christabelle felt unreasonably annoyed. If she had known they were staying at the hotel she would have worn a dress and shown off her long and shapely legs.

'Very well. I'm sure I'll find something appetising on the menu, although I have to warn you that I don't feel particularly hungry.'

'That's the jet lag. Give it a couple of days and you'll be back into a normal routine. Now, would you like a drink before we go in?'

'I don't drink,' announced Christabelle.

'Not even a glass of wine?'

Christabelle shook her head. 'I don't like alcohol. If you want a drink please go ahead. I'll have a fruit juice.'

Ben led the way into the bar, settled Christabelle at a table and ordered a whisky for himself and tomato juice for his companion. 'I can indulge myself tonight as I'm not driving. Cheers.'

Christabelle raised her glass. 'To my success,' she said.

Ben nodded. 'What are your plans for the next few days? Mike told me you wanted to do photographic modelling and commercial work whilst you were in London and asked me to help out.'

Christabelle looked at him quizzically. 'What do you mean – help out?'

'Basically to look after you and steer you in the right direction.' Ben smiled disarmingly at her.

'I am quite capable of fending for myself.'

'I'm sure you are, but look at it this way. You are an incredibly beautiful young lady. You will attract attention wherever you go, but there are parts of London that it would be very unwise for you to visit alone. If you start searching for modelling agencies you will have no idea by their address whether they are respectable establishments or a front for other activities. Once they have you through their doors they could make it very difficult for you to leave.'

'What are you talking about?'

Ben leaned forward. 'If you look in the advertising section of the newspapers you will see requests for escorts. A good-looking girl like yourself would be asked to accompany a visiting ambassador to a dinner. Sounds innocent enough, but at the end of the evening you would be expected to do him, and possibly some of his friends, a few favours before you were returned to your hotel. Your photograph would appear with him in a society magazine, but it's no more than high-class prostitution. There are many genuine agencies that would ask you to model, but you would find that the payment you receive would be far below the original figure quoted. A considerable amount would have been deducted for 'expenses' and you would probably find you could earn more as a shop assistant. There are others who would never pay at all. They declare themselves bankrupt and start up again under a new name. Photographs get 'lost' and mysteriously reappear in a few years time.'

'You're not serious?'

'I am extremely serious. This is London. I understand from Mike that you approached him, you went to one of the top magazines, but we work a bit differently over here. You need an agent. No one will employ you without.'

'So I need to approach agencies rather than magazines?'

Ben nodded. 'This is why Mike has asked me to look after you. I edit a magazine. We use a reputable agency and I can give you an introduction to them. You'll have to pay to have a portfolio done and a registration fee to be on their books, but any work you get will be genuine and you'll be paid promptly at the going rate.'

Christabelle sipped at her tomato juice. 'I have magazine adverts with me that I did in the States. I don't need to pay for a portfolio.'

Ben shook his head. 'They won't accept that. The registration fee pays their overheads, offices, studios, staff and the like. The portfolio is necessary to show to clients and goes towards their costs. The commission they get for each photo shoot makes up the rest of their money. Anyone who offered anything different is on a racket.'

'On a racket?'

'Crooked, cheating. Shall we go into the dining room?'

Christabelle rose obediently. She had expected to walk in to a magazine the way she had in New Orleans, using her beauty as a passport. Ben watched as she walked ahead of him. Mike had been right in his description of her. She was the most fantastic girl he had seen in a long time and she exuded self-confidence. In reality she was naïve and obviously thought the advertising world would fall at her feet just by looking at her. It was a pity she was wearing a trouser suit; he would have liked to see her in a cocktail dress, revealing more of her body.

'So what are your plans for tomorrow?' he asked as he tackled his steak with relish, and Christabelle pushed her smoked salmon around her plate trying to enjoy what, for her, should have been breakfast.

'I was planning to visit some of the magazines, but you've rather quelled my enthusiasm.'

Ben smiled easily. 'I didn't mean to put you down. You're probably going to feel pretty disorientated still tomorrow. How about if I meet you after lunch and show you a few of the London sights? I can give you directions to the places that interest you, Buckingham Palace, the Tower or the museums. Whatever takes your fancy. We could meet up again in the evening and I'll bring along the manager of the agency we use. Give you an introduction and you can take it from there. How does that sound?'

'I guess it makes sense,' Christabelle agreed. It would certainly be easier for her to use Ben than try to find work on her own. 'What do you get out of it?'

Ben looked at her in surprise. 'Nothing. Well, nothing financially. It gives me the opportunity to be seen with the best looking girl in town and a chance to play hooky for the day.'

'Hooky?'

'Be absent from my job.'

'Can you do that?'

'I'm the boss. I can do as I please. I usually do a nine 'til five, but no one will ask questions if I say I'm not coming in for the afternoon.' Ben smiled disarmingly at her. 'How's your food?'

Christabelle looked down at her plate. 'It's very good. I just don't feel very hungry.'

'Don't worry about it. Would you like a dessert?'

Christabelle shook her head. 'I couldn't do it justice.'

'Right. I'll ask them to bring coffee into the lounge, unless you'd like to go out for a while?'

'Maybe a short walk; provided it isn't too cold and wet. I'll need to get my coat from the cloakroom.'

'You do that whilst I settle up. I'll meet you again by the lift.'

Ben arrived back at the hotel the following afternoon as arranged and waited patiently whilst Christabelle made final touches to her

153

toilet before emerging from the lift. The rain had stopped, but the skies were still overcast and she wore her fur coat, again over trousers and a jumper. Ben wished she had visited England in the summer months. He ordered a taxi and helped her in, sliding in beside her on the back seat.

'I've asked the driver to give us a tour. Let me know what takes your interest and I'll give you details of the underground line or bus to get you there. The underground is quickest, but if you take a bus you'll see more. You can always grab a taxi, but they tend to take a tourist on the longest route available.'

Christabelle nodded. She had looked at a tourist guide in her room and already knew exactly where she wanted to go. The Tower of London to see the Crown Jewels, Buckingham Palace, the museums, Regent Street, Bond Street, Park Lane and Oxford Street for the shops, and, of course, visits to the many theatres. She tried to show interest as Ben pointed out landmarks to her as they drove past Marble Arch, through Hyde Park and into the city.

'This is Fleet Street,' he announced. 'At one time all the newspapers and magazines were based here. Now many of them have moved out.'

'Why?'

'Various reasons. With increased technology these old buildings were no longer suitable, or other premises were cheaper. A lot of them keep an office here, prestige value, but the printing work is done elsewhere.'

Christabelle looked at the grimy, old-fashioned buildings. She was not impressed by London. 'They look pretty depressing.'

Ben grinned. 'Don't be fooled by the facades. The interiors have been modernised, central heating, decent plumbing, carpet you sink into up to your ankles. If you have an address here on your notepaper it says you have money in the bank.'

'I think I'd rather live in New Orleans than here.'

Ben grinned. 'Give it a few weeks. London grows on you. By the time you've been here a few months you'll love the place.'

Christabelle looked at him dubiously. She thought it most unlikely she would grow to love the bustling city.

Before parting from Ben she had checked where they would be eating that evening and was relieved when he said at the hotel. She examined her wardrobe carefully and decided on a pale green sheath that ended just above her knees and left one shoulder exposed. She experimented with her hair and eventually swept it to one side where it covered the exposed shoulder and showed off a gold hoop earring on the other side. Satisfied that she would make an impression on the agent who was joining them for the meal she sat and looked at the magazine adverts she had brought with her until the telephone informed her that Ben had arrived.

He gave her an admiring glance as she walked towards him that was not lost on Christabelle, who was surprised to see a large, ungainly woman standing beside him. The woman looked her up and down critically and murmured something inaudible in Ben's ear. He gave her a quick smile before introducing her to Christabelle.

'This is Marsha. She's from the agency we use. You two can get to know each other during the evening and then make a formal appointment for your portfolio.'

Christabelle nodded. 'I'm pleased to meet you. Ben has spoken very highly of you.'

Marsha touched Christabelle's limp hand and led the way into the bar. 'May as well start with a snifter. I'll have my usual, make it a double, darling.'

Ben complied with her request, ordering a whisky for himself and orange juice for Christabelle. Marsha opened her bag and pulled out a packet of cigarettes. 'I presume we can still smoke in here, despite all these silly new regulations they're bringing in?'

Ben nodded. 'There's an ashtray on the table and no notices.'

Marsha exhaled a stream of evil smelling smoke and Christabelle edged away. 'Now,' the woman narrowed her eyes,

'Just because you've been a success in America, what makes you think you can be successful over here?'

'I have the looks.'

'I'll grant you that, but you need more than looks to get to the top. You need personality and a certain something that marks you out from the others. I have over two hundred girls on my books. Most of them look as good as you, but I know that only about half a dozen will make the big time.'

Christabelle forced a smile. 'I'm sure I can be a success in London. I'm prepared to work hard, maximum exposure, and I'm willing to learn the way you work over here and fit in.'

'So why come to London anyway if you're such a success in the States?'

'I've worked continually for the last six years and saved hard. I've always wanted to visit Europe and I decided I would turn it into a working holiday. I plan to spend some time here and eventually move on to Paris and Milan.'

Marsha raised her eyebrows. 'You speak French and Italian?'

Christabelle shook her head.

'You'll find it far more difficult to get any work over there if you don't speak the language. Unless you're willing to strip, of course.'

'Definitely not,' replied Christabelle firmly.

'What's your problem?'

'I will do underwear or bikinis, but I'm not prepared to be topless just to give dirty old men a thrill. It's disgusting when you see them sniggering over a woman in a magazine.'

'Not all nude work is pornographic. Much of it is art.'

'I'm not prepared to be exposed in that sense.'

Marsha stubbed out her cigarette. 'Well, we've got that clear for a start. Shall we go in? I'm ravenous.'

Christabelle accompanied her into the restaurant with Ben following. She already disliked this woman intensely.

'So,' Marsha looked at the menu and talked to Christabelle at the same time. 'Have you done commercials?'

'Yes. I did a number of them whilst I was in New York.'

'So I ask you to advertise a body moisturiser, you can't do that fully dressed.'

'I refuse and ask you to consider me for something else,' Christabelle retorted.

'You wouldn't be prepared to wear a body stocking and be air brushed?'

Christabelle shook her head.

'I have hundreds of girls on my books that have no such scruples. How do you expect to compete against them?'

'If you need a nude or semi-nude I suggest you use one of the other girls,' she replied tartly. 'I am not prepared to have photographs taken that could be misused if they fell into the wrong hands.'

'Do you make conditions about what clothes you wear? No low necks, no short skirts?'

Christabelle felt that Marsha was sneering at her and she took a deep breath. 'If you would care to look at some of the advertisements that I have brought with me you will see that I am very flexible. I just refuse to do modelling that could result in adverse publicity for me in the future.'

Marsha shrugged. 'I'll have clam chowder, followed by rack of lamb.' She placed the menu back on the table. 'I'm not interested in seeing what you've done in the past. Come in tomorrow at nine and we'll put you through your paces. If I think you're good enough I'll arrange a couple of minor shoots for you and see how you get on.' She passed a card across the table to Christabelle. 'There's the address. You'd better take a taxi or you'll be a couple of hours travelling from here. Ask for me when you arrive.'

'Thank you.' Christabelle looked at the address on the card. She had no idea where Finchley Park was, but she could ask Ben later.

Ben ordered for them and Christabelle was relieved when the food arrived and she could occupy herself by eating. Marsha kept up a steady flow of comments to Ben and Christabelle felt herself ignored. As soon as she decently could she excused herself, pleading that she was still suffering from some extent to jet lag.

'Probably explains why you've been so quiet all evening,' observed Marsha. 'Usually I can't shut you girls up. Want to tell me their life history.'

Christabelle smiled politely. 'I'm sorry if I've disappointed you.'

'Makes a change. How about another drink, Ben? I know a decent little bar round the corner.'

'Would you care to join us, Christabelle?' asked Ben.

She shook her head. 'Thank you, but no. I really would like to get to bed. I want to be at my best for tomorrow.' Christabelle gave Marsha a disarming smile. 'I'll see you at nine. I'll bring some outfits with me and I'm sure you won't be disappointed.'

Ben raised his eyebrows at Marsha. 'What did you think of her?' he asked as they left the hotel to walk to the bar.

Marsha shrugged. 'A strange one. Not the usual type. If she looks as good on paper as she does in the flesh she'll be a roaring success. She certainly knows what she's got to offer.'

'Pity she won't do nude,' observed Ben.

'Doesn't need to, by the sound of things. She's already made it in the States, so why take your clothes off over here? Most of the girls start as nudes and cover up as they get well known. Their problems start when someone digs up a few originals of them and their murky past gets discovered.'

'I don't think Christabelle has a murky past.'

'At her age, darling, she hasn't even got a past.' Marsha lifted her bulk onto a stool at the bar. 'I'll have my usual.'

Christabelle looked at the outside of the building with distaste. Litter was blowing around on the narrow pavement, paint was peeling from the door and the ground floor windows were heavily barred. She tried the door and it opened at her touch leading into a small room where a girl sat at a desk, a cigarette burning in the ashtray beside her whilst she typed.

'Yes,' she said without looking up.

'I'm Christabelle. I have an appointment with Marsha.'

'Miss Marsha,' corrected the girl. 'Go on through.' She inclined her head towards the door, picked up her cigarette and sucked greedily at it before returning to her typing.

The door led into a passage, desperately in need of a coat of paint, with a number of doors at intervals. Christabelle looked at the names crudely painted on them. *'Ladies', 'Gents', 'No. 1', 'No. 2', 'Lab', 'Marsha', 'Ferdi', 'Studio'*. Tentatively she knocked on the one with Marsha's name and was told to enter.

Marsha, wreathed in cigarette smoke, looked up from her desk. 'Good. You're on time. Formalities first. Fill in this form and then I'll introduce you to Jacob. He's our photographer.'

Christabelle looked at the form. It was quite straight forward, details of her name, date of birth, address, telephone number and a space for her signature at the bottom to say she agreed to her photographs being used for commercial purposes. She frowned.

'This place where I sign. It looks as if I'm agreeing to my photos being used without any payment.'

'These photos are for your portfolio. You pay us for these. We use them to show to clients.'

'Oh,' Christabelle felt she had shown her ignorance. 'It's a bit different in the States.' She signed the agreement and handed it back.

'Fine. Let's get started.' Marsha led the way from her room to the door marked *'Studio'* where Jacob was sitting reading a newspaper. He handed Christabelle a list.

'That's the order I'd like to shoot you in. Have you brought suitable gear?'

Christabelle read the list quickly and nodded. 'I think so.'

'In to makeup then. Quick as you can between shoots. I've other work to get through.'

Christabelle looked around. 'Where do I go?'

'Ferdi does make up and you can use No. 1. to change in. Come back as soon as you're ready.' Jacob picked up his newspaper and Christabelle felt herself dismissed. Marsha had already returned to her office, and Christabelle opened the door to '*No. 1.*' with some trepidation.

To her relief the room was clean, a table topped with mirrors ran the length of one wall whilst the other had rails at various heights to hang clothes, a rack for shoes and shelves for accessories. On the end wall was a large, full-length mirror to enable the girls to check their appearance before leaving.

Swiftly Christabelle unpacked her case and hung her clothes; pleased to see they were not creased. She looked at the list Jacob had given her and frowned. She was to start with evening wear, hair down, then smart, hair down, back to evening wear, hair up, then smart again with hair up. How stupid. It would be easier to do both the evening wear shots before the 'smart.' She would suggest it to him when she went in for the first photo.

Jacob looked at her. 'Who's taking the photos? You or me? That's the order I want, besides Mia would have to do your hair four times instead of twice.'

Christabelle shrugged. 'I just thought it could be quicker and easier to do it my way.'

'You're not paid to think. Just do as you're told.'

Christabelle felt flustered. She was not used to changing from one outfit to another in a short space of time, having her hair re-done and make up touched up after each few photographs. By the end of the morning she felt exhausted and was relieved when Jacob announced he was finished. She returned to the dressing room to find two other girls in a state of undress and hesitated in the doorway.

'I'm sorry. I thought this was my dressing room.'

'Come in. It's communal.' The girl removed her bras and began to search for a bikini top on the shelf.

'I can wait,' said Christabelle and began to back out.

'Wait? Don't be silly. Come in and get changed.'

'I'm used to a dressing room to myself,' protested Christabelle.

'Are you now? Well you won't get that here, will she, Nat? I suggest you come in now. There are four more girls arriving any minute and you'll be lucky to find standing room.' She fastened the bikini top and covered herself with an old dressing gown. 'I'm Anastasia, and this is Natalie. Who are you?'

'I'm Christabelle.'

'You're American?'

Christabelle nodded. 'My accent stands out a mile.'

'How long you here for, Chris?'

'My name is Christabelle.'

Anastasia shrugged. 'So? Mine's Anastasia and most people call me Ana, Natalie is known as Nat.'

'I am only known as Christabelle,' replied Christabelle firmly.

'Oh, get you! Have you got any mints, Ana? I meant to put a new pack in and I forgot.'

Anastasia passed a small container to her friend. 'So how long are you here for – Christabelle?' She accentuated the name intentionally.

'It depends. I'm on a working vacation. I'll probably stay a few months, maybe a year, then move on to Paris.'

'Why Paris? London is just as good.'

'It's an opportunity to see Europe and become as well-known over here as in the States.'

Christabelle removed her suit, donning a pair of trousers and thick jumper over her blouse as she talked. She placed the items from the rail into her case and hung her fur coat round her shoulders.

'Wow! Is that real?'

Christabelle nodded. 'I advertised some coats back home and was offered a discount. I bought the one I liked the most.'

'All right for some! All we ever get offered is strawberry yoghurt or shampoo. Come on, Nat, or Jacob will blow and say we're holding him up. After you, Chris.' Anastasia held the door open.

'Christabelle,' Christabelle corrected her as she walked through and heard the two girls giggle.

'So how did it go?' asked Ben when he telephoned Christabelle that afternoon.

'All right, I guess. I have to go along tomorrow to see Marsha.'

'I'm sure she'll be pleased with you. What time shall I collect you this evening? I thought you might like to venture out of the hotel and eat somewhere different.'

Christabelle sighed. She was not sure that she wanted Ben to be continually accompanying her, although he was obviously useful to have around. She also had to admit that she was quite nervous about going out on her own once it was dark having ventured out for a short walk during the afternoon and become hopelessly lost, finally having to hail a taxi to return to her hotel.

'About seven – if that suits you.'

Christabelle enjoyed the modelling work she was asked to do for the agency and by the end a month she was in continual demand. Her photographs could be seen in all the magazines, in shop windows and on their counters showing her using the product they were promoting. The first time she had seen herself in a television commercial in the New York she could hardly believe her eyes. She was only on the screen for a few seconds, but it was enough to whet her appetite for more television work and she approached Marsha tentatively. Each time she met her she seemed to dislike her more, but appreciated how necessary she was to her at present. It would be a different story when she left for Paris.

'I really did enjoy making commercials in the States. If there's an opportunity for more work in that line I'd like to do it.'

Marsha nodded. 'I'll bear you in mind. It depends what the producers ask for. It's not up to me. If they say a petite blonde there's no point in sending you.'

'Naturally,' replied Christabelle icily. She always felt at a disadvantage before the woman who was not impressed by her looks or American reputation.

'Can you sing or dance?' asked Marsha.

'No, but I'm willing to try.'

'Producers are not there to teach you how to do the job. They expect you to have the ability before you turn up on their doorstep. There's an opportunity for you to try out on the catwalk next week. It's a promotion in one of the shops in Oxford Street, no big deal. Provided you don't fall flat on your face I doubt if anyone will notice you.'

Christabelle nodded. She would make sure she was noticed.

Christabelle scanned the advertisements looking for a small apartment. She was horrified at the prices being asked, but knew it was impractical for her to stay at the hotel indefinitely. She would ask Ben if he knew of anywhere that might be available at a more reasonable rent.

Ben shook his head. 'Flats in London are like gold dust. Even out in the suburbs they command a price. I suggest you sit down and balance what you would pay at a small hotel against renting a flat. You have to take into account that you'll be paying for your gas and electricity, telephone, probably maintenance and a local council tax. If you take a flat that's way out you could find you spend two or three hours a day travelling to and from assignments.'

Christabelle frowned. 'Well I can't afford to stay in this hotel much longer. It's eating into my savings.'

'You should be able to find somewhere a bit more reasonable. You're partly paying for the location here. Two or three roads away and the prices will be less.'

'Would I be able to negotiate a price if I was planning to be a long term resident?'

'You can try. I'm sure some of them would be only too pleased to have you permanently.'

'Would you be able to come with me, Ben? You know the area. I don't want to end up living anywhere that has a bad reputation.'

Ben consulted his diary. 'I'm pretty busy all of next week. I'll tell you what; I'll ask my secretary to draw up a list of small respectable establishments within a three mile radius of where you are now. Check them out against a map to see where your nearest tube stations are located and telephone those that you think would be suitable. All you need to do is ask if they have availability and their weekly rates. I can spend a day with you the next week to check them out.'

Christabelle smiled at him gratefully. 'I really do appreciate all the help you give me, Ben.'

Rory returned to Kurt Schwaber. He was feeling more optimistic than he had previously and hoped his client would be amenable to his idea.

'Now,' Rory withdrew his note pad from his brief case. 'My friend made a few enquiries in the neighbourhood. He started at the drug store. The man who runs it did not remember seeing Miss Bartlett, but agreed it was his day for checking his stock and he could have been out in the back at approximately that time. His assistant did remember her. Miss Bartlett had chatted whilst she purchased some toiletries and her magazines. She said she hoped to be appearing in some of them fairly soon. The young lady wanted to know more and apparently Miss Bartlett was quite expansive regarding her ambitions. The assistant was not able to give an exact time that Miss Bartlett left the shop unfortunately.'

Kurt frowned. 'We know that was what she did.'

Rory nodded. 'Bear with me. My friend then spoke to the neighbours, and this I find interesting. Next door but one the woman was in her garden. She heard the Bartlett's door shut and looked up to see Miss Bartlett leaving. She saw you arrive and she also saw Miss Bartlett return with her magazines. She is adamant that Miss Bartlett did not enter the house until after you had left. According to her, Miss Bartlett stood behind a tree almost opposite and emerged as you closed the front door.' Rory sat back with a pleased smile on his face as he waited for Kurt to comprehend what he was saying.

'Why should she do that?'

'Why indeed? Would Miss Bartlett have known you planned to visit her mother that afternoon?'

Kurt shrugged. 'Maybe. If she was in she would have heard the telephone and possibly her mother's side of the conversation.'

'I want you to think very carefully about that conversation. Try to remember exactly what you said and Mrs Bartlett's replies. I don't expect you to do it now. Write down whatever you can remember and give it to me when I next visit. In the meantime I'd like to ask this friend of mine to do a bit more investigating. I need your permission to use him and his time costs money. How do you feel about the idea, and more to the point, can you afford to pay a private investigator?'

'I don't know. How much money are you talking about?'

Rory spread his hands. 'He charges a hundred dollars an hour. He's honest. He won't charge you for ten hours work when he's only done five.'

Kurt shrugged. 'Speak to my brother. See what he says. I can't think straight any more.'

Rory collected his papers together. 'Have you any idea when he next plans to visit you? It might be better if we talked face to face.'

'Probably some time next month. I'll ask him to call you.'

Bryony helped her grandmother into the car and stowed her case in the trunk. Despite the second hip operation her grandmother did not seem to be moving any more easily, although she said she had no pain.

'I just need to loosen up a bit. The joints need oiling. I'll be fine once I'm home and can move around as I please.' Annita spoke far more confidently than she felt. 'I hope Sharon has done the shopping as she promised.'

'I'm sure she will have. She's very reliable.' Bryony resolved to ask the woman for her telephone number so she could check on the progress her grandmother made during the week. 'You'll have to come over and visit us in a week or so. The railings are being put up on the roof tomorrow.'

'When are you off to Greece?'

'The end of September. I asked Marianne when it would be easiest for her and she said everywhere quietens down a bit then. A number of their visitors come from England and the children need to be back in school. We're having a stop over of two nights in London.'

Annita nodded. 'Not so hot either. August can be almost too much to bear.'

'You'll have to tell me where we should visit. We'll have almost three weeks and I don't want to miss anything.'

Bryony stepped onto the tarmac from the aeroplane and stopped. 'Oh!'

'What's wrong?'

'Nothing.' Bryony smiled. 'It's just the smell. It smells so different from New Orleans, and the heat. The heat is different. It feels lighter somehow, not so oppressive.'

Marcus felt a push from behind and took his wife's elbow. 'Come on. We're holding others up. You'll have plenty of time to stand and sniff the air later.'

'I hope I recognise Marianne. I haven't seen her for years. What will we do if she isn't there to meet us?'

'I'm sure she will be. If we don't see her we'll wait half an hour then take a cab. We have the address.' Marcus placed his passport in front of the officer and waited for it to be handed back to him. 'Where do we go to collect our luggage?' he asked.

'Follow the signs.'

'How am I supposed to read Greek signs?' muttered Marcus. Bryony giggled. 'It's written in English as well.'

'It's all right for you,' he grumbled, 'you know the language.'

'I can talk to Grandma, but I can't read it.' Bryony fanned her face. 'I shall be glad to get out of some of these clothes. If it hadn't been raining in London this morning I would have worn a short sleeved blouse.'

Bryony looked at the slim, tanned woman before her. She hardly resembled her twin sister Helena now. Helena visited the hairdresser and beauty parlour each week, wore designer jeans and expensive shirts. Marianne's hair was tied back, her face was devoid of make up and she was wearing a pair of old shorts and a T-shirt. Bryony felt well dressed beside her, despite the fact that her skirt was creased from travelling and she had a coffee stain on her blouse. She just wished she was as slim.

Marianne greeted her with outstretched arms. 'It's so good to see you. And you must be Marcus.' She planted a kiss on each cheek. 'Welcome to Crete.'

As they left the outskirts of Heraklion and drove towards the town of Malia, Marianne described the general area to them. 'So much more has been built since I first arrived. This used to be a pleasant drive, now it's just suburbs all the way.'

She took a mouthful from the bottle of water in the side pocket of the door. 'Would either of you like a drink? I brought some bottles with me. They're probably it a bit warm by now, but better than nothing.'

Bryony held out her hand gratefully. She was not enjoying the drive. The traffic seemed to be travelling far too fast for the width of the road. People riding scooters and motor bikes flashed past them, weaving in and out of the cars and lorries, making her shudder. She saw a sign giving the number of kilometres to Aghios Nikolaos and tried to work out how many miles that would be and how much longer it would take to drive there, finally giving up the puzzle.

Marianne swore as she found herself trapped on the inside lane behind a slow moving farm vehicle and a stream of traffic on the outside of her. Without warning, she swung the wheel to the left and turned off down a narrow road.

'This used to be the main road. Imagine what it would be like if they hadn't built the new one! With luck we should be able to bypass some of this traffic. You also get a view of the sea.'

Marianne slowed as she pulled her mobile phone from the pocket of her shorts and dialled a number before tucking it into the crook of her neck. 'Five more minutes,' she said and laughed at the reply.

Bryony caught her breath. As they rounded a corner and drove down a hill the view across the sea was magnificent, a small island shimmering like a mirage in the distance. To her surprise Marianne swung off the main road and through the gates of a large house. 'Here we are,' she announced as she drew to a halt and sounded the horn.

'I thought we were staying with you, not at a hotel.' Marcus looked surprised.

'This is our house,' smiled Marianne. 'Well, strictly speaking it's Uncle Yannis's house, but we live here.'

'It's so big!'

'Uncle Yannis built it to accommodate Aunt Anna and Uncle Yiorgo. He also made sure that he had enough guest rooms for his parents when they came over for a visit. There's Giovanni. Oh, good, John's here to meet you as well. They can get you all settled in whilst I open a bottle of wine.'

Bryony and Marcus looked at their bedroom with the bathroom en suite and Marcus raised his eyebrows at his wife. 'Well?'

'It's amazing. I was expecting an ordinary house in a village. I know Grandma said Yannis had done well for himself, investing in hotels, but I never expected anything as palatial as this.'

'Do you think they'll show us the rest of it? Maybe this is just the guest part and the rest of it is ordinary.'

'I'm sure they will – and I also think the rest of it will be as grand as this. I'll just have a wash and then we ought to find our way back to the patio where Marianne said she'd be waiting.'

Marianne had set out glasses and a bottle of wine on the patio table. Small bowls of olives and nuts were beside them and John was eating a packet of crisps. As Bryony and Marcus arrived she poured out a glass for each of them.

Bryony hesitated. 'I haven't had a glass of wine since I became engaged to Marcus.'

'The choice is yours. I'll not force it on you.'

Marcus looked dubiously at his glass. 'I really would rather stick to a fruit juice. You have a glass if you want, Bryony.'

Bryony shook her head. 'I guess I'll stick to fruit juice too.'

'I'll drink it,' offered John.

'You will not,' replied Marianne swiftly. 'You will have your usual half a glass diluted with water when we have our meal.'

John pulled a face. 'Can I have some more crisps, then? I'm hungry.'

'The answer to that is also no. You're always hungry. I've arranged for us to eat earlier tonight as I'm sure Aunt Bryony and Uncle Marcus will be tired and hungry after travelling. You pop in the kitchen and bring out some clean glasses and the fruit juice from the fridge. I'll take them in to meet Aunt Anna briefly when we've had a drink. Uncle Yannis and Aunt Ourania will be home at their usual time and Aunt Bryony and Uncle Marcus can always meet them tomorrow.'

Bryony frowned. 'I can't cope with this aunt and uncle business. It makes me feel so old. Please, John, just call us Bryony and Marcus.'

'Mum says you're nearly as old as she is.'

'That's not old!'

John slid off his chair and went through to the kitchen. 'Have I got time for a swim?' he called back over his shoulder.

'No. Tonight you will show some manners and sit and make polite conversation.' Giovanni spoke to his son firmly in Italian.

John scowled; then decided not to antagonise his father. He returned with a loaded tray, poured glasses of fruit juice for Bryony and Marcus and resumed his place at the table.

'What do you plan to do whilst you're here, Bryony?' He felt quite uncomfortable just using her first name. He had been brought up to call all adult relatives aunt and uncle. 'Are you going to spend all your time on the beach or go site seeing?' He smiled at them enquiringly.

Bryony looked uncertainly at her husband. 'We haven't really made any plans. We'd like to see Knossos, of course, and Grandma said we ought to visit Aghios Nikolaos.'

'Just tell us where you'd like to go and we'll take you.'

'Have you the time? Aunt Elena said you all seem to be working such long hours.'

Marianne smiled. 'We have to during the tourist season. It will slacken off soon and then there won't be any visitors at all. That's when we do our maintenance and catch up with friends. John's still on school holidays at the moment so he can take an extra turn up at the taverna and I can have some free time. Not having to look after Uncle Yiorgo now makes a difference.'

'We wouldn't want to spoil his holidays.'

'He always takes a turn up there once or twice a week. That's how he earns his pocket money.'

'Slave labour,' muttered John and grinned cheekily at his mother.

Marianne snorted. 'Be a good slave then and fetch some more nuts. The olives could do with topping up as well.'

John rolled his eyes, but rose uncomplaining from the table and did his mother's bidding. He had been dreading the arrival of his mother's cousins, imagining they would be like his Aunt Helena and Uncle Greg, but so far he had been pleasantly surprised.

'Take no notice of him,' Marianne said to Bryony. 'He's a good lad really and he enjoys being up at the taverna. It gives him a feeling of importance when he advises the customers what to buy to take home as gifts.'

Bryony and Marcus slept well and awoke early. 'Do you think we should get up or wait until we hear someone moving about?' asked Bryony.

'Might as well get up. They could think we're tired and sleeping in. I'm ready for some coffee. I'll shave whilst you shower. I'll shower whilst you're dressing.'

'What did you think of that old aunt?' asked Bryony as she walked into their bathroom.

Marcus looked at his wife, unsure of the answer she was expecting. 'Is she as old as your grandmother?'

Bryony smiled. 'A year younger.'

'You'd think she was ten years older! Is Grandma amazing or is her longevity due to living in America?'

'I think Aunt Anna probably worked every day until she was physically incapable. Having a farm would not have given you any time off. Grandma worked with Grandpa, but that wasn't manual work. She didn't even really look after her children. Her mother did that. In some ways I think she regards Sorrell and myself as her children rather than grandchildren. She did look after us in the school holidays, but even then she had someone to do the cleaning.'

Bryony raised her voice so her husband could hear over the sound of the running water. She drew the sheet back over their bed and replaced the cover. 'Should I clean the bathroom?'

Marcus shook his head.

'You can do it later. We ought to put in an appearance. It will only be us using it anyway.'

'I don't want Marianne to think I expect her to do it.'

'I'm sure she won't, but you can always tell her you'll do it later. What do you want to do today?'

Bryony shrugged. 'I don't really know. Why don't we ask Marianne just to drive us around? I really want to see her on her own. I want to tell her about my mother and Christabelle.'

Marcus frowned. 'Do you think that's a good idea? She'll probably tell her mother and sister and they'll tell grandma.'

'I'm sure she won't if I ask her not to.'

Marianne looked at her watch. 'Aunt Ourania and Uncle Yannis should be out soon. Aunt Ourania likes to have her shop open by ten and Uncle Yannis takes her into Aghios Nikolaos each day. She stays open until twelve and they come back for lunch and a siesta before opening up again from three until ten. That means we usually eat about ten thirty, but you must let me know if that's too late for you. After they have left we could drive along to Plaka and I'll show you our bungalows and taverna. Tomorrow I'll take you into Aghios Nikolaos. I can show you where Grandma lived before she went to Athens and also Aunt Ourania's shop. You can have a wander round on your own and I'll come back later to collect you. It's a pretty town. Then we can start to go a bit further afield. I'll give you a map and some leaflets and you just tell me where you want to go. I can take you anywhere provided it's not too far away.'

'Well, what do you think of our little complex?' Marianne slowed the car down to a crawl.

'It's anything but little! I'd like to see inside a bungalow.'

'At the weekend,' promised Marianne, as she waved to a family loading their beach equipment into their car. 'We'll have at least half a dozen free for a few hours.'

'What happens about cleaning them?' asked Bryony.

'When we first started I used to do them, but now we employ six women from Aghios Nikolaos. I had it down to a fine art. One hour per bungalow and they were ready for the next visitors. Just occasionally someone would leave one particularly messy and it would take me longer. I still help out if a woman is off.'

'When do you get a holiday?'

Marianne laughed. 'The winter is our holiday. We did manage to go to Rhodes for a week right at the end of the season the third year we were open. It seemed very strange to be a tourist again. Most years we go over to Italy and visited Giovanni's parents. Aunt Ourania likes to come with us and once Uncle Yannis made the journey.' Marianne drew to a halt before the taverna.

'This is where the family grew up. Most of the houses had fallen down and the owners were only too pleased to sell the land to us. We turned the farmhouse into a taverna and convenience store. Get out and then you can see properly.'

'Whose idea was it to have self-catering apartments?' asked Marcus.

'Giovanni's. There were some financial problems after he was shot and Uncle Yannis sold the hotels. That included the night club premises, so Giovanni had no work. There was a considerable amount of land around the farm and Aunt Anna and Uncle Yiorgo said Uncle Yannis could use it in return for looking after them. The bank agreed to lend Uncle Yannis some money and we started in a very small way. Each year we managed to add a few more bungalows and now we have a tennis court, crazy golf and water sports facilities.'

'Do you plan to continue to expand?'

Marianne shrugged. 'We'll wait and see what the figures tell us at the end of the season. The more we expand the more staff we have to employ and the more maintenance we have to do. That eats into the profits. I'd like to have extra paving in the area around the taverna so we could have more eating spaces outside, but that also means buying more tables, chairs and umbrellas. We've considered having it open as a taverna in the evening. I can cope with the cooking at the moment even if John or Giovanni are not in the shop, but I don't want to spend my evenings up here. We can't afford to employ a chef unless we have enough business to cover his wages and a bit over. Giovanni is keen to make a children's play area amongst the carob trees. We're not allowed to cut them down and we can't think of a more practical use for the area'

John was outside the taverna; sitting in the shade and studying the instructions for his camera.

'How's trade?' she asked.

John pulled a face. 'I've had a couple of people in. One lot bought some postcards and the other bought some stuff for a picnic. Dad said he was busy earlier. A couple wanted a full English breakfast!'

Marianne nodded. She accepted that once people had left the complex for the day there was little point in having the taverna and store open.

'Do you want to come back with us when Bryony and Marcus have looked around?'

'I might as well. I'll just take a few photos. Give me a shout when you're ready.'

Bryony and Marcus followed Marianne into the taverna. A large kitchen ran the entire length of a wall with a counter for serving food before it. The opposite wall was shelved and held an array of everyday commodities for visitors to purchase.

'There's not really anything of interest to see here. Would you like a drink? I can make some coffee or there's fruit juice.'

'Could I just have some water?' asked Bryony. 'I've only walked from the car to here and I'm already hot and thirsty.'

Marianne looked at her overweight cousin. If she lost a few pounds she would certainly find life easier. 'Same for you, Marcus?'

Marcus nodded. 'What's that photograph?' He pointed to the large framed photograph that adorned the far wall.

Marianne flushed. 'I think it is due to her that I have John and live over here. When Elizabeth and I were on holiday here I left her camera out on Spinalonga. I felt terrible about it and went over early the next morning to see if I could find it. I had planned to ask the first tourist boat to bring me back, but no one arrived. I didn't know there was a storm blowing up and they had been forbidden to go out to sea with tourists. Elizabeth called Giovanni and he came out to see if he could find me. I had taken some more photos and he had them developed for me. That one was amongst them. When I showed it to Manolis and Flora they said it was Anna.'

'What was she doing over there if there was a storm brewing?' asked Marcus.

'Not Aunt Anna. The girl that old Uncle Yannis and his wife had adopted. Anna died during the war. It must have been her ghost appearing to me.' Marianne felt the usual lump coming into her throat as she talked about the young girl who had died from blood poisoning.

Bryony crossed herself. 'I read about her in Uncle Yannis's book, but I don't see how she affects John.'

'I felt she was trying to tell me something, but I had no idea what. Giovanni and I,' Marianne reddened more, 'well, we were a bit foolish before he took me back over to the mainland. That night I had the phone call to say Dad was in hospital and I went rushing back to the States. I didn't realise I was pregnant until some weeks later. After I married Giovanni, I decided that was what she had been trying to tell me. Come back and marry him.' Marianne's eyes filled with tears and she brushed them away impatiently.

'Is that why the taverna is called '*ANNA'S*'?' asked Bryony, who had been listening avidly.

'Partly; and also after Aunt Anna. This was her home for

most of her life. It was the family farmhouse. Uncle Yannis lived here when he was a boy and Giovanni and his family used to come and stay,' replied Marianne, once again in control of her emotions.

'I guess it didn't look anything like this.'

'Not a bit. Ask Aunt Anna how it looked and what it was like living here. There was no electricity and all the water had to be drawn from the well over there. For years the toilet was a field at the back where the chickens ran.'

'What!' Bryony gasped in horror at the idea.

'It was the same for everyone. It was only after Uncle Yannis went into the hotel business that he converted a store room into a toilet.'

'We don't realise how spoilt we are in the States. I wish I had seen Greece fifty years ago.'

'I'll take you to some traditional villages. They have electricity, running water and a sewerage system now, but the buildings look much the same.'

'What about Spinalonga?' Marcus looked across the bay.

'Even Spinalonga looks very different now from the way it used to. There has been so much restoration, and there is an education centre in some of the old buildings. The main road looks like any other village now, but you can still wander around in the areas that haven't been touched and get a feel for the place. It's definitely worth a visit.'

'I'd love to go over. Do we have to book a trip?' asked Bryony.

Marianne smiled. 'I'll ask Giovanni and John to take you over early one morning, before the tourists start arriving. John loves going over. He's continually taking photographs of the houses. I think he hopes Anna will appear in one of them. He knows where everyone lived and likes to show off his knowledge to the tourists. He's proud to have had a relative who lived there.'

Bryony twisted her bottle of water between her fingers and looked towards her husband. 'There's something I want to tell you, Marianne.'

'I'll have a wander and see what John has found to photograph,' said Marcus rising from the table. 'I was quite interested in photography when I was a teenager.'

Bryony looked at her cousin earnestly. 'First you have to swear not to tell anyone else.'

Marianne frowned. 'I can't swear not to tell Giovanni.'

Bryony shook her head impatiently. 'You can tell him, but no one else, particularly your mother or sister.'

Marianne raised her eyebrows. 'I swear,' she promised.

Bryony dropped her voice to a whisper. 'I've never told Grandma that my mother is dead.'

'What!' Marianne was shocked. 'How? And when? You didn't write and tell me.'

Bryony shook her head. 'No one knows except Marcus and me. It's a strange story. You remember when we were all at Thanksgiving and there was that row between Uncle Andreas and mother?'

Marianne shook her head. 'We arrived just as your mother and Jeremy were leaving. All I ever knew was that Jeremy had left her and taken Saffron with him. I heard later that your mother had gone to Florida with a film star.'

'I don't know the details,' Bryony spoke miserably. 'Sorrell and I were sent back to boarding school and were told that mum would send for us when she had made a nice home for herself with this person called Rudi. Sorrell told me she was expecting his baby, but I didn't know if she was just being spiteful. Mum never did contact us and when I asked Grandma she always changed the subject.'

Bryony took another mouthful of her water. 'About eight years ago I had a telephone call. It was from a girl called Christabelle and she told me that her mother was dead. She'd found my phone number in an address book, but had no idea who I was. We met up and she's my half sister.'

'She didn't know about you?' Marianne found it hard to believe.

177

'My mother had never spoken to her about her family. As far as Christabelle was concerned she was an only child and had no relatives.'

'So why didn't you tell Grandma?'

Bryony's voice dropped even lower. 'Mother was murdered.'

Marianne was speechless.

'I know it must be rather a shock. That kind of thing happens in other families, not ours.'

Marianne snorted. 'Not always.'

Bryony continued as if she had not heard. 'Anyway, I talked it over with Marcus and he said we ought to meet her again and get to know her better before we told Grandma. She seemed lovely and very concerned about the effect the news could have on her grandmother. We decided not to tell Grandma unless it became absolutely necessary, after all, she was in her eighties, and we felt the shock could kill her.'

Marianne refilled her glass. 'So what happened? Has the murderer been caught?'

Bryony nodded. 'Apparently he was mother's latest boyfriend. Christabelle returned home just as he was leaving and found her on the floor. It seems they must have had a row and he hit her. She fell over and cracked her skull.'

'How awful for her. Have you kept in touch with Christabelle?'

'Only vaguely. She's a model. You've probably seen photos of her. She sends me an occasional postcard. She went to New York, then after the trial she went to England.'

'How sad. You'd think she would want to know she had family who cared for her.'

'I think she's too busy. She seems to be in every magazine that you open.'

'Hold on.' Marianne rose and went in to the kitchen area. She leafed through some magazines and returned with one folded open at a page advertising an evening dress. She held it out to Bryony. 'Is that her?'

Bryony nodded. 'She's known as '*Miss Christabelle*', never uses a surname.'

Marianne looked at the photograph carefully. 'She's beautiful. I'm only interested in the recipes they have inside so I don't usually take much notice of the adverts. You won't mind if I tell Giovanni? I won't say a word to anyone else of course, and I'll certainly not tell John. I don't actually buy magazines.' Marianne felt strangely guilty in admitting the fact. 'I usually ask friends to pass them on to me.'

'I feel ridiculously over dressed,' Marcus complained as sat on the side of the bed to remove his shoes and socks. 'I should have brought some shorts with me. I didn't realise it would still be this warm over here.'

'We're going into Aghios Nikolaos tomorrow so you could always buy some shorts and sandals. I'm going to buy a bathing costume.'

Marcus looked at his wife. He had never known her express any desire to go to a beach. 'Can you swim?'

'Of course I can. I learnt whilst I was at college. Besides, even if I couldn't, I would still want to lie on a beach and be able to go in the sea when I got too hot.'

'Maybe I'd better buy some swimwear.' Marcus folded his socks neatly and placed them inside his shoes.

'I'm sure Giovanni would have something that would fit you.'

'I wouldn't want to ask him.' Marcus hung his shirt over the back of the chair. 'I'd feel rather like the poor relation. We're already accepting their hospitality and they can't seem to do enough for us. I don't know how we're ever going to be able to repay them.'

'Maybe they could come to the States and stay with us?'

'They'd be welcome.' Marcus folded his trousers neatly into their creases and hung them up in the wardrobe.

Bryony yawned widely. 'Sorry,' she apologised. 'It must be this sea air.'

'Are you really tired?'

'Why do you ask?'

'The sea air seems to be revitalising me.' He slipped into bed beside her and took her into his arms.

'So what did you think of our island?' asked Marianne.

'It was amazing. I know I've read old Uncle Yannis's book, but I hadn't realised just how small it was. To have so many people living over there! It must have been larger than many of the villages on the mainland.'

'It was, and more advanced than many of them. They had electricity over there before Plaka. Aunt Anna can tell you how she went over there to see it. She thought it was a miracle to press a switch and have light. She and some of the other villagers used to go over there regularly after the war. It wasn't just to visit her brother. They staged plays, had puppet shows and even showed films once they had the electric generator. You know Giovanni's mother was married over there, don't you?'

Bryony nodded. 'John told us. To hear his description you would think he had participated! You're right when you say he knows all about the island. He showed us where old Uncle Yannis lived and pointed out the site where he built his first house. It's such a shame you can't see the ships that Anna carved on the shutters any more. Then he told us the romantic story of Flora and Manolis. He even made us climb right up to the top of the island, to that grassy plateau where you get a wonderful view of the mainland.'

'It was when Giovanni and I were sitting up there that he had the idea to make this holiday complex.'

'I'm surprised you didn't make it over there.'

Marianne laughed. 'We may think of the island as being 'ours', but it belongs to the government. Besides, it would be impractical. We would have to pull down all the old buildings and arrange for electricity, water and sewerage. Imagine if we had a storm and couldn't get people back to the mainland in time to catch their flight home?'

'I don't think I'd mind being stranded there for an extra week.'

'I think you would when the food began to run low and there was nothing to do.'

'You're probably right.' Bryony recalled how the islanders had been refused supplies and many had starved during the war time occupation of Crete. She gave a little shiver. 'We only see the romantic side, not the reality of living there.'

Bryony lay on the bed, no longer asleep but not quite awake. She could hear people moving around and the murmur of voices. A finger of fear clutched at her heart. Something had happened. She slid off the bed, trying hard not to disturb Marcus and pulled on her light wrap. Cautiously she opened the bedroom door and peered out into the passage.

She could see the door to Anna's room was open and there was a strange man standing in the doorway beside Ourania. Someone inside spoke and they both entered. Bryony assumed the elderly aunt had been taken ill and the doctor had been summoned. Swiftly she returned to the bedroom and shook Marcus's shoulder gently.

'Marcus, I think we ought to get up.'

Marcus grunted and Bryony spoke to him again.

'Marcus, wake up.'

'What time is it?'

'I don't know, but there's something wrong. We ought to get up and get dressed.'

Marcus opened his eyes and looked at the bedside clock. 'It's five thirty! What do you want to get up at this time for?'

'Something's happened, Marcus. I think Aunt Anna has been taken ill. We ought to be up and dressed in case we're needed.'

'I can't see that we'd be any help,' Marcus remarked as he placed his legs over the side of the bed and yawned.

'I could at least make coffee. I'll go and find out if we're needed or if they'd rather we stayed out of the way.'

Marcus nodded and lay back on the bed. He was not at his best in the early morning.

Bryony found Marianne and Giovanni in the kitchen. Marianne was dabbing at her eyes and Giovanni's looked suspiciously moist.

'What's wrong?' asked Bryony.

'Aunt Anna is dead.' Marianne gulped as she said the words and her eyes filled with tears again.

Bryony sat down abruptly in a chair. 'Dead? She seemed fine when I saw her last night. She was telling me about her brother Yiorgo and the fuss he made when the government wanted his land for the road.'

'She didn't wake up. When I settled her for the night she said she was tired and she seemed a bit breathless. I told Aunt Ourania and we both checked on her before we went to bed. She seemed to be sleeping peacefully and normally. I woke up just after three and thought I'd look in on her. I'm so glad I did. Her breathing was so shallow I could hardly feel a pulse. I called Aunt Ourania and we stayed with her until the doctor arrived.'

'Couldn't he do anything for her?'

Marianne shook her head. 'She wasn't ill, just worn out.'

'What happens now?'

'She will be taken to the morgue whilst we make the funeral arrangements. Uncle Yannis is talking to his mother and she and Victor will come over for the funeral. You won't be expected to come. You're on holiday, remember.'

Bryony looked at her cousin indignantly. 'Of course we'll come. She was as much my relative as yours. What would Grandma say – oh! Would you like me to telephone her with the news?'

'Would you? You know her far better than any of us. If you could call her first, then I'll telephone Mamma and Helena. I must 'phone Elizabeth and Nicolas also.'

'I'm so pleased we managed to meet her. There was so much I still wanted to talk to her about.'

'You were wonderful with her. She enjoyed the times you sat with her, and it certainly gave us a break. She had become so repetitious.'

'She kept mentioning someone called Michael. She spoke as if I should know him. At first I thought she meant Marcus, but when I corrected her she shook her head and said his name was Michael.'

'He was a resistance worker she met during the war. He visited with his family and planned to return to be with her. He was involved in a traffic accident and poor Aunt Anna waited and waited. It was years later that his daughter tracked her down and told her what had happened. Uncle Yannis and Giovanni know more about it than I do. I'm sure they'd tell you the details if you asked either of them.'

Bryony shook her head. 'It really is nothing to do with me. I was just curious because of the name. You'll have to tell me the procedure for the funeral service. I don't want to be an embarrassment to everyone. Will we wear black?'

Marianne nodded. 'I'll take you and Marcus into Aghios Nikolaos if you need to buy anything. If you've got a black skirt you'll only need a blouse. I can find you a scarf for your head. Marcus could borrow a shirt from Giovanni and wear a pair of grey slacks. Only Uncle Yannis and Giovanni need to wear a black suit and I still have the outfit I wore for Uncle Yiorgo. Somehow once you have worn it to a funeral you don't feel like wearing it on other occasions.'

Yannis drew Giovanni to one side. 'How is your father? Are you going back to Italy to be with him for a while? I'm sure your mother would appreciate having you there.'

'I'd like to. I haven't spoken to Marianne. I'll need to see how she feels about managing the end of the season alone.'

'Marianne will be able to cope. Provided you don't take any last minute bookings it shouldn't be too difficult for her. There's only two weeks left.'

Giovanni felt a surge of relief. He desperately wanted to be with his parents. It was obvious that his father would not be with them for very much longer.

Bryony walked with Ourania and Marianne along the road from the taverna to the church. She had been surprised that the funeral procession had started from there rather than the house.

'Uncle Yannis decided it would be more practical to go from here when we had Uncle Yiorgo's funeral. We don't usually arrive in cars at the church like you do at home and just go inside. It's traditional to follow the coffin to the church whilst the priest walks ahead.'

As they walked slowly along the road and up the hill to the small church more people seemed to be parking cars close to the taverna and joining them. Bryony looked behind, amazed at the number of people who were following them.

'Why are there so many people?' she whispered to Marianne.

'Aunt Anna was loved by everyone. People have long memories over here. She was well known for her knowledge of herbal remedies. People would ask her help to cure their ailments rather than visit a doctor. She was also the local midwife. Many of the people who lived in the villages locally would have been helped into the world by her. She delivered both Uncle Yannis and Giovanni's mother.'

The priest stopped at the doorway, crossed himself and swung the incense burner he was carrying. Still chanting he led the way inside.

'Just do as I do,' whispered Marianne and followed Ourania and Marisa to where the coffin lay.

Bryony searched for her husband's hand. She stood with her head bowed until the end of the short service. Bryony watched as each member of the family walked up to the casket where Anna lay and bowed solemnly before lifting the cross that lay on her chest and kissing it. They walked round the casket and back down the nave with their eyes on the ground. Bryony copied Marianne and she found she had a lump in her throat as she kissed the cross and said a final farewell to the old lady she had known such a short time.

Outside the men and women waited whilst Anna's coffin was sealed and she began her final journey. The priest led the way to the grave that had been prepared for her and began to chant the Trisagion. One by one the mourners placed a flower onto her coffin and said their own private prayers before moving to one side.

The people from the neighbouring villages who had joined them waited outside the churchyard whilst the family stayed to thank the priest. Yannis and Marisa walked over to where their mother was buried and tapped gently on her headstone before placing flowers at the foot. Victor seemed unable to move from Anna's grave and Marianne took pity on him.

'Time to go, Victor.'

Victor turned anguished eyes on his daughter in law. 'Always I love Aunt Anna.'

Marianne squeezed his arm, distressed by how thin it had become. 'She was very special. Everyone loved Aunt Anna.'

'Would you like us to come up to the taverna and help you this morning?' asked Bryony. 'I could at least see to the shop for you if you have to cook.'

'Would you? It would be such a help. We probably won't have any customers at all; but having said that some problem is bound to arise. Uncle Yannis is taking Aunt Ourania in to the shop and then going on to the airport to say goodbye. He'll take John back to the shop as Giovanni is flying back with his parents. He'll drive the minivan that we use to transport the visitors sometimes, so I shall have the car.'

'We'll enjoy it, won't we, Marcus.'

Marcus smiled at his wife benignly. 'I might be able to agree if I knew what you said. You two were speaking in Greek.'

'Oh, I'm sorry. I tend to forget that you can't understand. I offered our help up at the taverna this morning as Marianne will be on her own.'

'No problem. Just give me a shout when you want to leave.'

'We ought to go now.'

Marcus rose. 'I'm ready.' He slipped the book he had been reading into his back pocket. This could be a boring few hours.

'I'll just go and check with the maids to make sure all is in order,' said Marianne. 'If anyone comes in the prices are marked and there's change in the till. I'll only be about half an hour.'

Marianne unlocked the small door at the side of the taverna. 'Here are the keys to the patio windows. If you open them up customers will know that we're open for business.'

Bryony nodded. She was not sure if she really wanted to have customers and be responsible for charging them correctly and giving the right change. She settled herself behind the counter, then stood up again.

'I'll make some coffee. I can't just sit there doing nothing.'

'Why don't we sit outside until anyone comes,' suggested Marcus. 'I'm sure Marianne doesn't sit inside waiting for customers to appear.'

Bryony giggled. 'That will be really Greek. All the shop keepers tend to sit outside chatting to each other and only go into the shop if they have a customer.'

'There you are then. Shall I put up the umbrellas? I've brought my book and I'm sure Marianne won't mind if you borrow one from the shop.'

'I'll be happy to just sit. Somehow there seems to be more time over here. Marianne and Giovanni are obviously working hard but they always seem to have plenty of time. I wish I knew their secret.'

'I think it's called being Greek.' Marcus smiled at her. Bryony always seemed to have plenty of time when they were at home to sit and do nothing.

'Do you think John will be happy running all this eventually?'

'Who knows? They might decide to sell up when their aunt and uncle are no longer around.'

Bryony crossed herself. 'Don't say that, Marcus. We only buried Aunt Anna two days ago.' Thoroughly upset by her husband's thoughtless remark she marched into the kitchen area.

Marianne was gone a little longer than she had intended. A family had asked her how long it would take for them to drive to Rethymnon and another had wanted to ask what times the banks were open. Having given them the information they needed they seemed reluctant to let her go and finally asked her about Anna's funeral. She had hoped there would be no one around at the time they had chosen, but it seemed that the word had spread.

'She was my husband's great aunt,' she explained. 'She was nearly ninety so it wasn't unexpected.'

'There were so many people and they seemed so sad we were worried it was someone young.'

'Aunt Anna had lived here all her life and was well known and liked. She will be missed.'

The woman nodded. She had promised the family staying next to them that she would find out and she had been successful. She would certainly have something to tell her neighbours when she returned home.

Marianne excused herself and returned to the taverna where Bryony and Marcus were sitting. 'Any customers?' she asked.

'No one. We helped ourselves to coffee. Would you like one?'

'I'll have some water. I'm afraid today will be a bit dull for you. John will take a turn up here this afternoon; then I'll have to come back up for the early evening and lock up. It doesn't give me time to take you anywhere.'

Bryony shook her head. 'Don't worry about us. You've already taken us to so many places that we would never have found on our own. The only place I want to go again is Spinalonga and we can do that later in the week. We'll be quite happy to spend this afternoon on the beach, won't we, Marcus?'

'That's fine by me unless we can do anything to help.'

Marianne shook her head. 'The cleaning has been done and I think all the visitors have gone off for the day. I might as well lock up and we can go back to the house. I need to talk to Aunt Ourania about sorting out Aunt Anna's belongings. I expect most of it will go in the rubbish, but I wouldn't want to throw away anything Marisa or Uncle Yannis wanted.'

Bryony picked up their dirty cups and took them into the taverna to rinse. Marcus closed the patio doors and locked them whilst Marianne began to put down the umbrellas.

'Are you closed?' a woman called and Marianne turned to look at her. As she did so she let out a shrill scream of pain and both Marcus and Bryony rushed to her side.

'Put the umbrella up,' she gasped. 'My hand is trapped.'

Marcus pushed and Marianne screamed again as she lowered her hand, the tears rolling down her face.

'Let me look at that.'

'It's nothing. I'm just making a fuss. It's only pinched.' Marianne's face was drained of colour and Bryony pushed her into a chair.

'Let Marcus have a look.' Bryony felt quite faint as she looked at the torn flesh.

'You've done more than pinched it! Can you move your fingers?'

Marianne tried and grimaced again in pain, the tears coming to her eyes. She could feel herself getting hot and clammy. She blinked rapidly, trying to dispel the darkness before her eyes. She felt Marcus push her head downwards and did not resist.

Bryony soaked a couple of paper napkins with the water from Marianne's bottle and placed one on her neck and held the other to her forehead. 'Take some deep breaths. Keep your head down until you feel better.'

Marianne obeyed. Thoughts were running tumultuously through her head. How were they going to get back to the house? She would not be able to drive; her hand was far too painful. Who would open up the taverna and see to whatever was necessary? What would have happened if she had been alone up there?

The woman who had wanted a last minute purchase had disappeared.

Marianne sat up and took a mouthful of the water that was left in her bottle. 'I'll be all right now, thanks.'

Marcus sat down beside her. 'That hand needs a doctor's attention. There's a nasty gash that could need a stitch and your thumb could be broken, maybe a couple of other small bones are crushed. Where's the nearest hospital?'

'Aghios Nikolaos.'

Marcus nodded. 'When you feel ready get into the car – the passenger side. I'll drive, but I'll need you to give me directions.'

Bryony looked at her husband in consternation. He had expressed concern at some of the erratic motoring he had seen on Crete. 'Are you sure, Marcus? Couldn't we telephone for an ambulance?'

'It will be quicker if I drive. There'll be no problem if I take it steadily. Can you find something to make a sling?'

Bryony returned to the taverna and reappeared moments later carrying two clean tea towels and bottles of water. Deftly she wrapped Marianne's hand and made an improvised sling. 'Keep it up as high as you can. It will help it to stop bleeding.'

Marianne nodded. She felt totally light headed and accepted Marcus's arm as she made her way to the car.

'Promise me you'll not tell Giovanni when he telephones this evening,' begged Marianne. 'It really is nothing and I don't want him rushing back. His mother needs him in Italy at the moment.'

Yannis pursed his lips. 'He ought to be told. He doesn't have to come home.'

Marianne shook her head vehemently. 'Even if he didn't come home he would be worried. He'd want to know how I was going to manage the taverna and everything without him being here.'

'And how are you?'

'Bryony and Marcus are going to help. Marcus will drive me up each day and I'll sit in the taverna whilst Bryony checks on the maids and the bungalows. Customers will just have to make allowances for the fact that I have only one hand to serve them with at present.'

'What about cooking? You can't cook with one hand!'

'I'm sure I could, but Bryony says that Marcus likes cooking and so does she. We'll manage, Uncle Yannis. Just don't tell Giovanni. By the time he returns I shall probably be out of plaster and everything will be back to normal.'

When the doctor had given Victor the results of his latest tests Marisa had sat immobile, the tears rolling down her face. She had no recollection of Giovanni steering her out to the car and settling her in the back with her husband whilst he drove to their apartment.

Now Giovanni felt angry. Why should his father have to suffer? Why couldn't he have had a heart attack like old Uncle Yannis or gone to sleep like Aunt Anna? Quick and clean; it would have been a horrible shock for his mother, but she would not be forced to see her husband disintegrate daily before her eyes.

He poured himself a stiff whisky and gave a weaker one to his father. 'That may not do you any good, but I think you need it.'

'I'll have one also.' Marisa, her face drained of colour, turned large, sad eyes on her son.

Giovanni had never known his mother to drink anything stronger than wine, but complied with her request.

'Why didn't you tell us how ill you were? We would never have expected you to come over for Aunt Anna's funeral.'

Victor smiled. 'Of course we had to come to say goodbye to Aunt Anna. Your mother would never have forgiven me.'

'I'll have to telephone Marianne and let her know that I'm staying indefinitely.'

'Don't be foolish, Giovanni. The doctor said I could hang around for a good few months yet. You can't stay here all that time. Marianne needs you to help with the business.'

Giovanni shook his head. 'We close in a couple of weeks. Marianne will be able to cope.'

'Can you really stay?' Marisa looked at her son hopefully. 'I know Angelo will come down, but he won't be able to stay more than a few days.'

Giovanni nodded. He had no need to tell them that his stay would be of no more than a few weeks duration according to the doctor's prognosis.

'What's going to happen, Giovanni,' Marisa swallowed hard, 'when your Pappa's dead?'

Giovanni looked at his mother sadly. 'How do you mean?'

'I don't want to go and live with Angelo. I don't know anyone in that area.'

'What you mean is that you don't like Francesca.' Giovanni was also not enamoured of his brother's partner, whom he found over-bearing and demanding.

'That's beside the point.'

'What would you like to do, Mamma?'

A tear crept from the corner of Marisa's eye. 'I'd like to go home.'

'Home? You mean back to Crete?'

Marisa nodded. 'I don't want to stay here without your Pappa. His relatives have always been very kind to me, but they're not family.'

Giovanni took his mother's hand. 'If that's what you really want then it's no problem. There's plenty of room at Uncle Yannis's house.'

'What about Ourania? Would she mind me being there?'

'Why should she? You're her sister in law and you've always got on well together.'

'Maybe you should ask them before I make any decisions. I wouldn't want to come if I wasn't wanted.'

'Don't be silly, Mamma. You're family. You'll be welcomed.'

'Maybe you could ask them when you go back.'

'I'm not going back just yet. I'll telephone tonight and speak to Uncle Yannis. You're sure that's what you will want to do?'

Marisa nodded. 'I'm quite sure. I can't stay here without Victor.'

Marianne replaced the receiver and wiped her eyes with the back of her hand. 'That was Giovanni. They have given Victor no more than a month to live.' Her tears flowed more freely. 'He's planning to stay over there. His mother will need him. She and Victor were so close. They did everything together.'

'Oh, Marianne, I'm so sorry. Tell Giovanni when he next 'phones,' Bryony hesitated, 'well, tell him whatever one should say to convey sympathy.'

Marianne nodded. 'I will. However I put it Giovanni will understand what you're trying to say.' She frowned and looked at her hand. 'How long do you think it will be before I can use my hand again properly?'

'The doctor said at least two weeks in plaster and to start using it carefully after that. It will probably be about a month before you have the full use back in it.'

Marianne shook her head. 'It will have to be better before then. I have to get Aunt Anna's room redecorated.'

'There's no rush, surely. You've not turned out her possessions yet.' Marcus was surprised at her urgency.

'Giovanni told me that after his father dies his mother wants to come back here and live. We shall obviously go over for Victor's funeral. We haven't got round to redecorating Uncle Yiorgo's room yet; we'd planned to do it last winter but there didn't seem to be any rush. It would be most practical for Marisa to have Aunt Anna's room. It might even be comforting to her, but it will need a fresh coat of paint. I can't ask Uncle Yannis to start climbing ladders. Maybe John could do it.' Marianne rubbed her left hand across her forehead. 'Why did I have to be so stupid! If I hadn't looked over at that woman who asked if we were closed I wouldn't have crushed my hand. I know how quickly those umbrellas can come down unless you're careful.'

'Why don't I paint the room for you?' offered Marcus.

'But you're on holiday,' remonstrated Marianne. 'I can't expect you to do painting and decorating.'

'I quite enjoy it. I did our house. I didn't make too much of a mess, did I, Bryony?'

Bryony shook her head. 'You did a very good job. If we moved everything from Aunt Anna's room into Uncle Yiorgo's it should only take a couple of days. You and Aunt Ourania can go through everything later. At least the room will be ready for whenever Marisa arrives.'

Marianne considered the offer. 'Everything seems to have happened at once. Aunt Anna dying, now Giovanni's father being so ill, then my stupid hand. Your holiday has been well and truly spoilt.'

'It hasn't been spoilt at all,' Bryony assured her. 'I wish Aunt Anna hadn't died, and I'm so glad that we were able to meet her before it happened. If we'd been in America we would have written, but she would have been just a name to us. You've been terribly good about taking us out and around. We've been everywhere we wanted to go. Now we have a chance to repay you in a small way.'

Marianne smiled shakily at her cousin. She felt that she was very near to bursting into tears. Her hand was throbbing and she wondered if she was able to take some more of the pain killers the doctor had prescribed.

'This evening Marcus and I will move everything from Aunt Anna's room. Tomorrow I'll drive you up to the taverna, provided you feel well enough; and I'll stay up there with you. Marcus can stay here and start painting.'

Marianne shook her head. 'You can't do that. You've admitted that you are frightened of the traffic over here.'

'I'm only going to drive you up the road to the taverna. There's hardly any traffic, usually just the visitors leaving for the day. It's settled. Nothing more for you to worry about. Now, tell me what you'd planned for our meal this evening and I'll go and start preparing it.' Bryony smiled and rose from her chair. She would quite enjoying organising their next few days and feeling that she was in charge. Her only regret was that she would not be able to return to Ourania's shop as she had planned. She had found the goods for sale were fascinating

Marianne sat in the taverna. Despite the pain killers her hand still throbbed. Bryony had settled her with a cup of coffee before insisting that she would visit each bungalow and speak to the maids.

'Good job I still speak Greek. I'll be able to explain to them that you've injured your hand and tell them that you'll be at the taverna if there are any problems. Do you have any special instructions for them?'

Marianne shook her head. 'They all know their duties and they're pretty reliable. Most of them have been with us for a good few seasons now.'

'I have my mobile with me and there's the number.' Bryony anchored a piece of paper beneath Marianne's saucer. 'If anyone comes in wanting food give me a ring and I'll come back.'

Marianne nodded. 'You are good, Bryony. I'm sure Helena and Greg would not have helped out the way you and Marcus are.'

Bryony dismissed the compliment with a wave of her hand. 'I expect I shall be gone about half an hour or so. Do you want a magazine to look at?'

'I can't seem to concentrate properly at the moment. It's probably the pain killers.'

Bryony walked from bungalow to bungalow, explaining the situation to each maid and having a quick look inside each bungalow to ensure that the cleaning was up to standard. She was thankful that she could find no fault with the work and would be able to report back favourably to Marianne.

The shrill, raised voices of two women arguing in Greek attracted her and as she turned the corner she could understand their conversation.

'It's not necessary to make so much mess. I cleaned it up last week. I'm not doing it again.'

'You have to. It's our job to make sure everything is clean.'

'You do it then. I'm not.'

'Mrs Giovanni will sack you.'

'I don't care. There's only a couple more weeks of the season. I shall be out of a job then anyway.' The woman stood with her hands on her hips defiantly.

'I'm not doing it. It's not my bungalow to clean.'

'What's the problem?' Bryony moved forwards.

Both women turned and looked at her in surprise, taking her for one of the visitors to the complex.

'Is this your bungalow?' demanded the maid.

Bryony shook her head. 'I'm Mrs Giovanni's cousin. She's hurt her hand and I'm just helping her out for a couple of days. She asked me to check that all was in order and tell you that she's at the taverna if you need her.'

The maid stood undecided whether to go to complain to Marianne or show Bryony.

'What's she done to her hand?'

'She crushed it when she was putting down one of the

umbrellas. She's in considerable pain. If I can help I'd rather you didn't trouble her.'

'Come and see this, then.'

The maid threw open the door to the bungalow and pointed to the shower. 'She's dyed her hair again. It's everywhere. All down the curtain, in the tray, up the wall and on the floor, all over the towels. She did the same last week.'

Bryony looked at the brown streaks that were staining everywhere. 'Well I guess it won't take too long to clean up if we work together.'

'You'll do it?'

'Why not? Mrs Giovanni says she helps out if there is a maid off sick. There's no reason why I can't take a turn.' Bryony smiled. 'Have you got a spare shower curtain?'

The maid nodded. 'In the linen store.'

'You go and fetch that and some more clean towels. I'll take the old curtain down and make a start on the shower tray.'

It took Bryony longer than she had anticipated to scrub the stains from the tiles and shower tray. She was surprised at the length of time the maid was away collecting a clean curtain and towels and had an idea the maid was taking her time in the hope that Bryony would have finished the cleaning when she returned. Finally she rose from her knees and examined the shower critically. It was spotless. Now she would have to start on the floor.

'You were gone ages,' remarked Marianne when she finally returned to the taverna, hot and perspiring. 'What have you been doing?'

'I helped out one of the maids.' Bryony opened a bottle of water and drank thirstily.

Marianne's eyes widened in surprise. 'Why? Is one not well.'

'She's fine, but you nearly had a strike on your hands. One of the guests has dyed her hair for the second week in a row and left a filthy mess. I wasn't surprised the maid was annoyed about it. I sent her off for a clean shower curtain and towels whilst I did a bit of scrubbing. It's all sorted now.' Bryony smiled complacently.

'You really shouldn't have done that. You should have sent the maid up to me. I would have ordered her to do it or given her the sack.'

'She knew that and said she didn't care as it was nearly the end of the season. You can't afford to be short staffed at the moment, so it seemed the easiest way of dealing with the situation.'

Marianne felt tears welling up in her eyes and she brushed them away impatiently.

Marcus stood back and examined the wall he had painted critically. The job would take him longer than he had estimated as the room was larger than he had realised. He hoped Marianne would be satisfied and not regret not asking a professional decorator to come in. The door opened and John entered, his camera slung around his neck. He grinned cheekily.

'Can I take your photo?' he asked.

'Whatever for?'

'Just to prove to Pappa that you did the job,' he answered innocently. 'Just stand there by the tin of paint with the brush in your hand.'

Marcus did as he was asked. 'Where've you been? Up to the taverna?'

John shook his head. 'I went into Elounda. I needed to get some more film.'

'Quite a walk.'

John shook his head. 'I took the bike.'

'You rode up the hill?'

'The motor bike,' John corrected him.

'You're not old enough to drive!' Marcus was horrified.

'I've been riding that ever since I was tall enough. I only usually go up to the taverna if Mum or Dad can't take me. I was hoping the photographer would be there. I wanted to talk to him about digital photography. Do you know if it's suitable for close up photos of nature? I'd need a zoom lens and a timer.'

Marcus shook his head. 'I've no idea. Mine is pretty basic. You wouldn't be making a cup of tea, would you?'

John nodded. 'I could. Then I'll ride up to the taverna and relieve Mum and Bryony.'

Bryony hugged Marianne. 'We've had a wonderful time. Thank you so much for everything.'

'It's me who should be thanking you. I couldn't possibly have managed without your help.'

Bryony shrugged. 'It was nothing. I enjoyed being up at the taverna just as much as all the other things we did – and you could see Marcus enjoyed his painting.'

Bryony gave a little giggle. She had been most amused at the photograph John had produced of Marcus spattered with white paint.

'I can't wait to see Grandma. I've got so much to tell her and Marcus has loads of photos. I wonder if she'll be able to recognise any of the places? You will look after your hand, won't you? Don't forget to thank Giovanni on our behalf when you next speak to him and let me know about his father. You must come and visit us, try to make it next fall, it's not so humid then. Ask John to put some of his photos on the computer from time to time and send them on to us.' Suddenly Bryony stopped talking and her face crumpled. 'I don't want to go back to the States.'

Marcus looked over his wife's head to Marianne and gave a wry smile. 'Come on, Bryony. We need to go through. We'll come back. I promise.'

2003 - 2004

'It's time for me to leave, Ben,' said Christabelle as they sat over coffee after a leisurely meal.

'It's early yet,' he protested.

'No,' smiled Christabelle. 'I mean leave London. I want to move on to Paris.'

'What's the rush? You're being very successful here.'

'I know, but I more or less promised myself that I would stay no longer than three months and I've been here over a year. I'm pleased to have had the opportunity to visit Scotland and Wales, and I have grown to love London as you said I would; but now it's time for me to go.'

'Have you any contacts over there?'

Christabelle shook her head. 'I'll have to do as I originally planned over here. Go to the different agencies; I'm sure to be offered work.'

'I'm sure you will be.' Ben smiled at her confidence. 'The best I can do is to ask Marsha to write you a reference and see if she has any contacts.'

'That would be very good of you. I really appreciate all you have done for me, Ben.'

'I had hoped you would be staying longer. Maybe we could get to know each other better.' Ben placed his hand over hers and she withdrew it swiftly.

'There's no place in my life for relationships. I'm a career girl.'

Ben shrugged. 'There was no harm in me asking. I've grown very fond of you. I hoped you had some feeling for me.'

'Nothing more than friendship, Ben. I don't intend to marry and be saddled with a brood of children.'

'You wouldn't have to have children,' Ben persisted.

Christabelle set her mouth in a stubborn line. 'Could we talk about something different? Have you been to Paris? Can you tell me anything about the place?'

Her flight to Paris booked and her cases packed, the reference and list of contacts from Marsha safely in her handbag, Christabelle donned her fur coat and ventured out into the chill evening air. From the florists at the corner she purchased a large bouquet before hailing a taxi and asking the driver to take her to the photographic studio in Finchley Park.

She knocked tentatively at the door to Marsha's office and was relieved to hear the woman call to her to enter.

'I just came to thank you, Marsha, and to give you these.' She thrust the bouquet into the woman's arms. 'I can't stop. I have a taxi waiting to take me to the airport.'

Marsha looked at Christabelle in surprise. She had not been expecting more than a cursory word of thanks for the reference she had written. 'That's very kind of you. I really appreciate the gesture. I'm sure you'll do well in Paris. I'll always have you back if you change your mind.'

'Thank you.' Christabelle smiled. 'I really must go.'

Five minutes later Christabelle tapped again on Marsha's door. 'Can I ask you a big favour? The stupid taxi didn't wait for me. I have to be at Gatwick fairly soon or I'll miss my flight. Could you give me a lift to the nearest taxi rank, please?'

Marsha frowned in annoyance. She had planned to stay later at her office to finish her filing and have a clear start for the following week. She looked at the expensive bouquet and decided it would be churlish of her to refuse.

'Give me a couple of minutes. I must clear my desk first.' She began to place papers into folders as she spoke and Christabelle waited patiently.

Finally Marsha drained the glass on her desk, stubbed out her cigarette and declared herself ready to leave. She led to the way to where her car was parked and opened the passenger door. 'Bit of an old crock,' she apologised as Christabelle slid into the seat, kicking crisp packets and a half empty bottle of drink to one side. 'Gets me from A to B and that's all I ask.'

Christabelle pulled up the hood of her coat. 'I hope it won't be as cold as this in Paris.'

'Probably will,' Marsha spoke cheerfully as she put the car into gear and drew out into the road. 'Temperatures here and there are pretty similar. I can take you a fair way, there's a taxi rank close to where I live and it's the right side of the city for Gatwick.'

'I don't want you to go to any extra trouble,' murmured Christabelle.

Marsha shrugged. 'No trouble. Easier for me to drive towards home where I know the area. It's not out of your way.'

Christabelle waited until they had left the main roads and entered the suburbs where the traffic was less, which suited her purpose. She moved her hand forwards swiftly, pulling the brake upwards, bending her head down towards her lap as the car stopped immediately. Marsha was taken completely by surprise. Her head snapped forward and hit the windscreen as the steering wheel impacted her chest.

Carefully Christabelle raised her head. Marsha's limp form was slumped against the side window of the door, blood trickling from the wound on her head. From her handbag Christabelle took a cigarette and cheap lighter. The cigarette she placed on Marsha's lap and the lighter on the floor, throwing the rest of the pack of cigarettes near it. Christabelle opened the passenger door and climbed out carefully. She was totally unhurt. Two cars travelling towards them had stopped and a woman from the first car came across to her.

'What's happened? Are you hurt?'

Christabelle shook her head, feigning dizziness. 'I don't know. My friend – she's hurt.'

The woman looked through the window of the car. 'She needs help. Do you have a mobile?'

'No.' Christabelle swayed slightly.

The woman took her arm. 'Here, sit in my car. Maybe that man has one.'

The man from the second car had joined them and was already talking on his mobile. 'Emergency services are on their way,' he announced.

Christabelle sat and waited whilst the man and woman conversed together in low tones. She hoped she would not be detained for too long, as she needed to be at the airport by ten. It seemed an age to her before an ambulance and the police arrived.

An ambulance man approached her and asked if she was injured. Christabelle shook her head. 'I think my coat saved me. How's Marsha?'

'My colleague is dealing with her at the moment. If you're sure you're all right I'll go back and give him a hand.'

Christabelle gave a wavering smile. 'I just feel a bit shaky.'

The policeman was quiet and courteous. He invited Christabelle to move into the police car where he would drive her to the police station to make a statement about the incident and she agreed. She was given a cup of coffee and offered a cigarette as he commenced to question her.

After the formalities of identification, Christabelle explained that she had visited the photographic studio to give Marsha the flowers and Marsha had offered to drive her to a taxi rank where she could hire a taxi to take her to Gatwick airport.

'Where's your luggage?'

'I had it sent on earlier by the hotel.'

'You were going to be somewhat early for your flight,' observed the policeman.

Christabelle smiled at him. 'I had checked out of my hotel, so I thought I might as well get to the airport and have something to eat before I flew. I should be arriving in the early hours and I wouldn't expect the dining room at the hotel where I'm staying to be open.'

The policeman nodded. 'Now, can you tell me exactly what happened before the car accident?'

Christabelle sat back on the upright chair and closed her eyes. 'I'm really not sure. Marsha was just about to light a cigarette. I don't drive. Maybe she touched something accidently that she shouldn't have?' she suggested.

'Had she had any alcohol to drink?'

'I don't know. She finished a drink that was on her desk before we left. It looked like water, but it could have been gin. That was her usual drink.'

'Right. Did you smell alcohol on her breath?'

Christabelle shook her head. 'I didn't notice it, but she was smoking, so any other smell would have been masked.'

'I think we'll ask someone to call at the studios and see what was in the glass. As you say, it could have been water.'

'How is she?'

'I'm not a medical man. I can give you the name and address of the hospital where they will have taken her. They should be able to tell you. Now, is there anything at all that you can recall that might have made her make an emergency stop? A dog or cat running into the road? A bird or piece of newspaper blowing across in front of you?'

'I didn't see anything.'

'I'll ask you to read this statement and sign it. If you'd be good enough to write down the name and address of the hotel where you'll be staying in Paris; just in case we need to get in touch with you.'

'Of course. Am I able to leave now?'

'Certainly. We have no reason to detain you. I'll call a taxi for you and you can be on your way.'

'Thank you. I'm sorry I've been so little help to you.'

'Not at all. Here's the hospital address.'

Christabelle looked at the name. 'Is it far? Maybe I could call on my way to the airport? It would probably be easier than trying to telephone.'

'About ten minutes from here.'

'I'll go there first. I really would like to know how she is before I leave the country.'

The policeman shook her hand as he saw her into the taxi. 'Good luck in Paris. I hope you find your friend is all right.'

'Thank you.' Christabelle settled herself comfortably. That really had gone very well.

She found the hospital unhelpful. Marsha Everest was in surgery and they would not know the result for some time. If she would like to call the following day they might be able to give her some more positive information. Christabelle thanked them and taking a waiting taxi directed the driver to Gatwick. She would still have time for a meal before her flight was called.

Christabelle decided that it would be an unnatural reaction not to telephone Ben and tell him about the accident, but she also decided that he could wait until she was out of the country before hearing the news.

As she had anticipated, Ben was horrified when she called him from Paris the following morning.

'Why didn't you call me last night?'

'There was no time. I had to go to the police station and make a statement. I called at the hospital on my way to the airport. I nearly missed my flight.' Christabelle smiled as the lies slipped glibly off her tongue.

'I'll go to the hospital immediately. Give me your telephone number and I'll call when I have any news. Were you hurt?'

'Not a scratch,' Christabelle assured him. 'I was very lucky.'

Christabelle consulted the desk clerk at the hotel who spoke English and explained that she wished to visit various modelling agencies in the city. She was hesitant about telephoning to make an appointment, as she had no knowledge of French. The clerk was both charming and helpful. If she would give him the list he would telephone for her. He would have to fit the task in between his other duties, but if she cared to call back in the afternoon he was sure he would have been able to complete the three calls.

Satisfied that she would be able to trust him, she then asked him to call her a taxi as she wished to drive into the centre and understand where she was in relation to the city. She vacated the taxi at the Pompidou Centre and wandered leisurely through the shopping arcades, happy in the knowledge that heads turned as she passed.

Most of the women were smartly dressed, but she had a sneaking suspicion that their coats were made from imitation fur. She partook of a leisurely lunch at a small bistro, pointing to the items she wanted which were displayed behind the counter and the girl regarded her with a mixture of awe and amusement. She handed Christabelle the plate and asked her for thirty-seven Euros in English.

Christabelle looked at her in surprise. 'You speak English?'

'A little. It is necessary with the tourists.'

'Do most French people speak English?'

The girl shrugged. 'Some. They learn at school. If they need they can speak.'

Comforted by the information, Christabelle enjoyed her meal, although when she converted the Euros into the equivalent of the English pounds she had become accustomed to she thought it expensive. She consulted her watch and decided, as it was nearly three, that she would return to the hotel and see what progress the desk clerk had made with her appointments.

The clerk greeted her with a smile. 'I have made appointments as you wished.' He handed her the piece of paper and she studied it carefully. There was one for each of the following mornings.

'Did you explain that I do not speak French?' she asked anxiously.

'They will speak English,' he assured her. 'A gentleman telephoned you from England. He will call again.'

'Thank you very much.' Christabelle gave him a dazzling smile. 'You have been so helpful.'

The clerk smiled back. He hoped that would mean a large tip when she left.

Christabelle guessed her call from England was from Ben giving her an update on the condition of Marsha. She kicked off her shoes, removed her suit and lay down on the bed. She would wait for him to call back. Idly she flicked through an English magazine she had chosen from the bookstall, gratified to find an advert that featured her. She examined it critically. One eyebrow looked a little higher than the other. Was that due to the slight tilt of her head or did she really have uneven eyebrows? She stood at the mirror trying to recreate the exact pose and look at herself at the same time. After half an hour she decided that it was the pose that had created the illusion and returned to the magazine. She was almost asleep when the telephone shrilled insistently and she took a deep breath before answering.

'Hello?'

'Hi, Christabelle? It's Ben here.'

'Hi, Ben. Sorry I wasn't in when you called earlier. I've been investigating the agencies over here.'

'I just wanted to let you know the news.'

'Marsha?'

'She died on the operating table.' Christabelle heard Ben's voice break with emotion.

'Died!' Christabelle exhaled in relief.

'Yes. Internal haemorrhaging, due to the steering wheel crushing her chest.'

'How awful! Have they any idea how the accident happened?'

'They are still investigating. They may get in touch with you to ask you for the details again.'

'That's no problem,' Christabelle assured him. 'I gave the police the address of the hotel where I'm staying.'

'I'll let you know when the funeral will take place.'

'I'd like you to send some flowers on my behalf.'

'You won't be able to come back for the day?'

Christabelle shook her head. She did not plan to set foot on English soil again. 'To be honest, Ben, I don't want to. The only funeral I've ever attended was my mother's. I really don't feel ready to face another funeral yet.'

'I understand. I'll certainly send some flowers from you. Everyone at the agency is devastated. Marsha is totally irreplaceable.'

'She certainly was an incredible woman.'

'Everyone who ever worked for her spoke highly of her. She was a good friend to me.'

'She was very good to me also,' Christabelle agreed. 'I wish now I hadn't taken her the flowers, then she wouldn't have been giving me a lift.'

'Presumably the accident would still have happened. It was on her route home.'

'I'm sure you're right, Ben. I'll console myself with that thought.'

'I do wish you were still in London, Christabelle. We could have comforted each other.' Ben sounded thoroughly miserable.

'I wish I was still there also,' lied Christabelle, wishing he would end the conversation.

'Maybe I could come over and see you sometime?' he suggested.

'We'll have to talk about it. See when I'm not working.' Christabelle was horrified by the idea.

'Have you signed on with an agency?'

'I have an interview tomorrow. I have two others set up, but I doubt if I shall need them.'

'Let me know how you get on.'

'I will, and, Ben, I am sorry that you have lost your friend.'

'Thank you.' There was silence. 'I can't really think of anything more to say at the moment, Christabelle. I just feel numb.'

'I'm sure you do,' she replied gently. 'You'll feel better in a few days. Keep in touch, Ben, and let me know how things are going.'

Christabelle replaced the receiver without giving Ben time to reply. She had the information she required and she certainly did not wish to hear Ben extolling the virtues of the woman she had so disliked.

Bryony sat with her grandmother. 'Are you sure, grandma?'

'I'm sure it's the best solution. I've telephoned the manager at Green Vistas and she will let me know as soon as a place is available. Sharon is very good about doing my shopping and I have Jilly Jo doing my cleaning, but going up and down the stairs is such an effort. I seriously contemplated bringing my bed downstairs, but then I would have had to go upstairs to shower. Sharon suggested I had a stair lift put in or a shower installed down here, but it isn't practical. Now I can't drive any more I'm stuck here most of the time on my own and I'm lonely.'

'Surely you have neighbours who would come in to visit you?'

'Most of them are too busy with their own lives. They're trying to juggle work with bringing up children. There's going to come a time when I need to be looked after and I can't expect neighbours or you to do that. I've made up my mind, Bryony. Once I've moved into Green Vistas I shall sell this place. My savings won't last for ever so I shall need the money.'

'Suppose Marcus and I sold our house and came here to live with you?' Bryony felt depressed at the thought. She loved their house. The alterations they had made, the decor and the holiday to Crete had left them with a large loan from the bank, but felt she should make the offer.

'That would not be fair on you, besides, I'm sure Marcus wouldn't want to live with me. Provided you're willing to help me sort things out when the time comes and keep up your weekly visits I shall be happy enough. I'm sure to make some new friends there.'

'Of course I will. I enjoy visiting you.'

'Can't think why. A silly old lady like me!'

To Christabelle's surprise, a panel of two women and a man interviewed her. She exuded charm and professionalism, agreed readily to having her portfolio completed that afternoon and was assured that they would be able to use her. Knowing the reference from Marsha was a valuable introduction she insisted that the original was returned to her.

'It's sentimental,' she assured them. 'My poor friend Marsha died in a car accident just as I was leaving for the airport. Take a photocopy by all means, but I would like to keep the original. It's in her handwriting.'

Sympathy and understanding was immediately forthcoming from them; then one asked her how the accident had occurred.

'I really do not know,' replied Christabelle. 'A friend in England telephoned me with the sad news.'

Jacques Laverne looked at her steadily from beneath his bushy red eyebrows. 'I understood from the newspaper report that you were travelling with her at the time?'

Christabelle bit her lip. She had not realised the accident would be reported or that the news would have reached Paris.

'I was, but I still do not know exactly what happened. She was giving me a ride to pick up a taxi and for some reason she braked sharply. I knew she had hit her head and was suffering from concussion when she was taken to the hospital. I had no knowledge of the extent of her injuries. It was a terrible shock.'

'You were very fortunate to escape without injury.'

Christabelle agreed and Jacques continued. 'Marsha will be missed. I only knew her from telephone conversations, but I felt that we were friends. Will you be returning for her funeral?'

'I explained to my friend in England that I don't want to.' Christabelle allowed her voice to waver. 'The the only funeral I have ever attended was my mother's. I really do not feel I can ever face going to another. I would rather remember Marsha as she was when I worked for her.'

'Very understandable,' Simone nodded at her over her gold-rimmed glasses as Christabelle dabbed discreetly at her eyes. 'Maybe we could set a time for your photographs. How would three this afternoon sound? Would you have time to return to your hotel and collect some outfits? I'll tell Marcel to be ready for you.'

Relieved that the conversation regarding Marsha had been terminated Christabelle agreed readily.

'So, Lester, what do you have for me?' Rory placed his hands behind his head and swung back on his chair.

'I spoke to the woman who was gardening again. She couldn't help me any further, but stuck by her story. I asked why she hadn't told this to the police and she said she hadn't thought much about it at the time and they'd only asked if she had seen any strangers in the area.'

'Typical! Do you feel she's reliable?'

Lester nodded. 'I would expect her to be. Solid middle-class citizen.'

'Could she have got the days confused?'

'She says not. It was the day her daughter in law gave birth to her first grandchild. After that I went to the local school Christabelle Bartlett had attended and had a word with the Principal and her tutors. I said I was doing a story regarding her modelling success. Her tutors all told me much the same; intelligent, but lazy; good at the Sciences and Maths, average at the other subjects, showed no interest in sports or physical activities. Always received good grades for her homework, but participated very little in class and never achieved her potential in the exam work. The Principal then came up with something interesting. She seemed to have had only one real friend. The girl nearly died and the family moved away. After that Christabelle's homework grades went down dramatically and she seemed only interested in herself and the impression she made on others. She was always immaculate in her appearance and appeared to consider herself above her peers so it had been no great surprise to them when she had not returned to complete her grades and began working as a model.'

'What happened to her friend?'

'Nearly drowned, apparently. Went for a swim in the lake and got tangled up in the reeds. Christabelle held her up until help arrived. The girl was in such a state that her family decided to move out of the area altogether.' Lester held up his hand as Rory was about to interrupt him. 'I went along to the agency where she had worked. They gave her a glowing report. She was always charming, easy to work with, very ambitious. They were only too happy to employ her again when she came back from New York. Apparently she's gone off to Europe to try to make her name there. I felt that was a dead end, but something happened to make me think.'

Rory sat forward on his chair giving Lester his complete attention.

'I was chatting generally to Mike Able, asking how he had

come to employ the girl and she had approached them. Took along a portfolio of photos that Brajowski had taken. I asked to have a look at them, but they don't have them. They took their own. Mike Able happened to say that Brajowski was a bit of a dirty old man. Always insisted the girls needed some nude shots. Apparently this Miss Christabelle refused to do anything without her clothes on for them and said the nudes had been Brajowski's idea.'

Rory frowned. 'So?'

'I thought I'd just check out Brajowski, make the investigation complete, so to speak, and then I remembered. Brajowski is dead. He was electrocuted in his studio.' Lester sat back with a pleased smile. 'Now it begins to get interesting. I approached the police department and managed to persuade them to give me a look at the file. It appears that Miss Christabelle went along to the studio to collect some reprints on the day he died. In her statement she admitted going into the kitchen to make coffee and had difficulty in making the kettle work.'

'What did the police make of that?'

Lester shrugged. 'An electrical fault was found and Brajowski's death was classed as an unfortunate accident. Case closed. The Detective I spoke to remembered the girl. Said she was unforgettable. He also said she appeared genuinely shocked at his death.'

'Not much to go on,' Rory felt deflated.

'I agree, but suppose she fiddled around with the plug and manufactured a fault? She may not have meant to kill him. Probably just wanted to get her own back on Brajowski for taking the nude shots.'

'It's possible, but I don't see how it could be proved or how it could have a bearing on the case of my client. Her mother wasn't electrocuted.'

'She had an argument with her mother about giving up her education, according to Schwaber's statement.'

'Yes, she admitted that, but also said she and her mother had come to an agreement.'

'You only have her word for that.'

Rory nodded slowly. 'That's true. We need look a little more closely at this young lady. I suggest you trace the girl friend's parents and interview them. Then go back to Mike Able and see if he knows where she is now. Get her exact address if you can. It might be worthwhile getting a report from her current employer.'

Christabelle was enjoying Paris. She had ascertained that apartments at a reasonable rental were just as difficult to find in that city as they had been in London. Once again she sought out a small hotel and managed to negotiate a monthly rate that she felt she could afford and would cost her no more than renting. There was the additional benefit that she did not have to concern herself with cleaning, laundry or meals.

She had visited the Arc de Triomphe, Notre Dame and the Eiffel Tower before discovering La Galleries Lafayette. She enjoyed spending most of her free time wandering around the various departments, fingering the soft materials of the clothes on display and admiring the fashions. She was particularly taken with a diaphanous, sea green cocktail dress. Having tried it on and finding that it fitted her perfectly she decided she would make the purchase. It was too late to go to the bank and the shop was due to close within the next fifteen minutes. She would draw some money from the bank the next morning and buy it, regardless of the exorbitant cost. Maybe if she was contracted to model for the store she would receive a reduction in the price.

She approached Simone, trying to appear casual in her enquiry regarding modelling for the store and Simone had laughed at her. 'Only top models get an opportunity to appear at their fashion shows.'

'I am a top model,' replied Christabelle coldly. 'I've done live modelling in London. I'd like the opportunity to do some over here.'

'I'll bear you in mind for their spring collection. In the meantime there's plenty of other work.'

Simone spoke truly as hardly a day went by without Christabelle being offered an assignment. Often she worked alone, but on occasions a tall redhead, with a milk-white skin, that made Christabelle feel physically sick, joined her. In Christabelle's eyes Angelique was always given the more attractive clothes to wear, or had more shots taken. Christabelle began to collect the magazines avidly and count the number of times Angelique appeared and compared the total with her own exposures.

The rooms occupied by the photographic studio were on the third floor of an old building, the lift creaking and shuddering its way up and down. Christabelle noticed that whenever Angelique was there she always left by the fire escape and eventually asked her the reason.

'The lift – is slow. My car there.' She pointed downwards to where there was a small car park and Christabelle nodded. Maybe she would leave by the fire escape in future, although she had no car waiting for her. The first time she used the metal stairway she felt most unsafe, although Angelique ran down with practised ease, waving her hand to Christabelle as she reached the bottom. Christabelle took her time. It would be so easy to trip and fall.

With the Euros drawn from her bank account, Christabelle made her way to La Galleries Lafayette and approached the fifth floor where the cocktail dress was on display. She moved slowly through the expensive items on display until she reached the mannequin and gasped in horror when she saw the dress had been replaced with a long, electric blue evening gown.

Distraught she hurried over to a sales desk and asked for someone who spoke English to attend to her. A puzzled assistant went in search of the manageress, whilst the other girl smiled at Christabelle and wished her good afternoon. Christabelle ignored her, gazing around her wildly. Maybe the display had been changed around and she would see the dress she had set her heart on somewhere else.

Angelique emerged from the dressing room, the cocktail dress draped across her arm. 'I'll take it,' she said to the assistant in French. 'It's beautiful and just my size. I've been invited to a party at the Embassy and it's ideal.' She turned to Christabelle. 'I'm lucky. Only one. Expensive.' She rolled her eyes expressively and turned back to the assistant, continuing to speak to her in French, laughing with the girl and obviously delighted with her purchase.

Christabelle turned away. She was so furious that she felt physically sick. She wanted to snatch the dress from Angelique and rip it to shreds rather than let the girl have it. Just because Angelique had a car she had arrived at the shop before her and taken the one item she had wanted. Shaking with anger she made her way towards the lift, ignoring the call from the manageress to say she was available to deal with Madam's query.

Having been thwarted in her purchase of the cocktail dress Christabelle's dislike of Angelique increased out of all proportion. She could hardly bear to look at the girl and was relieved when she was told she would be working alone or with one of the other models employed by the agency. She brooded whilst alone in her hotel room. She would find a way to get her own back.

Ben continued to telephone her periodically from London, genuinely interested in her progress in Paris. She could always manage to talk about the advertisements she had appeared in and which magazines had featured her. He had not mentioned Marsha's funeral to her again and Christabelle did not ask.

'Maybe I could come over for the weekend?' he suggested.

Christabelle shook her head vehemently at the telephone receiver. 'Let me look in my diary. When did you have in mind?'

'I could probably arrange a time to suit you.'

Christabelle flicked through the pages. 'I've nothing free at present. I can't make any plans for too far into the future. I never know what will come up and where they will ask me to go. I'm actually taking a week out as I'm planning to go down to Cannes for the film festival. I thought it could be interesting and you never know who you might meet.'

'Lucky you!'

Christabelle selected from her wardrobe the clothes she thought would be most suitable for a visit to Cannes. She had no intention of trying to break into films. It was far too boring having to rehearse and spend the whole day doing the same scene over and over again whilst making a two minute commercial. She had made up the excuse on the spur of the moment when she was talking to Ben, but then decided that she would like to add the trip to her experiences. She could spend a few days in Cannes, or even less if she found nothing to interest her, and then go on to Monaco. Once there she would also visit a couple of their famous casinos although she had no intention of gambling with any of her money.

Without an invitation to any of the film events or a pass to give her admittance, Christabelle found she was pushed to one side and dealt with no differently than any other spectator. It was galling to be treated in such a way, but she also realised her naivety. She should have found out the protocol before she made the trip. She was just another amongst the many glamorous and well known figures and the knowledge did not please her.

She visited the shopping area and browsed. After Paris even the department stores appeared small and somewhat old fashioned, whilst the fashionable boutiques seemed to be catering for teenagers, reminding her of the clothing she had first modelled for magazines.

After two days she moved on to Monaco and found the Principality far more to her liking. She swept into the Casino, wearing a gold sheath dress and all heads turned to admire her. The opulence of the surroundings suited her. She was quite content to sit at the various tables and watched the proceedings, amused by the intensity of the dedicated gamblers. Only if she could ensure that she would win would she risk a few Euros at roulette or black jack.

By the end of the week she was quite ready to return to Paris. She would not admit to anyone that her visit had been somewhat of a disappointment to her.

Lester sat in Rory's office and sipped at a mineral water. 'I spoke to the Principal at the school again. She was reluctant to give me the address of Christabelle's girl friend, the one who had nearly drowned, but I assured her I could find out the name and address from the police department or the newspapers if the event was covered and she finally relented. It was quite a difficult interview with the parents at first.'

Rory nodded sympathetically. 'How did you approach it?'

'I told them I was ghost writing for a book by Miss Christabelle, describing her life and meteoric rise to fame. I said she had been most particular that I included her friendship with their daughter, Dolores. They told me how wonderful their daughter was; a credit to them. Very intelligent, she's at University doing child psychology. They had tried to persuade her to go for the sciences and become a medical doctor or chemist. I steered the conversation back to Christabelle, asked if she was as clever as their daughter.

The parents exchanged looks and Mr Lagazi said Christabelle came back some evenings and the girls did their homework together. If Christabelle didn't come back they usually spent a considerable time talking on the telephone. They seemed to feel that was the end of our conversation and were trying to show me the door politely. I decided to tell them that I was really interested in the incident at the lake. I said that Christabelle had made much of the fact that she had saved Dolores's life and definitely wanted that included in the book.

Their reaction was one of horror. They were adamant that the event was not to be mentioned. I really pushed them. Told them I would need a good reason not to include it. Mr Lagazi suddenly seemed willing to talk to me; almost as though it was a relief to tell someone. Apparently at some point the girls had fallen out. Dolores had finally realised that her friend was actually copying most of her homework, taking advantage of her better brain.'

'When did the falling out occur?'

'They said it was about two months before the incident. They couldn't be specific.

After a week or so Christabelle had arrived and asked to see Dolores. They had spent some time in the girl's bedroom talking. Christabelle had seemed quite happy when she left and Dolores said they were friends again, but Christabelle would not be spending so much time at the house. She also told her father that Christabelle had asked her for a loan to buy a suit to wear when she started to take her portfolio of photographs to modelling agencies and she had refused.'

'And?'

'They still met up most weekends and went off somewhere together. The weather was good and Christabelle suggested they went swimming in the lake. Dolores has always been a good swimmer so the parents had no qualms over the outing. They packed up a lunch and off they went. The Lagazis were expecting their daughter back by five as they were all going to a concert that evening. They were sitting out on their patio having a late lunch when the police arrived to say there had been an accident and she was in the hospital.

Christabelle was there with her and being hailed as the heroine of the moment as she had waded in and held her up until help had arrived. Apparently Christabelle is unable to swim. Dolores was bruised and in shock, and the hospital kept her in and sedated over night. She went home the next day.'

Rory held up his hand. 'If Christabelle was able to wade in to help her friend, why did she have to hold her up to prevent her from drowning? Surely the girl's head would have been above water.'

'I think people assumed she had stepped into a hole and become tangled in the reeds. Her mother said she was bundle of nerves. She could understand that at first, but she absolutely refused to see Christabelle. She wouldn't even speak to her on the telephone. She was petrified of going out alone and also about returning to school. Finally she confided to her mother that Christabelle had been trying to hold her under the water, not hold her up.'

Rory raised his eyebrows. 'Could she have been mistaken? If she was tangled up in the reeds she was no doubt panicking.'

Lester shook his head. 'I don't think so. She was suffering from nightmares. Screaming out *"let me go"*, *"Christabelle, please let me go."* It could be a coincidence. Certainly no one has ever suggested that it was anything other than an accident. The only real witness was the man who pulled her out. I could try to trace him if you thought it would do any good. It's so long ago now he could be anywhere and probably wouldn't remember any details clearly.

Anyway, the girl was in such a bad way mentally that the parents took her to a psychiatrist. He recommended they moved away from the area, so they relocated to Dallas. They particularly asked the school not to divulge their new address to anyone as they did not want Christabelle to contact her. She appeared to be terrified of her former friend.'

Rory frowned. 'You're telling me Christabelle tried to drown her friend and make it look like an accident?'

Lester nodded. 'Once they had moved away the girl made a full and rapid recovery. It seems to account for the good grades for Christabelle's homework until Dolores left the area. Presumably Dolores was still prepared to be a friend, but not to have her continually copying her homework and taking the credit. Maybe Christabelle was feeling vindictive when her friend refused to help her financially.'

'It's a bit extreme, isn't it, trying to drown someone because they refused to let you copy their school work or loan you some money?'

'Maybe it was her way of getting her own back. She probably didn't mean her to drown, just frighten her. It made me think. I went back to the school after I'd met with the Lagazis. I wanted to know if electricity was covered in the Science module.'

'And?'

'It was, about six months earlier.'

Rory nodded slowly. 'And Miss Bartlett was good at science.'

'I also contacted Mr Donaldson in London; asked him about Miss Bartlett. He gave her a glowing report, virtually the same as the one from Mr Able. There was just one thing that struck me. He said she had moved on to Paris and I asked him the date. He replied immediately. Said it was the evening before Marsha Everest died. She ran the agency where Christabelle was working. It appears she was giving Miss Bartlett a ride when she crashed her car.'

Rory raised his eyebrows. 'Were you able to get any details from him about the accident?'

'I didn't want to press too hard. I also wanted to get your instructions. Do you want me to telephone again?'

Rory shook his head. 'Not yet. I'll have a word with my client first. Put him in the picture. See if he wants you to proceed.'

Kurt Schwaber looked at Rory McMahon in disbelief. He shook his head. 'I can't believe Christabelle was involved.'

Rory leaned forward. 'We don't know yet that she was. All I'm doing is looking at the facts. The neighbour saw her go out and you go in. She also saw Miss Bartlett waiting across the road behind a tree until you left the house. She was absolutely certain that Miss Bartlett did not enter the house earlier, only after you left. She fell out with a girl friend, and shortly afterwards the girl nearly drowns when she is swimming in a lake, her companion being Miss Bartlett. The photographer, Brajowski, takes photographs of her and the day she collects some reprints he is electrocuted by using a kettle he has had for years. The day she leaves London to go to Paris the manager of the modelling agency where she has been working has a fatal car accident. All coincidences maybe; but coincidences that begin to add up.'

'But what reason would she have to harm anyone?'

Rory shrugged. 'Goodness knows. She could be totally innocent, of course. The problem as I see it is her mother. You insist that you didn't lay a finger on her and the only other possibility is her daughter.'

Kurt passed a trembling hand across his forehead. 'I know I didn't do it, but Christabelle! It's not possible!'

'Then who did?'

'I don't know. There must have been someone else, hidden in the house, maybe.'

'All right, we say there was an intruder. How long was it between you leaving the house and Miss Bartlett telephoning the emergency services? Ten minutes? Time enough for someone to commit murder, but when did they leave? The neighbour did not see anyone else come out of the house and the police obviously searched it.'

'Maybe they left by the back entrance?' suggested Kurt.

'They would still have to come round to the front of the house and leave by the side gate in full view of the gardening neighbour.'

'Perhaps she went inside at that moment?'

'She insists she was in her garden, pulling up dead plants and turning over the soil from one in the afternoon until the emergency services arrived. She went inside then, as she said she didn't want to appear nosey, and watched from behind her drapes.'

Kurt shook his head again. 'There must be another explanation.'

'Then you give it to me.' Rory folded his arms and sat back. 'Think about it and see if it makes sense to you. We'll decide on a course of action the next time I visit you.'

'Course of action?'

'If you are certain that Miss Bartlett could have had nothing to do with it then I'll get Lester to drop the enquiry. That will mean you have no defence to put before an appeal panel. Alternatively I ask Lester to do a bit more digging and see what else he's able to come up with.'

Kurt nodded slowly. 'I'll think about it.'

'Did you make the notes I asked for about your phone call to Mrs Bartlett?'

Kurt dug in the pocket of his prison uniform. 'I have them here. It's all I can remember.'

'I'll read them later.' Rory placed them in his briefcase. 'I'll probably make some notes and question you about details when I see you next. Here's Lester's bill up to date.'

Kurt hardly glanced at it. 'Send it to my brother. You have his address. He's dealing with my finances at present.'

Rory read the notes Kurt had made regarding his telephone call to Anna on the morning of her death and circled some of the sentences.

'I'll be over after lunch' and Anna's reply *'what time?'*

'I'm going to the airport to meet my brother,' and Anna's question

'what time is his flight?'

To Kurt's answer Anna had replied *'you'll need to leave about three to cope with the traffic.'*

Anyone who had overheard the conversation would have a pretty good idea of the time Kurt Schwaber planned to arrive at the Bartlett house and also when he would leave. Rory tapped his teeth with his pen. He was beginning to get a feeling about this case now.

Simone stood and waited until Marcel had finished his work with Christabelle. She had to admit the girl was good and she wondered how much longer she would stay in the modelling business. Maybe her visit to Cannes had been in the hope that someone would decide she would look good on the screen and offer her a part in a film. Whether she had the ability to act would not be an issue. Her looks alone would sell any films she was asked to make. She smoothed her sleek blonde bob, and pushed her glasses more firmly onto her nose.

'Christabelle,' she smiled. 'I think I have some pleasing news for you. Galleries Lafayette have sent me the date for their fashion show and asked me to send three girls. I have decided on Angelique, Nicolette, and you.'

Determined not to show her elation, Christabelle bobbed her head in acknowledgement. 'I am so grateful to you, Simone. I have dreamt of the chance to model their fashions. You'll not be disappointed in me.'

'I'm sure I won't. Angelique will be able to keep an eye on you and put you right if necessary. She worked there last year.'

Inwardly Christabelle seethed. She certainly did not need Angelique to keep an eye on her. 'That's very reassuring for me,' she answered demurely.

'There's an additional bonus,' Simone continued. 'If you wish to purchase anything you have modelled they will give you a generous discount.'

'That's very kind of them.'

'It gives you a chance to purchase something that could be out of your price range normally. Just make a note of the item and hand it to the wardrobe controller.'

'I'll remember,' Christabelle assured her. There was nothing

223

she would want now she was unable to have the sea green cocktail dress. She felt quite sick. If she had only reached the store before Angelique.

Rory looked at the unhappy man in front of him. 'Let me put it to you like this, Mr Schwaber. The argument between Mrs Bartlett and her daughter was far more serious than you realised. When you telephoned Mrs Bartlett, her daughter overheard the conversation so she knew exactly what time you would be arriving and leaving. She waited across the road until she saw you leave then she entered the house. Maybe their disagreement continued, within a few minutes it had got completely out of hand and Miss Bartlett reacted violently.'

'It's possible, I suppose, but their argument was the previous week.'

'Something triggered it off again. Had they ever argued in front of you?'

'Never.'

'Did you consider they had a close relationship?'

Kurt frowned. 'I never thought about it, but as I said, Christabelle tended to disappear when I arrived.'

'You said that Mrs Bartlett had discussed her daughter's decision to become a photographic model with you. Did she mention any of the actual photographs her daughter had in her portfolio?'

'No. Mrs Bartlett seemed very distressed at the idea and when I said to let the girl do as she pleased she accused me of not understanding. I really felt it was none of my business.'

'So she didn't say whether her daughter had been photographed nude?'

'No, but I suppose that could have accounted for her attitude. If Christabelle was planning to work for 'girlie' magazines I would expect her mother to be upset.'

'But Mrs Bartlett did not mention nude modelling to you? Would she have done so?'

Kurt gave a small smile. 'I have to admit that when she first started to tell me about Christabelle's ambitions I thought it was for 'girlies' and that was why Anna was so against the idea. She never mentioned that at all. It seemed to be the fact that Christabelle was not going to University to complete her education that worried her more than anything else.'

'You didn't mention 'girlie' shots to Mrs Bartlett?'

Kurt shook his head. 'In view of the state she was in I thought it better not to add to her distress by putting that idea into her head. From the magazines I've seen Christabelle featured in everything she has done has been in the best of taste. All magazines circulate around the prison and I've never seen her in a risqué pose in any of them.'

'Do you know the name of the photographer Miss Bartlett used for her portfolio?'

'Branowski? Balowski? Something like that. Anna told me the police had been round to interview Christabelle after he died. Apparently she had been at the studio that day, even used the kettle that had killed him.'

'How did Mrs Bartlett react to the news that her daughter might have been electrocuted?'

'She seemed more annoyed that the police had called whilst she was watching one of her favourite television programmes and she had been requested to turn it off.'

'And Miss Bartlett's reaction?'

'I've no idea. Her mother didn't say and I have to admit I didn't give it a lot of thought. The girl was uninjured and I didn't know the photographer.'

'Does Miss Bartlett drive?'

Kurt looked surprised at the unexpected question. 'Not to my knowledge. She didn't whilst she was living with her mother.'

'Did she have any knowledge of vehicles at all?'

Kurt shrugged. 'She never showed any interest, but you have to remember that I didn't know her well. Apart from the normal pleasantries we never really talked together. Why?'

'When she was in London she was involved in a car accident. Fortunately for her she was unhurt, but the driver was not so lucky.'

'I don't see how that has any relevance to my case.'

Rory smiled. 'Nor do I, but there is something niggling at the back of my mind and I want to find out what it is.'

Christabelle strutted, turned, smiled, swung her hips and generally charmed the spectators. She knew by the applause and approving nods that were given each time she walked out that she had stolen the show from the other girls and she felt triumphant. She had put Angelique Laverne in her place. The reviews in the fashion pages would ensure that her name was known throughout Europe.

She changed back into her own clothes and brushed the glitter from her hair. Another two weeks and she would announce to Simone her intention of moving on to Milan. She wondered if the woman would offer to give her a reference as Marsha had done. References certainly opened doors easily.

Angelique touched her arm. 'Was good, yes?'

Christabelle nodded absently. She needed to be at the airport at six that evening for a flight to Switzerland and she was looking forward to spending five days in Zurich.

'Next week, together.'

'Oh, yes. I'll see you on Wednesday.' Christabelle had almost forgotten she was due to be at the studio for a session with Angelique. At least she would not have to work with the objectionable girl for very much longer.

Christabelle approached Simone regarding her impending move to Milan and Simone was sincerely upset. She tried for half an hour to change Christabelle's mind, offering her more commission or a choice of assignments, but Christabelle was adamant.

'I need to move on again. My plan was to spend two years in Europe. I spent over a year in London and I've been in Paris for almost a year. I'm way behind with my schedule.'

'Do you have to keep to a schedule? Surely you can please yourself how long you stay in Europe.'

'I want to see more of the world. If I spend too long in any one place I won't achieve my ambition. I'm planning to take a holiday. I'm going to visit Portugal and Spain before I go on to Italy. There are so many countries in Europe that I've not set foot in yet and after that I will still have China, Australia and South America to visit.'

Eventually Simone was forced to accept that Christabelle was determined to leave. 'I can give you a reference, but I have no contact name in Milan. It may take you some time to find suitable work.' She frowned. 'If you have a problem we will welcome you back.'

Rory spoke to Lester over the telephone. 'I think it would be a good idea to speak to that man Donaldson in England again. See what you can find out about the accident. It's just a hunch I have.'

Lester frowned. 'Is it urgent? I'm tied up for a couple of days in court.'

'There's no rush. Do it when you can and get back to me. See if he happens to know where the girl is in Paris. Maybe she's kept in touch.'

Lester made some quick notes on his pad. 'Give me a week. After that I'm not going to be around. I promised the wife I'd take her and the kids to Disneyland and on to visit her mother.'

Rory chuckled. 'That's one advantage of not being married. No mother-in-law and no kids. Speak to you again soon.'

'I appreciate how good you have been to me. I have one more request before I leave you in peace.' Christabelle smiled at her employer. 'Can you tell me when Angelique will be working this week? I'd like to try and say goodbye to her, she's been very kind to me.'

Simone consulted the schedule in her diary. 'She should be here on Thursday afternoon. She's due at four and should be finished by about five thirty.'

'Thank you. I'll come over about five fifteen and wait for her.' Feeling extremely pleased with herself Christabelle left the office and went into the dressing room, leaving the building by the fire escape and walking carefully down the narrow, iron stairs.

Christabelle arrived at the studios and made her way to the car park. There were only two cars in evidence; Angelique's car was in its usual space, next to Marcel's. Christabelle climbed the fire escape until she reached the bend at the second floor. She sat down on the step and surveyed the area. There was no one around, the windows overlooking the car park had their blinds drawn down as usual, and the opposite building was a blank wall. From her pocket Christabelle took a reel of black twine and tied one end firmly to the base of the handrail. She stretched it across, fixing it to the opposite upright and repeated the procedure until she had six strands at varying heights. Stepping carefully over the trip wires she repeated the process on the next five steps. She studied the effects of her work carefully; the twine was almost invisible against the black of the metal. If everything went according to her plan no one would take any notice of any odd pieces.

She walked round the block to the florists, throwing the roll of twine into a rubbish container as she passed, and chose a large bouquet, asking for it to be gift wrapped. Carrying it carefully she returned to the studio just before five thirty and took the lift to the third floor. As she emerged she could hear Angelique laughing as she left Marcel and walked into the dressing room. Christabelle followed her and Angelique looked up in surprise.

'For you. To say thank you.' Christabelle pushed the bouquet into her arms.

Angelique looked both surprised and pleased. She placed the bouquet on the chair and flung her arms around Christabelle.

'Thank you. I miss you.'

'I'll miss you too,' smiled Christabelle as she drew away from the embrace. She sat down in the opposite chair and watched whilst Angelique removed the layer of make-up and slipped into her own clothes. Finally Angelique was ready to leave.

'So?' she said, raising her eyebrows. 'Milan? Good luck.'

Christabelle nodded. 'Good luck to you also.' She held out her hand. 'Goodbye, Angelique.'

After another quick hug, Angelique picked up her small case of clothes and the bouquet, cradling it in her arms, as she opened the fire escape door. She began to run down the stairs in her usual fashion and Christabelle followed her more slowly. The bouquet completely obscured Angelique's view and when her heel caught in the twine she tumbled forward, catching her other foot in the second trap and virtually catapulted down the stairs. Christabelle watched until she landed in a limp heap at the bottom, her neck twisted at an unnatural angle. Swiftly Christabelle proceeded to where the twine was still attached to the base of the handrail and cut through it at both sides with her nail scissors, leaving the loose strands to float down towards the ground.

Christabelle walked past Angelique's body without a second glance and almost ran out of the car park. Once she reached the front of the building she slowed to her natural pace and proceeded to wander along the road until she came to a bistro. She badly needed a cup of coffee.

Christabelle waited in her hotel room. She was expecting a call from the police and was prepared for them. When they finally arrived she opened her door and smiled at them. 'What can I do for you? I assure you my passport and work permits are in order.'

'It is not about your passport, Mademoiselle.' The Inspector spoke perfect English. 'It is about the sad death of a colleague.'

Christabelle opened her eyes wide. 'Death of a colleague? Who?'

'A young lady, Mademoiselle Angelique Laverne. You worked for the same agency, sometimes together.'

Christabelle sat on her bed. 'Angelique? My friend Angelique?' She feigned stunned surprise. 'What has happened to her?'

'A most unfortunate accident. She was leaving the premises by means of the fire escape and fell.'

'Oh, no. I always thought it was dangerous for her to run down as she did.'

'Why did she use that exit? There was no fire.'

'She always used it, most of us did. She had her car parked down below and the lift is very slow. It was quicker to leave that way.'

'You also used the stairway?'

'Sometimes. I didn't feel very safe on it. I don't like heights.'

'On the evening in question I am told you visited Mademoiselle Laverne. Is that so?'

Christabelle nodded. 'I'm leaving for Portugal the day after tomorrow. I wanted to see her to say goodbye and take some flowers. We had become friends.'

'What time did you arrive at the studios?'

Christabelle shrugged. 'I can't say exactly. I knew she should be finishing work about five thirty so it must have been near that time.'

'And at what time did you leave?'

'We talked for maybe ten minutes. I left her in the dressing room removing the last of her makeup.'

'And how did you leave the building?'

'I used the fire escape.'

The Inspector raised his eyebrows. 'And why was that? You said you did not feel safe, did not like the height.'

230

'I wanted to avoid anyone else in the building. I had only taken a bouquet for Angelique. It could have been embarrassing if I had met someone else. I had no gift for them.'

'So when you went down the fire escape you saw nothing unusual?'

'Unusual?' Christabelle was wary. Were they trying to trap her?

'An obstruction, something slippery, anything?'

Christabelle shook her head. 'I certainly didn't notice anything.'

'Did you happen to see Mademoiselle Laverne leave the building?'

'No. I don't know how long after me she left. I went for a coffee. I can give you the name of the bistro if you wish.'

'That will not be necessary.' The Inspector closed his notebook. 'Thank you for your help, Mademoiselle.'

Christabelle breathed a sigh of relief when they left. Now she must telephone Simone and express her shock, horror and sympathy, particularly to Jacques Laverne, Angelique's grandfather.

Annita walked slowly through the bare rooms on the ground floor. Over the preceding weeks the furniture had been sold or given away. Anything she valued she had packed up carefully and asked Bryony to deposit in the bank. Together they had sorted her clothes and two large cases stood ready in the hall way. All she carried with her was a photograph of Elias, her address book and jewellery.

There was no need to climb the stairs. The rooms up there were just as empty. Jilly Jo had promised to come in and dispose of the last few items of furniture and clean through before the new occupants arrived. Now it was time to leave she was being maudlin. How cross Elias and Yannis would be with her if they could see her. Even as his health failed Elias had continued to work, sure he would find a cure for leprosy; Yannis had been even more determined to survive when he had been exiled to Spinalonga. They would have no patience with a silly old woman who was getting emotional about leaving her house due to her old age.

Bryony gave a little gulp and tears came into her eyes. 'I shall miss coming here. I always loved this house.'

Annita felt the tears coming into her own eyes. The two women looked at each other and Bryony flung her arms round her grandmother. For a few minutes they clung together, their tears mingling.

Annita pulled herself from Bryony's embrace. 'There's no need for us to be sentimental. After all, it's only a house. Besides, if we stand here looking at it the only thing that will change will be me being late for my tea at Green Vistas.'

'Hi, Rory. I've spoken to Ben Donaldson, the man in England. Remember you asked me to get a few more details about that accident? Yeah, well, according to Donaldson the girl had gone to the studio to give the woman a bunch of flowers. She accepted a ride and during it the car stopped suddenly. Donaldson said the police had the car checked out and there was nothing faulty. When he spoke to Miss Bartlett she was unaware that the woman had died. She had seen her taken off in the ambulance, but as far as she was aware it was just concussion.'

Rory tapped at his teeth. 'Thanks, Lester. Did you manage to get the address where Miss Bartlett is staying in Paris?'

'I did, but it's no good. Donaldson says she's having a holiday in Portugal and Spain before moving on to Milan. He had wanted to go over to visit her, but she had a busy schedule and he never made it. She promised to keep in touch with him, but he hasn't heard from her yet.'

Rory sucked in his breath in annoyance. He would not be able to present any progress to Kurt when he visited him next.

'Do you want me to contact Donaldson again when I get back from my vacation?'

'Might as well. He may have an address for her in Milan by then. Find out from him who she was working for in Paris and we can find out what they thought of her, although I doubt if it will differ from her other employers. Have a good time in Disneyland. Don't get sick on the rides.'

Rory heard Lester snort in derision as he replaced the receiver.

ITALY 2005

Christabelle asked the taxi driver to take her to the most fashionable store in the city. He looked admiringly at the beautiful, well-dressed American woman. No doubt she had plenty of money and the journey was going to cost her dear. Christabelle paid him without demur and entered the store. She was pleased she had been able to dispense with her winter coat, as the weather had turned delightfully warm. Her peach sheath dress with bolero jacket showed off her figure and she knew that both men and women gave her admiring glances as she wended her way through to the fashion department.

'Do you speak English?' she demanded of an assistant.

'A little.' The girl smiled, hoping the customer was going to make a large purchase, which would add considerably to her monthly commission.

'I wish to speak to the department manager.'

The girl's eyes opened wide. She had understood the demand. Was the lady going to complain? 'I find,' she assured Christabelle and hurried away.

Impatiently Christabelle waited until the dapper Italian arrived. Christabelle extended her hand. 'Do you speak English?'

The man nodded and Christabelle proceeded to introduce herself. 'I'm Christabelle, the model. You've probably heard of me or seen some of my work. I've come to Milan to promote my career. Are you able to help me by recommending a reputable agency?'

The man looked taken aback. He was certainly not used to such a request. 'I am not sure, Madam. If you would care to come to my office I will speak with my assistant.'

Pleased to be treated with such deference Christabelle followed him through a door marked '*PRIVATE*' and up a flight of stairs. They passed through an office where three girls were working on computers and into a small, but comfortable room at the back. Mr Rosmini indicated a chair and offered her coffee or a soft drink. Christabelle declined. It was more difficult to promote herself with a glass in her hand.

Mr Rosmini pressed a button on his desk and within a moment a young woman entered. To Christabelle's amusement she was still wearing winter clothes and looked pinched and cold. Mr Rosmini spoke to her in rapid Italian and then turned back to Christabelle.

'I have asked Cinzia to bring me a list of all the agencies we use. They may be of use to you.'

'You do not give fashion shows in the store to promote sales?'

'Twice, three times a year, maybe. Cinzia will telephone an agency and they will send us suitable girls.'

'What about the fashion houses? When do they hold their shows for the buyers?'

'Usually four months before each new season starts. The manufacturers need the time to fulfil the orders.'

'So they should be holding their shows at any time now ready for the summer collections?'

Mr Rosmini nodded. 'This is your main interest?'

'I have done photographic, commercials and live modelling,' Christabelle assured him. 'I have become a household name in the States and well known in both London and Paris.'

Cinzia returned bearing a list that she handed to her employer and stood waiting for further instructions. Mr Rosmini spoke to her again and she began to point at various names on the list. He held up his hand, placed the list on his desk and began to write either 'P' or 'L' or both beside names and strike others through. Finally he checked with his secretary and handed the list to Christabelle.

'I think that may help you. 'P' for photographic, 'L' for live. Those I have struck through concentrate on footwear or toiletries.'

Christabelle looked at the list appreciatively. 'You have been very kind, Mr Rosmini. I have just one other question, are most of these establishments situated in one area of the city or are they spread over the whole?'

Mr Rosmini took the list back from her and placed a small cross against five of the names. 'They are near to each other. The remainder are in other areas.'

'You have been so helpful. Thank you so much.' Christabelle stood and held out her hand.

'Would Madam like a conducted tour of the store whilst she is here?' suggested Mr Rosmini.

Christabelle pretended to consult her watch and shook her head. 'Unfortunately I do not have the time. Another day I would be delighted.' She wanted to return to her hotel and begin to telephone and set up appointments as quickly as possible.

Mr Rosmini clasped her hand in his. 'I look forward to seeing you again in the near future. Please ask for me. I will conduct you personally and maybe we could have lunch afterwards? We have an excellent restaurant here.'

'What a lovely idea! I'll be only too pleased.' Christabelle withdrew her hand. She had no intention of returning to the store and receiving the personal attention of the little man.

The two letters, giving glowing reports of her previous work experience and how easy and amenable she was to work with, opened the door to the second agency Christabelle approached.

'We have no live modelling available,' Mr Mondolfo apologised. 'Our models are already booked for the live fashion shows, but I am sure we could use you for some of the magazines and mailshots.' He folded his hands complacently over his paunch and smiled benignly at her. 'Of course, should one of our girls become indisposed it is not inconceivable that you could take her place. Come and meet Roberto, our photographer. He knows our schedule for the next few months and may have something that would be suitable for you.'

Christabelle found that Roberto had many assignments that he considered suitable for her and she found herself at the studios most days of the week. Each time she met the photographer she found him more repulsive. He continually suggested that he take her for dinner, escorted her on a sightseeing trip around the city or accompanied her on a weekend to visit Florence or Venice. If she had to pass close to him he ensured that some part of his anatomy touched hers, making her shudder. Firmly and politely Christabelle rejected his advances. His moment would come, she decided.

'So, Lester, how was Disneyland?'

'The kids enjoyed it. That was good enough for me.'

'And the visit to the mother-in-law?'

'Not bad. A couple of whiskies in the evening loosens her up and she can be quite amusing.'

'Did you speak to Donaldson again?' asked Rory, the pleasantries complete.

'I did. He gave me the address and 'phone number of the agency in Paris and also the address of her hotel in Milan. I spoke to a manager at the agency, same glowing report, sorry she had to leave. They wished she could have stayed with them as they had just lost their top model,' Lester paused for effect. 'She died just before Miss Bartlett left for Milan.'

'What?' Rory sat bold upright in his chair. 'Say that again.'

'The top model of the Paris agency fell down the fire escape and broke her neck two days before Miss Bartlett caught a flight to Portugal.'

Rory could picture the smug smile on Lester's face as he imparted this information. 'An accident?'

'It would appear so.'

'Have you any details?'

'No, I didn't want to push too hard until I'd spoken to you.'

'Let me think about it for a day or two. Speak to my client. I'll get back to you. There's just one thing, Lester, don't take any long term assignment until you've spoken to me again.'

Puzzled Lester replaced the telephone. What did Rory have in mind for him that he had to keep himself free? He shrugged. Business was pretty slow, so he doubted that anything would arrive on his desk that would tie him up for too long.

'Mr Schwaber, so far I have managed to delay the date for your appeal twice by convincing the prosecutor that we are investigating some new leads. All the time you have an appeal pending the death sentence will not be carried out.'

Kurt shook his head. 'That doesn't make me feel any better. One day they'll decide to get rid of me.'

'I've spoken to your brother again and I have a proposal to put before you that I want you to consider very seriously. I know it's going to be expensive and we may not get anything conclusive from it, but I have a feeling it could be to your advantage eventually. I want to send Lester Harkonen to Europe to make some further enquiries. See if the police have missed anything, whether any suspicion can be thrown onto Miss Bartlett for these unfortunate accidents that she seems to leave in her wake. Even if we can prove nothing a jury might think it casts doubt on your guilt and throw the case out.'

'Do you think so?' A ray of hope shone in Kurt's eyes.

'I feel we should give it a try. Bear in mind that if you are finally released without charge you can sue the police department for wrongful arrest and ask for compensation for the amount of time you've spent in prison. That should certainly cover your legal expenses and probably give you something to help you make a new start somewhere.'

'How much is it going to cost?'

Rory shook his head. 'I can't give you a final figure.'

Kurt sighed. 'I just hope it will be worth it eventually.'

Lester landed at Heathrow on a clear, bright morning. He had managed to sleep fitfully during the flight, but checked into a small hotel to recover fully from his jet lag before he set up an appointment with Ben Donaldson. He needed to go over his cover story in his head and make sure Donaldson had no reason to mention his enquiries to the girl if he spoke to her. He awoke in the early hours of the morning, poured a cup of strong, black coffee and began to make notes, most of them ending with a question mark. An hour later he returned to his bed and managed to doze until the alarm call he had asked for roused him.

'Why have you come to see me?' asked Ben Donaldson.

Lester shrugged. 'Just a formality, really. I have to ascertain if there was any fault on the car for the manufacturer's insurance company. It means going over the ground covered by the police investigation to satisfy then that every possible enquiry has been made so they can disclaim any liability.'

'What is it you want to know?'

'Just tell me in your own words what you told the police, as near as you can remember.'

Ben frowned. 'I didn't give a statement to the police. Jacob 'phoned me to say Marsha had been involved in an accident and was in hospital. I telephoned the hospital to ask after her and they gave me the news that she had died. I then contacted Miss Christabelle to let her know. That's all.'

'Jacob is who? The lady's husband or partner?'

'No, the photographer.'

Lester nodded and made a note. 'And Miss Christabelle?'

'She was one of their models. She would be able to give you more details than I can. She was travelling in the car at the time; that was why I 'phoned to let her know about Marsha's death.'

'And where can I find Miss Christabelle?'

'She's in Milan.'

'Milan?' Lester feigned surprise.

'She left here to go to Paris and has now moved on to Milan. I can give you the address of her hotel.'

'I doubt if I shall need it, but I'll take it, just for the record.' Lester waited whilst Ben consulted the memory on his mobile and wrote down the details. 'Can you give me the address of this modelling agency? I'd better have a word with this man Jacob.' He exuded boredom with his job.

Ben complied readily and Lester left him not having learnt anything new. He found Jacob equally as unrewarding, the man having been contacted by the hospital from a calling card in Marsha's handbag.

'Miss Christabelle is the only one who could give you any real details. She was with Marsha at the time.'

'And where will I find this young lady?' asked Lester, knowing full well the answer to his question.

'She's gone to Paris.'

'Do you have her address?'

Jacob shook his head. 'No reason for her to leave it with us. She didn't plan to return to London.'

'There's just one more question, Mr Smethers, did Miss Everest ever mention that she had a fault of any sort on her car?'

Jacob shook his head. 'Marsha never said anything to me. I know she had it serviced regularly, because I would give her a lift whilst it was in the garage.'

Lester took his leave. He needed to speak to the police and the mechanic they had used to check the car over and then his work in England would be complete.

The police in London were helpful once he had shown his credentials as a private investigator. 'Miss Everest's family have asked me to make a few enquiries,' he lied. 'They feel there must have been a manufacturer's fault on the car for her to have a fatal accident. She'd never been involved in an incident before, not even a speed violation.'

'Trying to claim compensation? Everyone seems on to that these days. I think they'll find they've wasted your time and their money. There's nothing in the passenger's statement or the mechanic's report.'

'If I could just read the reports,' persisted Lester. 'Then I can tell them to let the case rest.'

'I can't let you take them off the premises.'

'No problem. I only want to read them,' Lester assured him.

Lester read and re-read the statement made by Christabelle. It was very plausible and it seemed there was no way she could have manufactured the accident. She had no idea how the accident had happened, but Marsha was just about to light a cigarette and may have taken her eyes off the road for a second. He made a note of the name of the police mechanic who had inspected the car and returned the files to the policeman.

'Does Jimmy Lyons still work for you, and if so where can I find him?'

'Doubt if he'll remember anything about it now.'

'I would hardly expect him to, but I don't want to be accused of not doing my job properly. The family could refuse to pay me if they thought I'd cut the corners.'

'Ask the desk sergeant on the way out.'

Lester ran Jimmy Lyons to earth in an unmarked garage in a side road and produced his credentials again. 'I know it's quite a while back now, Mr Lyons, and you've probably looked at a fair number of vehicles since then, but I have to ask if you noticed anything untoward when you checked out Marsha Everest's car.'

Jimmy Lyons pushed his hair back with a grimy hand. 'Can't say I remember it at all. I'll have to look up the records.'

Lester followed him into the cubby-hole that served as an office and the man took down a file from the shelf marked January 03. He flicked through the carbonised copies until he came to the one relating to Marsha Everest and read it through, following the lines with his finger and reading out the salient points to Lester.

'No sign of external impact. Been serviced recently and we checked that with her garage. Engine clean, brakes fine, lights working, tyres with regulation depth of tread, nothing that could be the cause of the accident.'

'So she didn't hit anything?'

Jimmy Lyons shook his head. 'No indication. No scratches on the paintwork or dents. She just appeared to have stopped so abruptly that the steering wheel impacted her chest.'

'Why would she have done that?'

'Who knows? An animal running out in front of her, maybe.'

'It said in the police report that she appeared to be in the process of lighting a cigarette when the accident happened. Would you know anything about that?'

Jimmy Lyons shook his head. 'I was only asked to inspect the vehicle for faults. The interior contents are nothing to do with me.'

With that Lester had to be content. He would telephone Rory and see if he wanted him to make arrangements for a flight to Paris.

Lester arrived in Paris at mid-day and by the time he had checked in at his hotel and had a leisurely lunch he decided he had no time to do anything that evening. He would telephone the modelling agency first thing in the morning and see if he could make an appointment for that day, ostensibly as a health and safety inspector who had been asked to check out the fire escape.

Simone greeted him without suspicion and he asked to be told exactly what had occurred. 'I cannot be sure, you understand, it is what we surmise happened. Miss Christabelle visited Angelique to say goodbye. She had bought her some flowers. Angelique left by way of the fire escape to reach her car and she must have tripped and fallen. Maybe the bouquet obstructed her vision? Marcel found her when he had packed away his equipment and went down to his car.'

'I have just a few questions, Madame. Miss Christabelle, who is she? One of your models or a friend of the deceased?'

'She was one of our top models. She is American. She came recommended to us by Miss Everest in England.'

Lester nodded. 'How long ago was that?'

Simone thought about the question. 'I am not sure of the exact date she started, but it would be in our files. She was with us for nearly a year and poor Angelique has been dead for almost three months now.'

'A tragedy,' sympathised Lester.

'Particularly for Monsieur Laverne. He is one of our directors and was also the poor girl's grandfather.'

'Truly dreadful.'

'He wanted to have the fire escape removed, but of course, we need to have it, regulations.'

'Exactly. That is why I am here. If I find anything wrong with it then you may have to replace it. If there is a fault due to negligence then you realise your company may be charged with manslaughter?'

Simone paled visibly. 'It has been inspected regularly. I'm sure all is in order. To be charged with manslaughter! Monsieur Laverne would never forgive himself.'

'I'm sure all will be in order, Madame. The man who found the young lady, does he work here?'

'He is our photographer. He also left by the fire escape and that was when he saw her. He immediately called an ambulance.'

'Is it usual for your employees to leave the building by the fire escape?'

'Only Marcel and Angelique used the fire escape on a regular basis. They would park their cars below and it was quicker for them than waiting for the elevator.'

'And yourself, Madame, where do you park your car?'

'My husband brings me to work and collects me most days. If our times do not coincide I take a taxi.'

Lester nodded. There seemed little to be gained by asking about the travel arrangements of all the employees. 'If I could inspect the staircase now, Madame.'

Simone led him to the dressing room and opened the door leading to the fire escape. 'I regret you will have to return by the front entrance. The door closes automatically. A fire precaution, you understand.'

'Of course. I will see you shortly, Madame and let you know the result of my inspection.'

Lester walked down the fire escape carefully. It was quite sound and there was nothing in evidence that could have caused the girl to fall. Having reached the bottom he began to retrace his steps and then he spotted where something appeared to have been attached. Tied to at least half a dozen uprights was a short length of black twine. He stood and looked at it. There was no way it could have been blown and become tangled and it had obviously been there for a considerable amount of time. Each piece was carefully knotted, some ends being longer than others. On two of the uprights there were a number of strands tied about six inches high.

Lester measured the distance with his hand and then tried to stand on his toes and measure the distance to his ankle. Balanced precariously on the stairs he gave up the exercise, but was convinced that his theory was correct. He took a photograph of the uprights and untied one of the threads, but left the remaining strands where they were. When he visited the gendarmerie later that day he would alert them to his discovery and ask them to take a sample of the thread.

He returned to Simone by means of the front entrance and the creaking lift to reassure her that there was no problem with the fire escape and no blame for the accident could be laid at the agency's door.

Lester telephoned Rory and updated him on his findings. 'The police seemed a bit sceptical about the thread, but they took a photograph anyway. What do you want me to do now?'

'I need you back here. The date of the appeal has been put forward and I shall need you here to present your findings. It's not much, but if we get a sympathetic judge he could delay the execution date to give us time to make more enquiries. I shall ask for a closed court. We don't want the press making up any sensational story.'

'What about the girl?'

'We haven't anything except circumstantial evidence against her at the moment. Unless the judge rules for a new trial for Kurt Schwaber, and I don't think that likely, we can't ask for her to be called back to the States. There's also a question of finance. I don't know how much more Schwaber can afford.'

Lester gave a sigh of relief. At least he should finally have the opportunity to have his bunions removed.

Christabelle examined herself carefully in the full length mirror. She was nearly thirty and she still looked good. She wondered how many more years she would have as a top model. One thing she was certain about was that she could no longer bear to work with Roberto. She debated the wisdom of asking Mr Mondolfo if he could provide her with an introduction to an agency in Rome or whether she should just ask him for a reference. She was not sure if she disliked Milan because of Roberto or if she was becoming bored with modelling the same goods time and again. She probably needed a break to recover her enthusiasm. Despite having visited Portugal and Spain after leaving Paris she had not stopped long in either country. Maybe it would be a good idea to holiday in Rome for a week or so and see what the market had to offer before she made a decision.

Christabelle clicked her tongue in annoyance. The recorded letter awaiting her was from the public prosecutor advising her that the date for Kurt Schwaber's appeal had finally been set for the second week in August. She was requested to attend. Uncertain whether she had the choice or if it was an order she telephoned Detective Mullen. He advised her to be in New Orleans and available if necessary.

'I have no idea what this new evidence is that they are planning to present, but it could be in your best interests to attend. You may wish to refute some of it.'

Christabelle sighed. This really did ruin her plans for modelling in Rome. She looked at the calendar. She was committed to working with the hated Roberto until the twenty second of June. That could probably be altered by a week and a couple of days later she would go on to Athens. She might just as well take advantage of visiting the city before returning to the States, and there was Roberto to be taken care off.

By now Christabelle was familiar with the city of Milan, having been photographed before most of their most famous buildings. She studied the map; she needed somewhere central, but also where she was unlikely to be observed. The idea came to her – the public gardens. She was sure there were plenty of secluded places in there.

It took her half an hour to walk from her hotel to the entrance of the gardens, wearing a pair of flat sandals. Once there she wandered through at a leisurely pace, noting the paths leading off between low bushes. Twice she disturbed courting couples as she left the main area to explore a little further afield. Close to the various entrances were bistros and snack bars and she selected one and sat at the table outside.

Having ordered an ice cream she sat deep in thought. She had no idea how strong Roberto was. She really must be prepared. It would be necessary to make a purchase as she returned to her hotel.

'Roberto,' Christabelle tied her wrap firmly round her as the young man gave her a broad smile, showing his perfect white teeth. 'Would you do something for me?'

'Of course.'

'I've found a delightful little restaurant. I had lunch there the other day and I was told that it's even better in the evening.'

Roberto nodded eagerly as she continued.

'The problem is, it's very close to the public gardens and I'm a bit worried about going there on my own at night. The gardens are so beautiful during the day that I would like to go there in the evening.' Christabelle spoke wistfully.

'You wish me to accompany you? Of course, it will be my pleasure. Tonight?'

Christabelle shook her head. 'No, I'm busy for the next few days. I thought maybe next Tuesday would be best, if you're free, of course.'

'For you, I am always free. What is the name of this restaurant?'

Christabelle frowned. 'I think it was called *Zucchis*.'

Roberto raised his eyebrows. He had never heard of the place. 'We will make it a date. I will collect you from your hotel at what time?'

Christabelle shook her head. 'I would prefer to meet you there. If I am seen leaving the hotel with you there will immediately be rumours and the press could become a nuisance. You know how they often turn up when I am doing location work. Besides, it would be more romantic to meet you there at the main entrance. How would nine thirty suit you?'

'It is no problem. You are sure I cannot collect you from the hotel?'

'Quite sure. I don't think I'm in again before then so I'll see you Tuesday evening.'

Roberto grinned delightedly as Christabelle bestowed a smile on him as she left the studio. His persistence had obviously paid off.

Christabelle waited until she saw Roberto approaching the entrance to the gardens and hurried towards him with a worried look on her face. 'Roberto, I'm so sorry. Look at me; I'm a scare-crow. I can't possibly go anywhere with you looking like this.'

Roberto looked at the drably dressed girl. Jeans, tee shirt and flat shoes, she certainly did not look like the glamorous model that he had photographed so often. 'You are still beautiful. It does not matter what you wear.'

'It matters to me. I like to do credit to my escort. A stupid man was painting his window and he dropped his paint pot just as I was passing. It splashed all over me. He was most apologetic, of course. Insisted I went inside and cleaned myself up, but my dress was ruined. I have it here and I doubt if the paint will come out.' She indicated the plastic bag she was carrying. 'The best he could do was to lend me some clothes that belonged to his daughter. I had no time to go back to the hotel to change before meeting you.' Christabelle's eyes filled with tears. 'I feel so awful.'

Roberto put his arms around her. 'Poor Christabelle. It is not a problem. No one will look at your clothes. They will look only at your beautiful face.'

Christabelle extricated herself from his arms and shook her head. 'I couldn't possibly eat anything. All I can smell is paint and that awful stuff you use to clean it off.' She looked at the disappointed young man beside her and took his hand. 'Come, we can at least walk in the gardens. I may feel better in a while and we could go and eat then.'

'Which way do you want to walk?'

'The restaurant is on the far side from here. I took a short cut when I came before.' Christabelle looked around, as if to get her bearings. 'This way.'

Roberto did not resist as she drew him away from the main path and into the gardens in the gathering dusk. Christabelle deliberately walked slowly and allowed Roberto to lead her deeper and deeper into the shadows. Finally she stopped and looked around. 'I think I am lost. Maybe we should make our way back to the path.'

'You are quite safe. You are with me.' Roberto drew her into his arms, crushing her body against his and making her feel physically sick as she felt his arousal. She pulled herself away and tried to give a little laugh.

'You will smother me. Do not hold me so tightly.' She turned her face upwards towards him, an open invitation for him to kiss her. As he bent towards her she swiftly brought up her knee between his legs and heard his quick intake of breath at the pain she had caused. Her strong hands fastened themselves around his neck and she squeezed with all her might, pushing his head back as far as she could. Roberto gave a groan and slumped towards her as she released him. Half choked and in considerable pain he fell in a crumpled heap at her feet. She put her hand into her jeans pocket and pulled out the knife she had purchased from a multiple store some days earlier. With one easy movement she slashed it across his neck, jumping to one side as the blood spurted out.

Roberto's eyes rolled in his head and a gurgling noise came from his throat. Christabelle looked at him with distaste and plunged the knife into his neck again with as much force as she could muster. There was blood on her hand and she wiped it on his shirt before pulling a handkerchief from his pocket and cleaning her hand more thoroughly. From the plastic bag she had been carrying she hastily donned an orange tunic over her tee shirt, wrapped the knife in the handkerchief and placed it in the bag. Straightening up she looked to get her bearings before walking rapidly away, hoping she was heading in the right direction for an exit to the gardens.

Dutifully Christabelle turned up at the studios on time for her day's photo session. After half an hour she went through to the reception area and asked if Roberto had called in sick. She was waiting for him and he was not usually late. The girl shook her head, only half understanding Christabelle's question, and Christabelle wandered disconsolately back to her dressing room. She would just have to wait and see what developed.

It was mid-morning before the receptionist knocked on her door and said there was a telephone call. Christabelle followed her back to the desk and picked up the receiver. 'Roberto no come today. Understand?'

'Yes. Thank you.' Christabelle was puzzled. Who had made that telephone call? It was no good trying to ask the receptionist, who was dabbing at her eyes and sniffing audibly. Presumably the caller had been able to give more information to the receptionist in Italian than he had to Christabelle in English.

Christabelle shrugged and turned away. She would get changed and return to her hotel. She would then go for a walk and it would be an ideal opportunity to dispose of the jeans and tee shirt, along with the knife. If confronted she would deny ever going to meet Roberto the previous evening, accusing him of romantic fantasies. She was sure people would believe her.

Carefully she washed and dried the knife before packaging up the items of clothing she had worn the previous evening into two parcels. She placed the knife, plastic bag and handkerchief in separate envelopes, and stowed them all into her vanity case before she left the hotel. Provided she deposited them in rubbish containers at discreet intervals there would be no reason for anyone to connect them with her.

Christabelle arrived at the studios the following day to find the Italian police in evidence. She tried to ask the snivelling receptionist what was happening, but the only word she was able to understand was 'Roberto.' She sat and waited as requested until an elderly police inspector finally approached her.

'Do you speak English?' she asked and was relieved when he nodded.

'That is why you have had to wait. I was told I was needed here. I have to ask you some questions, just a formality, you understand.'

'What has happened?' Christabelle decided it was wisest to feign ignorance, whilst her heart thumped against her ribs.

'You have not been told?'

Christabelle shrugged. 'I may have been, but if I was told in Italian I would not have understood.'

'The photographer who worked here, Roberto Verri, he was found stabbed.'

Christabelle opened her eyes wide in horror. 'Stabbed? How terrible! How is he?'

'Sadly he did not survive the attack. I am sure we shall very soon find his assailants.'

'I do hope so. What did you need to speak to me about?'

'The young lady on the reception desk informed me that you had planned to spend the evening in question with Mr Verri.'

'Me?' Christabelle shook her head. 'She must be mistaken. I have never met him outside of the studios.'

'Miss Carducci insists Mr Verri told her you had finally agreed to go to dinner with him. She said he was telling everyone.'

Christabelle thought swiftly. 'They must have misunderstood. I did agree to go out to dinner with him before I leave, but we had no date in mind.'

'You are leaving?'

'When I was first employed here they knew I would move on after a while.'

'Why was that?'

Christabelle smiled easily. 'I worked for some years in the States. I always dreamt of visiting Europe. I have worked in London, Paris and now Milan. I had planned to go to Rome and work there for a while but I have to be back in the States earlier than I expected. I still plan to visit Athens and possibly some of the islands before I return.' Christabelle shrugged. 'I will just have to take it day by day.'

'What is so urgent that you have to return to the States?'

Christabelle allowed her eyes to fill with tears. 'The terrible man who murdered my mother is appealing against his sentence,' she almost whispered the words. 'I have been told that I should be there.'

The Inspector nodded. He was really not interested in where she had worked before and the reason she was returning to the States. 'So when will you be leaving Italy?'

'I'm not sure now.' Christabelle frowned. 'I doubt if they will want me around if Roberto is not here to photograph me and it is pointless me staying here without work. I have seen all of Milan. It is an enchanting city.'

'And how long do you plan to stay in Athens?'

'Again, I'm not sure of my dates. Probably no more than two weeks, then I will make arrangements to visit some of the islands. I understand I have some relatives on Crete.' As soon as she said the words Christabelle realised she had made a mistake. Now she would have to contact Bryony and ask for their address.

'I hope you will enjoy your visit to them. This is such a tragedy to happen just before you leave our country.'

'It is most unfortunate,' agreed Christabelle. 'He was a very nice young man.'

'So I have been told. How did you spend your evening, Miss Bartlett?'

Christabelle wrinkled her brow. 'I went out for a walk, browsing around the shops, had coffee in a bistro, then returned to my hotel and ate in their dining room.'

'And after you had eaten? What did you do?'

'It was a beautiful evening so I went for another short walk.'

'So you did not see Mr Verri at all?'

'The last time I saw him was when he photographed me, last Thursday.'

'It was on the Thursday you agreed to go to dinner with him before you left the city?'

'Yes,' agreed Christabelle.

The Inspector turned the page in his notebook. 'Thank you. I doubt very much that we shall need to contact you again. Just as a formality I will have to ask you to report to the police in Athens to give them the address of the hotel where you will be staying. I will give you my telephone number and when you visit the islands I would like you to let me know where you are.'

'Am I a suspect?' Christabelle opened her eyes wide in horror.

The inspector shook his head. 'This enquiry may take some time. I may wish to verify something with you at a later date, so I do need to know where you can be contacted.'

'Of course. I understand.'

The Inspector left Christabelle feeling very unsettled. She should have known that Roberto would brag to the other employees that he was taking her out and she should have arranged an accidental meeting with him. She would certainly leave Milan as soon as possible and that would be the end of the matter.

Inspector Lorenzini lit a small cigar and looked at his computer screen. He had typed up his notes regarding the interviews he had conducted at the photographic studios. He read them through a second time, scrolled onto a clean page and began to type the questions that were worrying him.

'Receptionist certain R.V. dining with C. that night. Why say that if not true?

Deliberate lie? Misunderstanding?

Why should she lie?

If receptionist telling truth why C. lying? Check with hotel re meal and walks.

Does C. know area where body found?

If with R.V. was she threatened? Frightened?

He made a note at the bottom – *check restaurants in area for booking.*

Inspector Lorenzini picked up his cap. It was siesta time. He would pay a visit to the hotel later to see if anyone remembered the girl eating there or leaving for her evening walk.

Christabelle took a taxi to the store where Mr Rosmini was the manager and insisted she must speak to him. After a frustrating few minutes Cinzia appeared and made his apologies.

'He is in Rome. What is so urgent?'

Christabelle bit at her lip. She preferred to deal with men. 'I wanted to ask him to explain to the agency why I am leaving.'

'Leaving?'

Christabelle nodded. 'Do you know the terrible thing that has taken place?'

Cinzia shook her head and Christabelle continued.

'The photographer, Roberto, he was found dead a few days ago. He had been murdered. It is so horrible I can't bear to think about it.' Christabelle shuddered dramatically. 'I was due to work for them for another week before I left for Athens. I don't want to stay here any longer. This has spoilt Italy for me.'

'The photographer? Murdered?'

Christabelle nodded. 'Please will you telephone the studios and explain why I am leaving? There is no one there who speaks English well enough now Roberto has gone. I relied upon him so much to help me.'

'When do you leave?'

'As soon as I can book a flight. Tonight, maybe or tomorrow. I was going to visit Venice and Rome, but I've changed my mind.'

Cinzia raised her eyebrows. 'The studios do not know this?'

'They know I am leaving, but not so soon. I would like you to thank them and explain my reason. I've been very happy working for them.'

Cinzia nodded. It was really not her affair. 'I will telephone for you. Also I will telephone Mr Rosmini. I am sure he will understand.'

Christabelle relaxed and smiled. 'Thank you, Cinzia. Please thank Mr Rosmini for all the help he gave me. Without him I don't think I would have been able to find any work over here. I did not realise how difficult it would be, not speaking Italian.'

Returning to her hotel Christabelle placed a call to the airline office and booked a ticket for an evening flight to Athens. Relieved, she telephoned down to the reception and asked them to prepare her bill, which she would pay after dinner that evening and commenced her packing. Tomorrow she would be in Athens. Once there she would have to telephone Bryony and ask her for the address of their relatives on Crete. If the police decided to check on her movements it would add credence to her story. There was even the possibility that her grandmother had died since she had last spoken to her and that would be a bonus in her eyes.

Inspector Lorenzini sat in the hotel manager's office and sipped at the coffee he had been given.

'These are just routine enquiries,' he assured the manager. 'Nothing to do with the hotel; just one of your guests. Miss Christabelle Bartlett, the American woman. She has been staying with you for some months now.'

The manager nodded agreement. 'She is a beautiful young lady, so gracious.'

'I understand she is a model. Unfortunately the young man who photographed her regularly was found murdered a few nights ago, Tuesday, to be precise.'

The manager held up his hands and expressed his horror at the news.

'Are you able to tell me the movements of Miss Bartlett that evening?'

'Surely, you do not suspect her?'

Inspector Lorenzini shook his head. 'I am just trying to clear up some confusion. I was told that Miss Bartlett had arranged to meet the gentleman for dinner. Miss Bartlett insists that she ate here and went for a short walk afterwards. Are you able to confirm that for me?'

'I can try. Give me a moment.' The manager left his office and returned with a ledger containing computer printouts. 'In here we have the number of meals we have served and a record of the room numbers, to make up their bill, you understand. If the young lady paid cash for her meal there will be no record, but if it is to be added to her bill – ah – I have it here. She definitely ate in our dining room.'

'Do you have any idea of the time she took that meal?'

The manager shook his head. 'I cannot say with any certainty. The entries are made after the dining room has closed. There are people entered both before and after her. At a guess I would say between eight and nine thirty, but it is only a guess.'

'The waiter would not remember?'

'He might. He will be on duty this evening. I can ask him and let you know tomorrow.'

Inspector Lorenzini nodded. 'When this young lady went out for her walk after dinner, would anyone have seen her leave?'

The manager spread his hands. 'Maybe, maybe not. It would depend upon the night clerk. If he heard the elevator come down he would have looked up, but if he had been on the telephone or dealing with other guests he would probably not have noticed.'

'What time does he come on duty?'

'He works from eight in the evening to eight in the morning.'

'And he stays awake all night?'

The manager looked pained. 'I have to trust him to do so. I cannot sit and watch him.'

'Of course. I understand. With your permission I will return this evening and ask him myself if he saw Miss Bartlett either leaving or returning. Maybe I could speak to the waiter at the same time?'

'Certainly.'

'Do you have a fire escape?'

'Of course. It is law.'

'Could anyone have returned to their room by that route?'

The manager shook his head. 'It would not be possible. The doors open only from the inside and close automatically. They could leave that way, but certainly not return.'

'Suppose it was wedged open?'

'That is not possible. An alarm would sound and there would be an investigation immediately.'

Inspector Lorenzini finished his coffee. 'Thank you. You've been very helpful. I'll return this evening and have a word with the two men in question; then I shall be able to leave you in peace.'

'If there is anything else we are able to help with, please, do not hesitate.'

'I doubt if we shall need to trouble you again.'

'Elizabeth, that's awful. How long do the doctors say she will take to recover?'

'They can't put a time on it. Apparently Glandular Fever is a strange thing. You feel better only to have a relapse if you exert yourself. It can even come back in future years if you are run down or over tired.'

'What about the rest of you? Are you likely to catch it?'

'They say not. We've all been tested and told we are clear. It's just poor Eleanor. She just has to rest. I've spent hours reading to her and doing puzzles, anything to keep her laying down and not actually doing anything physical.'

'She will recover, won't she?' asked Marianne anxiously.

'Oh, yes, but it can take a long time. We just hope she'll be well enough to return to school in the fall. If she drops behind the others it will stress her and probably give her a relapse. It just seems to be a vicious circle.' Elizabeth sighed deeply. 'We're going to have to cancel our visit to you. The journey would be too much for her at the moment.'

'I'm disappointed, but I understand. Eleanor's health must come first. If she recovers quickly jump onto the first flight you can get. There's always a welcome here for you and we have plenty of space.'

'I appreciate it, Marianne.' Elizabeth's voice was shaky. 'I'm just so worried about her.'

'Of course you are. I would be if it was John. Is there anything we can do from a distance?'

'I'll take advantage of you when I feel really down and 'phone for you to cheer me up.'

'Any time. I do mean that, Elizabeth.'

'I know you do. You're miles away, but you're still my best friend.'

Marianne relayed the news miserably to Giovanni and John. 'I always look forward to seeing Elizabeth so much. The summer won't be the same without them.'

John frowned at his mother. 'Does that mean Nick won't be coming?'

'I told you, Eleanor is ill. They can't come.'

'That shouldn't stop Nick from coming. Surely it would help Aunt Elizabeth if Nick came over here for the whole of her vacation. Aunt Elizabeth wouldn't have to worry about her and could give all her attention to Eleanor.'

Marianne considered her son's proposal. 'I suppose it would be possible. If they would let her fly out on her own. She is only sixteen.'

'Would you let me go over to them?'

'You couldn't possibly go and stay with them. It would be too much for Elizabeth.'

John shook his head. 'I'm not asking if I can go over there. I'm simply saying that if the occasion arose would you let me travel that far alone?'

'I don't see why not.' Marianne frowned.

'That's settled, then. Ask Aunt Elizabeth if Nicola can come out for the whole vacation.' John smiled complacently.

Marianne looked at Giovanni doubtfully. 'Do you think Elizabeth and Nicolas would let her? She could be terribly bored. I won't have the time to keep her amused and I shall need John at the taverna and shop as usual.'

'She can always go up there with him and give you a hand. The rest of the time I'm sure they'll be quite happy together on the beach.'

'Sorted and settled,' beamed John. 'You get back on the phone and speak to Aunt Elizabeth. Once she's agreed I'll phone Nick.'

'You will not! I know just how long that call will be. If Elizabeth agrees you can e-mail Nicola.'

John pulled a face. He and Nicola corresponded regularly, often two or three times a week by e-mail. His parents had forbidden him the use of their telephone after a bill for nearly one thousand Euros arrived and they saw the long calls that had been made to America.

Inspector Lorenzini despatched one of his junior officers to the area where Roberto had been found with instructions to check all the restaurants in the vicinity of the gardens for a booking in the name of Verri for the previous Tuesday evening. It seemed a strange area for a young man to take a lady like the model for an evening out, most of the eating places were little more than snack bars. Maybe the restaurant he had chosen belonged to friends and they had promised him a special meal.

At eight he returned to the hotel. A quick inspection of the dining room showed him that Christabelle had decided on an early evening meal. There was no mistaking her, sitting alone and smiling graciously as other visitors entered. She certainly seemed unconcerned and relaxed.

The night porter tried to be helpful. He had seen the lady in question return to her room from the dining area. She had passed by his desk and smiled at him on her way to the elevator. He thought it was probably about nine, as shortly after that a coach party had arrived as arranged, and he had been busy organising their luggage to be taken to their rooms.

'You didn't happen to notice the young lady leaving the hotel after that?'

The night porter shook his head. 'I was busy. The elevator was going up and down with the new arrivals and their luggage.'

'You didn't, I suppose, see her return later in the evening?'

'I can't be sure. I was very busy until at least ten thirty, but I think I caught a glimpse of her getting into the elevator.'

'What makes you think it was her?'

'She was wearing a bright orange tunic top when she left the dining room. A perfect colour for her; that was why I noticed. As I came out of the down elevator I caught a flash of orange as the doors closed on the up elevator. Once the hotel had quietened down at about ten thirty I would have seen her if she crossed the lobby.'

Inspector Lorenzini thanked the man, asked him to contact him should he remember anything and took his leave. No doubt it was a casual knifing, robbery probably being the motive. That was something he must add to his list. Had the young man been robbed?

Lester flew into Milan and took a taxi to a small hotel. Having checked in he decided that as it was almost the siesta hour he might as well take advantage of the comfortable bed and try to sort out an agenda for the following day. He decided he would try the agency where she was working, spin them a story about doing a promotion on her for when she returned to the States and see what information he could glean. He would then visit her hotel and see if he could pick up on her movements when she was not working.

When he woke a couple of hours later he telephoned the number of the modelling agency and listened to the recorded message. He did not understand a word. Deciding they could still be on their siesta, he tried again an hour later, only to hear the same message. Maybe they had closed early for the weekend. He lay with his hands behind his head. If his wife and children were with him he would have been in his element, as it was, he felt faintly irritated. It was all very well for Rory to say he had a 'feel' about the girl, but as yet there was absolutely nothing that could be directly connected to the accidents and her.

Lester took a taxi to the hotel where he understood Christabelle was staying. He wandered into the reception area and settled himself in one of the seats, hoping the employees who passed him would think he was waiting for a guest. Two hours later there had been no sign of Christabelle and a desk clerk approached him.

'May I help you, sir?'

Lester smiled. 'I'm waiting for a friend. Maybe you could page her for me? Mrs Markham. I don't know her room number I'm afraid.'

'Mrs Markham?' The clerk frowned. 'I do not recognise the name.'

Lester followed him over to the reception desk where he ran his finger down the guest list. 'I'm sorry, sir, we have no Mrs Markham staying here.' He looked at Lester suspiciously.

Lester frowned. 'She must be here. I arranged to meet her this morning and go to the museum. This is the *Roman Palace*, isn't it?'

The desk clerk smiled and shook his head. 'You are in the wrong hotel, sir. This is the *Roman Palazzo*. The *Roman Palace* is further down the road.'

Lester banged his hand on the desk. 'What a fool I am! I'd better get down there straight away. She'll think I've stood her up. Is it right or left from here?'

'Right. About five minutes walk.'

Lester thanked him and left the foyer. There was no way he could hang around the hotel any longer without arousing suspicion. He wandered slowly down the road, wondering how to pass the day before he could return to the hotel for an evening drink.

'So,' Inspector Lorenzini raised his eyebrows. 'Mr Verri had booked a table for two at *Zucchis*. A very strange choice. Did he know the owners?'

'The manager said he had never set eyes on him before. Said the man seemed quite excited, said he was bringing a very beautiful young lady with him and would expect their best.'

'What's this restaurant like?'

The officer shrugged. 'Small, looks clean enough, but nothing special. The menu was pretty unexciting. Plenty of pizza and spaghetti dishes.'

'If you were taking out a young lady, would you go there?'

The officer shook his head. 'There are plenty of much better restaurants in the city.'

Inspector Lorenzini drummed his fingers on his desk. There seemed no explanation for the murder of the young man. His body had shown no trace of drugs and nor had he been robbed.

Lester spent a frustrating weekend. He hung around the hotel as much as he dared without attracting attention to himself. He visited the bar for drinks on the Saturday evening and returned on the Sunday for dinner, but there was no sign of Christabelle. He telephoned Rory on Sunday evening and reported his lack of success.

'Maybe she's moved to another hotel. Try the agency where she's working.'

'I tried them when I first arrived. All I got was an answering machine. I reckon they were closed for a long weekend.'

'She might have gone away if that was so. Probably decided to visit Florence or Venice. See what you can get from them tomorrow and check out the hotel again then. She might well turn up.'

Lester telephoned the agency after eating a leisurely breakfast. To his annoyance he heard the same message in Italian again. Maybe they had changed their telephone number? In desperation he approached the reception desk and asked them to place a call and interpret the message for him. The receptionist obliged and wrote a brief note on his pad.

'The agency is closed until after the funeral,' he announced.

'Funeral? What funeral? What did the message say exactly?'

'The message said the agency was closed due to the unfortunate death of Mr Verri. Out of respect for him they will stay closed until after the funeral.'

Lester rested his elbows on the desk and leaned forward. 'It is very important that I speak to someone from the agency. Do you have any idea how I can contact them?'

The receptionist shook his head. 'I regret you will have to be patient, sir.'

Lester telephoned Rory and reported the information regarding the agency. 'Another unfortunate death. What do you want me to do?'

Rory tapped his teeth with his pen.

'I think you'll have to come out into the open at the hotel where she was staying. See if she has checked out and if they have a forwarding address. Show your credentials if they refuse and say you'll go to the local police.'

'Do you think it's possible that she's on her way back to the States?'

'She could be, but somehow I think it's unlikely. I'm due in court in an hour and will be there for the next week, but you can call me at home in the evening if you have any information.'

Lester strode into the *Roman Palazzo* and up to the desk, relieved that the clerk who had spoken to him before was not in evidence. In answer to the receptionist's query he asked for Miss Bartlett's room to be telephoned and say she had a visitor waiting in the lobby.

The receptionist frowned and consulted the register. 'I regret I cannot do that, sir. Miss Bartlett checked out last Thursday.'

Lester raised his eyebrows. 'Did she give any reason? I understood she was to be here for at least another week.'

The receptionist shook his head. 'I did not check her out. She left in the evening.'

'Did she leave a forwarding address?'

'There is nothing recorded. It is not obligatory.'

'I understand. That does leave me with a big problem. I understood she was working at the Matteoti agency and they are closed until after the funeral of Mr Verri. It is very urgent that I contact her.'

'A moment, please, sir.'

Lester waited until the receptionist returned with the manager. 'I understand you are trying to contact Miss Bartlett? How may I help you?'

Lester heaved a deep sigh. 'I need to speak to Miss Bartlett very urgently. A family bereavement, you understand. I was told she was staying here and working for Matteoti. They are closed and you tell me she has left the hotel. What am I going to do?'

The manager pursed his lips. He did not believe the man's story and he certainly did not want to be involved. 'I can only suggest that you visit the police station. Ask for Inspector Lorenzini. He spoke to Miss Bartlett before she left and she may have given him a forwarding address.'

Lester beamed. 'Do you think that likely? Well, it's worth a try, better than nothing. Can you tell me which station I should go to and how to get there?'

The manager obliged by writing down the address and offered to call a taxi. Mopping his brow, more with relief than the heat, Lester accepted gratefully.

Inspector Lorenzini was surprised when he was told he had an American waiting to see him.

'He will have to wait,' he said. 'I'll be busy for another half an hour. He probably just wants to complain that his wife was harassed or he has lost his camera.' He continued to add to the report on the death of Mr Verri the information he had gleaned regarding the restaurant. He looked at his list and crossed off the last item. It could help if they could find the murder weapon, but so far a search of the area had drawn a blank.

Lester waited in the cool reception area and watched the leisurely activity around him. Nothing seemed to hurry the police in their duties, often two or three of them conferring together, before one returned to continue dealing with the complaint on hand.

Inspector Lorenzini closed the file, drank a glass of iced water, and decided he could not put off meeting the American any longer. Replacing his cap he strode out into the reception area where Lester was pointed out to him.

'What can I do for you, sir? I regret that you had to be kept waiting.'

Lester shook the Inspector's hand. 'I'm hoping you will be able to tell me the whereabouts of a Miss Bartlett.'

Inspector Lorenzini's eyebrows shot up. 'Miss Bartlett? Why should you wish to know where the young lady is?'

Lester took his credentials from his pocket and handed them to the Inspector who examined them carefully. 'Maybe we should talk in my office.' He barked out an order to one of the young officers who nodded and saluted.

Inspector Lorenzini settled Lester into a leather armchair and took his place behind his desk. 'Why are you interested in this young lady? What made you come to the police?'

'The manager at the hotel where she had been staying thought you might be able to help me. He had no forwarding address for her.'

'And you think I may have?'

'He said you had interviewed her, something to do with the death of a Mr Verri?'

Inspector Lorenzini nodded. 'I do have an address for the young lady. Her intention was to move on to Athens.'

Lester smiled. It was a start. 'Are you able to give me any information regarding Mr Verri? I understand he was connected to the Matteoti agency where Miss Bartlett worked.'

'Mr Verri was the photographer at that agency.'

Lester sat forward in his chair. 'Are you able to give me any details of the case? Was his death unexpected? Suspicious?'

Inspector Lorenzini studied the man before him. 'I have seen your credentials, but may I ask what your interest is in this affair?'

Lester considered. The Inspector was more likely to be forthcoming if he thought Christabelle was under suspicion for other deaths that had taken place. 'It will be confidential, you understand?'

'Of course. If it has no bearing on this case I shall simply pass her address on to you and forget our conversation. A glass of water?'

Lester accepted gratefully. 'About eleven years ago Miss Bartlett fell out with a close girl friend. The friend nearly drowned whilst swimming. Miss Bartlett was hailed as a heroine for rescuing her, but the girl told a different story. Miss Bartlett had some photographs taken with the idea of becoming a model. The day after she collected some prints the photographer was found electrocuted. The death was officially recorded as an accident. Shortly before Miss Bartlett commenced work her mother was found murdered. There is a man in custody who denies all

knowledge of the act and I am in Europe on behalf of his lawyer.'
Lester took a mouthful of water. He could see he had the
Inspector's full attention.

'Miss Bartlett became very well known in the States and
decided to visit Europe to promote her career. She worked in
London for almost eighteen months. She decided she would leave
the city and visit France. A colleague agreed to drive her to the
airport and they were involved in an accident. The woman died.
Miss Bartlett worked in Paris for nearly a year before coming to
Milan. In Paris a young model fell to her death shortly after Miss
Bartlett had visited her to say farewell. Now in Milan a young
man, again from a modelling agency, has died.'

'You think Miss Bartlett is involved?'

Lester shrugged. 'I don't know. It could just be coincidence.
There's nothing positive to link her to any of the incidents.'

Inspector Lorenzini switched on his computer and brought up
the file marked "VERRI" that he had been working on. 'According
to our information Mr Verri was assaulted and stabbed. There
was extensive bruising both in the genital region and around his
neck. The evidence from the vertebrae shows that considerable
strength was used to force his head back. There are two stab
wounds to the neck. One wound would have been sufficient to
cause his death through loss of blood. We have conflicting reports
regarding his reason for being in the area. The receptionist at the
agency insists that Mr Verri was taking Miss Bartlett out to dinner
that night and a booking was made in his name at a nearby
restaurant. Miss Bartlett assured us that there must be a misunderstanding. She had agreed to accompany the gentleman to
dinner, but not on that evening.'

Lester raised his eyebrows. 'Her movements for that evening
have been checked out by you, of course?'

'Of course.' Inspector Lorenzini sighed and turned sorrowful
eyes on Lester. How did he think Italian police investigated crime?
'Miss Bartlett ate a meal at the hotel, this is confirmed. She said

she had been for a walk before her meal and another afterwards. According to the meal register she was in the dining room between eight and nine thirty. They cannot be more precise about the time. She was seen by the night clerk when she left the dining room. He thinks that would have been about eight thirty as shortly afterwards some guests arrived and he was then occupied with getting them settled in. No one saw her leave the hotel. The night clerk was still busy with new arrivals, but he thinks he may have seen her just after ten entering one of the lifts. I, personally, questioned the night porter.'

'The knife that was used?'

'As yet it has not been found, but of course, it could be anywhere. We may never find it.'

'And the apparent motive?'

Inspector Lorenzini shook his head. 'There does not appear to have been a motive. I suspected robbery myself, but Mr Verri's wallet was found in his pocket, containing a considerable amount of money.'

'The other deaths seemed motiveless, also.'

'Tell me about these accidents again. Maybe between us we will see something that has been missed by others.'

Lester spent the next hour relating all the information he had about Christabelle and how she had travelled during the years of her career. Inspector Lorenzini continually made notes and when Lester had finished he smiled at him.

'I do not envy you your task. So far there is little to link the deaths. A girl friend nearly drowns, a photographer dies due to an electrical fault. When she left London she took a bouquet of flowers to her employer and again in Paris to a girl she had worked with. She was a close friend of each, yes?'

Lester shook his head. 'On the contrary. She gave the impression to her other colleagues that she did not like either of them very much. She doesn't appear to make friends very easily. Seems to spend most of her time alone.'

'How sad. Why is that do you think?'

'I'm no psychiatrist,' laughed Lester. 'Maybe it's due to her being an only child or maybe she's frightened of rivalry.'

'Maybe indeed.' Inspector Lorenzini nodded his head slowly. 'Surely she would not have expected any rivalry from a young man? What reason would she have to dispose of him?'

'Maybe she let him take a few indiscreet photographs and then he refused to let her have them,' suggested Lester. 'It doesn't fit into her character, but you never know.'

Inspector Lorenzini made another note on his pad. 'I shall ask for all his negatives to be examined from the time that she commenced to work for the agency. You may be right.'

'You think she may have been involved?'

'After the story you have told me I am convinced she is involved. Mr Verri told the receptionist at the Matteoti agency that Miss Bartlett was going out to dinner with him that night. According to her he was most excited. He booked a table at a very poor restaurant close to the public gardens. Hardly the act of a man who was trying to impress a famous model.'

Lester frowned. 'You'll have to forgive me. I don't know Milan at all. How far away from the hotel is the restaurant where Mr Verri made the booking?'

'It would not be a long walk, maybe twenty minutes, half an hour.' Inspector Lorenzini smiled.

'What about a taxi?'

'In view of the story you have told me I am going to ask for information from the taxi drivers. I'm sure that if one of them gave her a ride they would remember her. It will probably take some time for our enquiries to be completed. We have a lot of taxi drivers in Milan, you understand.'

Lester drank more of his water thoughtfully.

'We really need to find two taxi drivers. One who took her to the area of the restaurant, and one who brought her back to the hotel.'

'Of course, although I think it would be hardly likely, if she were involved, that she would ask a taxi driver to drop her at the door.'

'I have some news for you, Mr Harkonen. Would you care to come to my office tomorrow morning? Eleven? Would that suit you?'

Lester agreed with alacrity. He had appreciated his free time and spent most of the day sight seeing. When he spoke to Rory the attorney was annoyed.

'You don't get paid for sight seeing? Why haven't you followed the girl to Athens?'

'I'm waiting for information from Inspector Lorenzini. You never know what he might come up with.'

'We don't want the girl arrested in Italy,' Rory spoke in alarm. 'We need her back here in the States, but with evidence against her.'

'Don't worry. By the time they had the paper work in order to extradite her from Athens she would be back in the States anyway. They certainly won't arrest her without concrete evidence. Imagine the out-cry! All America would be up in arms.'

Rory was forced to smile. 'Just remember that Kurt Schwaber and I are relying on you. Don't get carried away and think of it as a holiday jaunt.'

Lester arrived promptly for his appointment with Inspector Lorenzini and accepted the glass of iced water he was offered. 'So what have you found out?'

'All in good time, Mr Harkonen. The information will not go away. I have had it translated for you.' Inspector Lorenzini handed Lester a closely typed page.

Inspection of negatives – nothing found.
No taxi driver had collected her from the hotel that evening.

No taxi driver had returned her to the hotel.

Taxi driver from the next square had picked up a young lady fitting her description.

She had waved him down. Appeared to be in a hurry.

Dropped her two streets away from the restaurant at approximately nine twenty.

Said the photograph looked like his passenger, but decided he was mistaken.

The girl he took was dressed in an old pair of jeans and tee shirt.

Second taxi driver had picked up a girl who fitted the photograph, wearing jeans and orange tunic top.

Waved down one road away from gardens.

Dropped her half a block from the hotel at approximately ten twenty.'

Pair of jeans, American label, found in parcel in rubbish bin.

'May I keep this?'

Inspector Lorenzini nodded. 'By all means.'

Lester read the information through again. 'How can the taxi drivers be so certain of the times?'

'We have a number of clocks in the city that chime up until midnight. The men also know their routes and the time it will take them, provided the traffic is not too heavy.'

'Do you have the jeans? May I see them?'

'They are with our forensic team. I am hoping they will they will find something incriminating on them.'

'Blood?'

'It would be useful if we found blood and could prove it came from Mr Verri and the jeans belonged to Miss Bartlett.'

'Not proof, though?'

'Not proof that she committed the crime.' Inspector Lorenzini shook his head sadly. 'I am convinced this young lady had a hand in his death. Maybe she lured him there and someone else committed the crime?'

'It's possible, I suppose.' Lester sounded doubtful. 'Well, there doesn't seem any more I can do over here. I'd better get over to Athens and see what she's up to there.'

Inspector Lorenzini copied down the addresses that Christabelle had given him. 'I cannot guarantee you will find her there. She may have decided to move on to the islands. She said she had relatives living on one of them. She also, of course, could have no intention of going there at all, but has returned to Paris or London.'

'Under the circumstances I don't think she'd do that. It's my guess she'll stick to her proposed schedule. A way to convince you of her innocence, she has no reason to run or hide.'

'Good luck, Mr Harkonen. I would be interested to know the outcome of your case.'

'Of course.' Lester handed him a card. 'You can contact me anywhere on my mobile, but I shall return to the States as soon as Miss Bartlett books a ticket.'

The two men shook hands and Lester returned to his hotel to telephone the airlines, pack and pay his bill. He doubted he would be lucky enough to have time to go sightseeing in Athens. Maybe he would be able to bring his wife over to Milan for her fiftieth birthday. It was only another eight years away and he would enjoy showing her the city.

GREECE 2005

Christabelle was not impressed by Athens. The city centre was far smaller than the centre of Milan and although there were fashionable shops they were few and far between. It seemed hardly worth her while to have come to the city as she would not be able to stay long enough to work, but she had needed to leave Italy. Slowly she walked up and down, gazing into the shop windows, gratified when she heard someone mention her name, although she had no idea what was said about her.

After three days of visiting the tourist sights and window-shopping, she decided to leave the smog and heat of Athens behind and make for the islands. She had five more weeks before she must return to the States. Originally she had planned to work in Athens for six months or more and then take a trip to Egypt. Now that would have to wait until a later date. She would fly across to Crete and visit her relatives, then move on and visit some of the other islands before booking a flight back to England and on to America.

With a sigh she telephoned Bryony and outlined her plans, asking for Marianne's address.

'I'm so envious; I would love to go back there again. They live in a most idyllic spot,' enthused Bryony. 'It's out of the town, right by the sea. They even have their own private beach. You'll need to go to Plaka. Unless you stay with them I suggest you find a hotel in Aghios Nikolaos. That's not too far away and very

273

pretty. It's where Aunt Ourania has a wonderful gift shop and Grandma lived when she was a girl.'

Christabelle listened to her, trying to curb her impatience. 'How is Grandma?' she asked finally, remembering that Bryony would expect her to enquire.

'She's fine. Being in *Green Vistas* has given her a new lease of life. Although she had her second hip operation and felt considerably better, it really slowed her down. She has sold her house and the furniture. Now she's settled I'm busy helping her to sort out her papers.'

'What papers?'

'I don't know. She gave me a large envelope the other day and said it was to go into her strong box at the bank. We then sat down and sorted through a whole load of receipts, guarantees and a pile of old letters. She decided to send the letters to the bank. She said they had come from old uncle Yannis years and years ago. Whilst you're at Plaka you ought to go over to see Spinalonga. That's where old Uncle Yannis lived and it's an amazing island.'

'I'll make a note.' Christabelle rolled her eyes. She was thoroughly bored with the conversation and Bryony appeared willing to talk for hours. 'I really must go, Bryony. I have a photo shoot in an hour,' she lied. 'I have to get there in plenty of time for make-up.'

'Of course. I mustn't keep you. I'll 'phone Marianne and tell her to expect you.'

'There's no need ...' The telephone line went dead and Christabelle clicked her tongue in annoyance.

Christabelle landed at Heraklion airport and wrinkled her nose. The island looked unattractive. She took a taxi to a hotel in the centre of the city, deciding that she was not impressed. Heraklion seemed even more polluted and congested than Athens had been. She could not imagine wanting to spend very long here.

The shops in Heraklion were smaller than Athens and they all seemed to be selling cheap tourist souvenirs. Everywhere she turned there were shops selling jewellery, the price tags turned so she could not read them, and she was not at all sure whether the items were real or good imitations. Despondently she returned to her hotel and examined the brochures left in her room advertising the various attractions. A guided tour of Knossos. She ringed the advertisement. She would pay a visit to the site as it was so famous. A day walking the Samaria Gorge. Certainly not. A boat trip to Spinalonga, departing from Aghios Nikolaos. She recalled Bryony telling her about the island. Some old relative had been incarcerated over there as he suffered from leprosy. She might consider a quick visit, provided she did not have to spend too long travelling on the sea. Snorkelling or Deep Diving could be undertaken in certain bays and golf or tennis could be played by those not interested in the sea. Sports were definitely not on her itinerary. They held no interest for her. She would find out where her relatives lived, visit them for the day and move on, probably to Santorini.

The desk clerk was helpful. Plaka was beyond Aghios Nikolaos. The only way to reach there was by bus and she would need to change at Aghios Nikolaos. Few buses went through to Plaka, they mostly stopped at Elounda and from there she would have to take a taxi. Christabelle clicked her tongue in annoyance. Why couldn't her relatives be civilised people who lived in the town?

'How long does this journey take?' she asked.

'The bus will take almost two hours from here to Aghios Nikolaos. I do not know the times of the buses for Elounda. Maybe three, three and a half hours for you to reach Plaka.'

'That is ridiculous. How long would the journey take by taxi?'

The clerk shrugged. She had no idea. She had never travelled that far in a taxi. 'A little less, maybe two and a half or three hours. The alternative would be for madam to spend the night in

Aghios Nikolaos. The journey from there to Plaka then would be no more than an hour.'

Christabelle nodded. 'That sounds more reasonable. Do they have any decent hotels down there?'

'Very good hotels. Very pretty town. Much night life.'

'Book me into the best hotel for two nights. That will be long enough.'

'I will try. The hotels could be fully booked. It is our summer season.'

'I shall expect a room for two nights booked for me by the time I return from Knossos this afternoon. Make sure it has air conditioning,' Christabelle demanded imperiously.

The clerk looked surprised at her attitude. 'I will do my best, madam.'

'I shall retain my room here for when I return. I plan to leave Crete within the week. I would like a taxi booked for ten tomorrow morning to take me to Aghios Nikolaos and that also must have air conditioning. I am not prepared to spend my time sitting in an oven.'

Christabelle found Aghios Nikolaos more to her liking than Heraklion. The journey in the air conditioned taxi had taken just under two hours, giving her time to shower and change before eating lunch. Carefully dressed in white shorts, turquoise blouse and a pair of very high-heeled sandals, she strolled up and down beside the lake, soaking in the admiring glances. To her gratification people obviously knew who she was. She examined the address and instructions that Bryony had given her over the telephone, wishing yet again that she had never mentioned relatives to the Italian police inspector.

Lester arrived in Athens and immediately felt stifled. The heat was as oppressive as in New Orleans. He drank greedily from his bottle of water and mopped his face whilst he waited for a taxi to take him to the hotel he had booked in the centre. His first question when he had made the booking was to confirm that they had air conditioning.

He spent a pleasant evening wandering around the old area and climbing the hill to the Parthenon, hoping he would have the opportunity to visit it properly before he had to leave the city. As arranged he telephoned Rory to say he had arrived and agreed to look for Christabelle the following day.

'I expect I can get a coffee at her hotel, maybe breakfast. If not I'll have to hang around outside until she puts in an appearance.'

'Nothing more from the police department in Milan?' asked Rory anxiously.

'Lorenzini promised to contact me if the tee shirt or knife turned up, but he's pretty doubtful that they'll find them. He seems to be pinning his hopes on discovering some hoodlum she paid to attack the photographer.'

'I rather hope he doesn't find anything until she's back on American soil.'

'The way things are going it won't make much difference. We have absolutely nothing we can pin on her at the moment.'

'I'm hoping that when we confront her with these 'accidental' deaths she may crack.'

'I wouldn't count on that. They could be truly accidental.' Lester spoke gloomily.

Christabelle rose early. Despite the air conditioning she had found the night hot and she had slept restlessly. She showered and presented herself in the breakfast room, automatically attracting preferential service before those who had arrived earlier. She ate leisurely, not looking forward to spending a day with relatives. Despite Bryony's glowing account of the holiday she and Marcus had spent with them they no doubt they lived in a stuffy little hovel in some out of the way spot. She wished she had never found her mother's address book and telephoned Bryony in the first place.

Finally unable to delay her breakfast any longer she returned to her room, donned shorts and a tee shirt over her bikini, placed her towel, sunscreen and some magazines into a beach bag and set off in search of a taxi with a driver who spoke English. She would spend an hour or two sunbathing on the beach before the dreaded visit.

'Where do you want in Plaka?'

Christabelle looked at the address. According to Bryony they spent most of their day up at a taverna. It could be sensible to try there first. '*ANNA'S taverna.*'

'Oh, Giovanni's place. Are you staying there?'

'No, just visiting. Is there a beach nearby?'

'Many beaches. Which one do you want?'

'The nearest one to the taverna.'

'It's a private beach.'

'Fine. It should be less crowded, then.'

The driver shrugged. It was up to her. There was a notice at the top advising visitors that it was private and they faced being prosecuted. To his knowledge the threat had never been carried out, but it kept the beach relatively quiet and secluded for the people who stayed in the self-catering apartments.

Christabelle eyed the beach with satisfaction. There were no more than eight people and no children. A number of beach umbrellas were free and she walked across the hot sand and placed her bag beside one. To make quite sure that everyone on the beach saw her she walked down and wriggled her toes in the water. She had no intention of getting herself wet, but the water was cooling. Slowly she walked back to her umbrella, stripped off her tee shirt and lowered her shorts to the ground. She took a mouthful of water; then opened the magazine she had purchased and began to look through it in the hope that she might be featured in one of the advertisements. Gradually the sun rose higher in the sky and Christabelle adjusted the umbrella to ensure that she was still in the shade, before lying down and closing her eyes. She would have a short siesta; then set about finding her relatives.

John looked appraisingly at the girl lying beneath the umbrella. It could be worth his while to try to get a photograph of her.

'Excuse me, would you mind if I took a photograph of you laying there?'

Christabelle lifted her sunglasses and looked at him coldly. 'Yes I would. People make appointments to photograph me and then they pay for the privilege.'

'Oh!' John was taken aback by her attitude. 'You do realise that this is a private beach and I have the authority to ask you to leave?'

'Really? How are you going to make me leave? Pick me up and carry me? Try putting one finger on me and you'll be in court for assault.' Christabelle replaced her sunglasses.

'This really is a private beach,' persisted John. 'It is only for the people who are staying in the self catering apartments. You could be served with a summons for being here. Let me take your photograph and I'll pretend I didn't see you.'

'I really do not care if you saw me or not. You are not taking my photograph. I'm Christabelle.'

'Hi,' John squatted down beside her and extended his hand. 'I'm John.'

'You really do not understand, do you? I'm Christabelle, the model. No local boy takes a photograph of me to gawp over in their bedroom.'

'It wouldn't be for my bedroom. It would be for the summer brochure for my father's business.'

'Professional photographs have to paid for with a professional fee. Do go away. You're beginning to annoy me.'

'If my father offered to pay you, would you let me photograph you?'

'I might consider it if the price was right.'

'What is the price?'

'One thousand dollars.'

John threw back his head and laughed. 'You must be joking! Who would pay that kind of money for a photograph! Forget it. I'll find someone else who will be happy to have a meal and a couple of drinks.'

'You do so. Just leave me in peace.'

'I can't do that. As I said, you're on a private beach. There's a sign at the top which says trespassers will be prosecuted.'

Christabelle shrugged. 'Then prosecute me.'

John looked at her perplexed. 'The fine for trespassing is one thousand dollars. Let me have the photograph and we'll call it quits.'

'What is the fine for harassment? In the States you can receive a prison sentence. Go away and leave me alone or I'll say you were spying on me as I undressed and assaulted me. I shall have the marks to prove it.'

'You're mad!' John was genuinely amazed at her reaction. 'I don't think my father would want a photograph of a mad woman advertising his accommodation.' John rose to his feet. 'Quite mad,' he murmured as he walked away, turning at the top of the low cliff and focusing his camera very deliberately on Christabelle. He took his time adjusting his zoom lens, whilst Christabelle glowered at him. Finally satisfied he had convinced her he had taken her photograph he raised his hand to her and continued back up the road towards the taverna.

Christabelle was furious. She was sure he had taken a photograph and suspected it was of herself. She was quite unable to settle again. Maybe her relatives would know the young man and she would certainly report him to the police and accuse him of taking photographs of her without her permission. Shaking with anger she replaced her shorts and tee shirt, and began to walk up the beach.

It was only a short walk to the taverna and she sat at an outside table, requesting an iced orange juice and their menu.

'We only serve snacks,' apologised the woman, 'Not full meals.'

'A snack will be quite sufficient,' Christabelle assured her. 'An omelette, salad and bread, please.'

Marianne returned to the kitchen and gave the order to the young girl who was working there. 'Yuk, I hate making omelettes,' she muttered.

'I hate making beds,' Marianne rejoined with a smile as she poured the orange juice and added chunks of ice.

'I hate that too,' Nicola agreed, 'and cleaning showers'.

'You do the salad, I'll make the omelette.'

'Yeah? You're the best.' Nicola beamed at Marianne.

'With a bit of luck she'll be the last customer wanting anything to eat today. You scoot off and meet John. You'll be able to have the afternoon on the beach.'

'Truly? John said he'd take me snorkelling again today.'

'Where is John?'

'Wandering around somewhere with his camera, I expect. You know what he's saving up for? A camera that he can use under water.'

Marianne looked at Nicola in surprise. 'What does he want that for? To photograph the fish?'

Nicola nodded. 'He said that if you go out to Spinalonga around the rocks there are all sorts of interesting fish you don't see around here.'

'Is that where you're going today?'

'I don't know. I leave it up to him. Here, the salad's ready.'

Marianne flipped the omelette over expertly and placed it onto a plate. 'Put that on the tray for me with the other things and I'll take it out.'

Christabelle enjoyed her meal more than those she had eaten in the town, deciding it must be the sea air that made the difference. She mopped her lips with her serviette and signalled to Marianne that she would like the bill. Counting out the Euros carefully and adding a tip she called Marianne back to her again, rather than walking away as was the usual custom.

'I wondered if you could help me. I'm looking for Mr and Mrs Pirenzi. I'm told they live somewhere close by.'

'I'm Mrs Pirenzi,' said Marianne. 'What can I do for you?'

Christabelle studied the woman. She bore no resemblance at all to Bryony and looked decidedly Greek. 'Are you? Do you work here?'

'My husband owns the taverna. We all work here during the season.'

Christabelle raised her eyebrows. She would not have thought that a small taverna serving only snacks would have been busy enough to employ a family. 'I suppose I should introduce myself, I'm Christabelle.'

Marianne frowned. 'Should I know you?'

'I thought my sister, Bryony, had told you about me and might have telephoned you to say I planned to visit.'

'Your sister Bryony? You mean you're that Christabelle? I'm sorry. I didn't mean to be rude. I wasn't expecting you and my brain didn't connect.'

Christabelle smiled easily. 'I presume you are my cousin, yet I can see little likeness to Bryony.'

Marianne sat in the seat opposite. 'I'm pleased to meet you. Bryony told me about you when she and her husband came out for a vacation. She was so happy to have found one of her sisters. She told me you were working in Europe and I asked her to pass on an invitation to visit us if you were ever in Greece. I'd virtually forgotten, what with the summer rush and everything else that has been going on. She said you were a model, that's right, isn't it?'

Christabelle nodded. 'I have been modelling for over ten years. I am very well known in the States and also in Europe. You can hardly open a magazine or walk into a shop without seeing me advertising something.' She pulled a magazine from her bag and thumbed through to a photograph of herself advertising a gold necklace. 'That was when I was working in Milan,' she explained.

'Very nice, and so is the necklace.' Marianne closed the magazine. 'I don't get much time for reading, I'm afraid.'

Christabelle looked at her in surprise. 'Don't you buy magazines?'

Marianne shook her head. 'I pick up an occasional one left by the tourists and flick through those. I never buy them. I'm really only interested in the recipes. So how is it that you are in Crete? Are you modelling here?'

Christabelle shook her head. 'No, I'm really just passing through. I finished my contract in Milan and decided I would go to Athens, then look you up before I go on to Santorini and Rhodes. I shall then return to the States.'

'You'll like those islands. They're so much smaller than Crete; more intimate and friendly.'

'Do you go there often?'

Marianne laughed. 'Goodness, no. I've been to Rhodes once and found it beautiful. We used to go to Italy each year when my in laws lived there. We haven't had the chance of a proper holiday for years. We're just too busy.'

'With the taverna?'

'The taverna and the apartments are a full time job in the summer months. Then we have to do the maintenance and prepare the advertising in the winter. We live with my husband's relatives, Aunt Ourania and Uncle Yannis. They're both in their seventies now, fit and well, I'm pleased to say, but slowing down a bit. My mother in law came back to Crete after she was widowed and lives with us also. Quite a trio to keep an eye on.'

Christabelle looked at the taverna. It certainly did not look large enough to house such a collection of people. 'Where do you live?'

'You will have passed the house if you came from Elounda. It's the one built down by the sea.'

'You mean the big one?'

Marianne nodded. 'We all live there. It's more than big enough for all of us. Uncle Yannis designed it years ago when his old aunt and uncle were alive. They lived up here when this used to be a farmhouse. The family has lived here for generations. Your grandmother used to visit here when she was a girl. It was very different then, of course; just a small village. Gradually the people moved away, mostly after the war, and Uncle Yannis bought up a lot of the land. When Giovanni had his idea about making a self-catering holiday centre here he rented the land from his aunt and uncles. When Aunt Anna and Uncle Yiorgo died they left their land to Giovanni. We still think of it all as being Uncle Yannis's land as no one was ever sure where the boundaries were.' Marianne stopped to draw breath. 'I'll get some more orange juice, unless you'd prefer coffee.'

'Juice would be fine.'

Despite used to being the centre of the conversation Christabelle was interested. This was the side of the family that Bryony had seemed to know very little about when they first met, although she had spoken of them in glowing terms when Christabelle had asked for their address. They certainly seemed to have done well for themselves. She was not sure how many of the small apartments the couple owned, but they spread all along the shoreline and up into the surrounding hillside.

'Do you do all the work up here yourself?' asked Christabelle as Marianne returned with a large jug of juice and glasses.

'I did when we only had two or three, but I couldn't possibly manage it now. I have a dozen girls who come in during the season and do most of the cleaning and change the beds. I spend most of my time up here at the taverna, sorting out the bookings and seeing to whatever the guests want. I'm lucky this year. Nicola has come over for a holiday and is willing to work some of the time. She's the daughter of my friend in America. It's really through her I met my husband.'

Marianne chattered on non-stop, and Christabelle was deciding how she could decently take her leave and escape back to Aghios Nikolaos, when a large car swept round the curve in the road and stopped abruptly. Marianne greeted the driver rapturously.

'Giovanni, look who's here; my cousin Christabelle from America.'

Giovanni strode forward and extended his hand. 'Welcome. I am pleased to meet you.'

Christabelle's heart sank. Now, no doubt he would want to tell her how hard he had worked and how successful he was.

Marianne spoke to him in fluent Greek and Christabelle looked at her in surprise. 'You speak the language?'

'Of course. I was brought up speaking Greek. We both were, but my sister remembers very little now and certainly hasn't passed it on to her boys. Bryony is quite fluent still and had no problem when she was here.'

'It never occurred to me to ask her. I've not been able to see that much of her really. I am always so busy, my modelling career, you know.' Christabelle tried desperately to turn the attention back to herself. 'They have great plans for me when I return to the States.'

She began to elaborate on mythical deals for magazines, commercials and finally films, all of which were in the process of being finalised. 'I'm very well known now, but eventually I shall be a household name throughout the world,' she boasted.

Giovanni said something in Greek to Marianne and she smothered a giggle. 'I'll go and replenish the orange juice,' she managed to say.

John and Nicola lay side by side on a flat rock, soaking up the sun after their swim.

'Stay still, Nick, absolutely still.'

Nicola obeyed and heard the familiar click of John's camera. 'Can I move now?'

'Yes, the way you were laying the sun was shining through the drops of water on your back and making a rainbow of colours. If it comes out well it will be a masterpiece.'

Nicola smiled and closed her eyes. 'So long as you're happy with it.'

John replaced his camera carefully into the carrying case. 'What do you want to do when you leave college, Nick?'

Nicola gave an almost imperceptible shrug. 'I don't know. I could run for President, become a famous film star or be a long distance truck driver.'

John looked at her in amazement. 'You're not serious?'

'Of course I'm not, you idiot. I really don't know. I'd like to be a translator, but my Greek isn't good enough. I'll probably end up doing something with computers.'

'Why do you say your Greek isn't good enough? You're fluent.'

'When I talk I'm fluent, but translating is a different matter. You need to know the official and legal jargon that's used. Besides, they usually like you to have more than one language. I don't even know what you and your father are saying when you speak in Italian.'

John grinned. 'Nor does Mum. That's why we do it. I'm going to be a photographer. I'd like to work for National Geographic and travel the world photographing exotic and rare animals.'

'Now there's a surprise!'

John never travelled without his camera and Nicola had become used to seeing notices on the fridge door warning that there was an insect of some sort in a container inside. John would leave it there until its reactions had slowed with the cold, then remove it and place it where he wished to take a photograph. One he was satisfied with the result he would leave the insect in the sun to recover and go on its way.

'What about getting married and having children?'

Nicola opened one eye. 'Not yet!'

'I mean in the future. I think about twenty five is the right age to get married. By then you're usually established and have some money behind you.'

'I guess so; but why wait until then if you know you're with the right person?'

'It gives you time to gain experience of the world and make sure. No one wants to rush in to marriage and make a mistake.'

'I can understand your reasoning, but why ...'

John cut across her. 'That's settled then. I'm going for another quick swim before we go back. Fancy joining me?' He walked to the edge of the sea.

Nicola shook her head. 'I'm nearly dry. I can just slip my shorts and top over my bikini.'

John bent down and scooped up a handful of water, throwing it over Nicola's back. 'You're not now, so you might as well come in again.'

'You beast!' Nicola scrambled to her feet, but John was gone, striding into the sea before she could catch him. He stood at a safe distance from her and splashed her vigorously as she approached.

'John and Nicola are on their way.'

A cloud of dust could be seen coming along the road and from it emerged a scooter driven by the young man Christabelle had encountered earlier on the beach. On the pillion was the girl with glasses who had served her earlier. They came across and Giovanni introduced them. Nicola smiled, showing the braces on her teeth.

'Wow, fancy really meeting you, and knowing that you're John's relative. Wait 'til I tell them that back at school.'

Christabelle smiled. This was the kind of reception she was used to receiving.

John frowned. 'You're the girl I spoke to on the beach. The one who wouldn't let me take her photograph.'

'Maybe you understand now. I don't allow people to take casual photographs of me, not even for a meal and a couple of drinks,' answered Christabelle tartly.

Giovanni turned to his son and spoke to him in Greek. 'Did you really offer her that?'

'She said she wanted a thousand dollars for a photograph to go in your summer brochure. She was on the private beach and I told her the fine was a thousand dollars and if I took her photo we'd be quits.'

Marianne laughed. 'You are awful, John.'

'No, I'm not. She shouldn't have been there, she's not a guest, and besides, what's a photo anyway?'

Christabelle looked from one to the other of them. She guessed they were discussing the incident on the beach. She felt fury boiling up inside her. He was an obnoxious little boy. She would teach him a lesson.

'May I see your camera?' asked Christabelle. 'It looks very expensive.'

John handed it to her and watched as she turned it slowly in her hands.

'It's certainly a very good one.' Christabelle tripped a clip at the back and the light flooded in across the film. 'Oh, dear, what have I done? I do hope I haven't ruined your snapshots.'

John took the camera back from her. He objected to his photographs being classed as snapshots. 'That was very clumsy of you. Luckily it was a new film that I put in after I left the beach, so there's no harm done.'

Christabelle drew in her breath. She should have dropped the camera and trodden on it, squashed it, ground it to dust.

John hung the camera around his neck. 'I'm going for a shower. I'll see you all later. We'll come down on the bike. Coming, Nick?'

Nicola agreed and they strolled off together, their heads close together as John was telling Nicola something confidential. She drew away from him.

'No! I don't believe it, John.'

'You'll come and eat with us tonight, won't you, Christabelle?' asked Marianne. 'Giovanni can drop you back at your hotel and can return later to collect you. He'll take you back again, of course. You'll be able to meet Uncle Yannis and Aunt Ourania. Giovanni's mother will be there also. She lived in Turin for many years so she'd be interested in hearing about Milan.'

'Does she speak English?' asked Christabelle.

'Goodness, no. She speaks only Greek and Italian. Giovanni can always interpret in either language.'

Christabelle could think of no pressing engagement at that moment to decline the invitation. 'Thank you. I should like that. I really ought to go soon. I shall need to wash my hair as I've been on the beach.'

'Did you swim?' asked Giovanni.

'Oh, no.' Christabelle looked at him in horror.

'The swimming is good around here. You should take advantage of it.'

'I prefer to sunbathe. I am ready whenever it suits you, Giovanni.'

'I'll just wash my hands and I'll be with you.'

'I'll let John know we're leaving now. He and Nicola can lock up.'

Christabelle rose and picked up her beach bag. 'I'll wait by the car for you.'

Swiftly she went over to the elderly scooter that John had ridden earlier. With all her strength she pulled at the brake cable, finally feeling it come away in her hand and she twisted it back so that the damage hardly showed.

John smiled to himself. He had caught her in the act on his video camera.

'We're going now, John,' called Marianne.

'Hold on a second. We've changed our minds. We're coming in with you.' John took hold of Nicola's arm. 'Don't say a word. If she knows I've got her on film she'll try to destroy it again.'

'Take it out, then,' suggested Nicola practically.

'I haven't got a spare.'

'Then leave your video and take your other camera. I doubt that you'll need the video this evening anyway.'

John looked reproachfully at Nicola. 'You never know.'

Christabelle spent a boring evening smiling graciously at the three elderly people who were obviously going to such pains to put her at ease and make her welcome. She could not understand a word they said and had to rely on Marianne for interpretation. Giovanni spent most of the time conversing with his uncle, but John and Nicola said very little. Marianne had given her a conducted tour of the house and she had been impressed by its size and tasteful decoration, although she would not admit it.

'Uncle Yannis and Aunt Ourania live in that wing. Giovanni, John and I live here, and Marisa lives on the other side. Nicola is also staying that side in the guest room. That wing is where Aunt Anna and Uncle Yiorgo lived,' explained Marianne. 'That way we all have our privacy. It also meant that when Aunt Anna and Uncle Yiorgo needed to be looked after there was always someone on hand. They became a full time job for Ourania and me towards the end.'

'What was wrong with them?' Christabelle felt obliged to ask.

'Mainly old age. Uncle Yiorgo had cataracts and was almost blind. He became very senile. He lived in the past, couldn't remember one minute from the next. Would eat his breakfast, leave the room and return five minutes later asking where his breakfast was. We used to laugh amongst ourselves, but it was sad. He worried continually about his sheep.' Marianne shook her head sadly. 'He decided one wet night that he must go and bring them down from the hills. He managed to walk a short distance along the road before he collapsed and I found him lying there soaking wet. He never recovered. Aunt Anna was not quite so bad. She lived in the past a good deal of the time. She continually muddled up our names or forgot them completely. We were never sure if she thought we were her brothers and sisters. She had been a mother to Uncle Yannis and his sister when his own mother died and he was very fond of her.'

Christabelle nodded. 'Mothers are very special.'

'I agree. I didn't like to say anything, Christabelle, but Bryony told me how you found your mother. That must have been quite awful for you.'

'It was. I'd rather not talk about it if you don't mind.'

'I do understand. I just wanted to let you know how we all feel for you.'

'Thank you. I appreciate how kind you were to me today, and all the time you spent telling me about the family. Bryony is going to be very envious of me.' Marianne detected a note of triumph in Christabelle's voice.

'She and her husband are welcome to come and stay again whenever they wish.'

'I really don't think they could afford it,' Christabelle dismissed them. 'I understand they are still paying back the loans they took out for their house although they are both working. And talking of working, I must go. I need my regular beauty sleep or I shall certainly not be working when I return to the States, and you, no doubt, have a busy day ahead of you.'

Marianne agreed. There was something unnerving about this beautiful girl. Outwardly she appeared to be charming, but there was a falseness about her that Marianne could not quite put her finger on. 'Would you allow John to take a family photograph before you leave? I know Aunt Ourania and Uncle Yannis would like a souvenir of your visit and so would we.'

'You mean a family group?'

Marianne nodded eagerly.

'It will stay in the family. It will not be published anywhere?'

'Of course not.' Marianne was surprised. 'You know how we like to have photographs of all the family around us.'

'Would I be able to have a copy? I would like to show it to Bryony.'

'Of course. I could look out a few others for you also. There must be some from Thanksgiving and parties, when we all used to go over to Grandma and Grandpa. If you don't want them I'm sure Bryony would appreciate having some of her sisters.' Marianne frowned. 'Can I look them out later and drop them in to your hotel tomorrow?'

'Of course. I'd be very grateful. Now, where do you want me for this photograph?'

John, accompanied by Nicola, examined his scooter carefully the next morning. 'You see,' he announced. 'She did pull out the brake cable. I was sure she had.'

'Whatever would she do that for?'

'To get her own back on me as she thought I had taken her photograph on the beach.'

'It seems a bit extreme.'

'She tried to ruin my film, but didn't succeed. I'm glad I had changed it, or I'd have lost those other shots. All I lost was the price of a new film.' John photographed both ends of the brake cable. 'Right, now I'll mend it. Mum wants me to take over those photographs later. I'll give her a surprise by arriving safely on my scooter, brakes in perfect working order.'

'I'm coming with you,' announced Nicola.

'Mum will need you here.'

'She'll have to do without me for an hour. I'm not letting you go to her hotel on your own. Goodness knows what she might try next time. You're right when you say she's mad.'

John drew up outside the hotel in Aghios Nikolaos and found Christabelle sitting beside the pool. She looked up in surprise when she saw him and Nicola.

'How nice. I was beginning to think Marianne had forgotten her promise.'

'Mum never breaks a promise,' John assured her. 'Are you planning to sit here all day?' he asked as he handed her a slim envelope.

'Maybe. It's very pleasant here.'

'I thought you might like us to take you out on the boat? We could take you over to Spinalonga. We have family connections there.'

'I'm not very fond of boats. I tend to be seasick.'

'No one could be seasick on a day like this. Your great grandfather was a fisherman. You should have inherited some of his seafaring genes.'

'I don't think I have. No, I'm quite content to stay here for my last day. Did you come down by boat?'

'No, we rode my scooter. It's much quicker than by boat.'

Christabelle's eyes narrowed. She was sure she had broken the brake cable. 'Well, thank you for delivering the photographs, and for the offer of a boat trip. Have a safe journey back.'

'Oh, we will,' John assured her.

Lester took up his position outside the *Greco Palace*. He was grateful that there was an open-air bar opposite. He bought a paper and sat at the table nearest to the road, pretending to read. All morning he sat there, drinking coffee and finally ordering lunch. This really was a total waste of time. Either the girl was staying in her room or was not at that hotel. He would spend a few more hours there; then give up. If he had still not spotted her he would have to approach the hotel management the following day and ask them to page her, using the bereavement story as a cover.

He visited the *Greco Palace* in the evening, hoping Christabelle would be in the dining room and asked if he could have an evening meal, only to be politely refused by the dining room manager. The dining room was open to residents only, but he was welcome to use the bar. He had a solitary drink and returned to his own hotel for a mediocre meal before retiring to his room to try to follow the Greek news on the television.

The following morning saw him at the *Greco Palace* asking for Miss Bartlett. The desk clerk shook his head regretfully at him. 'I am very sorry, sir. Miss Bartlett stayed with us for only one week.'

'Have you any idea where she may have gone? I'm her agent and I have a contract I need her to sign urgently.'

'None at all. She did not say. She was American, so maybe she has returned home?'

Lester shook his head and thanked him. He would consult with Rory and no doubt he would be winging his way to Crete to see if the elusive woman was staying with her relatives.

Glumly Lester packed his bags. He had refused the seat he had been offered on a night flight to Heraklion, preferring to travel the next morning. He would spend one more night wandering around the city that he found just as fascinating as Milan. He telephoned Inspector Lorenzini and told him of his plans.

'The girl has moved on again. I just hope I catch up with her; otherwise I might as well go back to the States now. Have you found the tee shirt or knife?'

Inspector Lorenzini had to admit that neither item had turned up. He also confessed that the crime had been placed in the 'unsolved' file to be dealt with again at a later date when time became available.

'If any new evidence comes to light we shall obviously open it immediately. I'll let you know if that happens. Enjoy yourself in Greece.'

Lester groaned. Enjoy! He begrudged the hours he sat doing nothing, hoping Christabelle would put in an appearance, when he could have been sightseeing or laying on the beach.

Christabelle spent a frustrating time on Santorini. The island was so small and the shopping centre seemed only to sell tourist goods. Within two hours she had walked from the main square in Fira to the end of the town and looked in every shop that sold clothes, accessories and jewellery. She had returned to her hotel and asked when the next flight left for Rhodes, only to be told that she would have to wait for three days, unless she wanted to make a twelve hour ferry trip. Shuddering at the thought, she visited the airline office and booked her ticket for an afternoon flight.

She studied the brochures in the hotel foyer. How was she going to fill her time for three days? She could take a taxi ride to the next village, but she doubted there would be any more to interest her than there was in Fira. Taking a boat trip and walking across the volcanic island in the bay did not appeal to her. Maybe she would take the coach trip they advertised go to Akrotiri. It would be an opportunity to see more of the island and also fill the day.

The coach trip to Akrotiri brought into perspective just how small the island was. From a high point the passengers alighted and almost the whole of the island could be seen. The tourists avidly took photographs, Christabelle moving well away from their lens and skilfully avoiding being part of their picture.

She found the visit to the site of Akrotiri interesting, but hot and dusty. She would have preferred to be alone to wander as she pleased, but was forced to stand and listen to their guide relating the history of the site and its discovery at great length. Relieved when they finally boarded the coach she thought they would now be returning to Fira and she would be able to shower and siesta. After only a few kilometres drive they stopped at a taverna and it was announced that they were expected to lunch there before visiting the wine factory in the afternoon.

Christabelle was annoyed that she had not read the advertisement more closely. She had no interest in visiting a wine factory. She finally tracked down their guide who was eating inside a taverna with the family who owned it.

'Would I be able to catch a taxi from here back to Fira?' she asked.

The guide looked at her in surprise. 'Are you not feeling well?'

'I have no interest in the wine factory. I would prefer to return directly to Fira.'

'I think you will find the factory interesting. They have a spectacular view and an excellent gift shop. You will not be expected to purchase wine.'

'I would still prefer not to visit. Please can you tell me where I could find a taxi?'

'There are no taxis here. You would have to ask for one to drive down from Fira. It would probably be quicker for you to stay with us.' The guide frowned. She was not used to such a request.

Christabelle shrugged and turned away. She obviously had no choice.

She stood by the window in the gift shop and had to admit that the view was spectacular. The expanse of glass gave an unrestricted panorama across the low vines, then over fields and finally the deep blue sea.

So engrossed was she in the view that she did not realise someone had approached her until she felt an arm around her waist.

'You are admiring my view and I am admiring the most beautiful visitor who has ever stood here.'

Christabelle took a step back, away from the encircling arm. 'Excuse me.' She began to walk away, but the man caught her arm.

'Please, I was being complimentary.'

Christabelle looked at the man coldly and walked further away.

'Ladies and gentlemen,' he announced, 'If you would like to follow me, I will now show you where we turn our delicious grapes into even more delectable wine.'

Christabelle trailed along at the rear of the group as they were taken up and down stone steps and were shown where the different processes for making grapes into wine took place. Whichever way they turned the man always seemed to be close to her and able to touch some part of her body. Desperately she tried to avoid him, but to no avail.

On the lowest level stood the enormous vats that held the wine whilst it matured, with a tap at the base to release the fermented liquid into bottles. Their guide released the stop cock to withdraw a small amount of the golden liquid to show to them.

'You would not want to drink this for at least another year. It would taste like vinegar.'

In the room next door there was a conveyor belt where the bottles were stacked for corking and labelling. The visitors seemed inordinately interested in the whole process and Christabelle was pleased that at least her tormentor was forced to stand in front of the group and answer their questions.

She was relieved when they finally returned to the gift shop and she was able to sit at the table where their guide had remained sipping coffee whilst the group had completed the tour.

'Did you find it interesting?' she asked.

'I'm pleased I came. It was very informative. I have decided I shall have to return as I am not sure I understood everything I was told.' Christabelle smiled sweetly at her. 'Does the trip run again tomorrow?'

'It runs every day.'

'Then please book me a seat for tomorrow.'

'Certainly.' The guide looked at her in surprise. What a strange woman. Why would she want to return the following day when she had not wanted to visit in the first place?

Christabelle took a magazine with her to look at whilst on the journey to Akrotiri. She had it carefully folded so that an advertisement featuring her was clearly visible. She did not bother to get off the coach to admire the view of the island and the guide did not urge her to join the others.

At Akrotiri she wandered around the site in the wake of the other tourists, disregarding the knowledge the guide was giving to them. She had heard it only the day before. She lingered over one or two spots that had caught her interest; then would catch up with the group again. When they stopped for their lunch she went for a walk along the coarse, gritty black sand. She needed to think carefully.

In the gift shop she tried to stay in amongst a group of the tourists, but the owner spotted her and gave a wink and a wide smile. She had obviously returned to see him again. He led them through the various passages and into the concrete rooms. Christabelle made sure that she stayed close to the other people until they reached the cellar where the vats of wine were stored and then she dropped back.

As she passed a vat she tried to turn the tap. It was stiff, but she felt it give a little. She dared not wait to see if she had been successful, but moved on and did the same with the next, gratified to see that a few drops collected and began to drip into the trough below. At each vat she turned the stop cock and by the time the party began to mount the stairs she could hear the sound of a faint dripping.

As the group mounted the steps slowly in the wake of the owner she retreated and rapidly pushed two taps into the 'on' position, hearing the wine begin to gush out. Dreading that it would begin to splash over her sandals or the owner would hear and return, she hurried to the steps and emerged with everyone else into the gift shop.

The owner was kept occupied by the tourists and their purchases, Christabelle leaning on the end of the counter and smiling encouragingly to him each time he came close. She finally pointed to a small book.

'I would like that, please.'

'I'm afraid we only have that in German at present. We are waiting for our delivery. It should be here tomorrow. Maybe I could bring it to your hotel?'

Christabelle shook her head. 'How very kind of you to offer. I regret that I am leaving tomorrow.'

'Maybe there is something else I could show you?'

'I think not. I wanted that as a gift for a friend.' Christabelle turned her back and walked over to where the guide was waiting. 'Are we leaving now?' she asked.

'If everyone is ready.'

'Well I certainly am.' Christabelle had achieved her objective for the visit and was quite ready to leave before the owner returned to the lower floor and found the damage that she had inflicted.

Lester stayed the night in Heraklion. He had decided it was pointless to go chasing half way down the country in the evening to try to find the relatives Christabelle was supposed to be visiting, besides, it was an ideal opportunity for a visit to Knossos during the afternoon. He passed an enjoyable three hours and ate at the taverna opposite, sitting there until it was quite dark.

'What time does the bus come?' he asked.

'There are no more buses tonight. You will need a taxi.'

Inwardly cursing, Lester asked for one to be called, and was not at all sure that the driver took the quickest route back to his hotel as the return journey certainly had taken considerably longer than the bus. He handed over his Euros reluctantly and did not give the man a tip.

He decided it was too late to call Rory, and as he had nothing of interest to report, he would wait until the following day. He pulled his book from his case and settled down to read. A rare luxury; usually restricted to when he was on an aeroplane. When you were supposed to be watching for someone you could hardly read the book you were holding in your hand.

Lester enjoyed the bus journey down to Aghios Nikolaos and booked into a small hotel. Again he decided it was too late to start yet another journey of indeterminate time to find where Christabelle's relatives lived.

He wandered around by the lake, gazed in the shops and ate at a taverna like any ordinary tourist. He asked for directions to

Plaka from the hotel and decided he would once again take a bus. He was enjoying the scenery and he doubted if a few hours either way would make any difference to finding the whereabouts of Christabelle Bartlett.

At Elounda he found his journey was terminated and he had the choice – a long, hot walk in the sun or the local taxi, alternatively he could wait for a couple of hours until the bus that served the self-catering apartments went through. He chose the taxi, remembering to ask him to put his meter on as he got in.

'Where you want in Plaka?'

'The taverna,' answered Lester firmly. The place was sure to have one, however small, and it was a good starting point for finding people. The driver nodded and took off at a fast pace along the winding road.

Clutching alternately at the seat and the seat belt, Lester was relieved when they arrived and was pleasantly surprised by the immaculate small building. He took a seat beneath an umbrella and asked for a beer, being even more surprised when the girl spoke with an obvious American accent. He sipped at his glass appreciatively. This was a pretty spot. Having spent most of the summer months in the cities he relished the opportunity to be beside the sea, if only for a few days.

The girl passed by to serve another customer and Lester stopped her.

'Another?' she asked.

'Maybe later. Do you know where I can find Mr or Mrs Pirenzi?'

'Mrs Pirenzi is in the kitchen,' she replied, laughing at him.

'Would I be able to see her? I have a couple of questions I need to ask her.'

Nicola frowned. The man was certainly not Greek. Maybe he was from a travel firm. 'I'll ask her to come out when she's free.' She turned on her heel and left him wishing now he had asked for another beer.

Lester studied the other customers in the taverna. They all looked as if they had just left the beach, sporting their suntans, with only shorts or a sarong over their swimsuits. He felt a pang of envy. It must be good to go away on holiday with your family and know that no one would page you with an urgent job. The girl went backwards and forwards with plates of food, and Lester managed to catch her eye and indicate that he was ready for a second beer. To his surprise a young man brought it out to him and sat in the vacant seat opposite.

'Am I able to help you?' he asked. 'My mother is cooking for this crowd at the moment. She probably won't be free for another half an hour or so.'

'You are?'

'John Pirenzi.' John held out his hand. 'Nick said you wanted Mr or Mrs. My father's not here this morning and I wondered if I could be of any help.'

'Maybe. I'm from the States, as you've probably guessed. I'm trying to track down Christabelle Bartlett. I understand that she planned to come to visit you.'

'Who told you that?'

'Oh, friends of hers,' replied Lester airily.

'Why are you looking for her?'

'I've got a contract sitting in my pocket. I need her signature as soon as possible,' lied Lester glibly.

'So how come you don't know her address?'

'She's been moving around. I can't seem to catch up with her.'

'Why didn't you try sending a Fax to her hotel?'

'We tried, but we kept missing her. You don't happen to know where she's staying over here?'

John shook his head. 'She was at the *Nicolas Hotel* in Aghios Nikolaos, but I don't think she's there now. She was talking about going on to Santorini and Rhodes.'

Lester sighed. 'I guess I'll have to trail over to those islands and see if I can find her.'

'I doubt if you'll manage it. They're full of tourists at this time of the year. She said she was returning to the States in a few weeks. I suggest you wait until she gets back.' John rose. 'I'll ask Mum if she left a forwarding address.'

John returned to the kitchen where his mother was removing a pizza from the microwave. 'I've just spoken to that man. He's American. He wondered if you had a forwarding address for Christabelle; says he has a contract for her to sign.'

Marianne raised her eyebrows. 'If what she was saying were true, and I have no reason to doubt her, he probably has. She didn't give me any addresses, not even in the States. See if he wants anything to eat, will you?'

John returned to where Lester was sipping his beer. 'Mum says would you like anything to eat?' He handed Lester the typed menu and waited. 'The calamari is good. I caught it yesterday.'

'You caught it?'

'I was out by the rocks and saw a couple. I decided they would look better on a plate.' John grinned.

'Are you a fisherman?'

'No. I was just swimming around and took advantage of them.'

'I'll take a chance as you say it's fresh. What does it come with?'

'Salad and bread. I'll tell Mum. By the way, Christabelle was only staying at the *Nicolas Hotel* in Aghios Nikolaos for a couple of nights and then returning to Heraklion before going on to the islands. She didn't give Mum any forwarding address.'

'Thanks.'

Lester took out a pad from the pocket of his shorts and wrote down the name of the hotel. John continued to weave his way through the tables, replenishing drinks, handing out bills and collecting the money. He placed Lester's meal before him and retired to a small table at the side, all the time watching Lester, who would eat a mouthful of food and add a note to the pad beside him. When the man finally wiped his plate with his bread, John approached him.

'How was the calamari?'

'The best I've ever had,' replied Lester truthfully.

John sat down in the seat opposite him again. 'A lot of places serve up the frozen stuff. It doesn't have the same flavour. Would you like another beer?'

Lester nodded. 'I'll need to use your rest room.'

'Over there.' John pointed and watched until Lester disappeared through the doorway.

Once Lester was out of sight, he rose and went to the other side of the table to read what the man had been writing down. There were the dates Christabelle had entered and left the various countries and the hotels where she had stayed. Beneath that were names and the dates when their death had occurred and the subsequent conclusion. Inspector Lorenzini's private telephone number was also recorded.

John flipped over the page and read the notes Lester had made recently.

'Nicolas Hotel – Aghios Nikolaos'
'Boy said planned to move to Santorini and Rhodes'
'Has she left? – Find out.'
'If left phone Rory for instructions.'
'Go straight to Rhodes?'
'Ask immigration for help?'
'Require her to register name of hotel?'
'Hold her on technicality?'

John flipped the pad closed and moved away from the table as Lester exited the toilet, but not before Lester had noticed. He frowned in annoyance. He should have taken it with him.

'What do you think you're up to? That's private.'

John raised his eyebrows. 'I just wanted to check something out. You see, I don't believe your story about having a contract for Christabelle. What do you really want her for?'

Lester looked at him in exasperation. 'That's none of your business.'

John looked at him levelly. 'I think you're something to do with the police. If she's in trouble I could probably give you some evidence that would help.'

Lester looked at him scathingly. 'Assuming I am something to do with law enforcement, what could you possibly have that would help me?'

'A video of a certain person snapping the brake cable on my scooter.'

'What!'

John nodded. 'How about you settle your bill and we go and have a quiet chat?'

Lester nodded slowly. 'How much do I owe?'

John returned to the kitchen with the Euros. 'I'm giving the American a lift to Elounda. I'll call in on Uncle Yannis and Aunt Ourania. Is there anything you want me to take down?'

Marianne frowned. She was relying on her son to clear the tables as they became vacant and load the dirty dishes into the machine. 'Are you able to finish up here first? I need some help today.'

'I'm sorry, Mum. He needs to go now. It's rather important. I'll explain later.'

John exited swiftly before his mother could detain him and raced up to his room to fetch his video. He grinned at Lester as he led him towards his scooter.

'This is the best I can offer in the way of transport, I'm afraid. I have mended the brake cable. It's quite safe.'

Lester looked at the elderly machine dubiously. 'Are you old enough to drive this?'

John shook his head. 'Not officially as I haven't taken my test yet. Provided I only go along this coast road as far as my uncle's house no one will stop me. Strictly speaking it's a private road, for the use of people staying in the accommodation.'

'How long have you been driving?' asked Lester suspiciously.

'Since I was twelve. You'll be quite safe, I promise.'

Lester perched himself on the pillion seat and put his arms around John's waist. 'Take it steady. I'm not used to being a passenger on one of these things.'

John did drive steadily and Lester had just begun to enjoy the experience when John cut his speed dramatically and swung the machine off the road and onto a driveway.

'Wait here for a couple of minutes. I'll be back.'

Lester stood and looked around. A palatial villa stretched along the side of the bay, on the landward side was a landscaped garden and overlooking the sea was a wide patio. Lester drank in the view, a large island gave shelter to the bay, the turquoise sea was dotted with small craft belonging to holidaymakers and towards his right he could just see the small marina at Elounda.

John returned; bottles of beer and glasses in his hand and beckoned to Lester to follow him. He skirted the house and they walked onto the patio, selecting an umbrella and table at the far end.

'If you find it too hot here we can go into the gardens where it's shady,' he offered. 'I brought out a beer, there's wine if you'd prefer it.'

'Beer's fine,' agreed Lester. 'Is this a hotel?'

John shook his head. 'This is where we live. The house belongs to my aunt and uncle, but we all live together in different apartments that interconnect. Uncle Yannis built it that way when he had his old aunt and uncle to look after. They lived down at the taverna and he lived in Aghios Nikolaos. He was forever being called over to them, so decided this was the solution.'

'Is it all right for me to be here?' Lester had an idea that an armed guard would accuse him of trespassing at any moment.

'Of course. I told you, I live here. I can bring back whomever I please. I told Uncle Yannis you were here when I went in for the beer, just out of courtesy, you know. He'll probably come out at some point just to say hello, which is an excuse to look you over and make sure you are not leading me astray.'

Lester smiled at the self-confident young man. 'Where did you learn your English?'

'My mother, mainly. She's American Greek; my father's an Italian Greek.'

'Do you speak Italian?'

'Not according to Dad.' John grinned. 'But I can get by.'

Lester nodded and took a mouthful of his beer. 'I'm Lester Harkonen, by the way. What was it you wanted to tell me?'

John gave him a measured glance. 'I'd like to ask you a few questions first. For all I know you could be Christabelle's ex, trying to track her down, or a hit man carrying out a contract.'

Lester laughed. 'You've seen too many American films. I'm neither of those.'

John pulled a face. 'Shame. I was hoping you were a hit man.'

'I gather you were not impressed by the lady when you met her?'

John shook his head. 'I wasn't, but I'd still like to know exactly what your interest is in her before I tell you anything.'

Lester sighed and pulled his official identification from his pocket, handing it over to John in the leather wallet. John read it carefully. His eyes shone. 'This is exciting. You're a private eye!'

'That's just between you and me.'

'I can tell Nick, can't I? After all, she saw what I saw.'

'Who's Nick?'

'Nicola, the American girl at the taverna. We're kind of related. Her sister's sick so her parents couldn't come as they'd planned, so she's spending the summer out here; a working holiday.'

'We'll talk about that later. Tell me about this brake cable that you say was broken deliberately.'

John drank half his glass of beer. 'I'd better tell you what happened on the beach first.'

He related to Lester his encounter with Christabelle and her reaction when he had wanted to take her photograph. 'I couldn't believe it when she turned up at the taverna and was a relation.

She then ruined the film in my camera. It was quite deliberate; she opened the back to let the light in. I told her it didn't matter as it was a new film.'

'What was her reaction to that?'

'She looked furious. I think she damaged my scooter to get her own back on me. Maybe she didn't know it was the brake, just thought she'd pulled a cable out and I wouldn't be able to start the thing.'

'You said you had a photograph of her doing it.'

John nodded. 'I said I was going in for a shower. It was really an excuse to take a video of my parents sitting out there talking to her. I knew they'd like to have a photograph and I thought it unlikely she would let me take one of her. I was just about to put it away when Nick came over to see what I was doing. My parents said they would get ready to go down to Elounda and left her alone. She immediately rose from the table and walked over to my scooter. I was a bit intrigued and kept on filming. She deliberately pulled out the brake cable. She must be pretty strong. It's not an easy thing to do. By the time my parents came back out she was standing by the table.'

'Any chance of me seeing this film?' asked Lester.

John tapped the video that hung round his neck. 'I've got it with me. You'll have to see it through the viewer. I've not had it developed yet.'

'So what happened after that?'

'I called out to my mother that Nick and I had changed our minds and would come down here in the car with them. We usually come back down on the scooter; then it's here ready for the next day. We drove down here and Dad dropped us off whilst he took Christabelle into Aghios Nikolaos to her hotel. He collected her again later and we all had a meal together. She said she planned to leave the following day.'

'Did you see her again?'

John nodded. 'Mum agreed to look out some old photographs

of the family and I said I would drop them down to her the next morning. I mended my scooter and Nick and I went down together.'

Lester raised his eyebrows. 'I thought you were not supposed to ride off the private road?'

John grinned. 'I drive carefully, don't draw attention to myself by doing anything stupid and no one has stopped me yet. I'm due to take my test next month anyway.'

'So you went to the hotel to pass on these photographs?'

'She was sitting by the pool, making sure everyone could see her. We offered to take her out in the boat, a visit to the island, but she refused. She must have read my mind. I'd planned to give her a soaking! She asked if we had come down by boat and I told her we had used the scooter. She even had the nerve to wish us a safe journey back.' John swallowed the rest of his beer. 'Fancy another?'

Lester nodded absently and waited until John returned. John handed him another bottle and sat back in his chair. 'So now you tell me why you're looking for her.'

Lester considered. 'I can't go into detail, you understand. Let's just say that tragedy seems to follow the young lady around. A number of people that she has known have been involved in fatal accidents.'

'I bet she did it. I said she was mad when I met her on the beach. I suppose I was to be another fatal accident!'

'It's a possibility,' agreed Lester.

John removed his camera from around his neck and switched it on. He pressed the rewind button until he reached the small section that featured Christabelle and handed it across to Lester.

'See what you think. You can just about hear the sound. Press that button if you want it to stop.'

Lester screwed up one eye and looked through the viewfinder. The picture was of a typical holiday scene of two women and a man sitting beneath an umbrella at the taverna. The man rose, announcing he was going to wash his hands and the woman followed, saying she would tell John they were off and ask him to lock up when he left. The frames clearly showed Christabelle going over to the scooter and pulling the brake cable loose and twisting it back so that a casual glance would not detect the damage.

Lester handed the camera back to John. 'Can you rewind it? I'd like another look.'

John obliged and this time Lester froze the frames where Christabelle was at the bike and studied them carefully.

'I would say that was pretty deliberate sabotage,' he said finally. 'If she had done it accidentally she would have looked shocked or guilty; as it is she looked pleased and triumphant.'

'I wish I'd taken the look on her face when I told her we had arrived at her hotel by bike. She obviously couldn't believe it. Why would anybody be so vindictive over a photograph?'

Lester shrugged. 'It's beyond me. Would you be able to get this printed up and get a copy for me? I'd pay, of course.'

'On one condition,' John smiled at the man before him. 'Tell me about the other accidents.'

Lester tipped the remains of his beer backwards and forwards in his glass whilst he considered.

'I'll get you another.'

John retreated to the kitchen and returned with another beer, but this time he had water for himself. 'Don't want to be picked up for driving over the limit,' he grinned. 'Well? Tell me.'

Lester shook his head. 'I can't. Part of the job of being a private detective is being confidential.'

John looked disappointed. 'Nothing I can say will make you change your mind?'

'Nothing,' said Lester firmly.

'Oh, well,' John shrugged. 'It was worth a try. I'll drop you down in Elounda when you're ready and take this film in to be developed. Where are you staying? I could bring it in to you tomorrow.'

Lester wrote down the name of his hotel and John pocketed the information.

Lester calculated the remaining days that Christabelle had before returning to the States. He decided that if she had visited Santorini as she had intimated she would probably have left the island by the time he arrived. He sighed and made some more notes on his pad. He would have to speak to the immigration department and ask them to detain her on a technicality if she arrived on Rhodes, they would then be able to make her register the address of the hotel where she planned to stay and he would have a starting point. He telephoned Rory, telling him about the video film, and also his plan for travelling directly to Rhodes.

'Buy yourself a video camera. It could be invaluable. You can pretend to be a tourist. There will be hundreds of people there filming.'

'She's hardly likely to do anything suspicious if she knows there are people filming,' protested Lester. 'Besides, I've never used one.'

'Get the boy to give you a few lessons. It's not difficult. I'm relying on you, remember, so is Kurt Schwaber; and the time is getting short.'

John arrived on his scooter at the appointed time with the processed film and handed it to Lester. 'There's no need to return it. I got them to make a copy.'

'I'm not likely to lose it,' protested Lester.

John shrugged. 'Look on it as a safety precaution for you. Actually I want what is on the beginning of the reel.'

'How much do I owe you?'

'A beer.'

'Come to think of it, if you're not legally old enough to ride a scooter, you're not legally old enough to drink.'

John grinned cheerfully. 'I've been doing that since I was ten,' and signalled to the bar tender.

'Actually, I've another favour to ask of you. My boss has asked me to go straight to Rhodes. He also wants me to buy a video camera and get instructions from you how to use it. Can you take me to a camera shop and choose something simple for me?'

John looked at him doubtfully. 'Have you never used one?'

Lester shook his head.

'It's not that easy for a novice. It takes practice to be able to zoom in and adjust controls without having to break off from filming and look at what you're doing. The first few reels of mine are appalling; a lot of shots of my feet and the paving stones. How long do you have to learn?'

'I ought to leave tomorrow if I can get a flight. If Christabelle runs true to form she won't stay in Santorini more than a week. I need to be there at least a day before her so I can contact immigration and get them to find out where the girl plans to stay.'

'You speak Greek?'

'No.'

'You're going to have a job on your hands.'

'They must speak English over there.'

'Oh, they do,' John assured him 'when it suits them. They'll keep you hanging around for days waiting to see the right person.'

'What do you suggest, then?'

'That I come with you.' John sat back with a pleased smile on his face.

Lester burst out laughing. 'You're not serious.'

'I'm quite serious. I can negotiate for you in my mother tongue and do all the filming for you. It makes sense.'

'Your parents would never agree.'

'Of course they would. You work for National Geographic and your photographer has gone sick. They wouldn't deny me such a wonderful opportunity.'

Lester shook his head. 'The girl knows you. She'd immediately suspect something and be on her guard.'

John leaned forward. 'I can assure you that even my mother would not know me. Christabelle has seen me in shorts and a tee shirt. She hasn't seen me as a hippy tourist and wearing a hat. I'll speak only in English and call you Dad.'

Lester was forced to smile at the young man's enthusiasm, but he shook his head again. 'I couldn't take you up on your offer without consulting my boss.'

'Then 'phone him. Get the okay from him for me to go with you and also for you to tell me what this is all about.'

'Why are you so keen to come? Do you have ambitions to become a private detective?'

John shook his head. 'I want to make underwater films. After what that girl did to my scooter I'd like to get my own back. It's what could have happened to Nick that worries me. She often uses the bike. Just imagine how my mum would have felt if anything had happened to her best friend's daughter.'

'Did you tell your parents about the brakes?'

'I didn't see the point. Luckily there was no harm done. Thank goodness it was me that upset her. Had they done so she would probably have come back and torched the taverna!'

'I hadn't thought of that,' Lester frowned. 'If she does recognise you, she could well come back here and exact some sort of revenge on them.'

John shook his head firmly. 'I guarantee that she won't know me. You make that 'phone call. Once we've spoken to my father I'll get on to the airport and book a flight then I can get packed.'

Marianne shook her head vehemently. 'There is no way he can go off alone with this man. We don't know him. He could be a paedophile and we'd never see John again.'

'John seems to think it's the opportunity of a life time for him.'

'I can't help what John thinks. The answer is still no. If you're not prepared to tell him, I will.'

'Calm down, Marianne. I agree with you. He can't possibly go off to Rhodes with a stranger. I'd be unhappy about him going up to Heraklion with him. I'll go and explain that John is far too young to go away without either of us escorting him.'

John glared at his father as Giovanni sat and calmly explained that neither parent was happy about the proposed trip.

'It's very important, Dad. I really need to go.'

Giovanni shook his head. 'Your mother and I have said no and that's an end of the matter. Goodbye, Mr Harkonen.'

Lester rose. 'Maybe I could have a few words in private with you.'

Giovanni shrugged. 'If you wish, but it will make no difference to our decision. Go and help your mother, John.'

Sulkily John rose. He had been so excited about the prospect of helping Lester Harkonen.

Lester mopped his forehead. 'I understand all your misgivings, Mr Pirenzi. I can assure you I have no evil intent whatsoever towards your son. I'm married with children. I know that makes no difference to some sick people.'

He held up his hand as Giovanni was about to interrupt. 'Please, hear me out. You can check on my credentials with the police. I am nothing to do with National Geographic Magazine. I'm actually a private detective.'

'Why didn't you say that in the first place?'

'In my line of business you don't tell people your true occupation unless it's strictly necessary. I can't go into the details of the case I'm working on, of course, but an innocent man's life hangs in the balance. I am trying to catch up with a certain person and make a record of their activities. When I spoke to my boss in the States he suggested I bought a video camera. I've never used a video. I spoke to John, who I understand is a keen photographer, and he says it takes quite a bit of practice. I haven't the time. I need to be in Rhodes as soon as possible and I doubt if I shall be there for more than a week, ten days is the most John would be away. He can telephone you to let you know where we are staying and call you regularly to reassure you that all is well.'

Giovanni looked doubtful. 'How would I know it was the police I was speaking to? You would give me the number.'

'John tells me you speak Italian. I made the acquaintance of Inspector Lorenzini in Milan. I can give you the number of the police station there and you can ask to speak to him. He will assure you that I am genuine.'

Giovanni glanced behind him to where Marianne was watching him from the taverna. 'If we did agree to him accompanying you to Rhodes, you wouldn't be going into the red light district?'

Lester shrugged. 'I can't say for certain as I have no idea where it is. I certainly wouldn't envisage that we would have occasion to go there. I'm sure the person I'm interested in would only be visiting the usual tourist attractions.'

Giovanni pulled his mobile phone from his shirt pocket. 'Give me the number of the police station.'

John arrived at the hotel in Aghios Nikolaos where Lester was staying, a holdall strapped to the back of his bike and looking no different from the young man Lester was acquainted with.

'I thought you said she wouldn't know you?'

'I'd rather be conventionally dressed going through the airport. I don't want to be stopped and searched. Besides, you want to speak to immigration and they'll take more notice if I pass myself off as your assistant. I have to be decently dressed to do that. As soon as we reach our hotel I'll change. Have you booked anywhere?'

Lester shook his head. 'There seem to a fair number of hotels in Rhodes Town. Seems to be the only place of any size.'

John nodded. 'When we arrive I'll ask a taxi driver where he recommends. It's early in the season, we should have no trouble finding a vacancy somewhere.'

'What happens at the end of the season?'

'Everything closes down. The tourists go home, a good many people go over to Athens to find work, and it rains.'

Lester looked at him in disbelief. 'Rains?'

'You might not believe it now, but by the end of October you'll be carrying an umbrella whenever you go out. We ought to make a move. We don't want to miss this flight or we'll be waiting all day for the next one.'

Lester could hardly believe the ease with which they passed through the formalities at the Heraklion airport and again when they arrived in Rhodes.

'Right,' said John, 'Now we want the immigration authorities.' He looked around the airport. 'I'll start with the security girl over there.'

John held a long conversation with the attractive young Rhodian girl. They seemed to be laughing and joking like old friends by the time John shook her hand and returned to where Lester was waiting.

'We need to go upstairs and speak to the security police. She also gave me the name of a good hotel, run by her aunt.' John winked. 'We could do worse. At least I know where to come and complain if we're not satisfied.' He led the way up the stairs and along a passage until he came to a room marked 'SECURITY' where he stopped and knocked deferentially before opening the door.

John spoke to the man inside in Greek, who frowned and looked doubtfully at the two men before him. 'Show him your credentials, Lester. I'll do the talking.'

The security officer examined Lester's papers minutely, demanded to see his passport and John's, despite both having been cleared to enter Rhodes. Finally he nodded and, to John's relief, agreed to alert the airport. If Christabelle entered the country they would have instructions to obtain details of her proposed accommodation but nothing more.

John steered Lester back down to the main body of the airport. 'Now for the hotel.'

'Shouldn't we visit the port and put out an alert for her there?'

'I think it unlikely that she'll use a ferry or hydrofoil. She told me she wasn't a good sailor.'

'I still think we should cover them.'

'If you say so. We've plenty of time. We'll go to the hotel first, book some rooms, then I can 'phone back here so that our friend upstairs knows where to contact us.'

Lester followed John out of the airport and climbed into a waiting taxi, giving the driver the address of the hotel. Lester looked around in interest as they drove towards the main town. This island was very different from Crete.

'Do you know your way around?' asked Lester.

'No,' replied John cheerfully. 'I've never been here before. We'll pick up a map and do some exploring on our own. The first flight in from Santorini is due tomorrow morning; the second is three thirty in the afternoon. I can't see Christabelle getting up at the crack of dawn to make an early flight, so we should have at least twenty-four hours before she arrives.'

'Unless she's already here or decides not to come,' said Lester despondently.

'According to your reckoning she couldn't be here yet. There's only one flight day a week from Santorini to Rhodes. She would have had less than a day on the island if she were here already.'

John booked himself and Lester two separate rooms at the small, unpretentious hotel in the centre of the newer part of Rhodes Town.

'I'll get myself sorted and see you in about an hour. I suggest you find the nearest place that sells a map and start looking at it. Mum and Dad came here a few years ago and said the Old Town was a rabbit warren. Fascinating, but easy to get lost! There's a bar downstairs. You can sit and have a beer whilst you study it.'

John retired to his room and found his scissors and razor. He ran his hand across the stubble on his chin, having deliberately refrained from shaving before leaving home. Taking up the scissors he cut his hair as short as possible and then began to run the razor across his head until nothing remained of his dark curls. He studied the effect in the mirror, pleased at the unfamiliar face that stared back at him.

He stripped off his tee shirt and began to place the henna tattoos onto his arms. He waited for them to dry before changing from his shorts into a pair of jeans and replaced his shirt with a vest. He flexed his arm muscles tentatively and grinned to himself. His mother would have a fit if she could see him now! He donned a pair of reflective sunglasses that hid his eyes completely and picked up a baseball cap, turning the peak towards the back of his neck.

Arriving in the foyer of the hotel he could see Lester sitting at a table, a beer at his elbow and a frown of concentration on his face as he studied a map of the island. Ignoring the man, John took a table opposite and ordered a beer from the waiter. Lester gave him a cursory glance and returned his attention to the map. John smiled to himself. If Lester did not recognise him it was hardly likely that Christabelle would do so.

Picking up his glass he walked over to Lester's table. 'Do you mind if I join you?'

Lester looked up in surprise. 'I'm waiting ….. John! What the devil have you done to yourself? I didn't recognise you.'

'Good. That was the idea. Nothing is irreversible.' John removed his cap. 'My hair will grow back pretty soon and the tattoos only last about six weeks before they wash off. A quick shave and the stubble will have gone.'

'What will your mother say when you go back?'

John shrugged. 'What can she say? It's done. I've called home to say we are safely here and where we are staying. I've also 'phoned he airport and spoken to Mr Tasamados and given him this address. He's promised to 'phone the hotel when Christabelle decides to arrive. Now, I think I'm entitled to know exactly why you are trying to find Christabelle.'

Lester had been waiting for John to start to question him. 'She had a disagreement with a school friend and the girl nearly drowned when they went swimming together. She had a portfolio of photographs done in the States and the day after she collected some reprints the photographer was found dead. Accidental death, there was a fault on his kettle. She accepted a lift from a woman at the modelling agency in London and during their drive the woman made an emergency stop and the steering wheel pierced her chest. She died on the operating table. One of the models she had worked with in Paris fell down the fire escape steps and broke her neck. A photographer she worked with in Italy was assaulted and stabbed to death.'

John raised his eyebrows. 'You think she was responsible?'

'I don't know.' Lester made no mention of the twine attached to the fire escape.

'Who asked you to make enquiries?'

'You know she found her mother murdered?'

John shook his head. 'She didn't tell us that. How awful. Maybe that pushed her over the edge. I think I'd want to kill everyone in sight if my mother was murdered.'

'The man who has been accused insists he is innocent.' Lester waited for John to realise what he was saying.

'You don't mean…..?'

Lester shrugged. 'I don't know. I've just been asked to make enquiries and see what I can turn up.'

'It's not possible.' John shook his head in disbelief. 'I know I said she was mad, but she really must be insane if she would do a thing like that. Is that why you wanted my film?'

'It's about all I've got that could cast any doubt on her. The attorney I'm working for believes his client. The case is coming up for appeal in about three weeks. The best he can hope for, even with your film, is that doubt is thrown on her story and his appeal is upheld due to lack of incriminating evidence.'

John frowned. 'If you use the film she'll probably admit to damaging the scooter, but insist that she didn't know it was the brake cable she had broken. You can't prove otherwise.'

Lester sighed. 'It's a slim chance, but it's all I have to show for chasing over half of Europe after her.'

John nodded sombrely. 'Do you want another beer or do you fancy a walk up in the Old Town? See if we can get our bearings?'

Lester enjoyed walking through the cobbled streets and looking into the gift shops. John seemed to have an uncanny knack of knowing his way instinctively and his knowledge of the language made it easy for them to avoid the invitation of every restaurant-owner who declared their taverna was the best and only one to eat in.

'We'll find somewhere decent tonight,' John promised. 'Have you eaten proper Greek food?'

'I've eaten at the hotels.'

'That's tourist food,' John replied scornfully. 'I'll find out from our hotel where they recommend and you can sample the local cooking. I don't suggest you go for calamari unless we eat down by the harbour. It will probably be frozen. Have you seen enough up here? Shall we go down and look at the yachts?' Without waiting for Lester's answer John led the way through an arch and onto the waterfront. 'Wow, I wouldn't mind one of those.'

'Which one?'

'More or less any one would do me. They make ours look like a rowing boat.'

Lester smiled at the boy's enthusiasm. 'No doubt if you become a successful under water photographer you will have something like this.'

'There isn't a reward, I suppose, for capturing Christabelle doing something awful on film?' asked John hopefully.

Lester shook his head. 'You're getting a free holiday, young man. Don't push your luck.'

John shrugged his shoulders. 'I'm not complaining. Oh, look at that beauty!'

Lester followed in John's footsteps as he made his way along the harbour arm, admiring and commenting on every sailing craft that was moored there. The boats held no interest at all for him and he would have preferred to be back up in the Old Town wandering the streets. He consoled himself with the thought that he would hardly have to repeat the experience, as Christabelle was unlikely to consider a sea trip.

As darkness fell John led the way back to the hotel where they washed and changed, John donned a long sleeved shirt that hid the tattoos on his upper arms and a pair of well-pressed slacks. 'I can't do much about the hair,' he apologised, 'but at least I don't think we'll be thrown out as undesirable.'

'Where are we going?'

'The owner of the hotel recommends a little place up by the Old Town. It's in one of the side streets and only Greeks eat there. The tourists probably wouldn't give it a second glance even if they found it.'

Lester nodded, willing to follow the boy's directions, just hoping it was clean and free of cockroaches. He was pleasantly surprised when John stopped before a small courtyard in a dark side street. Inside were tables, laid with clean clothes and glasses, some already occupied, the people eating a variety of foods.

'I'll order for us,' John said. 'There's no menu; just whatever they've cooked today.'

Lester listened to the boy reeling off various strange sounding names, the elderly man who was waiting on them either agreeing or shaking his head. Finally John checked whether Lester would prefer wine or beer and the waiter retired to the small kitchen to pass on the order to his wife.

It was no more than ten minutes before dishes began to appear on the table and John explained what each of them contained. 'Try all of them. If you don't like it you don't have to eat it.'

Lester followed John's example of placing a small quantity from each onto his plate, but before he had a chance to sample a mouthful more plates began to arrive until most of the table was covered. As they emptied the plates John stacked them up and within minutes they were cleared away. 'It's easier that way or you run out of space.'

Lester looked at the amount of food still on the table and thought he might very well run out of space in his stomach. John raised his glass of wine in salutation. 'Here's to a successful mission!'

Christabelle turned on the television in her room and spent an amusing few minutes watching the coverage on the Greek news of the disaster that had overtaken the largest wine producer on Santorini. Two of the stop cocks on the vats of wine had been turned on and he had lost hundreds of gallons before it had been discovered when he took his next group on a conducted tour. Although she could not understand a word, Christabelle could tell that the owner was furious. She shrugged. It served him right. He should not have been so familiar with his hands on her first visit. She locked her cases, checked she had her passport and ticket, and called down to the reception desk. It was definitely time to leave the island.

To occupy her time whilst sitting at the airport Christabelle began to examine the photographs that Marianne had given her. Wrapped around each one was a piece of paper that identified the subjects and she looked at Helena, Marianne's twin sister with interest. They were very alike when they were younger and she wondered if they still resembled each other so closely.

Bryony was recognisable to her, she had retained her round face and slightly surprised air, but it was the other two girls that really interested Christabelle. Saffron, only a child, she realised she would probably never recognise, as she would have matured and changed over the years, but Sorrell was a different matter. It was like looking at a younger version of her mother.

Christabelle landed at Diagoras Airport and was annoyed when she was asked to step inside a small room by immigration control.

'It is just a formality, Madam. All visitors are requested to fill out a landing card. You should have been given one during the flight. It will only take a moment.'

Christabelle looked at the card before her; requesting her full name, date of birth, passport number and the address where she planned to stay, followed by her departure date. Sighing heavily, she entered the details and handed it back to the young woman who checked her passport number and gave her a smile.

'Thank you. That is all in order. Enjoy your stay on Rhodes.'

Christabelle swept imperiously from the room and headed towards the waiting taxis, knowing everyone was looking at her and murmuring her name.

At John's instigation Lester hired a scooter and drove nervously around the corner where he relinquished the driving to John. They parked the scooter outside their hotel and spent the remainder of the morning on the beach, alternately swimming and sunbathing, finally returning to their hotel for a shower and a snack lunch.

They sat on the balcony of Lester's room, grateful for the shade it afforded, and waited for the telephone to ring. John answered immediately and wrote the name of the hotel on Lester's note-pad.

'Now the fun starts,' he grinned. '*Imperial Palace Hotel.* I'll find out where it is and we can take the bike up and park outside. We can walk around and see where the best place is to wait to see her when she comes out.'

'I suggest you take a book with you. It could be a long wait. She probably won't even come out tonight, but stay in the hotel for the evening.'

John nodded. 'We can take it in turns to read or doze, provided we don't have to stand on a street corner.'

John drove steadily up to the top of the hill where the *Imperial Palace Hotel* was situated. He parked the scooter a short distance away and he and Lester strolled along on the opposite side of the road.

'We are in luck.' The *Imperial Palace Hotel* stood back from the main road, surrounded by a low wall that gave a clear view of the entrance. Across the main road was the old city wall. The ground between the wall and the pavement had been turned into a dusty garden with seats interspersed beneath the wilting trees. 'We'll even have a bit of shade.'

They wandered along the paths until Lester finally chose a seat and sat down. 'You go for a walk on the other side of the road and see if I'm instantly visible.'

John did as he was asked and returned to assure Lester that with the continual traffic flow and the tourists passing by he was hardly noticeable. He also handed the man a bottle of water that he had bought from a kiosk as they settled themselves for a tedious few hours.

By eight thirty there was still no sign of the young woman they had seen check in earlier and Lester was becoming restless. 'I think it's unlikely she'll go out tonight. It's dark and she isn't familiar with the area so she'll probably eat at the hotel. I suggest we go back to our hotel, have a shower and go for a meal.'

John did not argue. He was stiff and bored.

Nine the next morning saw Lester and John taking up their position on the seat opposite the *Imperial Palace Hotel*.

'I don't see that we needed a scooter to drive up the hill,' complained Lester. 'We could walk up in a few minutes.'

'True,' agreed John, 'but if she decides to go off in a taxi we can't follow her on foot.' He settled back, his cap pulled low over his eyes. 'You can read if you want, Lester. I'll watch out for her.'

It was after eleven when Christabelle finally walked down the steps from the hotel and looked around to get her bearings. John tapped Lester on the leg. 'Here she comes. What now?'

'We wait and see where she goes. She'll probably just wander around as we did yesterday.'

Christabelle was a striking figure as she stood at the junction waiting to cross the busy main road. Dressed in a pair of apple green shorts, white sleeveless blouse and wearing a wide brimmed sun hat, heads were turning as she waited for the traffic lights to change. She walked slowly across, giving everyone ample time to admire her, then stopped on the pavement and consulted her map. Immediately a man stopped and offered to assist her and John sniggered.

'Careful,' warned Lester. 'She'll probably look this way in a moment.'

Christabelle walked a short distance down the hill towards the next set of traffic lights.

'Right,' said Lester, rising with alacrity. 'We'll make sure we're on the opposite side of the road and a good distance behind her. We're not likely to lose sight of her.'

They hurried to where Christabelle had crossed and saw her disappearing through the archway towards the newer part of the town. She walked slowly and deliberately along the pavement, finally stopping to check her map again. Lester and John found it difficult to match their pace to hers, finally having to stop and pretend to consult their own map.

'It's my guess she's going into the New Town to check out the shops,' said John. 'I think we shall be in for an exciting day!'

They watched Christabelle stroll down one side of the street looking into every window. She ignored those selling tourist gifts and concentrated on fashion shops and jewellers. John began to study the window of a photographers and Lester nudged him.

'You're supposed to be watching her.'

'I am. The window is acting like a mirror. Besides, if we both stand here staring after her she'll soon spot us. If we were genuine tourists we'd be window shopping, same as she is.'

By the time they had followed Christabelle down two roads and back up again they were familiar with her routine.

'I suggest we sit here,' Lester indicated a small café with tables and chairs on the pavement. 'We can have something to drink and wait for her to come up the other side.'

Christabelle took her time. She was disappointed in the shops. There was nothing she would consider purchasing to wear in any of them and wondered if she was in the right area. She consulted her map again and decided there was nowhere else except the New Agora and the Old Town. They could wait until the next day. She had certainly done enough walking up and down the hills. It was nearly three, definitely time for her to return to her hotel and spend a short time by the pool before beginning her toilette ready for the evening.

John and Lester sat again in the gardens overlooking the hotel where Christabelle was staying until ten thirty, finally deciding she was not planning to venture out during the evening and they returned to their own hotel.

'Is it always like this?' asked John. 'Just wandering around watching what someone is doing?'

Lester nodded. 'A good bit of it is repetitive and monotonous. You can spend hours doing absolutely nothing.'

John pulled a face. 'I don't mind sitting for hours waiting for a good photograph, but at least I have something at the end of it. This just seems like a waste of time.'

'You were the one who insisted you wanted to come with me,' Lester reminded him.

'Well you wouldn't have got very far without me,' John retorted. 'I doubt if you'd even know the name of her hotel. I'm going for a shower. I'll meet you in the bar when you're ready.'

Christabelle was disappointed in the New Agora. Everywhere

she looked the shops were selling cheap tourist souvenirs and the smell of greasy food was making her feel quite ill. She would walk on to the Old Town and if that was no more interesting she might well move on somewhere else for the last two weeks before she had to return to the States. Surely Madrid or Seville would have a better class of shops than those she had seen so far on Rhodes.

She exited the Agora and found herself down on the waterfront, the walls of the medieval city spreading out before her. She crossed to walk by the harbour and followed the road round until she saw an entrance in the massive stone walls. She debated whether to take a chance, walk into the road and force the traffic to stop for her, then thought better of it. She might have to run for a few yards to avoid a vehicle. Instead she walked to the crossing and waited with the other tourists until a car finally slowed and allowed them to cross the road.

Once inside the Old Town Christabelle was surprised at the size of it. She tried to ascertain her whereabouts from her map and gave up. She would wander and look for jeweller's shops; she could always find her way back to the harbour when she was ready to leave. To her gratification, the jewellery on display was of a far higher quality than she had seen anywhere before, and almost every other shop was a jewellers. It took her almost half an hour to peruse each window and Lester and John were quite happy to sit at a taverna where they had a good view of the shops in the vicinity and could keep Christabelle under easy surveillance.

Finally Christabelle looked at her watch, surprised to see it was nearly four. She would have to leave and return the following day. Turning to retrace her steps she realised she had no idea where she was in relation to the entrance she had used. She looked at her map. She would have to go up the hill to return to her hotel and there was an entrance clearly marked not far from it, so that would seem the most logical way to go.

It was not until after she had started out that she realised the map was not truly to scale, numerous side streets ran off it, and even the wider roads seemed to twist and turn. Finally hot and exhausted, Christabelle turned into a small square and walked over to a taverna. She ordered a drink and had to admit that it was extremely pleasant there, with trees in the centre providing shade. She looked at the other occupants of the taverna. There were a varied collection of tourists, others appeared to be local workmen and a woman leaning on a table, her head down on her arms as if asleep. She waited until the bar man passed her table.

'Excuse me, do you have a rest room here?'

'Yes, we rent rooms. None free at the moment.'

Christabelle sighed in exasperation. The woman raised her head.

'It's down that passage. We call it a toilet over here.'

'Thank you.'

Christabelle returned a short while later. 'That would be closed down if it was in the States.'

The woman shrugged. 'You're not in the States. Be thankful I speak English or you would still be wanting it.'

Christabelle scowled at her. 'You're not Greek.'

'I didn't say I was.'

'Where do you come from?'

'The States, same as you.'

'Are you on holiday?'

'No, I live here.'

'Here, in this taverna?'

'No, close by. What are you doing here? Holiday?'

Christabelle nodded. 'I'd been in Athens for a couple of weeks so I thought I'd visit the islands for a while.'

The woman examined Christabelle closely. 'You're that girl, aren't you? The one in the magazines.'

Christabelle smiled. She did love to be recognised. 'That's right.'

'Is your name really Christabelle?'

'Yes, that was what my mother called me. Why?'

'Just wondered. It's an unusual name.'

'I'm an unusual person.' Christabelle sipped at her drink. 'So what is there to do on this island?'

Sorrell shrugged. 'Depends what you want to do. Plenty of sun bathing, there's museums and shopping.'

'Shopping! You call this collection of tourist rags shopping? I've walked through the old and new town and I was certainly not impressed.'

'We have some of the best fur coats in the world and also some of the cheapest jewellery. We have a great variety of shoes and they're well made and very good quality.'

'I thought Turkey was supposed to be cheaper for jewellery?'

'If you want imitation go to Turkey. If you want quality you shop here.'

'I doubt if I'll bother. I usually buy my clothes in Paris or Milan.'

'Lucky you to be able to afford it, or do you get them free when you've soiled them by wearing them for ten minutes?'

'Sometimes,' admitted Christabelle.

'I used to have nice clothes like yours.' Sorrell shook her head. 'It seems a long time ago.'

Christabelle looked at her in utter disbelief. 'You did? You were a model?'

Sorrell shook her head. 'No, but people often thought I was.'

'What did you do?'

'A number of things,' Sorrell replied airily.

Christabelle looked at the drab woman sitting opposite her. There was something so familiar about her face. 'I don't think you've ever been off this island.'

'Really? I've probably been to more places than you have. New York, London, Amsterdam, Paris, Rome, Milan, Athens, Cyprus, Egypt, most of the Greek islands.' The different countries rolled glibly off her tongue.

'So how come you live here?'

Sorrell shrugged. 'Circumstances.'

'Like what?'

'Like none of your business.'

Christabelle did not like to be snubbed. 'You don't have to talk to me.'

'It makes a change to have a conversation in one's own language.'

John and Lester sat at the taverna beneath the trees watching Christabelle on the opposite side of the narrow road. As she began her conversation with the woman Lester stiffened.

'Start taking some photographs, John. It might be interesting to find out who she's met up with.'

Obligingly John rose to his feet and photographed the two women sitting at the taverna opposite; he walked across the square until he was able to take close up shots of both women. Christabelle heard the buzzing of the camera and turned immediately. As she did so John swung the camera round to take the derelict building and boarded up fountain, altering his position as if filming the buildings opposite, but training the camera once again on Christabelle and her companion.

He returned to Lester with a worried look on his face. 'I'm sure I know the woman she's met, but I can't place her.'

Lester raised his eyebrows. 'How's that? You said you'd never been to Rhodes before.'

John leaned his chin on his hands. 'She just looks so familiar. You remember I said I had delivered some photographs to her hotel? I had a good look at them when Mum gave them to me. I've a good memory for faces and I'm sure that woman looks just like one that was in the photos.'

'Do you think this was a pre-arranged meeting?'

'From the conversation I picked up I wouldn't think so.'

'I think it's just a coincidence,' Lester was sceptical. He looked over at the two women again. 'They appear to be leaving together.'

They walked across the square, Sorrell shortening her stride as Christabelle walked languidly at her side, and disappeared through the arch at the far end.

'You go on, Lester; I'll pay and catch you up.'

By the time John reached the arch he could see Christabelle walking alone with Lester following her. There was no sign of the woman she had been talking to. John turned in the opposite direction, as he looked up the first side street he could see the woman almost at the top and he hurried after her. She exited into a small square and then entered another small road. He followed her at a distance, making a note of the doorway she entered. As he drew level he could see her in a small courtyard, written above the entrance in red lettering was the name *'Suzi'*. John sucked in his breath. Above all the doorways there was the name of a girl and it was obvious that he was in a most undesirable area of the town. His parents would not be pleased if they ever found out about that.

He was in a dilemma. If he retraced his steps there was no guarantee that he would see either Christabelle or Lester, yet if he continued he had no idea where he would finally be in the Old Town. He decided to walk on, taking a wide road to the right, against the old medieval wall, until he came to a narrow street that led out to one of the main thoroughfares. He hurried along. If this were a main road he would eventually join up with the others where they met at the top of the hill. He would wait at the top for fifteen minutes and if neither Lester nor Christabelle had appeared he would return to the seat in the landscaped area opposite Christabelle's hotel.

To his relief the road did lead to the top of the hill and he also knew exactly where he was. He scanned the busy roads, thronged with tourists, but saw no sign of his quarry. He debated the wisdom of asking one of the shopkeepers if they had seen Christabelle pass by and decided against it. He consulted his watch. In reality no more than ten minutes had passed since he had left the taverna in the square. Unless Christabelle had taken a different route she was hardly likely to be there before him due to the pace she walked.

John read the menu at the taverna, looked in the jeweller's shop, examined the items for sale in the gift shop on the corner, alternately looking down the hill for any sign of Christabelle. He gave a sigh of relief when he saw her white, wide-brimmed hat coming into view, although there was no sign of Lester. He walked a short distance along the street, ostensibly looking at the items for sale, then returned on the other side. Christabelle had stopped and was fanning herself gracefully, before proceeding towards the main gate. John walked past her and down the hill until he met Lester on the way up.

'Where did you get to?' asked Lester.

'I followed the woman. Thought it might be a good idea to see where she was going.'

'And?'

'I guess she went home. Assuming it is where she lives and that she wasn't visiting. Her name is Suzi.'

'How do you know that?'

'It's written above her door. She's a prostitute.'

Lester stopped in surprise. 'I wonder if Christabelle knows that?'

John shrugged. 'Who knows? Ah, she's moving again.'

'I assured your father we'd have no reason to go near that area.'

'Well, he doesn't have to know and we'll probably not have to go up there again.'

Christabelle returned to her hotel feeling distinctly hot and disgruntled. It had been a long climb up the hill and the sun had been relentless, despite being late afternoon. She refused to carry water with her and should have stopped again to have a drink, but she wanted a second look at the photographs John had delivered to her. The face of the woman she had met haunted her.

She shook them out of their packet and examined the one that showed Anna and her three daughters. The oldest was certainly the image of her mother and the woman she had talked to that day was certainly very like her. She also came from the States, and her accent was definitely from the south. Christabelle looked at them and debated within herself. Did she really want to meet another half sister?

During her shower and whilst washing her hair, Christabelle turned the question over in her mind. It could be interesting to find out if the woman was her half sister and why she had never contacted any of her family. What had they done that had turned her so against them? Finally, whilst eating her meal in the hotel restaurant, she decided she would pay a return visit to the small taverna the next day. If the woman was there she could ask her the best place to buy jewellery and see what she could find out. If she were not there, then she would not pursue the idea and put the resemblance down to imagination.

Christabelle examined her finances. When she had left the States she had more than twenty million dollars in her bank account. Her European tour had been financed by the work she had done whilst in the different cities and due to the commission she had received her bank balance had stayed almost the same. She could afford to buy a really good piece of jewellery as an investment. Once she returned to the States and Kurt Schwaber was behind bars for the rest of his life she would move back to New York. She should be able to make more lucrative deals there and she would rent a small apartment until she decided to retire. Surely her grandmother would be dead soon and then she would be able to sell the small house where she had lived with her mother. Then the world would be her oyster and she could choose where she lived and the society she moved amongst.

Sorrell sniffed at the powder she held in the palm of her hand. Despite all the attempts she made to try to kick the habit she really needed it to help her think clearly. She was sure her mother had called her youngest daughter Christabelle, and the girl she had met would be about the right age. She was obviously wealthy, and it could be a good idea to get to know her. Maybe she could tell her a hard luck story and extract some money from her, or even better sell her a couple of the uncut diamonds that still sat in the heel of her evening shoes. She had never told Joseph about those, or he would have managed to sell them long ago. If she could sell those she would have enough money to buy a passport, leave Joseph and start again, maybe in Turkey or Algeria. If she could sell Christabelle three of the diamonds she would even have enough money to put into a bank account for when she was no longer able to work. To sell her four would be even better. She would not have to work. There would be enough money for her to pose as a rich American widow. The daydreams continued as she washed and changed ready to receive her regular customers.

Christabelle wandered across to the Old Town followed at a discreet distance by Lester and John. Once they were amongst the other tourists who thronged the narrow streets they thought it highly unlikely Christabelle would notice them. They crossed to the opposite side of the road, stopping whenever she did, and gazing into a shop window. Finally she turned into the garden of a restaurant, selected a table, ordered an orange juice and asked for the menu.

Lester and John chose a table a good distance away from her and ordered a beer. 'We won't order food,' announced Lester. 'She may decide to move on without eating.'

John relaxed back into his chair. 'If there's one thing I've learnt in the past few days it's never be a private detective. So far these have been the most boring days of my life. All she does is look in shop windows at jewellery and clothes.'

Lester grinned at him. 'Most of the work is boring. You just sit and watch, or wander around after someone, hoping something will happen that will make it all worthwhile. It's called patience and perseverance.'

'How will we know when she does plan to do something?'

Lester shrugged. 'She may not. We could be on a wild goose chase. Ah, she is eating here. Make your beer last, unless you want another.'

John shook his head. 'One's enough at mid-day.'

Christabelle ate her meal leisurely and looked at the map of the Old Town. She was not sure of the location of the taverna where she had met Sorrell the previous day and decided she would ask the waiter when he brought her bill. He had hardly taken his eyes off her since she had given him her order and he returned to her table with alacrity when she signalled to him.

'I'm looking for a taverna where I have to meet a friend,' she smiled at him. 'I wonder if you could tell me where it is from here?'

'What is the name, Madam?'

Christabelle shook her head. 'I didn't notice. It is situated at the side of a small square. There's an archway opposite and some large trees in the centre.'

The waiter frowned. 'I think you are speaking of *The Grapevine.* May I write on your map?'

Christabelle pushed it towards him and watched as he marked the restaurant where she sat with a cross and drew a line along the streets. 'That would be your most direct route. If you get lost ask in one of the shops and they will redirect you.'

Christabelle thanked him, paid her bill and rose. There was no rush, the woman might not be there, she could continue to look in the jewellers shops on the way, as yet she had seen nothing that she felt compelled to purchase.

John took some Euros from his pocket, looked at their bill, and placed the money in a small glass. 'Time to go, I guess.'

'Will that be safe there?'

'Perfectly,' John assured him. 'It's quite acceptable to leave your money and walk out.'

Once again they separated, one on each side of the road,

following Christabelle's slow progress, until she finally reached the square where *The Grapevine* was situated.

Christabelle wandered across the square and looked at the occupants. There was no sign of the woman. She checked the time on her watch. It was considerably earlier than the previous day. She would retrace her steps up the hill and visit the Grand Master's Palace to while away and hour or so.

Both men enjoyed their visit to the Palace in the wake of their quarry, keeping a group of chattering Japanese tourists between them.

'Well, that beats jewellers' shops any day,' remarked Lester as they returned to the main courtyard. 'I just hope she decides to visit some of the museums.' He threw his empty water bottle into a rubbish bin. 'Can you buy another bottle for me when we get to the shops?'

Christabelle made her way slowly towards *The Grapevine* and Lester and John stood at the archway, gratified to see that the woman was already sitting at a table.

John pressed a button on his camera and handed it to Lester. 'I've set it to record. You go down to the taverna and sit fairly close to them. Put the camera on the table and it should be able to pick up their conversation. I'll go round the other way and go to the taverna in the centre of the square. When they decide to leave I'll follow Christabelle and you follow the woman. We can meet up outside her hotel.'

Lester nodded, placed the camera strap around his neck and followed Christabelle across the square. He stopped half way and pretended to film the archway before continuing to *The Grapevine* where he chose a table one away from the two women and placed the camera beside him.

Sorrell waited until Christabelle sat down opposite her. 'Managed to find your way here again, have you?'

'I hoped I would see you.'

'Why?'

'I thought that as you lived here you might be able to tell me the best place to buy jewellery.'

Sorrell shrugged. 'Depends what you want and how much you want to pay.'

'I was thinking of an investment. Something good that will appreciate over the years,' replied Christabelle cautiously.

'Gold or platinum?'

'No preference.'

'Did you want plain jewellery or something with stones?'

'I'd prefer stones, but not some of this awful garish, multicoloured rubbish that I've seen in the shops.'

Sorrell nodded and pretended to consider. 'I think I could probably help you with a very good deal. We can't talk here. Do you know your way to Mandraki Harbour?'

'I think so. I have a map.' Christabelle was doubtful.

Sorrell held out her hand. 'I'll show you.' She spread the open map on the table and traced the road with her finger. 'You can't really get lost. Go down and to your left until you reach the Street of the Knights. Carry straight on, through the archway, down the road to the second arch and you'll be at the end of the harbour. Keep left, past the taxi rank and the New Agora until you come to the post office. Cross over the road to the harbour and wait for me to join you by the statue.'

Christabelle looked at her suspiciously. 'How do I know you're not planning to attack and rob me?'

Sorrell threw back her head and laughed. 'I'd hardly choose such a public place! I'd ask you to meet me when it was dark in some secluded, unlit square. I just can't talk here,' she added quietly. 'I'll explain later.' She pushed back her chair. 'I must be off. See you around.'

Christabelle folded the map and replaced it into her pocket. She waved Alecos away as he came over to ask what she would like to order. 'I only came to ask for some directions,' she smiled at him. 'Maybe I'll come for a drink later.'

Lester hurriedly gulped down the last of his beer and left the money on the table, hoping the bar tender would not call after him to say he had not paid. He followed Sorrell as she strode across the square and through the archway at the opposite side. He saw John pay his bill and pretend to consult his map before following in the footsteps of Christabelle.

Sorrell reached Mandraki Harbour long before Christabelle and took a seat close to the statue. Lester strolled past, examined the exterior of the church and continued on, looking at the building that flanked the road and finally walking through to the seaward side, where he doubled back and stood in the shelter of an archway to watch Sorrell.

It was a good twenty minutes later that Christabelle arrived and sat beside her.

'What took you so long? I was just about to leave.'

'I don't know my way around like you do,' grumbled Christabelle, 'and it's hot. Why was it necessary to drag me all the way down here?'

'The bar tender at *The Grapevine* knows me. If he overheard what I was talking to you about he'd tell Joseph.'

'Who's Joseph?'

'The man I work for.'

Christabelle shrugged. 'I don't see what it has to do with him if you recommend a jeweller to me.'

Sorrell looked up and down the harbour. She knew a number of the men who worked on the boats, taking people for trips around the harbour or over to the neighbouring island of Simi, but they were not in evidence. She bent her head towards Christabelle confidentially.

'I know someone who has some uncut diamonds that you might be interested in buying.'

Christabelle looked at her in disbelief. 'What do you take me for – a gullible fool? You don't know anyone with any uncut diamonds. They've probably got a couple of pieces of glass. No doubt you make money by selling them to unsuspecting tourists. I'm not interested.' Christabelle rose to go.

'No, please, listen.' Sorrell placed a hand on Christabelle's arm. 'When I was about nineteen I was in Amsterdam with my fiancée. He gave me some uncut diamonds that were intended for my engagement ring. Unfortunately we had to part, but I kept the stones. I still have them, but I want to sell them. Joseph doesn't know I have them. If he did he'd take them away from me and sell them himself.'

Christabelle raised her eyebrows. 'If you want to sell the stones why don't you take them to a jeweller?'

Sorrell shook her head. 'They don't do that kind of work over here. The stones are imported ready cut and polished. I'd have to go to Turkey.'

'Turkey isn't very far away. I've seen day trips advertised.'

'You need a passport and I haven't got one, besides, I wouldn't know where to go or who to ask.'

Christabelle was sceptical. 'You must have a passport or you wouldn't have been able to come to Greece in the first place.'

'I did have, but it was stolen from me, along with everything else I possessed.'

'So why didn't you go to the police?'

'I couldn't. The man who had stolen everything from me had threatened me. He said if I went to the police he would accuse me of stealing from him and I'd be sent to prison.'

'I don't believe you.' Christabelle made to rise again.

'It's true. I swear it's true.'

'So if he took everything you possessed how is it you still have your uncut diamonds?'

Sorrell passed a hand over her forehead. 'I came over here with a friend on his yacht. I didn't know, but he was smuggling drugs onto the island. When the police came he tried to protect me by sending me off to stay with a friend of his. He was no friend. He literally held me prisoner for some weeks and treated me very badly. I managed to escape and came looking for Joseph. I knew he would help me. I didn't know that the same man had tried to have Joseph murdered. Alecos, the bar man at *The Grapevine* and his sister, Nadia, helped me. They kept me hidden whilst the police were looking for me. Alecos even managed to get my clothes back for me, but my passport and jewellery were missing, except for the diamonds that I'd managed to hide. I couldn't go to the police or the embassy. I was too frightened of being arrested, so I stayed here and worked for Joseph. The trouble is, I know Lakkis is going to be released from prison soon and I don't want to be here when that happens.' She leaned forward earnestly towards Christabelle. 'If I could sell the diamonds I would be able to buy a passport and leave the island. Start again somewhere else, somewhere that Lakkis couldn't find me, return to the States, maybe.'

Christabelle looked at her companion with something akin to amusement. 'Is this the story you tell to all the tourists? I don't believe a word of it. You're trying to con me into buying some worthless pieces of glass.'

'I swear I'm not. You could take them to any jeweller on the island and he would authenticate them.'

'Because you would have asked him to do so, no doubt! I'm sorry, but I'm not as stupid as people think.'

'I thought you might be willing to help me, under the circumstances.'

'What circumstances? On the strength of a wild story about drug smuggling and people trying to murder each other? Forget it.'

Sorrell shrugged. 'I can't make you believe me. If you change your mind I'll be in *The Grapevine* tomorrow afternoon.' Sorrell rose and began to walk back towards the Old Town.

John retrieved his camera from Lester, rewound the film and tried to listen to the conversation that had been recorded. It was faint, but intelligible and John shook his head at Lester.

'Waste of time. Christabelle asked the woman where she could buy jewellery; then they arranged to meet down here. Pity we couldn't hear their latest conversation. It could have been more interesting.'

Lester frowned. 'Why should they need to meet down here to discuss buying a piece of jewellery?'

'Maybe it's stolen?' suggested John.

'Possible, I guess. She's off again.'

The two men followed Christabelle to the taxi rank where she spoke to the driver and climbed in. Lester muttered beneath his breath, but John steered him into the next waiting taxi and asked to be taken to the *Imperial Palace Hotel*. The taxis followed each other up the hill; the one Christabelle was in stopping outside the hotel.

'Drive on, please. I'll tell you when to stop,' ordered John. 'Here is fine. How much?'

John paid the driver whilst Lester climbed out. 'Good thinking on your part,' he acknowledged. 'What made you suspect she would come back here?'

'It just seemed logical that she wouldn't climb up the hill again. Had she continued on we could have either picked up the scooter or continued on in the taxi. Are we going to spend the rest of the afternoon sitting on that seat?'

Lester nodded glumly. 'I guess so.'

'I'll go and buy some giros. We've not eaten, remember.' Before Lester could answer John had walked off down the road towards the new town, and Lester had to admit that now John had mentioned it he was hungry.

Christabelle looked carefully at the photograph. She was almost certain the woman she had met was her oldest half sister. If that were so, she should be able to trust her, and uncut diamonds could be a very profitable investment. She did not for one moment believe the story Sorrell had told her. Although she had not gone into detail, it was too far-fetched and melodramatic to be true. She would visit *The Grapevine* the following afternoon she decided, if only to show her the photograph and see her reaction.

Sorrell was surprised when she approached the taverna to see Christabelle already seated with a tall glass of orange juice before her. She sat down opposite and raised her eyebrows.

'So? Changed your mind?'

Christabelle looked at her steadily. 'Maybe. Who are you?'

'What has that got to do with it?'

'I like to know who I'm doing business with.' Christabelle opened her purse and withdrew the photograph. 'Do you know any of the people in the photo?'

Sorrell took a quick glance, frowned and looked up at Christabelle. 'Where did you get this?'

'From a relative of mine. That is you, isn't it? Next to the little girl.'

Sorrell shrugged. 'What if it is?'

'It would make you my half sister.'

'Big deal!'

'It might help me to believe your story about the diamonds.'

'Don't mention that here,' hissed Sorrell. 'We can talk business down at Mandraki, where we met yesterday.'

Christabelle shook her head. 'I want you to tell me who the people are in this photograph before I decide whether to trust you or not.'

Sorrell began to point at the various people. 'Grandma and Grandpa, Bryony, Saffron, Jeremy, my step-father, my mother, Aunt Elena and her girls and another aunt. I expect my uncle was taking the photograph.' Sorrell handed it back. 'Good enough?'

Christabelle nodded. 'I'll finish my drink and meet you down at Mandraki.'

'I don't take orders.'

'Fine. We can talk business here. It's more convenient for me than having to traipse all the way down there.'

Sorrell rose immediately. 'I'll meet you in half an hour.'

Alecos had been watching the two women closely. It was an unlikely friendship, and today was the third time they had met. He picked up his mobile 'phone. It could be a good idea to speak to Joseph.

Sorrell sat down beside Christabelle on the seat overlooking Mandraki Harbour. 'What made you decide to show me that photograph?' she asked directly.

'I was struck by the likeness between you and my mother.'

'Our mother,' corrected Sorrell. 'How is she?'

'She's dead. Died about ten years ago.'

'Oh!' For a moment Sorrell was struck dumb. 'Had she been ill for very long?'

'No, she was murdered.'

'I don't believe you!'

Christabelle shrugged. 'It's true. I came in from shopping and found her.'

'Did the police catch the person who did it?'

'Oh, yes.' Christabelle gave a secretive smile. 'There was no doubt about that. It was her boyfriend. He's sitting on death row, but has decided to appeal. I have to go back to the States in a few days to testify.'

Sorrell shook her head. 'Mother never changed. She didn't deserve to be murdered, though. What about everyone else?'

'I only know what Bryony has told me. She's married. Grandpa died a long while ago, but Grandma is still alive apparently.'

'Don't you know?'

'I've only ever met Bryony, oh, and a cousin, Marianne, when I was in Crete.'

Sorrell raised her eyebrows. 'Why's that?'

'Until mother died I had no idea I had any relatives. I only discovered Bryony when I went through an old address book. I've met up with her and her husband a couple of times and she gave me Marianne's address in Crete. I spent an afternoon with her before coming over here. She was the one who gave me the photograph.'

'They really did cut mother out of their lives. Why did you decide to look for me?'

'I didn't. It was pure chance that I went to *The Grapevine* and you spoke to me. I've managed very well without any relatives up until recently so I have no reason to go looking for them.'

'I knew who you were from your photographs in the magazines.'

'You knew I was your sister?' Christabelle looked at Sorrell in surprise.

Sorrell nodded. 'I read an article about you. It said you were Christabelle Bartlett from New Orleans.'

'What else did it say?'

'I don't remember. It was just your name that caught my eye.'

'Which magazine was it in?'

'I've no idea now. It was a while back.'

Christabelle was disappointed. She would have liked to read the article for herself. 'Is that why you offered me the diamonds?'

Sorrell nodded. 'I thought you'd give me a fair price – being my sister.'

'That story you told me, it isn't true, is it?'

'Absolutely. That's why I want to get away from this island.'

'Why don't you just move to another one? You don't need a passport to travel between islands.'

'You need money.'

'You must have some.' Christabelle spoke scornfully. 'You said you were working.'

'Joseph takes most of my earnings,' replied Sorrell simply.

'Why do you let him?'

'You don't understand. I don't have a choice.'

'Of course you do.' Christabelle spoke vehemently. 'I wouldn't let anyone take my money. I'd get rid of them.'

Sorrell shrugged. 'It's not that easy. Joseph's crippled. It was part of the deal that I looked after him.'

'What deal?'

'I told you, Alecos and his sister hid me from the police and Lakkis. Alecos lets us live in one of his houses. I know that when Lakkis is released from prison he'll come looking for Alecos and to save his own skin Alecos will tell him where we are.'

'So you and Joseph want to move on?'

Sorrell shook her head. 'Only me. I don't want Joseph to know my plans.'

Christabelle looked at Sorrell doubtfully. 'I don't know. It all sounds very dubious to me. I'd have no proof of purchase and I don't want to be arrested for breaking the law.'

Sorrell leaned towards Christabelle and spoke earnestly. 'If you buy from me – I have six – I'll show you how to take them out of the country in such a way that no one gives them a second glance.'

'How much are you asking for them?'

'Eight hundred thousand.'

'Dollars?'

Sorrell laughed. 'Don't be silly. Euros.'

Christabelle shook her head. 'I couldn't possibly afford that much.'

'Six?' asked Sorrell hopefully.

'Four – and that would be the limit – if I decided to buy.'

Sorrell kept her eyes downcast, not wishing to show the avaricious gleam in them. Five hundred thousand dollars was probably nearer to their true value, but she had no intention of selling all of them. 'You could be saving my life,' she said quietly. 'I'd be grateful to you for ever.'

'Really?' There was a hint of mockery in Christabelle's tone.

'Well, as I said, I'll think about it. I'll meet you at *The Grapevine* tomorrow and let you know my answer.'

'There's just one thing,' Sorrell frowned. 'Don't call me Sorrell. I gave that name up a long time ago. I'm known as Suzi over here.'

'Whatever.' Christabelle shrugged. It made no difference to her what the girl called herself.

'So what are you up to? You'd better tell me the truth, Suzi. I know you've been meeting this girl down at *The Grapevine*. Why?'

'Let go of my arm, Joseph. You're hurting me.'

Joseph tightened his grip. 'You tell me, the truth, mind; then I'll let you go.'

'I'm trying to con her out of some money. She's got plenty.'

'How are you doing that?'

Sorrell thought wildly. 'I'm trying to sell her my evening dresses. I've told her they're collectors' items.'

Joseph snorted in derision. 'Those old rags!'

'They were exclusive models when I bought them.'

'That was years ago,' sneered Joseph.

'That's what makes them collectors' items,' persisted Sorrell. 'Let me go, Joseph. I'll be bruised.'

By way of an answer he twisted her arm viciously before releasing his grip. 'It had better be the truth. When are you meeting her again?'

'Tomorrow.'

Joseph nodded. 'I'll come with you, just to make sure you get a good deal.'

'She's only going to tell me her decision tomorrow. If she agrees I'll arrange to bring her back here to see them. You can supervise the deal then.'

Sorrell sat in *The Grapevine* and waited for Christabelle to arrive. She had cleaned up the mean, back street house that she shared with Joseph as best she could in anticipation of Christabelle returning with her, and hung the old evening dresses out in the courtyard. With luck Christabelle could be persuaded to go along with her story to Joseph and she would arrange for her to make an evening visit to view the diamonds when Joseph would be out.

Lester and John followed Christabelle at a discreet distance and realised that once again she was making for *The Grapevine*.

'Shall we get in front of her and be there when she arrives?' suggested John and Lester nodded. He was convinced that Christabelle would eventually realise they were following her.

The taverna owner greeted them as old friends, offering his menu, which they declined, and ordered only a beer each. Lester watched as Sorrell bent her head close to Christabelle's and talked quietly. Finally Christabelle nodded and the two women walked across the square, Sorrell shortening her gait to keep pace with Christabelle's slow, languid steps.

'It's my guess that she's going back to the woman's house,' said Lester. 'I'll wander up after them. You wait here, but let me have the map. I can always claim to be lost.'

Christabelle looked at the exterior of the houses that were crowded cheek by jowl along the narrow road. She read the names above each door and turned to Sorrell, disgust written all over her face.

'You're a prostitute!'

'I was forced into it,' Sorrell assured her.

Christabelle looked at her scornfully. 'No one is forced into being a prostitute.'

Sorrell stopped and looked at her half sister. 'You may have no need to sell yourself to put food in your mouth and keep a roof over your head, I had no choice. If I had refused Alecos would have handed me over to the police and I'd be sitting in jail for ever more.'

Christabelle shook her head. She would spend no more than five minutes inside, declare herself not interested in the dresses and leave. The diamonds were a different matter, but she certainly did not want to visit the area during the evening. She had a suspicion that there would be a number of undesirable men hanging around and she certainly did not want to be accosted by any of them. She stepped into the courtyard gingerly, immediately seeing the man in the wheelchair and shuddering.

His once handsome face was bloated, his arms were muscular and his hands looked over large as he rested them on his thin, wizened knees. He looked at Christabelle with a mixture of curiosity and lust and she shrank back behind Sorrell.

'This is Joseph,' Sorrell introduced him perfunctorily.

Christabelle nodded at him and he held out his hand. Reluctantly she moved forward to shake it; then backed away again. 'Where are the dresses?' she asked, although she could quite clearly see them hanging on the washing line.

'There. Have a look at them. Examine the shoes,' Sorrell added in an undertone.

Christabelle went forward, conscious that Joseph's eyes were on her back. She pretended to look at the dresses whilst her eyes were on the pair of evening shoes with diamante in the heels. She shook her head. 'No, I'm not interested. Sorry.'

'Why aren't you interested?' Joseph's voice rasped as he spoke.

Christabelle took a deep breath. 'I don't think I'd have any use for them. They're rather old fashioned in style. They would need to be cleaned and they might fall to pieces due to their age.'

Joseph wheeled his chair closer to her and held Christabelle's arm in a firm grip. 'Suzi tells me you're a model. You must have plenty of money. I think it would be in order for you to make a gift to Suzi before you leave, after all, she's spent her time bringing you up here.'

Christabelle tried to stay calm and in control of herself. 'It was her idea, not mine. Let me go.'

Joseph grinned. 'When you've given me a little donation. Have a look in her purse, Suzi. See how much she's carrying around.'

'No.' Christabelle clutched at her purse tightly. 'I shall complain to the police that you robbed me.'

'Me? A cripple in a wheelchair. How am I supposed to do that?'

'Take your hands off me,' shouted Christabelle, trying to wrench her arm free.

'Don't be a fool, Joseph. Let her go. We don't want any trouble.' Sorrell looked at Christabelle fearfully. This could ruin her chances of selling the diamonds. 'He doesn't mean any harm, Christabelle.'

'If you do not take your hands off me immediately I am going to the police. I shall accuse you of assault and attempted robbery.'

Joseph laughed. 'What a little spitfire you are.' He released her arm and gave her a resounding smack on her bottom.

Christabelle was almost speechless with indignation. 'How dare you do that to me.'

Joseph continued to grin. 'I've bet you've had a lot worse than that done to you. I'd show you a thing or two if I wasn't confined to this chair.'

Christabelle gave him a venomous look and walked towards the doorway, her head held high. He would regret his treatment of her. Walking more quickly than usual she made her way down the narrow street to the small square where a tourist sat studying his map. She was shaking with anger as she heard Sorrell berating the man in Greek and his voice raised in reply.

'Christabelle, please, wait. I'm sorry Joseph behaved like that.' Sorrell hurried after her and caught at Christabelle's elbow. 'You understand now why I want to leave him, to get away.'

Christabelle shook off Sorrell's hand. 'Don't touch me. I'm going back to the hotel for a shower – to get rid of the filth from both of you.'

'You will come tonight, won't you? To see the diamonds properly. Joseph won't be there, I promise you. He goes out every evening whilst I'm working.' Sorrell pleaded with her.

Christabelle hesitated. 'Where does he go?'

'*The Grapevine*. Leaves just before my first customer and comes back about four in the morning. He and Alecos play cards when the taverna is closed and Alecos pushes him back up the hill. You may have to wait a while for me if I'm busy.'

'I have no intention of waiting around anywhere near where you live,' replied Christabelle firmly. 'I certainly don't want to be mistaken for a prostitute.'

Sorrell shrugged. 'All right, where can I meet you?'

'I thought you said you couldn't bring them out with you?'

'I can when Joseph's not there. Please, Christabelle. You're my only hope for getting away from Joseph and starting a fresh life.'

Christabelle walked on in silence, she was determined to get her revenge on the disgusting man who had dared to slap her bottom. She gave a deep sigh.

'I suppose you could come to my hotel.'

Sorrell shook her head. 'They wouldn't let me in.'

Christabelle clicked her tongue in annoyance. 'I'll meet you in the gardens opposite. What time will you be there? I like to be in bed by eleven.'

'I can't say for certain. My first appointment is for nine. If he's quick …'

'I really do not need to know the details of your trade,' replied Christabelle icily. 'I will wait for you from nine thirty until ten thirty, no longer.'

Sorrell swallowed her rising indignation. Who did this girl think she was, talking to her in such a way? 'I'll be there.'

Lester had seen Christabelle enter the garden door into Sorrell's courtyard and hung around long enough to hear her shouting at Joseph. He retraced his steps to the small, deserted square and sat down on a crumbling wall, his map spread out on his leg. As the women passed him he listened eagerly to their conversation as he folded the map and began to walk back down the road behind them.

They were almost at the main thoroughfare when he heard Sorrell say 'I'll be there,' and he hurriedly held his map in his hand looking alternately at the name of the street and the map as if trying to find his location. Christabelle walked past him and Sorrell retraced her steps, her head bent.

'Well,' said Lester to John. 'At least we won't be sitting on that park seat half the night in vain. They've arranged to meet up there between nine thirty and ten thirty.'

John looked at Lester eagerly. 'Yeah? They must be up to something.'

Lester nodded slowly. 'Will you be able to film them? It will be dark by then.'

'No problem,' John assured him. 'I have a setting for night shots, and provided I'm close enough I'll be able to pick up their conversation.'

'I wish I could have seen what was going on in the courtyard. Christabelle was shouting her head off at one point and the other woman was telling someone called Joseph to stop.'

'Why don't we take a little walk up there?' suggested John.

Lester shook his head. 'I don't think that's a good idea. Sooner or later one of them is going to realise that we always seem to be around wherever they are. I think we could have the rest of the day off. I really am sick of trailing round whilst Christabelle window shops.'

Sorrell returned to the small house and looked contemptuously at Joseph. 'Well, you made sure you ruined that deal.'

'She wasn't going to buy them.'

'I may have been able to talk her into doing so.'

'Don't be stupid. Where's she staying?'

'I don't know,' lied Sorrell.

Joseph shrugged. 'Should be easy enough to find out. I'll have a word with Alecos tonight. Maybe we could set a little ambush for her and relieve her of some of her surplus Euros.'

Sorrell turned away. Christabelle could take her chance after the way she had spoken. She would take the shoes to her tonight and show her the diamonds. If the girl agreed to buy them she would replace the diamonds with the original diamante stones. Christabelle would probably not know the difference, and by the time she found out Sorrell would have disappeared.

Christabelle sat on the side of her bed. She would certainly not buy the diamonds now, but she did want to know if Sorrell spoke the truth about Joseph being at *The Grapevine* in the evenings. She would meet her as arranged, feign interest and promise to meet her the following evening with the money. In the meantime she needed to think and plan carefully.

John dressed himself in black trousers, sweatshirt and black cap. He tried to insist that he went alone to the park, assuring Lester that he would be able to hide behind a tree or bush and be unseen by the women.

'If they do spot me they'll think I'm just a peeping Tom.'

Lester shook his head. 'I'm not letting you go up there alone. I'm responsible for you. I'll hang around at the bus stop at the other side of the road.'

'There are no buses at this time of night.'

Lester shrugged. 'I'm a tourist. How am I supposed to know that?'

Lester was surprised how quickly John merged with the background of trees and low shrubs to become virtually invisible. He took up his stance at the bus stop and ignored the taxis that slowed as they approached him, hoping for a fare. He saw Christabelle as she waited for the lights to change to allow her to cross the busy main road and hesitate before she ventured from the pavement into the gardens. Within a few moments she returned and stood close to a streetlight, obviously feeling safer. Every few minutes she looked at her watch, glanced along the road and walked a few steps in both directions. Eventually Lester saw Sorrell round the corner from the Old Town and hurry over to where Christabelle was waiting.

The two women walked into the gardens to a seat well away from the road and Lester strained his eyes to see if he could discern whether John was anywhere near. From Lester's position at the bus stop he had no idea what was taking place and he felt unreasonably annoyed.

Christabelle examined the shoes. Sorrell shone a small torch onto their heels and showed her the diamonds. In the small amount of light afforded her Christabelle had been totally unable to make them out clearly but she nodded her head. 'I'll buy them. Four hundred thousand Euros. I presume you want cash?'

'Of course. When will you get it?'

'I'll meet you up here tomorrow. It will have to be later. There are too many people still around at this time.'

'I thought you had to be in bed by eleven?' mocked Sorrell.

'I'll make an exception,' replied Christabelle coldly. 'I'll be here between one thirty and two. If you don't arrive the deal is off.'

Sorrell replaced the shoes into a cloth bag. 'I'll be here. Make sure you have the money.'

Without waiting for Christabelle she returned to the pavement and walked towards the road leading to the Old Town, breathing a sigh of relief. Once she had the money she would take a ferry to Kos. She should be able to find someone there who could furnish her with a false passport and she would be able to leave Greece for ever.

Lester waited for Christabelle to walk back to her hotel and John to reappear from the greenery. To his surprise Christabelle walked along the road and took the turning for the Old Town. Within minutes John was beckoning for him to join him on the other side of the road. Without waiting for the traffic lights to change, Lester took advantage of a lull in the traffic and ran across.

'Any idea what they were up to?' he asked eagerly.

'The woman is selling something to Christabelle. I couldn't see what it was and I doubt if the camera has picked it up, but it must be something valuable. She's agreed to pay four hundred thousand dollars and is meeting her again tomorrow night.'

'Where's she off to now? She doesn't usually wander around at night.'

John stuffed his cap into his pocket and pushed up his sleeves as they followed Christabelle at a distance seeing her leave the road and cross over to the entrance to the Old Town.

Christabelle's progress puzzled both of them. She walked to the top of the Street of the Knights and took a long look down the hill before walking past the back of the clock tower and up to the main road taking the fork to the left that would eventually lead her to *The Grapevine*. She entered the square through the archway and took the first vacant seat at the taverna on the far side. She sat back in the chair and made no attempt to attract the attention of the waiter.

John and Lester wandered through and over to *The Grapevine* without giving a glance in her direction. John rewound the film in his camera and checked the sound before he handed it over to Lester to examine. Lester waited until Alecos had brought them their beer before lifting it to his eye. The pictures of the two women were quite clear, but whatever Sorrell had brought to show Christabelle was too dark and indistinct to discern, although John had tried to zoom in.

'Any way of getting it any larger?' asked Lester.

'Not without a screen to project on to. What do you think it is?'

'I've no idea. It's fairly large as whatever it is she took it out of a bag and then shone a torch on it. It's just possible it's a piece of jewellery.'

'Maybe we'll find out tomorrow.'

Christabelle looked at the occupants of *The Grapevine*. Three tables were obviously occupied by tourists, but at the far end, sitting alone, was the man in the wheelchair. From time to time Alecos would go across and stand by the table to chat before moving off to serve his customers. She went over the route in her mind. She would have to leave the square by means of the passage, as she would never manage to get the wheelchair over the high step at the archway. What excuse could she use to convince the man that he needed to leave with her? She would have to accomplish the task before the taverna closed or the bar tender would offer to push the wheel chair and she needed to have Joseph alone.

Finally the waiter spotted her sitting at the furthest table and approached for her order.

'What time do you close?' she asked.

He shrugged. 'When the customers leave.'

'I'll just have coffee, thank you.'

'There is time for a meal if you wish.'

Christabelle shook her head. 'Coffee is fine. I've already eaten.' She sat with her chin in her hands, deep in thought, until finally she emitted a deep sigh of satisfaction. She knew what would persuade him and she would act tonight. The opportunity might not be there tomorrow.

She finished her coffee, left the money on the table, and walked languidly across the square to where Joseph was sitting. 'He looks like a malevolent toad,' she thought and shuddered.

'Hi,' she said, as she reached him, smiling charmingly. 'I thought it was you sitting here. I'm so pleased I've found you.'

Joseph looked at her in surprise and with suspicion. 'What do you want?'

'I thought you might like to know that your girlfriend is planning to run out on you.'

Joseph's face darkened. 'What do you mean?'

'Didn't you know that she had some rather valuable uncut diamonds in her possession? She's offered to sell them to me.'

'Rubbish!'

354

Christabelle shook her head. 'She's asked me for four hundred thousand Euros. I don't think she'll hang around here with you once she has the money in her hand.'

'I don't believe you.'

'Please yourself. I'm on my way up to your house with the money now.'

Joseph looked at Christabelle's voluminous handbag. It could well hold a large amount of money.

'Show me.'

Christabelle shook her head. 'Not here in front of people. I don't want to be mugged. Why don't I take you back up to your house? You'll see I'm speaking the truth and you'll be able to ask Suzi for your share.'

'I can't get back up the hill on my own.'

'I could push you,' offered Christabelle.

'Would you be able to manage? It's not easy over the cobbles.' He eyed Christabelle dubiously.

'I'm far stronger than I look,' she assured him. 'I may have to take a slight detour if I find it too difficult.'

Joseph finished his glass of wine. He wondered if Suzi would be working and they would have to hang around outside until her client left. This was going to be easy money. He called over to Alecos in Greek.

'I'm going back to the house for a short while.'

Alecos raised his eyebrows. 'How are you doing that? I can't leave here yet. I've still got customers.'

'The girl is going to take me.'

Alecos frowned. 'Can she manage? You're no light weight.'

'She says she can.'

'Are you coming back?'

Joseph grinned. 'Shouldn't be more than half an hour or so. Maybe I'll be prepared to raise the stakes tonight.' He released his handbrake and turned the wheels with his hands until he reached the step where Alecos manoeuvred the chair down to the ground and Joseph began to propel himself towards the passage.

Christabelle shook her head. 'It will be easier for me if we go out the other way. Most of the way is paved and I'll take you out of the gate and up the main road. When we reach the Athanasiou Gate I'll turn back in to your house. If I went the direct route I'm not sure if I could manage those narrow turns without bumping you into the walls. It could be a good idea if you put your safety belt on. I'd hate to hit a cobble and throw you out.'

Joseph fastened his belt and turned his wheel chair around. The route Christabelle had proposed made sense.

'This is an unexpected development. I presume we're following?'

Lester nodded. 'You follow them and I'll follow you. You're less likely to be noticed dressed the way you are.'

They waited until Christabelle had rounded the corner with Joseph. John slipped out of his seat whilst Lester took his time about placing the Euros for their beer on the table before following him. Once on the cobbles the wheelchair moved less easily and Christabelle struggled to keep it in a straight line. She was relieved when they were once more on a paved area and Joseph was able to propel himself.

She followed Joseph's instructions down and through the old streets until she could see the gate the vehicles used to gain access to the main road. She followed the passage through and turned right up the hill.

John waited in a pool of shadow at the bottom of the hill as Christabelle struggled to push the heavy man. She stopped frequently to recover from her exertions, although Joseph was helping as best he could by turning the wheels with his hands. John followed slowly until he saw them turn into the entrance that led back into the Old Town, then hurried to catch up.

With the twists and turns of the road and the high walls he was almost upon them when he realised they had stopped.

'I need a rest,' he heard her say to Joseph. 'Put the brake on for a moment.'

John shrank back into the shadow of an archway, frustrated by being unable to see or film whatever was happening. Within a few minutes John heard the sound of the wheelchair moving again. He waited until he was sure they would have rounded the next bend before moving forwards.

Reaching the main thoroughfare Christabelle began to move swiftly again. To John's surprise she did not turn off into the narrow passage that led to his house, but took a turn to the left and struggled up the cobbled hill until the road eventually levelled out again. At this time of night the area was deserted and if she decided to turn round there was no way he could remain hidden from her. He moved cautiously from doorway to doorway.

Christabelle was relieved to see that no one was around in that area, although she thought it unlikely anyone who did not know Joseph would ask her about his condition. They would probably assume he was drunk, the way he was lolling in the wheelchair.

John followed her silently, moving from one shadow to another, taking film of her progress whenever he was able. He had no idea if Lester was keeping up with his progress and wondered exactly where the girl was taking the crippled man, who was slumped to one side of the wheelchair.

Christabelle turned down the wide road that led to the Grand Master's Palace. John felt happier filming here. If she did see him she would take him for an ordinary tourist filming the castle walls where they were floodlit. With wooden scaffolding erected around the building opposite he was afforded plenty of shadows in which to conceal himself.

Christabelle moved swiftly past the Palace to the top of the Street of the Knights. John stood in the shadows and took the opportunity to focus his camera lens on her. At the top of the Street Christabelle hesitated and glanced swiftly behind her, checking that there were no late night tourists or workers around before pushing the wheelchair with all her strength down the steep, cobbled road. The wheelchair rocked and lurched as it gathered speed, finally toppling over onto its side, Joseph's head bumping along the ground as it finally came to a halt. Christabelle smiled and turned away, running back towards the main exit and her hotel, whilst John stood riveted to the spot, aghast at the scene he had just witnessed. He was not sure if he should go and see if he could help the wheelchair victim or follow Christabelle and he started violently when Lester touched his shoulder.

'She pushed him down the hill,' he muttered, as much to himself as to Lester.

'Did you get it on film?' asked Lester and John nodded.

'By the time I realised what she'd done it was too late. I should have tried to stop her and help him.'

'You can't blame yourself. You weren't to know what she planned.'

'Should we go and help him?'

'No.' Lester was very definite. 'There's someone coming round the corner now and we don't want to get involved. We could be held up for hours by the emergency services, besides, we would be obliged to show the authorities the film and I need that.'

Slowly the two men walked back to their hotel, Lester feeling triumphant that at last he had something that Rory could use to defend his client, whilst John's emotions were in turmoil. Although he was convinced that Christabelle was mentally unstable and he knew she had tried to injure him by damaging the brakes on his scooter, it was altogether different to see her push a helpless cripple in their wheelchair down a steep hill.

Christabelle stopped at the reception desk of the hotel on her way in. 'Are you able to telephone the airport for me and enquire about the times of flights and availability of seats to Athens? I have to return to the States as soon as possible; an unexpected bereavement. I am going to pack now and as soon as I come down I should like to pay my bill and have a taxi to the airport.'

'I will do my best. I hope you have enjoyed your stay on our beautiful island.'

'Very much. It has been memorable.' She gave the receptionist a charming smile and swept into the lift.

'What now?' asked John, as he and Lester sat in their hotel room and Lester had viewed the film a third time.

'That's it,' replied Lester. 'We'll check out tomorrow and go to the airport. We may have to hang around a bit, but we should be able to get flights. I need to get back to the States as soon as possible.'

'Can I go with you?' John asked eagerly and was disappointed when Lester shook his head.

'You've been absolutely invaluable to me. I'm going to put in a bill on your behalf for your time. It should cover the cost of that underwater camera you're saving up for, but I can't justify taking you back to the States. There's just a chance you'll be called on at a later date to give evidence, but don't count on it.'

John shook his head despondently. 'Life is going to seem pretty dull after this.'

Sorrell woke just before mid-day. She lay in her bed and stretched lazily. What a surprise Joseph and her customers would have in twenty-four hours. Before she met Christabelle she would pack a few belongings and take them with her. She could then book into a small hotel for the rest of the night and catch the first ferry to Kos in the morning. Joseph wouldn't miss her until the afternoon and by then she would be long gone. She smiled happily. This was like her earlier days when she had enjoyed moving around, living on ill-gotten gains and her quick wits.

A persistent knocking on her door roused her from her dreams, and clutching her wrap around her she stumbled across the courtyard to answer, determined to turn whoever it was away. She only worked nights. They would have to find one of the other girls.

To see a policeman and woman standing there made Sorrell go cold. Surely after all this time they had not realised she was the woman they had wanted to find all those years ago? Her mouth was dry and her legs were shaking.

'May we come in?' asked the policewoman, and without waiting for Sorrell's reply pushed the gate wider. 'Maybe we could talk inside.'

Sorrell shook her head. 'I'd rather stay out here. It's hot in the house.' She indicated the low wall that ran around half of the courtyard.

'Is Mr Konstandides here?'

'He's still asleep.'

The policewoman nodded. 'Would you be kind enough to check on that for us, please?'

Sorrell felt relief flooding through her as she walked into the house and opened the door of Joseph's bedroom. It was empty and the bed had obviously not been slept in that night. She looked at it in surprise. Joseph had never stayed out all night, however long his card games with Alecos had gone on. She returned to the courtyard.

'He's not there.' Sorrell licked at her dry lips. It must be Joseph they wanted. Had he met up with Christabelle and robbed her or had she made up some story about him assaulting her?

'I'm very sorry to have to be the bearer of bad news, but there's no easy way to tell you this. I'm afraid Mr Konstandides met with an accident last night.'

'Joseph?'

The policewoman nodded. 'He appears to have lost control of his wheelchair in the Street of the Knights. By the time he was found there was nothing that could be done for him.'

Sorrell waited for the policewoman to continue.

'You understand what I am telling you, Mrs Konstandides? You are Mrs Konstandides, aren't you?'

'Yes. No. Not really.' Sorrell felt completely confused. 'Joseph's had an accident. How is he?'

'He's dead, Mrs Konstandides. I'm so sorry. I wish I could have broken the news more gently to you.'

'Joseph – is dead?'

The policewoman nodded. 'Unfortunately we will have to ask you to come with us to make a formal identification.'

'But you know who he is.'

'We were given his name by a shopkeeper who found him when he was on his way home. We do need positive identification. We'd also like to ask you a few questions about his movements.'

'Can I get some water?' Without waiting for their answer Sorrell walked into the alcove that served as her kitchen and ran her hands under the tap, splashed her face liberally, then took a long drink from a bottle of water. At least she felt awake now. 'What did you want to ask me?'

'Just about yesterday evening. Did you know Mr Konstandides had left the house?'

'Oh, yes. He went out every evening. I used to push him down to the turning where the church is. It was difficult for him on the cobbles, but he could manage well enough where it's paved.'

'And about what time did he go out last night?'

Sorrell shrugged. 'Half nine, twenty to ten. No later.'

'Where did he go in the evenings?'

'To *The Grapevine*. He plays cards with Alecos, the bar tender.'

'How does he get home? Do you fetch him?'

'No. Alecos lives close by and he brings him up.'

'What time is that usually?'

'I don't really know. I don't wait up for him.'

'Where else does he go in the town?'

Sorrell frowned. 'What do you mean?'

'Mr Konstandides was in the habit of visiting *The Grapevine*. Did he go to other tavernas?'

'Not on his own and certainly not regularly.'

'Have you any idea why he would have been in the Street of the Knights?'

Sorrell shook her head. 'He would have avoided that hill – and I can't think why he would have been there anyway. There aren't any tavernas down there.'

The policewoman looked at her companion who nodded. 'I think that's all, Mrs Konstandides. We'll speak to the man at *The Grapevine* and see if he can help us. He may know why Mr Konstandides was in that area. He may even have taken him up there.' She smiled sympathetically at Sorrell. 'If you'd like to get dressed we can take you into town in our car and bring you back afterwards.'

Alecos eyed the policeman who entered *The Grapevine* suspiciously. They usually came in small groups if they were about to raid him, but he'd become clever at hiding the drugs he dispersed in the most unlikely places and only once had they found any.

'What do you want?' he asked abruptly.

'Just a chat.' The policeman eased himself into a chair. 'Did Joseph Konstandides come down here last night?'

Alecos nodded.

'What time did he leave?'

Alecos shrugged. 'I don't know. I didn't look at the time.'

'Approximately?'

'Eleven thirty, maybe quarter to midnight.'

'So you didn't take him home?'

'Not last night. Said he needed to go back to his house. I still had customers so I couldn't take him. The girl said she would.'

'What girl? His wife?'

Alecos's lips curled in derision. 'No, the model girl. Been in here quite a bit recently. Seemed to be friendly with Suzi. She came down here last night and talked to Joseph, then he said he had to go back home and would be back later.'

'And did he come back later?'

Alecos shook his head. 'No. I waited for him for about an hour after I closed up, but he didn't appear. Why? What's he done?'

'Unfortunately Mr Konstandides had an accident last night. He lost control of his wheelchair in the Street of the Knights.'

'What was he doing up there? It's nowhere near his house.'

'That is what we are trying to find out. Mrs Konstandides says she brought him down as usual to come to your taverna and to her knowledge he did not return to the house.'

'Odd.' Alecos frowned. 'I can't think what he'd have been up that way for. How is he?'

'I'm afraid the accident was fatal.'

After making the formal identification of Joseph's body, Sorrell was asked to return with the police to the station. Despite the warm July sunshine she shivered. What would happen to her if they found out she had been living on the island illegally for years and was also wanted in connection with drug trafficking and murder? She continued to shiver uncontrollably as she was taken into a small interview room and asked to sit down.

The policewoman was sympathetic. 'You're obviously suffering from shock. We won't keep you very long. My colleague spoke to the bar tender at *The Grapevine*. He confirms that your husband was there yesterday evening, but shortly before midnight a young woman spoke to him and he told Alecos he had to return to his house. Did you send anyone down there with a message for him?'

'Definitely not.' Sorrell spoke firmly.

'Have you any idea who the woman would have been?'

Sorrell shook her head.

'According to Alecos you had met this woman on a number of occasions at *The Grapevine*. You appeared to have struck up a friendship.'

'Oh, it must have been Christabelle.'

The policewoman raised her eyebrows. 'Can you tell me more?'

Sorrell thought quickly. She did not want to admit to Christabelle being her half-sister, or that she had met her earlier in the evening. 'She's the American model who has been staying on the island. She visited *The Grapevine* one afternoon when I was in there. We started talking and happened to meet on another couple of occasions.'

'Do you know where she is now?'

Sorrell shrugged. 'At her hotel, I presume, or wandering around the Old Town. She asked me the best place to buy jewellery.'

'Do you know which hotel was she staying in?'

'The *Imperial Palace*.'

'Thank you. We'll send someone up there to speak to her. You've been a great help. If you do think of anything that could be of help to us, please don't hesitate to get in touch.'

Sorrell looked at her in surprise. 'You mean I can go now?'

'Of course.' She smiled for the first time. 'We will notify you when Mr Konstandides's body will be released and you can make the necessary arrangements. In the meantime please accept my condolences. Do you have a friend you can spend the rest of today with? I really do not feel you should be on your own.'

Sorrell nodded. 'I shall be all right. I have a friend down the road. I can visit her.'

Lester spent eight hours at Athens airport waiting for a flight to Heathrow to pick up his connection to the States. It took him two hours to write up his report and had just finished e-mailing it to Rory when he received a call from Inspector Lorenzini in Milan.

'I have some news for you. The pair of jeans that were found in a rubbish bin, you remember?'

'Yes?' answered Lester eagerly.

'There was a stain on them and it has been identified as the same blood group as Mr Verri, the photographer. The jeans themselves, we are able to link with Miss Christabelle.'

'How's that?'

'When an item of clothing is modelled it has additional marking on the label. The item cannot be replaced into their stock and sold as new. The girls are offered the clothes, either as a gift or very cheaply. This pair of jeans was modelled by Miss Christabelle and subsequently given to her.'

Lester raised his eyebrows. 'Well, that might give my client something to work on.'

'Do you know the whereabouts of Miss Christabelle?' asked Inspector Lorenzini.

'Not exactly. I believe she's on her way back to the States.'

'We shall be sending someone over to interview her. We may even ask for her extradition if we feel we have sufficient evidence.'

Lester chuckled to himself. 'I wish you luck, Inspector.'

John telephoned the taverna when his plane landed in Heraklion. 'Is there any chance of a lift home from the airport, Dad?'

Giovanni breathed a sigh of relief that his son was back on Cretan soil. 'I'll be there as soon as possible.'

'I'll keep a look out for you. You may not recognize me.'

'What do you mean? What's happened to you?'

'Nothing happened. I shaved my head. You'd better warn Mum. I'll explain later. 'Bye.' John replaced the receiver. Now he must decide exactly what he was going to tell his parents about the week he had spent on Rhodes.

Rory read Lester's report regarding Christabelle with growing amazement, finally picking up his telephone and speaking to a friend who happened to be a retired police officer.

'I'm after a big favour. Some string pulling. Is there any way you can find out if the model, Christabelle, has landed in the States? If she has, can you pick her up and hold her? I've some vital evidence that implicates her in a murder and I don't want her disappearing.'

Aldo frowned. 'Any idea which flight company she's using?'

'I don't know. She's been in Greece so she'll have to change at Heathrow.'

'When did she leave?'

'Probably early this morning from Rhodes to Athens.'

Aldo consulted his diary and the time difference. 'Hardly likely to be at Heathrow yet. Are you sure she's coming over and not staying in Europe?'

'She has to be here by next week. She's subpoenaed to appear at Kurt Schwaber's trial – for the prosecution. With the new information I have the case is likely to be thrown out. I want that decision before we reach the court.'

'Tell me more.'

'Not over the 'phone. I'll meet you for lunch. The *Ophelia* at one thirty.'

Christabelle was gratified to be paged at Louis Armstrong airport and escorted, along with her luggage to a waiting limousine. Obviously word of her return had gone before her. She settled herself back in the luxurious seats and looked at the familiar streets. They seemed so poor and mean after the European cities.

She would certainly move back to New York as soon as she had spoken to Mike Able and secured work for herself in the city.

The limousine came to a halt and Christabelle craned her neck to see the name of the hotel; then frowned. It was not a hotel, but the precinct police station. The chauffer opened the door and she shook her head.

'This is not the right place. I am going to the *Astoria*.'

'I have to ask you to get out here, madam. Someone wishes to ask you a few questions.'

'Rubbish. Take me to my hotel at once.'

'I'm sorry, I can't do that. My orders were to bring you here.'

'I don't care what your orders were. I am ordering you to take me to the *Astoria Hotel* immediately.'

'Madam, I am requesting you to get out of the car and accompany me inside.'

'I absolutely refuse.'

'In that case I regret that I have to arrest you.'

'Arrest me? Whatever for? Are you out of your mind? I'm Christabelle.'

'The police would like your help with some enquiries they are making. I suggest you come inside quietly with me now or I shall be forced to serve the warrant. I am sure you would like to avoid the unpleasantness that entails.'

Christabelle felt fear for the first time. She felt cold inside and shivered. It could only be about that awful cripple, Joseph. Maybe he hadn't died. She should have checked before she had pushed the wheelchair down the hill.

'Very well. I suggest you keep the engine running. I should only be a few moments.'

The chauffer helped her from the car and Christabelle had no choice but walk into the police station. The man she had taken to be a chauffer threw his hat on the desk. 'Where would you like her?'

'Interview room two.' The desk clerk did not even look up.

Christabelle was escorted down the stone corridor to a small room and offered a chair. 'Someone will be with you shortly, ma'am,' she was told and she did not deign to reply as the door was closed and locked.

Christabelle was kept waiting for nearly half an hour before the door was opened and she was asked to accompany the police officer down the corridor to a larger room where three men and a woman sat at a large table. Before them were note pads, tape recording machines and a film projector. She was again asked to be seated and offered a drink, which she declined.

'I really just want to be at my hotel. I've had a tiring journey.'

'Quite.' The man who spoke regarded her with hard, grey eyes and she felt her stomach lurch. 'I am Mr Langley, the Chief Prosecutor; this gentleman is Rory McMahon, attorney for Mr Kurt Schwaber. Miss Solomon is here as an independent witness to ensure that correct procedures are carried out, and the other gentleman is Lester Harkonen, a private detective who has been employed by Mr McMahon on Mr Schwaber's instructions.'

He switched on a tape recorder and spoke into the microphone, entitling the tape 'Interview One with Miss Christabelle Bartlett', giving the date and time and the names of the people present.

'First of all, before we ask you any questions, Miss Bartlett, would you like to have your solicitor present?'

Christabelle looked at him in surprise. 'I don't have a solicitor.'

Christabelle listened as he read her rights out to her. 'Are you happy for us to conduct this interview without anyone representing you being present?'

'Yes.'

'Very well. In that case I will proceed with my questions.'

Mr Langley consulted his notes and removed his glasses. He leaned forward on the table and studied Christabelle carefully.

'Much of what I will ask you will be purely routine; but I regret we have to go through the formalities.'

Christabelle nodded and replied to his questions regarding her full name, date of birth, address in New Orleans and the company she had worked for before visiting Europe.

'You went first to London, I believe?'

'Yes.'

'And you found work there which was to your liking?'

'Yes.'

'Yet you stayed little more than a year?'

'I wanted to move on to Paris. The firm knew I only intended to stay for a short while.'

Mr Langley nodded. 'I believe that on the evening of your departure you were in a car belonging to Miss Marsha Everest when a fatal accident occurred?'

'I did not know that it was fatal at the time. I thought Marsha was just concussed.'

'So what did you do then?'

'After I had given a statement to the police I proceeded to the airport and flew to Paris. I did not know she had died until I had a telephone call from Mr Donaldson.'

'You did not go to Miss Everest's funeral I understand.'

'That's correct.'

'And why was that?'

'I was in Paris.'

'It is only a short journey by 'plane.'

Christabelle shrugged. 'I didn't feel it was my place. I worked for Marsha, but we were not really friends.'

Mr Langley nodded. 'I think I understand. Now, whilst you were in Paris you again found work as a model. How long did you stay there?'

'About seven months. Just time to establish myself in the public eye.'

'And you enjoyed your work?'

'Very much.'

'The young ladies you worked with, did you become friendly with any of them?'

'Not particularly. I do not speak French and they spoke only a little English.'

'How about Miss Laverne? Were you more friendly with her than the other girls?'

'We worked together on a number of occasions.'

'I understand that you took Miss Laverne a bouquet of flowers on the afternoon that she met her death.'

'Yes.'

'Did you take flowers for any of the other girls you had worked with.'

'No.'

'Why was that?'

Christabelle shrugged. 'I knew her better than any of the others.'

'And when did you know that she had suffered an accident?'

'The police called at my hotel. I telephoned to give my condolences.'

'Once again, you did not attend the funeral?'

'By then I was in Milan.'

Mr Langley tapped his fingertips together. 'According to our information there was another incident whilst you were in that city. A young photographer was stabbed.'

She nodded. 'The police called at my hotel to inform me.'

'And you promptly left the city and went to Athens. Why was that?'

'I had planned to leave in a week's time. I didn't think there would be any work for me in that final week, due to Mr Verri's death, so it seemed most practical to leave immediately.'

'You then spent some time in Athens before you flew to Crete and visited relatives on the island.'

'Yes.' Christabelle frowned. Why were they suddenly so interested in her movements?

'And how long did you spend with these relatives?'

'An afternoon and the evening. The following day I returned to Heraklion and then flew on to visit Santorini.'

'Had you met these relatives before?'

'No.'

'What made you decide to pay them a visit?'

'My half-sister had asked me to do so if I was in the area.'

Mr Langley nodded. 'Can you tell me exactly what happened on the day that you visited them?'

Christabelle looked puzzled. 'I went to a taverna in Plaka and asked for Mrs Pirenzi. It turned out she was the owner. I spent the afternoon chatting to her and her family. Mr Pirenzi, Giovanni, drove me back to my hotel and collected me later to take me to their house for an evening meal. He then drove me back to my hotel again afterwards.'

'And that is all that happened?'

'Yes.'

'Apart from Mr and Mrs Pirenzi, who else did you meet that day?'

'Their son and an American girl who was some kind of relative, then their uncle and aunt in the evening. Mr Pirenzi's mother was there also.'

Mr Langley raised his eyebrows. 'I understand that you met Mr John Pirenzi on the beach earlier that day.'

'Oh,' Christabelle gave a small laugh. Surely they were not going to prosecute her for trespassing. 'I could hardly say that I met him. I had no idea who he was and he was very rude to me. He threatened to prosecute me for being on their private beach.'

'And what was your reaction to that?'

'I told him not to be so silly and to go away.'

'And did he?'

'Yes.'

'When did you next see Mr John Pirenzi?'

'At the taverna.'

'Did he mention the incident on the beach?'

'Not to me.'

'And he attended the meal you had at their house?'

'Yes.'

'Did you see Mr John Pirenzi again after that evening?'

'He delivered some photographs to my hotel the following morning.'

'Were you surprised to see him?'

Christabelle shrugged. 'Yes and no.'

'Can you clarify that?'

'I thought his mother might forget her promise.'

'Was that the only reason you were surprised to see him?'

Christabelle frowned. 'Yes.'

Mr Langley relaxed back into his chair. 'I suggest you were surprised to see him because you had pulled the brake cable from his scooter. Had he tried to ride it in that condition he would almost certainly have had a very nasty accident.'

Christabelle shrugged. 'I know nothing about scooters.'

'But you did go over to the scooter and detach something?'

'Why on earth should I do that?'

'That is what I should like to know, Miss Christabelle.' Mr Langley fixed her with a penetrating stare and Christabelle did not answer. 'Now, moving on, you left Crete and flew to Santorini. What did you do whilst you were there?'

'There was very little to do. I visited the site of Akrotiri. It's a very small island. I would have left after a couple of days but there were no flights.'

'And from Santorini you went to Rhodes. What made you go to those islands?'

'I was in the vicinity. I had two weeks before I needed to return to the States for Mr Schwaber's appeal hearing. There was not enough time to visit Egypt as I would have liked so I thought I might as well see some other Greek islands.'

'And whilst you were in Rhodes, how did you occupy your time?'

'I spent most of it in the Old Town.'

'Did you meet anyone there?'

'No.'

Again Mr Langley fixed Christabelle with a look of disbelief. 'I understood that you met a woman at a taverna on a number of occasions.'

Christabelle shrugged. 'They were coincidental meetings. We happened to be in the same place at the same time.'

'And the photographs that you showed her?'

A look of amazement crossed Christabelle's face. How did they know she had shown Sorrell the photographs she had been given by Marianne?

'They were photographs of me modelling in various places. She is a great fan of mine.'

Mr Langley nodded. 'Now, if we could return to the time you spent in Milan. You modelled a variety of clothes, I presume?'

Christabelle nodded.

'Please answer 'yes' or 'no'. The tape recorder cannot record a nod.'

'Oh, yes.' Christabelle had forgotten every word she uttered was being recorded.

'Evening wear, swim wear, casual clothes, jeans?'

'Yes, all of those.'

'And what happened to these items after you had modelled them?'

'We returned them to the wardrobe.'

'Suppose there was an item you particularly liked. Were you able to purchase it?'

'We could purchase anything we liked at a discount. Sometimes they gave us the clothes.'

'And did you purchase anything on this occasion?'

'I don't remember doing so.'

'Were you given any items?'

'Probably.'

'You don't remember?'

Christabelle shook her head. 'I have an extensive wardrobe. Some items I do remember buying, but a good deal would be gifts.'

'And did you always keep these gifts?'

'It would depend whether I liked them.'

'If you decided you would not keep them for yourself, what did you do with them?'

'I usually left them in my hotel when I moved on. I expect someone there would be grateful for them.'

'Did you leave anything behind when you left Milan?'

'I have no idea. Maybe.'

'Right, now we have established that, let us go back to Rhodes again. You met a woman by chance on a number of occasions. What was her name?'

'She told me it was Suzi.'

'She told you it was Suzi? Do you have any reason to doubt her word?'

Christabelle smiled condescendingly. 'She told me she was known as Suzi. I found out subsequently that she was a prostitute. I assumed that Suzi was probably the name she used in her – er – business.'

'And when you found out she was a prostitute, what was your reaction?'

'I was shocked and disgusted.'

'Did you see her again after she had disclosed her profession?'

'Certainly not,' replied Christabelle indignantly.

'You felt she was not a suitable person to have as a friend, is that so?'

'Yes.'

'Do you have any friends, Miss Bartlett?'

'I have a great number of acquaintances.'

'Acquaintances are not exactly friends. I'm talking about someone to share your problems with, confide in.'

'No. I used to confide in my mother. I was badly hurt by her death. I don't feel ready for any form of relationship yet. It is also difficult with my work. You meet so many people briefly.'

'From what I understand you do not have a relationship with anyone. No close girl friend since your school friend moved out of the State.'

'I prefer to keep my own counsel. I've never been one for 'girlie chats' in corners.'

'I suggest that is because you feel superior to everyone else that you meet.'

Christabelle shrugged and did not answer.

'What about a boyfriend? Surely a young lady as beautiful as you are must have had a number of offers?'

'Maybe I haven't met the right person yet.' Christabelle tried to laugh the question off. 'I'm only twenty nine. There's plenty of time to think about boyfriends when I retire from my career.'

'Many young ladies of your age are already married and have a family.'

'That is their choice. My choice is to stay single.'

'Going back to the time you spent on Rhodes. You felt the lady you had met to be unsuitable for you to associate with, yet you arranged to meet her on a number of occasions; once you went to her house and another time you met late at night. Why was that, Miss Bartlett?'

'I had asked her advice about buying some jewellery.'

'You felt this lady was undesirable yet you were willing to take her advice about the purchase of jewellery and meet her in a deserted area at night?'

Christabelle shook her head. 'I had nothing to lose except possibly my purse containing a few hundred Euros.'

'Why did you think that?'

'She was desperate to escape the clutches of the awful man she had been forced to work for. He took all the money she earned each night. She had some jewellery that she wished to sell and he did not know about. I had no intention of buying it. It was probably stolen. I went back to her house to look at it, but he was there at the time so it was impossible. I agreed to go along with her charade of meeting clandestinely and had planned to give her a present.' Christabelle sat back, desperately hoping they would believe her story.

'How much had the lady asked for this jewellery?'

'Oh, a ridiculous amount; four hundred thousand Euros.'

'And how much did you intend to give her as a present?'

'I felt a couple of hundred Euros were quite sufficient.'

'Apart from the occasion when you visited the lady at her house, did you see her gentleman companion again at any time?'

Christabelle shook her head. 'He was in a wheelchair. I doubt that he left the house. I assumed that was why she asked me to meet her elsewhere.'

Mr Langley looked at the three silent men who sat at the table with him and they nodded agreement.

'Well, Miss Bartlett, I regret to say that we are going to have to arrest you.'

'Arrest me? Whatever for? Associating with a prostitute is hardly a crime. You can't arrest me for that.'

'I'm afraid we have no choice. We have had an urgent communication from Inspector Lorenzini of Milan. He is coming to New Orleans to question you further about the death of Mr Verri. It appears that a pair of jeans, which at one time were your property, was found in a rubbish bin. The smears of blood on them match Mr Verri's blood group and the Inspector is looking for an answer.'

'I told you, I left items of clothing that I didn't want in the hotel.'

'According to you that was when you left, Miss Bartlett. Mr Verri was killed whilst you were still in Milan.'

'One of the hotel staff probably stole them from me. I would not have noticed.'

Mr Langley raised his eyebrows, but made no comment. 'There is also a problem with the Rhodian police. They would like to question you regarding the death of Mr Joseph Konstandides. He was found strapped into his wheelchair at the bottom of a steep hill. According to a bar tender there you were the last person to see him alive.'

'I know no one called Joseph Konstandides,' replied Christabelle firmly.

'So you deny offering to take him back to his house – the one he shared with the woman known as Suzi?'

'Of course.'

Mr Langley sighed. 'Miss Bartlett, we have irrefutable evidence that you not only removed Mr Konstandides from the taverna, but you also assaulted him and finally pushed him down the hill where he subsequently met his death.'

'If anyone says they saw me they have to be lying. That Suzi and the bar tender probably did it between them and are trying to blame me.' Christabelle's voice was a little shrill as she tried to think of ways to defend herself.

'Why should they want to harm Mr Konstandides?'

'I have no idea, but what reason would I have?'

'That I would very much like to find out.' Mr Langley's eyes bored into her. 'You understand that we have to keep you under arrest until such time as Inspector Lorenzini has satisfied himself of your innocence. Assuming he does so, the Greek police will be sending a representative to interview you regarding Mr Konstandides. We will have to hand over to them the evidence we have and as a result it is almost certain that you will be deported to Greece to stand trial for murder.'

'You are being quite ridiculous. You cannot have any evidence against me. I demand that you release me immediately.' Christabelle rose, but a hand on her shoulder pressed her back down into her chair.

Mr Langley held a very quiet conversation with the three men who had sat silently, listening to the exchange. He returned his attention to Christabelle.

'We are prepared to show you the evidence we have against you. Maybe when you have seen it you will decide to be a little more co-operative.'

Christabelle's lip curled. 'You have no evidence. I'm Christabelle. Be warned, I shall sue you for wrongful arrest.'

Lester Harkonen took a reel of film from his pocket and placed it into the projector on the table. He nodded to Miss Solomon who rose and dimmed the lights.

A picture emerged on the white wall of Christabelle sitting at a table at the Plaka taverna. The conversation between the three people could just be heard; then the man and woman rose, leaving Christabelle alone. With surprising speed she walked from the table to the scooter.

'Stop it there, please,' she ordered and scanned the still shot of herself critically. 'I really must not wear those shorts again. They do not do my legs justice.'

'Miss Bartlett, this is not a film of you modelling. Proceed.'

The film showed the vicious tug Christabelle gave to the brake cable and how she had twisted it back to disguise the fact that it was broken. Swiftly she had returned to the table and was waiting when the couple emerged from the taverna.

'That shows you quite clearly tampering with the brakes on the scooter,' said Mr Langley.

'Oh, dear,' she murmured. 'Was that the brake cable? I only went to look at the bike and when I touched something it came away in my hand. I was far too embarrassed to tell them.'

Mr Langley did not answer her. He waited for the film to wind on until it showed Christabelle on Rhodes and meeting Sorrell at *The Grapevine*.

The scenes continued, recording her subsequent meetings and the conversations that had been picked up. The meeting with Sorrell in the grounds opposite her hotel was obviously taken at night, but John had not been close enough to record the conversation clearly.

Finally it showed Christabelle wheeling Joseph up the road to the old town and through the entrance towards the Street of the Knights, stopping at the top of the steep hill and hitting Joseph viciously on the temple. Her violent push of his wheelchair was recorded and then she was seen running swiftly back up to the main thoroughfare.

Lester switched the projector off and Mr Langley looked at Christabelle. 'I do not think the Greek police will treat that kind of evidence lightly.' Mr Langley turned to Rory and Lester. 'Do you have any further questions, gentlemen?'

The two men shook their heads.

'In that case we will conclude this interview. Miss Bartlett will be held in custody pending the arrival of Inspector Lorenzini from Milan.'

Rory looked despondent. 'She'll not be able to avoid the charges of the Greek police, but it doesn't actually get us any nearer to getting my client exonerated.'

Philip Langley passed a shaky hand over his forehead. 'Who would have believed it? A beautiful young woman like that! I'll recommend psychiatric reports.' He turned to Rory. 'I'll get the date for your client's appeal to be deferred. When Miss Bartlett's lawyer tells her she will be extradited to Greece and probably spend the remainder of her life in prison out there she may decide it's in her best interest to claim manslaughter of her mother due to diminished responsibility. At the moment the evidence against her is as circumstantial as it is against Schwaber so it would not be in the interest of justice to proceed with his case.'

'Thank you, sir. You'll keep me informed, of course.'

Christabelle sat on the edge of the unmade bunk in the small cell. How dare they lock her up as if she were a common criminal? She was Christabelle. It was inconceivable that someone should have taken a film of her without her knowledge. She would sue them for everything they possessed. As the idea came into her mind so did the identity of the cameraman. It had to be that obnoxious boy who had tried to take her photograph on the beach. That was the only explanation, but how had he managed to follow her to Rhodes and take the film without her recognising him and being aware of his actions? She began to think about returning to Crete and this time she would manage to dispose of him and his films. How dare he film her! She began to pace up and down the cell. How long would they keep her locked up here? It was so undignified. Didn't they realise that she was a world famous model and should be treated with respect?

John took the newspaper to his father and pointed out the small paragraph. Giovanni read it with a mixture of sadness and relief. The police were investigating the death of a man known as Joseph Konstandides. Since his death it had become known that his real name was Joseph Pirenzi. He had been implicated in the murder that had taken place sixteen years earlier at the *Athenia De Luxe Hotel*. They described how he had fallen over the castle wall and spent the rest of his life as a cripple. It appeared he had lost control of his wheelchair whilst trying to negotiate a steep hill in the Old Town.

'Was he a relative, Dad? Was he your brother? ' asked John.

Giovanni shrugged. 'It's a very long story. Let's just say he was no good.'

John frowned. 'That was Uncle Yannis's hotel. Did Uncle Yannis sell it because of the murder?'

'It was a long time ago. Best forgotten now.'

'I'd like to know more about him,' persisted John.

Giovanni shook his head. 'Believe me when I say he was not a relative to be proud of. I don't ever want to hear you mention his name again.' Giovanni tore the item out of the paper and crumpled it in his hand. 'There's no need for your mother to know about this and under no circumstances do you tell your grandmother. It would only upset both of them.'

John watched as his father walked away, longing to know more about the murder in the hotel, the details of his uncle's life and the reason his father had for classing him as 'no good'. Maybe if he had to confess that he had filmed Christabelle pushing the man down the hill to his death, his father would be more forthcoming.

AUGUST 2005

John opened the small parcel curiously. He had never before received a package that had needed his signature. Inside was a folded newspaper and in a separate envelope were a cheque and a letter from Lester.

He read the letter eagerly.

Just a brief note to thank you for your help.
Subject sent for psychiatric examination and reports.
Diagnosed as having Narcissistic Personality Disorder.
Explains her actions, but does not excuse. Whilst undergoing examination she boasted about her other victims and how clever she was to cover her tracks.

K.S. released without charge and currently suing the police for wrongful arrest and the length of time he spent in prison.

I have enclosed your fees for the photography and I'm sure K.S. will add to it eventually.

In the meantime he sends his grateful thanks.

John looked at the cheque in delight. It would more than cover the cost of an underwater camera. Maybe life as a private detective was not so terrible after all if that was the kind of pay cheque you picked up for a week's work. He smiled to himself. In retrospect he had enjoyed the experience, but photography was his first love.

He spread the newspaper out in front of him and looked at the large headlines.

'WORLD FAMOUS MODEL IS SERIAL KILLER'

It was an article from a psychiatrist explaining that Narcissistic Personality Disorder meant that the subject was obsessed with fantasies of unlimited success, power and brilliance. In the psychiatrist's estimation, Christabelle was convinced that she was the most beautiful woman in the world and was not prepared to let anyone stand in the way of her rise to fame. That her mother had opposed the idea of her becoming a model at the age of eighteen had caused Christabelle to kill her and she had deliberately timed the crime to coincide with a visit from Kurt Schwaber to throw suspicion on him.

The knowledge that she had escaped detection for the electrocution of the photographer, Brajowski, had given her a feeling of invincibility. She admitted manufacturing the accident that had killed Marsha Everest, as she had not liked the way the woman spoke to her.

She confessed that she had tied trip wires to the fire escape in Paris, hoping that the model, who had purchased an evening dress that she had set her heart on, would fall. When talking to the psychiatrist she was reported to have giggled and said how funny Angelique looked as she fell, arms and legs flailing all over the place.

At least she appeared to have a better reason than a dispute over an evening dress when she murdered Roberto Verri, the Italian photographer. According to her he had made lewd and suggestive remarks to her repeatedly which she regarded as insulting and degrading.

There were just a couple of lines about snapping the brake cable on a scooter belonging to a young man who had tried to take her photograph without her permission, but he had discovered the damage. John was relieved when he read this that there was no mention of his name.

By killing Joseph Pirenzi she considered that she had done the community a service. According to her he was a violent pimp who had hit her and tried to rob her. The world was better off without him.

The psychiatrist summed up by saying that as she had been successful in escaping detection for the murder of the photographer this had encouraged her to murder again. Her ego was such that she thought she was far too clever to be caught and the psychiatrist was convinced that she was criminally insane and could not be charged with any of the crimes. Instead he recommended she be confined for the rest of her life in a mental institution, as he doubted if she could ever be rehabilitated into society.

John folded the newspaper and placed it in his pocket. He would hide that and only show his parents and Nicola the letter and cheque from Lester.

'Mad, quite mad,' he muttered. 'I knew it.'

If you have enjoyed reading *Christabelle*, you will be pleased to know that the next book in the continuing saga – *Saffron* – is planned for publication in June 2010.

See overleaf for a 'taster' of what is to come.

For up-to-date information, have a look at the author's website:

www.beryldarbybooks.com

1976 - 1991

When Jeremy packed his belongings and those of his daughter, Saffron, he had no clear idea of his intentions. He needed to leave and put as much space as possible between himself and his wife. Their relationship had deteriorated over the ten years they had been married and this time he was not prepared to forgive and forget. Anna had gone too far.

On previous occasions when he had accused her of being unfaithful to him she had cried and pleaded for another chance, assuring him it would not happen again, but he was not prepared to pretend to be the father of the child she was carrying. The responsibility he felt for his daughter weighed on him and it was a haggard man who booked them into a motel on the outskirts of the town.

He had explained to Saffron that he could no longer live with her mother for various reasons and in future she would be living solely with him. Saffron had cried, not for her mother, but for her two stepsisters, Bryony in particular. Holding her to him, Jeremy assured her that it would not be for ever and when she was older she would be able to spend time with them again.

A difficult telephone call to his office had followed and he had agreed to visit the firm to discuss his options. They were more sympathetic than he had dared to hope and offered him a transfer to their London branch. He had accepted gratefully, not sure what the future would hold for him in a strange country, but willing to take the opportunity of building a stable environment where his daughter could grow up. He regretted cutting the ties with Anna's parents, who had always been good to him, but the break from his wife had to be final.

Now he looked around the small flat he had rented and wondered if he should have stayed in America. Everywhere seemed so cramped and dark by comparison and was certainly more expensive. He smiled as Saffron entered the lounge that doubled as his bedroom.

'How's my girl today?'

'I'm okay. Did you sleep all right on that thing?' She pointed to the couch where Jeremy had slept.

'Better than I have for weeks,' he lied. 'Now, plans for today. We need to go round some of the local schools to get you enrolled and see how soon you can start. Once we have done that I think we'll start looking for somewhere better to live. This flat is adequate at the moment, but I don't want you to be embarrassed when you start to bring friends home.'

Saffron shrugged. She knew she would have to go to school, but she did not relish the idea. She was an American and had no idea what would be expected of her. Would the pupils laugh at her accent? Would she be able to make any friends? She thought of her close friend Gina in America and felt tears coming into her eyes.

'I'll go and get dressed.'

Jeremy watched her leave the room and hoped once again that he had done the right thing in uprooting her from all that was familiar in her life.

Jeremy sat at the table in the staff rest room and ate his sandwiches morosely. Financially he could not refuse the offer from his employers. They might even declare him redundant if he did so. If Saffron were older there would be no problem leaving her alone, but she was only twelve. He had felt guilty expecting her to arrive home at least an hour before him each evening, although she had assured him she used the time to complete her homework and an hour alone did not worry her.

Now he was being asked to spend two weeks in Ireland to go through the accounts of a firm that seemed to be on the brink of bankruptcy. He could not leave her alone in their flat, but nor did he want to take her with him and leave her in a hotel room all day. There was also her education to consider. She had settled so well at the secondary school, but a two-week absence could be detrimental to any friendships she was making as well as keeping up with the work.

He returned to his desk and frowned at the note he found there. He had sent the file to his secretary the previous day. Why did she need to see him about it? He crumpled the note and threw it into his rubbish bin. He doubted it was important. The ringing of his telephone interrupted his scrutiny of a new file. He answered it automatically.

'Jeremy Bartlett. How can I help you?'

'It's Marjorie, Mr Bartlett. I left a message on your desk asking you to see me about the Coltrane file. Can you spare me a few minutes?'

'What's the problem?'

'I really need to see you, Mr Bartlett.'

Jeremy sighed. 'Very well. Come in now.'

Marjorie entered, clutching the file she had been sent the previous day. She placed it on his desk and opened it at a page she had marked. 'I know I'm not an accountant, but these figures don't make sense, Mr Bartlett.'

Jeremy scowled as he re-calculated the column and checked it against the final balance. Marjorie was right. The figures were incorrect by a considerable amount.

He turned to the previous page and looked at the figures he had written there. They were wrong also. He would have to go through the whole file again.

'Leave it with me, Marjorie. I'll go through it again. It was well spotted by you.' He tried to smile at her.

'I was asked to make sure it went into the post tonight.'

'I'll give it priority.'

As Marjorie left his office Jeremy gave a deep sigh. It was already two thirty, to check the whole file would take him at least two hours. The post was collected ten minutes before Marjorie left at five and there was no way she would be able to have it ready. It was Friday, that would mean it did not go until Monday. Coltrane, one of the firm's largest customers, was depending upon the accounts to present at their shareholders' meeting the following week.

He groaned and placed his head in his hands. It was concern over his forthcoming trip to Ireland that was making him lose his concentration.

Marjorie entered without knocking. 'I thought .... What's the matter, Mr Bartlett? Aren't you well?'

Jeremy lifted his head and gave a wan smile. 'I've rather a lot on my mind. I'm never going to have this ready for the post and we promised Coltrane. It's already been delayed by a month due to their accountant taking sick leave.'

'There's a late collection from the main post office. I don't mind staying on a bit and taking it to the post myself.'

'Would you really? It would be one worry off my mind.'

'Just let me know when it's ready.'

Jeremy worked doggedly, checking and re-checking the figures until he was finally happy that they were correct. It was nearly six when he entered the small separate room where Marjorie worked. She looked up at him with a smile.

'I've got a template ready. All I need to do is insert the new figures. If you read them out to me it will be quicker still.'

Jeremy obliged and watched as her fingers sped over the keys. 'You are the most efficient secretary I've ever had. You must claim overtime for this.'

Marjorie shook her head as she stuffed the papers into the envelope. 'You know the firm hates paying overtime, besides, the tax man will only take it away from me.'

'Would you accept a gift from me?'

'Don't be silly; of course not. Just buy me a drink some time.'

'You're on. Let me know when you're free. Now, I must rush. My daughter is on her own until I get home.'

'Is that what's on your mind?'

Jeremy shook his head. 'She's used to being home from school before me. The firm wants to send me to Ireland for a couple of weeks. I can't afford to refuse, but I don't know what to do about her. She's too young to leave alone.'

'Haven't you any relatives who would look after her for a couple of weeks?' Marjorie shrugged herself into her coat and picked up the envelope.

'All her relatives are in America.'

'A neighbour, maybe?'

'I don't know my neighbours. We pass the time of day if we meet, but I don't know any of them well enough to ask them to look after her.'

'A school friend?'

'She has no particular friend. She only started secondary school a short while ago.'

Jeremy picked up his jacket and held the door for Marjorie. 'Thanks for the suggestions, anyway.'

Marjorie approached Jeremy hesitantly. 'I don't want you to think that I'm interfering, but I spoke to my mother last night about your daughter. She said she could stay with us for a couple of weeks.'

Jeremy looked at his secretary in disbelief. 'You don't mean it?'

Marjorie nodded. 'If you're both happy with the arrangement, of course. We've got a spare room and we're no further from her school than you are. She'd be company for Mum until I get home.'

'She won't have a choice.' Jeremy spoke firmly. 'She's a pretty good kid. She can manage to behave for a fortnight. I'll pay you, of course. She can eat for ever; hasn't got to the age of watching her weight yet.'

'I think you ought to bring her over to meet us. Come this evening and have a meal. That will give us time to get to know her and you can tell us the rules and regulations.'

'There aren't that many; straight home from school, homework done each night before the television goes on, bath and bed by nine thirty at the latest.'

'Sounds easy. What does she like to eat?'

'Just about anything except sprouts.'

'Fine. Shall we say six thirty for seven?'

'We'll be there – and, Marjorie, I can't tell you how grateful I am.'

Saffron looked up from her homework. 'Granny Harris, do you know how to do trigonometry?'

'Trigonometry? What's that?'

'It's something to do with dropping perpendiculars and measuring angles. I don't understand it.'

'Didn't your teacher explain?'

'Yes, but I found it hard to concentrate.' Saffron giggled. 'She kept writing things on the blackboard and when she finished she would stand back and say to us "now watch the board whilst I run through it." Every time she said it we all laughed and she didn't know why.'

Mrs Harris smiled. 'Maybe your dad can help you. We didn't do complicated things like that when I was at school.'

'I really wanted to get this finished before he and Marjorie came home.'

'Haven't you something else you can get on with?'

Saffron shook her head. 'I've done everything else. I did my biology first because I like that best of all. I want to be a doctor.'

She closed her exercise books and placed them into her satchel.
'Can we play a game of cards until they come?'
　'If you want; you know where they're kept.'

to be continued...

Beryl Darby

YANNIS

A continuing saga

First book

The compelling story of Yannis, who comes from the village of Plaka on the island of Crete. He attends school in the town of Aghios Nikolaos and gains a scholarship to the Gymnasium in Heraklion.

Whilst in Heraklion, he is diagnosed with leprosy, shattering his dreams of becoming an archaeologist. He is admitted to the local hospital for treatment and subsequently transferred to the hospital in Athens. The conditions in the hospital are appalling: overcrowding, lack of amenities, poor food, and only basic medication. The inmates finally rebel, resulting in their exile to Spinalonga, a leper colony just across the water from Yannis's home village.

The book tells the heart-rending account of his life on the small island, his struggle for survival, his loves and losses, along with that of his family on the mainland from 1918 to 1979.

Beryl Darby

ANNA

The second book in a continuing saga

Second book

In this, the second book in a continuing saga, Anna is left to care for her invalid mother and her sister's children when the Germans invade Crete. A battalion of Italian soldiers is billeted in the village to prevent a seat of resistance being formed on Spinalonga, the leper village opposite the village.

There are resistance workers in the area.

How will she protect strong-willed Marisa from the Italian soldiers, and impulsive Yannis from joining the resistance?

Unwillingly she becomes involved with the resistance and has to draw on all her resources and ingenuity to fool the Italians, finally risking her life to save the man she loves.

Beryl Darby

GIOVANNI

The third book in a continuing saga of a Cretan family

Third book

Yannis has become a successful businessman with a number of hotels. He has taken his resourceful nephew, Giovanni, into partnership. Giovanni is full of ideas to improve the business. He has only one failing – he is susceptible to a pretty face.

His younger brother, Joseph, is resentful of Giovanni's success and determined to avenge himself. With the help of a beautiful woman, he schemes and plans to bring about his brother's disgrace. His final act of revenge has dire results for all involved.

Marianne, Annita's granddaughter, visits Athens with her friend and meets relatives who were previously unknown to her. Elizabeth finds the city romantic in many ways. Later they both visit Crete, which has unexpected consequences for Marianne.

Yannis's loyalty to his extended family saves all of them from shame and humiliation.

Fourth book

Joseph has moved to Rhodes. He lives and works in a warehouse that is a centre for drug distribution and is responsible for taking the money to Turkey each week. He becomes over ambitious and has plans to become a wealthy man.

Sorrell is searching for Joseph to wreak her revenge. She accepts the offer of help from a millionaire hotelier and enjoys a life of idleness and luxury before she finds herself in the clutches of a ruthless criminal. She is both used and abused. Fearing for her life she finally has to ask Joseph for help and protection.

Events take an unexpected turn and a number of people find they are under the scrutiny of the police. Both Joseph and Sorrell are able to evade the law, but they are unable to evade their ultimate fate at the hands of their associates.

SAFFRON

Book 6 in the continuing saga is scheduled
for publication in June 2010